D0050332

Also available from
Julia London
and HQN

A Royal Wedding

The Princess Plan

The Cabot Sisters

The Trouble with Honor
The Devil Takes a Bride
The Scoundrel and the Debutante

The Highland Grooms

Wild Wicked Scot
Sinful Scottish Laird
Hard-Hearted Highlander
Devil in Tartan
Tempting the Laird
Seduced by a Scot

JULIA LONDON

A Royal KISS & TELL

HQN

ISBN-13: 978-1-335-13697-8

A Royal Kiss & Tell

Recycling programs
for this product may
not exist in your area.

HQN
22 Adelaide St. West, 40th Floor
Toronto, Ontario M5H 4E3, Canada
www.Harlequin.com

Printed in U.S.A.

A **Royal**
KISS & TELL

CHAPTER ONE

Helenamar, Alucia
1846

It is an absolute truth that men and women alike desire the earnest vow of someone to love and cherish them all their days, and that nothing elicits joy in the breast of all mankind quite like a wedding.

Recently, the most joyous occasion was the wedding of the universally admired Lady Eliza Tricklebank and His Royal Highness Sebastian Charles Iver Chartier, the Crown Prince of Alucia.

The bride entered Saint Paul's Cathedral in the Alucian capital city of Helenamar at half past twelve. She wore a gown of white silk and chiffon. It was fashioned in the Alucian style, cut close to the body and featuring a customary train thirty feet in length. The train was hand stitched in silver and gold thread with the symbols of Alucia and England, including the famous Alucian racehorses, the mountain buttercup and the Chartier coat of arms. England was duly represented in the Tudor rose, the lion and the English royal banner. The Alucian national motto, Libertatem et Honorem, *was embroidered in tiny scalloped letters around the hems of the sleeves.*

The bride wore a veil anchored with a diamond

tiara with a center stone weighing ten carats, lent to her by Her Majesty Queen Daria. Around her neck she wore a pearl necklace comprising twenty-three pearls, one for each of the provinces in Alucia, a gift from His Majesty King Karl. On her breast Lady Tricklebank wore a sapphire-and-gold brooch, a wedding gift from her fiancé, Prince Sebastian.

The prince was dressed in a black frock of super-fine wool, worn to midcalf, a white waistcoat embroidered in miniature with the same symbols of Alucia and England as the bride's train, and a silk cravat trimmed in silver and gold thread. He wore the crown bestowed on him at his investiture as crown prince.

After the ceremony, the newlyweds rode in open carriage to Constantine Palace through a throng of well-wishers that lined the avenue for three miles.

The king granted the prince and his new bride the titles of Duke and Duchess of Tannymeade. They will reside in the port city at Tannymeade Palace.

♌—Honeycutt's Gazette of Fashion and Domesticity for Ladies

THE PROMISE INHERENT in any wedding was delightful, but if it were a *royal* wedding, the paroxysms of joy might very well result in smiles permanently frozen to all the cheerful faces. It would turn the most jaded heart to gold. And if the beatific royal bride were one's dearest friend, it would provoke cascading waves of unbridled happiness.

Lady Caroline Hawke was over the moon at the good fortune of her dearest friend, Eliza Tricklebank, who was, at that very moment, swearing her love and fealty to Prince Sebastian. Until a scant few months ago, Eliza had been determined to be a spinster and care for her blind father for the rest of his days. She spent her days in plain gowns and aprons, alternately reading to her father or engaging in her curious hobby of repairing clocks. But then Eliza was invited to a royal ball, and a man was murdered, and she was given some gossip that pointed to the identity of the killer, and the next thing Caroline knew, her Eliza was marrying a man who would one day be king of this country. Which meant Eliza would be *queen*

It was so improbable, so impossible, that it went well beyond even the wildest fairy tale Caroline had ever heard or had the capacity to imagine.

Seated in the front row of the cathedral, a place of honor awarded to her as Eliza's dearest friend, Caroline was a little misty about it. Eliza radiated happiness. Caroline had never considered herself the sentimental type, but here she was.

She shifted her gaze to Prince Leopold, standing beside his brother, Prince Sebastian. She wondered what he thought of the occasion and the happy couple. He was quite tall and had a robust and muscular figure. The broad shoulders of his coat tapered to a slim waist, then flared out again. He looked so regal and masculine that Caroline allowed herself a bit of a daydream—she imagined walking down this very aisle on his arm.

She refused to ruin this pleasant little dream by recalling his wretched reception of her at the royal banquet. At that august event, he'd looked at her as if she were a servant come to take away his soiled clothing. He'd done it again during a morning ride through Klevauten Park that had been arranged for the wedding guests. On that day, when she'd galloped up beside him and his friends, he'd frowned and said, "You must be lost, madam." As if she were some ragamuffin who had slipped into a royal party!

Fortunately for him, Caroline had a forgiving nature and, in spite of her pique, could still imagine what it would be like if Prince Leopold were to smile at her the way Prince Sebastian smiled at Eliza. What joy it would be to walk down the aisle with him while wearing a gown as beautiful as Eliza's, which, naturally, Caroline had helped the royal dressmakers to design. She had a keen eye for fashion.

Next to Eliza stood her sister, Mrs. Hollis Honeycutt, the matron of honor. Hollis had the help of eight little cherubs to oversee the elaborate train affixed to Eliza's wedding dress. The cherubs were dressed identically to Eliza, without the train, of course, because only the most seasoned of ladies could maneuver in them. Instead, the girls wore flower crowns on their heads. There were no bridesmaids.

If it were Caroline's wedding, she would have had a fleet of bridesmaids.

But in Alucia, Eliza explained, that was not the custom. "Flower girls," she'd said. "They come from all over the country. It's quite an honor to be named a flower girl, as I understand it."

"But why can't you have what *you* like?" Caroline complained, assuming, of course, that Eliza liked what she liked. Since the day of Eliza's betrothal to Prince Sebastian, Caroline had also assumed, quite incorrectly, that she would be the principal bridesmaid. After all, she and Eliza and Hollis had been entwined in one another's lives since they were very little girls.

"I am content with flower girls, honestly," Eliza said. "I'd be content with a very simple affair. I was *content* with the civil ceremony. But Queen Daria prefers otherwise."

"Naturally, she does. *This* is the wedding where you will be seen by all the people you will rule one day."

Eliza snorted. "I will not rule, Caroline. I'll be fortunate if I can find my husband in this massive place." She'd gestured to the decorative walls around them. It was not an exaggeration—Constantine Palace appeared to be bigger than even Buckingham.

"Let me be the maid of honor," Caroline had begged her. "I am much better equipped to see to your train than Hollis is."

"I beg your pardon! I am her *sister*," Hollis reminded Caroline.

"The train is thirty feet, Hollis. How will you ever manage? You've scarcely managed your own train since we've been in Alucia. And *my* gown should be seen. I spared no expense for it."

Eliza and Hollis looked at Caroline.

"I mean, of course, after *your* gown is seen."

The sisters continued to stare at her.

Caroline shrugged a very tiny bit. *"Obviously,"* she added.

"I rather thought that's what you meant," Eliza said charitably.

The three of them had gleefully adopted the Alucian style of dress since arriving a month ago in Helenamar. The English style of dress—full skirts, high necks and long sleeves—was hot and heavy. They'd admired the beautiful Alucian gowns that fit the curves of a woman's body, with the long flowing sleeves, and, most of all, the elaborately embroidered trains…until they discovered that the unusually long trains were a bit of a bother to wear.

"I will manage," Hollis had insisted. "No one has come to this wedding to see *your* gown, Caro."

"Well, obviously, *Hollis*, they haven't. But they will be

delighted all the same, won't they? And by the bye, there's no law that says the attendant of honor must be one's sister."

"There is no law, but she *is* my sister and she will be the attendant of honor," Eliza said. "And besides, if you were to stand with me, I'd fret the entire ceremony that you were too enthralled with Leo to even notice my train." She'd arched a golden brow directly at Caroline.

As if Caroline had done something wrong.

She most certainly had not. "Leo? Is that what we're calling him now?" she drawled. *Leo* was Prince Sebastian's younger brother. His Royal Highness Prince Leopold.

Prince Leopold, as everyone knew, had spent the last several years in England, "attending" Cambridge, which meant, in reality, that he spent more time at soirees and gentlemen's clubs and hunting lodges than studying. Caroline had encountered him last summer in Chichester at a country house party. They'd engaged in a charming little exchange that Caroline recalled perfectly, word for word. Prince Leopold, on the other hand, remembered it not at all. Worse, he didn't seem to remember *her*.

The archbishop's voice suddenly rose into a chant of some sort, drawing Caroline's attention back to the ceremony. Oh dear, she was thinking about Prince Leopold again when she should be watching her best friend marry a *prince*. At that moment, Eliza slipped her hand into Prince Sebastian's hand and held on tightly as the archbishop asked her to repeat after him in English. *To love, to honor, to protect and defend.*

So romantic.

Caroline glanced to her right. She was seated next to her brother, the baron Beckett Hawke. He was older than her by half a dozen years and had been her guardian since she was eight and he was fourteen. She leaned against him. "Isn't she lovely?" she whispered.

"Ssh."

"I think she is lovelier than even Queen Victoria on her wedding day," Caroline whispered. "Her gown is beautiful. It was my idea to use the gold and silver thread on the train."

Beck pretended not to have heard a word.

"Do you know, I think I could have made that train."

Her brother put his hand on Caroline's knee and squeezed as he turned his pale green eyes to hers. He frowned darkly.

Caroline pushed his hand away and glanced around her. It was massive, this Saint Paul's Cathedral. Painted ceilings soared overhead with visions of angels and other godly images. All the fixtures were gold plated, particularly the pulpit, which looked more like a monument than a stand for the Bible. There was so much stained glass that the morning light fractured across Eliza's long train, turning it into a moving rainbow as sunlight shimmered through the panes.

Every seat in the massive cathedral was taken, filled with beautiful people of varying skin tones and colorful costumes and glittering jewels. They had come far and wide, Caroline understood, from countries she'd never even heard of.

In a cove above the altar, a choir of young men and boys sang the hymns that had accompanied Eliza down the center aisle to meet her prince. It had sounded as if the heavens had parted and the angels were singing for this bride.

The ceremony, almost an hour of it now, was filled with a lot of pomp and circumstance. Caroline wasn't entirely certain what was happening, as the ceremony was con-

ducted in Latin and Alucian and, for the parts Eliza had to
say, in English. It seemed to her that Eliza and Sebastian
were up and down quite a lot, one minute on their knees
with their heads bowed, and standing the next, staring
starry-eyed at each other. There was a somber moment
when Eliza was directed down onto her knees alone. It
looked as if she were knighted or anointed in some way,
and when it was done, the archbishop put his hand to her
head, the king and queen stood, and then Prince Sebastian lifted her up and pinned a gorgeous sapphire-and-gold
brooch to her breast.

"She's a real princess now," Caroline whispered to Beck.
Predictably, he ignored her.

Eliza *looked* like a princess, too, and Caroline wished
Eliza's father, Justice Tricklebank, could be here. Alas, his
advanced age and blindness had made it impossible for
him to attend. There had been a smaller, private ceremony
in England—the first civil union—before Sebastian had
returned to Alucia. That ceremony, which her father had
attended, had been necessitated by the fact that Eliza and
Sebastian could not seem to keep their hands from each
other for as much as a few hours.

There was another civil union once Eliza had arrived
in Alucia so there would be no question of impropriety,
as the heat between Eliza and her prince had only grown.
It was embarrassing, really.

But neither ceremony had been anything like this. *This*
was a pageant, a feast for the eyes and hearts of roman-
tics everywhere.

Caroline's mind drifted, and she wondered if all these
people would be at the ball tonight. She hoped so. She had
a beautiful blue Alucian gown trimmed in gold that was as-

toundingly beautiful. She'd made the train herself. The ball would be her moment to shine...next to Eliza, of course.

Yesterday, Eliza had nervously counted out the heads of state that would attend the wedding and the ball and had turned a bit pale as the number mounted. Caroline's pulse had leapt with delight.

"I can't bear it!" Eliza had exclaimed, unnerved by the number of dignitaries, of the many kings and queens, "What if I say something wrong? You know how I am. Have you any idea how many gifts we've received? Am I to remember them all? I've never seen so many gold chalices and silver platters and fine porcelain in all my life! What if I trip? What if I spill something on my gown?"

"My advice, darling, is not to fill your plate to overflowing," Hollis had said absently. She was bent over her paper, making notes for the periodical she published, the *Honeycutt's Gazette of Fashion and Domesticity for Ladies*. The twice-monthly gazette covered such topics as the latest fashions, domesticity and health advice, and—the most interesting part—the most tantalizing on-dits swirling about London's high society.

Hollis could hardly keep up with the ravenous demand for society news now. She was planning to publish a gazette that would be twice the length of her normal offering with all the news of the royal wedding the moment she returned to London. She'd been busily dispatching letters to her manservant, Donovan, for safekeeping throughout the month they'd been in Alucia.

She was so preoccupied that her advice, while offered freely, was not offered with much thought, and Eliza took exception. "I beg your pardon! I've hardly eaten a thing since I've arrived in Alucia. At every meal the queen looks at me as if she disapproves of everything I do! I'm afraid to do anything, much less eat," Eliza complained. "They'll *all* be looking at me. They'll be waiting for me to do something wrong, or speculating if I'm already carrying the heir. You cannot imagine how much interest there is in my ability to bear an heir."

"Well, of course!" Caroline said cheerfully. "You'll have to be a broodmare, darling, but after you've given them what they want, you may live in conjugal bliss for the rest of your days surrounded by wealth and privilege and many, *many* servants."

"They won't *all* be looking at you, Eliza. At least half the room will be looking at your handsome husband," Hollis had said with a wink.

Caroline was once again jolted back into the present when the archbishop lifted a heavy jeweled chalice above the heads of Eliza and Prince Sebastian. Surely that meant they were nearly done? Prince Sebastian took Eliza's hand, and they turned away from the archbishop, facing the guests with ridiculously happy grins on their faces. They were married!

Hollis turned, too, and even from where Caroline sat, she could see Hollis's dark blue eyes shining with tears of joy. The guests rose to their feet as the prince and his bride began their procession away from the altar. Rose petals rained down on the couple and their guests from above. The little flower girls fluttered around behind Eliza like butterflies, flanking her train as they followed the couple down the aisle. Prince Leopold offered his arm to Hollis, and she beamed up at him. Caroline felt left out. Hollis and Eliza were near and dear to her heart, the closest thing to sisters she'd ever had, and she longed to be with them now.

Eliza and Prince Sebastian floated past Caroline and Beck without any acknowledgment of them. That was to be expected—the two of them looked absolutely besotted. They were so enthralled with each other, in fact, that Caroline fretted they'd walk into any one of the marble columns that lined their path.

Oh, but she was envious, filled to the very *brim* with envy. In England, she rarely gave marriage any thought except on those occasions Beck complained she ought to settle on someone, *anyone*, and relieve him of his duty. But he didn't really mind his duty, his protestations notwithstanding. Caroline rather suspected he liked having her underfoot. So she flitted from one party to the next, happy to enjoy the attentions of the many gentlemen who crossed her path, happy with her freedom to do as she pleased.

But looking at Eliza, Caroline realized that she did indeed want one day to be in love with a man who would be as devoted to her as Prince Sebastian was to his bride. She wanted to feel everything Eliza was feeling, to understand just how that sort of love changed a person.

Prince Leopold and Hollis passed by Caroline and Beck. Hollis's face was streaked with happy tears. Prince Leopold happened to look to the guests as they passed, a polite smile on his face. His gaze locked on Caroline's—well, not *locked*, really, as much as it skimmed over her—but nevertheless, she smiled broadly. She began to lift a hand but was suddenly jostled with an elbow to her ribs. She jerked a wide-eyed gaze to her brother.

"Stop gawking," he whispered. "You'll snap your neck, craning it like that."

Caroline haughtily touched a curl at her neck.

Beck turned his attention to the procession. The king and queen were passing them now. Beck leaned toward her and whispered, "He's a *prince*, Caro, and you are just an English girl. You're indulging in fairy tales again. I can see it plainly on your face."

Just an English girl? She very much would have liked to kick Beck like she used to do when she was just a wee English girl. "Better to dream in fairy tales than not dream at all."

Beck rolled his eyes. He stood dispassionately as the archbishop and his altar boys followed the king and queen.

Just an English girl, indeed.

CHAPTER TWO

The newly married Duchess of Tannymeade is greatly admired by the citizens of Alucia, and indeed the world. Following the wedding ceremony, the couple was feted in a private ceremony by the duke's family and specially invited guests, during which time the duchess was presented with wedding gifts, including a ruby necklace from Emperor Ferdinand I of Austria, a gold-plated and porcelain casket from Sultan Abdülmecid and the people of Turkey, and a pair of dancing horses from Prince Florestan I of Monaco. Our own Queen Victoria and Prince Albert have gifted the duke and duchess Crawley Hall, a country residence in Sussex, the keys to which were presented to the couple by the Right Honorable Lord Russell, who traveled to Helenamar in the queen's stead.

The Duke and Duchess of Tannymeade were not the only ones to receive attention at the ceremony. Some observers noted a very close kin of the duke invested his considerable attentions on a Weslorian heiress rather than the newlyweds.

᠍—Honeycutt's Gazette of Fashion and Domesticity for Ladies

THIS WEDDING WAS quite possibly the longest ceremony in the history of all mankind. Even a Greek bacchanal could not have lasted as long as this. The neckcloth around Prince Leopold's neck felt too tight. The medals he wore as part of his formal attire seemed to be pulling oddly at the fabric, causing him to move his shoulder every so often to right his coat. What time had his guard, Kadro, rolled him into bed this morning? Four? It was all but a hazy memory now. It was not Leo's fault, really. It had been a dare of some sort, to drink *la fée verte*, or the green fairy, as the Swedish ambassador had called it.

At the end of the newlyweds' procession from the cathedral, they stepped into a small vestibule to sign the parish marriage registry. Leo, Mrs. Honeycutt and the archbishop followed them to witness. Leo watched his brother sign *Sebastian Chartier* with the familiar thick and sure stroke of his pen. He realized he was tapping his finger against his pant leg with impatience as Eliza took the pen and signed next. Her hand was shaking, and she managed to leave a smear of ink under the broad, flourishing strokes that formed *Eliza Tricklebank Chartier*. As soon as she put down the pen, she and Mrs. Honeycutt clung to each other and laughed as if they were mad, Mrs. Honeycutt's dark head pressed to Eliza's fair one.

Sebastian and Leopold exchanged a look. Or rather, Leo looked at Bas, and then at the clock just over his brother's shoulder. He didn't want to be impolite, but his head was pounding and his mouth dry. For a fortnight, there had been ceremony after celebration after official event after reception. He'd attended them all, dutifully fulfilling his obligations as prince and best man and whatever else they wanted him to be, all the while drinking to numb his tedium. He chafed to be done with this, to be with friends.

Leo preferred a life far from Alucia, in England, with

friends. Not this princely one where he was no use to anyone, a prop at one ceremony after another.

"You are to witness, Mrs. Honeycutt," Leo said, to hurry things along, and he picked up the gold pen and handed it to her in case she was unclear what witnessing meant.

"Yes, of course," she said nervously, and let go her sister. Beneath Eliza's smear, she deftly wrote her name.

Leo affixed his, as well—dashing it off in his haste to carry on—then stood with his hands clasped at his back as the archbishop offered one last blessing. How many blessings did one couple need?

But at last, they exited the cathedral, and Bas and Eliza stepped into an open carriage. On this beautiful sunlit day, the happy couple would be escorted by palace guards down the long avenue en route to the palace so that the throngs of people waiting for a glimpse of their new crown princess would have opportunity to wave. Eliza had become quite popular since arriving in Alucia. The people saw her as one of their own, a commoner who had charmed the crown prince through no particular effort, other than being just as she was. Leo understood their fascination—it was a tale of hope and fantasy. He understood that most people worked quite hard to provide the necessities of life, and that life in a palace was merely a dream. She was one who had broken through the thick walls of royalty and privilege, and they loved her for it.

It held no fascination for him, however. He did not like the gilded cage that surrounded him in Helenamar. He resented the many rules that governed his behavior, like to whom he spoke, where he sat and so forth. In England, people knew he was a prince, of course, but most of the common people did not, and moreover, no one expected him to *be* anything. Which suited him, as he wasn't anything. He was nothing but a man with a fat purse and a pair of guards to protect him. In England, he moved about as he pleased, hunted when he liked, caroused with his many friends as the mood struck him, rode his horse, wooed women, sat wherever the hell he liked. All without bother.

Or rather, he *had* enjoyed his life without bother until his brother had come to London to negotiate a trade agreement, and his private secretary had been murdered, and then suddenly, everyone in England knew a pair of unmarried princes moved among them. His life had changed somewhat since then. More people in England were aware of him now. He sincerely hoped that when he returned to England, the excitement of an Englishwoman marrying an Alucian prince would have died down, and he could resume his dissolute life.

Unfortunately, there were miles to go before he could board that ship and sail away. But today, after the private reception for family and what he supposed would be hundreds of their closest friends, Leo was to meet friends from his youth for a little respite before the final royal ball this evening. More drinking would be a hard go after last night's debauchery, but if Leo was accomplished at anything, it was revelry.

Leo and Mrs. Honeycutt joined his parents in the gold carriage and followed behind the newly married couple. Mrs. Honeycutt seemed genuinely intimidated by it all—she sat stiffly, her hands clasped so tightly together that he worried she might break a finger. He wished he could assure her that she needn't have worried—his parents ignored her for the most part and, aside from a few pleasantries exchanged about the wedding, turned their attention to the crowds. Leo knew how his parents viewed Mrs. Honeycutt. She was a foreigner, a commoner. She would return to England soon. There was nothing to be gained by knowing her.

But Leo felt sorry for her and her nerves and smiled at her. He could imagine this day had been as overwhelming for her as it had been for her sister. Frankly, there were times the massive crowds still overwhelmed him. What it must be like to be a man simply standing in the crowd, watching a royal carriage roll by. What it must be like to go to the pub afterward and drink to the prince's marriage, then home to his wife and his children and his bed.

He'd warned Bas that Eliza might experience difficulties in adjusting to this life. "Take care of your bride," he'd said yesterday in a rare moment they'd found themselves alone. "This is a new world for her."

"I will," Bas had said, and though he'd said it casually, there was fierceness in his eyes that suggested he loved Eliza more than anything else in this world.

Thank goodness for it, because she would need his protection. The Alucian nobility looked down on her. The English nobility who had come for the wedding seemed appalled by her. Eliza herself was at turns both unnerved and then charmingly joyous. Her sister seemed ill at ease more often than not.

The only person on the side of Eliza who appeared completely unaffected by the trappings of royalty was Lord Hawke's sister. That woman would take no notice of her nerves even if they rose up and wrapped themselves around her throat. Oh, quite the contrary—she seemed emboldened by unfamiliar and formal situations. She sailed through them with a wide, warm smile and rosy cheeks and spectacularly blond hair. She did not go unnoticed—she was exceedingly attractive and taller than average. It was impossible *not* to see her. She was that rare social butterfly who thought nothing of chatting with anyone and everyone in her path. She delighted in being heard, and all were fair game to her—be one a duke or a butler, a queen or a chambermaid. She particularly seemed to enjoy butting into any conversation to offer an opinion, and she didn't care who was on hand to hear it.

The attention she received seemed to invigorate her and compel her to step out of her bounds. She'd certainly thought nothing of approaching him at the royal banquet two nights ago as if it were a trifling thing. Either she didn't understand that one did not approach a royal prince without proper introduction at a formal event or she didn't care—all he knew was that he was in the midst of a conversation, feeling pleasantly inebriated, when he suddenly realized she was at his side, smiling as if there were only the few of them in this room. "Good evening!" she'd said brightly, her green eyes shining. "Is this not a *glorious* event? I am so very impressed with the reception Eliza has received in Helenamar, aren't you?"

"She is well liked," Leo confirmed blandly. He was not surprised by the lady's approach, but his companions, all of them hailing from the highest reaches of Alucian society, had stared at her as if she were a curiosity from a circus, and her breach of proper royal etiquette was to be examined and discussed. In particular, Lady Brunella Fortengau's eyes had gone wide with shock, and she'd looked at Leo as if she thought they were being invaded by a plague and he ought to do something about it.

Well, there was nothing to be done about it, that much Leo had deduced long before this evening. As Lady Brunella had looked on disapprovingly, Hawke's sister had taken a glass of champagne from a servant's tray and said to the poor man, "Oh dear, *should* I?" as if she expected him to answer. "I had a glass of champagne at the bridal luncheon, and much to my dismay it had gone off. Have you tasted this?" she'd asked, putting the glass up to her nose.

The servant flushed. "No, madam."

She'd sipped, narrowed her eyes and stared upward as she assessed the champagne, then smiled brightly at the servant and declared it divine. Then she'd offered to hand Lady Brunella a glass, encouraging her to sample a most excellent vintage.

Judging by the dip of Lady Brunella's eyebrows, she did not care to be told by this lively Englishwoman that she "simply must try" the champagne, and Leo had made the decision to hasten the woman along when she asked if he would like to taste the champagne.

"Thank you, but I shall wait until the king and queen arrive."

She'd laughed. "Then you might be in for a long wait, no? They were *quite* tardy last night, weren't they?"

"I beg your pardon?" With a nod of his head, he sent the servant scurrying along.

"I'm making a jest," she'd said. "Except that they were rather behind schedule." And to the stunned looks of his friends, for who would dare remark on the king and queen's tardiness, she'd explained, "We're acquainted," and had gestured to herself and Leo.

"Not exactly," Leo had said.

"In England," she'd clarified with a pert smile.

"Perhaps in passing," he'd offered politely, still miffed that she insisted on making the ridiculous assertion about a meeting at a house party in Chichester. How could he possibly remember anyone he'd met at that house? Given all that he'd drunk, it was remarkable he recalled Chichester at all. With a small and subtle lift of his finger, he'd summoned the head butler, who smoothly interceded.

"Madam? If I may," the butler had said, and gestured vaguely in the direction of her seat.

At first, when the wedding celebrations had begun, Leo thought Hawke's sister merely naive, something like a country bumpkin come to a grand wedding. But the more he saw her over the course of the wedding celebrations, the more he determined that she was a mix of intrepid spirit with a sprinkle of insolence, a dash of presumption and a dollop of cheeriness for whomever she met, whether it was warranted or not, all delivered with a pretty smile and a bit of laughter in her green eyes.

She was exactly the sort of person royal courtiers did not care to find in their midst. Courtiers were typically annoyed with anyone who took attention that they desperately sought for themselves. And when one was foreign and beautiful and annoying, *beautifully* annoying, they tended to revile that person on general principle.

At last, the cortege of wedding carriages arrived at the royal palace to more trumpets and crowds, disgorging all the people dressed in cumbersome military regalia and medals. The royal family and their dozens of friends were ushered into a private reception room, where Bas and Eliza would welcome foreign dignitaries.

When presented to the king and queen in the salon, Eliza dipped into a much-improved curtsy beneath a glittering crystal chandelier. When she'd first come to Alucia, she had a tendency to lean to one side to such a degree that Leo feared she was in danger of toppling over if she dipped any lower.

Bas was beaming. Leo had never seen his stoic brother as happy as he was in this moment. He was always so reserved, and so proper. Courtiers used to remark that it was the difference in training for the brother who would be king and the one who would not. While Bas had been off learning how to comport himself, Leo had been learning how to enjoy himself.

Bas grabbed Leo's elbow and squeezed it hard, grinning. "I'm a married man now, Leo."

"*Je*, Bas, I stood beside you as it happened."

Bas laughed as if Leo had said something hilarious. The expression on his face reminded Leo of an occasion many years ago when they were boys, living under the watchful eyes of governesses and tutors, but rarely their parents. They'd stumbled upon a litter of wiggling, floppy-eared black-and-brown puppies in a sack that someone had clearly meant to dispose of. When they'd released the puppies, they were besieged by a tangle of big paws and fiercely wagging tails. Sebastian had been delighted with the find, and to this day, Leo could recall Bas's utter joy as he'd lain on his back and let the puppies wiggle and squirm around him, fighting one another to lick his face.

The puppies were returned to the palace with them and homes found for them at Bas's insistence. One of the puppies became a constant companion to Bas until the dog's death fourteen years later. Bas was as devoted to Eliza as he had been to Pontu.

"Look at her," Bas said, nodding to a point behind Leo. Leo turned around, his gaze landing on a small group of women that included his new sister-in-law, Mrs. Honeycutt; an Alucian heiress he'd met once or twice; and, of course, Hawke's sister. That one waved at him, as if they'd been separated at a country fair.

"She's beautiful," Bas said. "I can't believe I found her. Much less married her."

Neither could Leo, frankly. Eliza Tricklebank and her coterie were as far removed from the sort of woman he and Bas had been raised to expect to marry as she could possibly be. Leo would never forget the first time he'd met her. In a modest townhome with yapping dogs, an insolent cat and the many, many clocks.

"I always thought it would be someone from Alucia," Bas mused. He suddenly grinned. "I suppose the Alucian bride will be yours."

"Don't even say it," Leo muttered, looking around them. "I'm quite content with my bachelor lifestyle, thank you. In fact, I can scarcely wait to return to it."

"I won't say it, but you may trust our father will soon enough. When are you setting sail?"

"Two days' time."

Bas was still smiling when he did something completely uncharacteristic and put his arm around Leo's shoulder and squeezed him into an affectionate hug. "Not a moment too soon, I'd wager. Good luck to you, Leo. We are to Tannymeade, where I intend to honeymoon like a beast in the wild for several days." And then, remarkably, his very proper brother laughed and elbowed him in the side.

That was not unlike something Leo might have said himself, and before Eliza, Bas would have chastised him for it. "Is this what marriage does to a man? Turn him so bloody randy?" Leo asked.

Bas laughed loudly, and people turned to look, their expressions as surprised as Leo felt.

No one was happier for Bas than Leo, but he'd be much happier when the ceremonies finally ended and Bas and Eliza turned their attention to the important task of creating heirs. He'd be wild with joy when he could divest himself of this bothersome neckcloth and the bloody weight of these medals, and perhaps take a headache powder. But until that last congratulatory remark had been made, the last gift received, the last cake cut and the last dance danced, he had to endure the attentions of parents and unmarried women, all of them eager to make an advantageous match. All of them eager to do for their daughters what Eliza Tricklebank had done all on her own.

Speaking of Eliza, she had made her way through the throng of guests with her companions in tow. "You must try the champagne!" she said, holding a flute aloft to Bas. "It's very fine."

"Ah, the gift from the French ambassador," Bas said.

"That kind man? He also sent the wine, didn't he? We must make friends with him right away," Eliza declared, and looked around them, as if seeking the gentleman.

This did not appear to be Eliza's first glass of fine champagne of the day.

"Here we all are, like a band of merry troubadours!" Hawke's sister announced and looped her arm around Eliza's shoulders. Her eyes were on Leo, twinkling with what he suspected was at least as much champagne as Eliza had enjoyed. "Well, Your Highness?" she asked Leo. "What did you think? The ceremony was perfection, wasn't it?"

"It was, *je*," he confirmed. He wondered how long he would be forced to make proper small talk before he could make his escape.

"I'm so glad you thought so! I fretted for you—you looked rather glum standing there beside your brother."

He had to think a moment about what she'd said. He'd looked glum? "Pardon?"

"Caro!" Eliza said with a bit of a laugh. "What a thing to say!"

"It's true!"

"I am certain His Highness's nerves were on edge, like mine," Mrs. Honeycutt said. "It's terrifying to stand before all those people."

This amused Bas, and he looked at his brother. "Were you terrified, Leo?" he asked with a wink.

Leo had not been terrified. He'd been trying to remain upright, frankly. "I was observing the solemnity of the occasion."

"The solemnity!" Hawke's sister laughed as if he'd meant that to be amusing. "But it is a *joyous* occasion! It's the happiest I've ever seen our dearest Eliza. So happy that it made me long for the same."

"The same what?" Eliza asked.

"The same as you, darling! A stroll down the aisle in a stunning gown, like you, on the arm of a handsome gentleman. Like you." She winked.

No one said anything. Leo was astonished. Who spoke like that, laying her feelings so bare to all and everyone?

Hawke's sister looked around at them all, noting their surprise. "What? Am I not to imagine it?" She laughed. Before anyone could think of a suitable response, she said, "Were the flower girls not adorable?" She looked directly at Leo, as if she expected him to answer.

What was the matter with this woman? Why was she speaking to him of these things? But now they all turned to look at Leo, as if they wished to know his opinion of the young girls that he'd scarcely even noticed. Bas smiled devilishly, enjoying this attention to Leo.

"I, ah...*je*. From what I recall," he muttered, and looked away from Hawke's sister.

But she was undaunted and continued to natter on, as he was learning she was wont to do. "I had said to Eliza that she ought to have bridesmaids, but she said it is the custom here for flower girls, and I wondered how that would appear in a venue so grand as the cathedral, but I must admit I—"

"I beg your pardon," said a deep male voice.

Leo hadn't seen his father join the group until he stepped up behind Hawke's sister. She at least had the sense to stop talking when the king made an appearance. She moved aside and curtsied. "Your Majesty," she said solemnly.

"I have no wish to interrupt your celebration, but I should like a word with my son, if I may?"

"Of course," Bas said.

"Not you, Sebastian—enjoy the reception. My other son," his father said, and smiled at Leo.

Leo was instantly suspicious. He glanced curiously at his smiling father, thinking he should have made his escape sooner. His father rarely needed to speak to him alone, saving his weighty conversations for Bas.

"Well, Leopold?"

"Je," he said, and with a nod to the others, he joined his father and moved away from the group.

The king's eyes crinkled at the corners with his smile as they strolled away, generally an indication that he was in a very good mood. As if to confirm it, he said, "The day has been excellent in every way. Your mother and I could not be happier that our Bas is, at long last, married." He smiled again but turned his head and looked at Leo.

The slightly calculated curve of that smile caused a small knot to form in Leo's stomach. He was usually quite adept at avoiding the conversation he knew was about to burst forth from his father's mouth, but with all the wedding celebrations and drink and that beautifully annoying woman talking about flower girls, of all things, his reflexes seemed to be compromised.

His father stopped near one of the large windows. On the grounds, enormous crowds were still milling about, hoping for another sight of the newlyweds.

"Now the crown prince has married," his father said, shifting closer to Leo, still smiling, "your mother and I might turn our attention to you."

"What? Me?" Leo felt exposed, as if he'd gone off to war without any armor or even a sword. "I'm...I'm to England in two days," he quickly reminded his father.

His father's smile did not waver. He gestured to a passing footman, took two flutes of champagne from his tray and handed one to Leo. Leo didn't realize he'd even taken the glass until he saw it in his hand. He was flat-footed, taken aback that his father would use the opportunity of Bas's private wedding reception, with the ink not yet dry on the marriage registry, to beat this drum for him.

"Hear me out, Leopold," his father said congenially, and drew him even farther aside. "I want this to be as easy and painless as possible for you. There have already been discussions."

Both of those things sounded alarm bells in his brain. Big brass bells, clanging loudly. His marriage would be easy and painless? The king made it sound as if Leo were a dog to be put down—Leo saw nothing easy or painless about shackling himself for the rest of his life to a woman he hardly knew. There had already been discussions? With whom? Certainly not *him*. "I would like to—"

"We have made some progress with Wesloria, have we not?" his father quickly continued before Leo could beg off from the discussion.

The knot in his belly tightened. *Had* they made progress, really? It hadn't even been a year since some Weslorians and traitorous Alucians had plotted to kidnap Bas.

The two nations had a history of war and distrust, but his father was referring to recent attempts to ease the ongoing tensions between the neighboring kingdoms.

At the crux of the dispute were two royal half brothers. When Leo's father, Karl, had taken the throne some forty years ago, Uncle Felix had been banished from Alucia... mainly because he believed he had a more legitimate claim to the throne than Karl did.

The question of the rightful succession had its roots in a sixteenth-century civil war, when a Chartier had first assumed the throne. Felix's ancestors, the Oberons, had lost that war and retreated to Wesloria, propping up Weslorian kings and nobles along the way. They'd long held that the Chartier claim to rule Alucia was not as legitimate as theirs, and military skirmishes along the border had been plaguing the countries for years.

Felix and Karl were the result of Leo's grandfather attempting to bring unity to the two countries after his first wife died. His second wife, a distant cousin and an Oberon, had been a bit of a schemer. She'd thought to insert herself into the mix for the throne with the birth of her son. That had not worked out for any of them, quite obviously.

Uncle Felix made a lot of noise in Wesloria. It was well known that he kept the Weslorian king under his thumb. Felix had promised to unite Wesloria and Alucia under one rule if he was successful in gaining the Alucian throne, and with the many loyalists dedicated to the Oberon cause, the threat of war hung over the heads of the two nations. The Chartiers sought to suppress anyone who was rumored to be sympathetic to Wesloria, which had caused a lot of strife and stymied economic growth in both nations. There were myriad rumors every week of this noble or that wealthy merchant plotting to overthrow King Karl.

Sebastian had wanted to unite Wesloria and Alucia, too. But his idea had been to strike a trade agreement with England. He'd wanted the Chartiers and Oberons and their fellow countrymen to unite in the strength of industrialization and shared prosperity—not by the ravages of war.

Unfortunately, not everyone shared his desire for peace. A plot had unfolded while Sebastian was in England that had involved treachery at the highest reaches of Alucian government and had resulted in the murder of Sebastian's personal secretary. But in the way tragedy had of revealing a silver lining, his brother had met and fallen in love with Eliza.

Today was the happiest of occasions, but the threat of war and attempts at a coup still surrounded the royal family outside the ivy-covered walls of the palace. No one had forgotten it. Least of all, the king.

"We can make greater progress with Alucia if we align ourselves with the right Weslorians," his father said, glancing over his shoulder.

"The *right* Weslorians?"

"Those who have no desire to unify," his father said, glancing around. "There are many advantages to keeping our borders and our sovereignty."

Leo didn't know what those advantages were and really didn't care to learn them. He liked not knowing the advantages of sovereignty. It all seemed unduly complicated.

"A highly placed minister in the Weslorian cabinet is very keen to foster better trade and economic arrangements with Wesloria. He is the minister of labor, and there is every reason to believe he will be the next Weslorian prime minister." His father waggled his brows. "A marriage with his daughter would serve us well, indeed."

Us. His father said the word without hesitation or hint

of irony, as if his parents and even Bas and Eliza would walk down the aisle with him. "I understand," Leo said as he tried to quickly think of a way out of this corner. "But I'm not—"

"You will make her acquaintance tonight, at the ball. You'll want to be certain to do it publicly, where everyone will see. Dance with her."

Leo could feel what little blood was left in him after last night's festivities draining from his limbs. So it really had been *all* arranged.

It was, in some ways, quite galling to him. When Leo was a young man, he'd wanted this sort of responsibility. He'd wanted to be a prince with a cause and had begged to be useful. But his father had given all real responsibility to Bas. Leo still recalled being denied the opportunity to join the cavalry because Bas was to join. He was still bitter about begging his father for something with purpose and being proclaimed the royal patron of the town criers. The bloody town criers.

There had been other things, and somewhere along the way, Leo had ceased to care about purpose. Purpose, he'd learned, was for Bas.

"Do you not want to know who she is, then?" his father asked jovially.

The king was proud of himself for this arrangement, and it clearly didn't matter how Leo felt about it. He shrugged.

"Lady Eulalie Gaspar."

Leo didn't know any Gaspars, much less any Eulalies.

His father smiled coolly at Leo's lack of enthusiasm and put his hand on his shoulder. He squeezed as if Leo was being a precocious child. "It's already been arranged, Leopold. We mean to make the formal announcement when you've returned from England with your things well be-

fore the summer ends. You will court her properly for a
few weeks and a formal announcement will be made by
end of summer. But for all intents and purposes, you may
consider yourself affianced."

"I'm to consider myself affianced before I've even met
her? Before I've even *kissed* her?" Leo asked coldly.

His father sighed and dropped his hand. "You know
very well how these arrangements are made. Your mother
and I ask very little of you, and this is something I need
you to do."

That they asked very little of him was at the heart of
his discontent. "It's not as if you are asking me to walk
your dog," Leo said.

"Son," his father said sternly. "You always knew this
day would come. You needn't look as if I've commanded
your head to be lopped off. It's just a woman, for God's
sake."

Just a woman. Not a wife, not a companion. Just a woman.

"Now go and speak kindly to the ambassador from
Wesloria." He nodded in the direction of the ambassador.
"Ask after his horse—he claims to have a gelding who
has clocked a faster speed than any horse known in this
part of the world." His father winked in a manner that was
completely uncharacteristic and walked on, sipping his
champagne before being swallowed up by people seeking his attention.

Leo stood in the same spot where his father had left
him, stung and inwardly outraged. His father was right—
he had known this day would come. But he'd thought there
would at least be some discussion, that his desires would
be taken into consideration.

He needed a drink and looked around for a footman.
Not wine, thank you. Something heartier. Gin. Whisky.

He turned to see where the Weslorian ambassador was standing and spotted him in lively conversation with Hawke's sister. Or rather, she was holding audience, her slender hands animating whatever tale she was imparting to the circle of gentlemen around her. Always attracting a crowd, that one. She suddenly tossed back her head and laughed loudly.

The ambassador seemed taken aback by it

That woman. Gregarious and loud. She laughed carelessly; she told tales that apparently required the expansive use of her hands. She touched an arm here, a back there. She was in a royal palace at a royal reception, having the time of her life with not a single care for how she appeared. Meanwhile, he was an impotent prince, where the rules of society and royal protocol dictated what he said, what he ate, who he bloody well would marry. He was the one commanded to make small talk about a bloody horse with someone he hardly knew and didn't want to know, while she breezily chattered on about God knew what.

Leo must have been standing and staring for too long— he slowly became aware of people looking in his direction. People who looked as if they might want a word. A "word" generally led to unusual requests and introductions he did not want to make.

No. Leo wanted to escape this palace and everything that went with it. But since he couldn't do that, he determined he would escape to meet his friends as planned.

In a poor attempt at self-encouragement, he told himself that all he needed was time. Just a little bit of time to figure out how to postpone his fate a little longer.

CHAPTER THREE

Celebrations of the royal nuptials were held all over the city of Helenamar, including at the Foxhound Public House, a unique gathering place in the center of Old Helenamar, where it was rumored Prince Leopold made an appearance. Monsieur Bernard, a notorious Frenchman who is believed by some Alucians to be plotting with the Weslorians, was also spotted at the Foxhound in the company of Prince Leopold.

White satin boots are on the feet of every discerning Alucian woman in the evenings. They are often decorated with beads and ribbons to complement the gown, and the heels so high that the casual observer fears the lady may topple right off.

๑—Honeycutt's Gazette of Fashion and
Domesticity for Ladies

SHORTLY AFTER ELIZA and Bas made their escape from the afternoon's private reception—no doubt to find a room, as their esteem for each other had now become notorious in every corner of the palace, if not the entire city—Leo managed to take his leave, too.

He'd been looking forward to this reunion with old friends since arriving in Helenamar. It was unavoidable that so much ceremony would attend any event that included the royal family, and it was unavoidable that he would chafe at it. But he was fortunate in that he had a pair of palace guards who had been with him for many years and were accustomed to arranging these outings for him.

The Foxhound was situated between a pair of stately gated homes, and across from a public stable. It enjoyed a rare and curious mix of clientele—this was the one place in all of Helenamar where aristocrats mingled with ordinary residents of the city. It was the one place Leopold could go without being beset by men or women who wanted something from him. It was the one place he could hear the news of the country that hadn't been filtered for him or painted in a most pleasing light by palace personnel. The truth won out at the Foxhound.

His friends were all on hand today, and already three tankards into the afternoon. When he entered, a rousing cry of delight went up.

"What of the evening's festivities?" Leo laughingly asked, gesturing to the empty tankards scattered among them.

"There's plenty of time to sober up and make ourselves presentable," Francois said, and threw a collegiate arm around Leo's shoulders as he bellowed for the barmaid to bring more ale.

Francois was a Frenchman who had immigrated to Alucia at a very young age and had attended the same hallowed halls of education as had Leo and Bas. With the fringe of dark ginger hair that hung over one eye, he was charming and always jovial. He was a raconteur as well, and today he'd brought an entertaining tale of an encounter with a dance-hall girl.

Leo and his friends drank more ale, toasted his brother and his bride, reminisced about their school days and laughed uproariously at bawdy jokes. At some point in the afternoon, Leo found a barmaid seated on his lap. He didn't recall the specifics, but there she was, casually stroking his hair behind his ear.

It would seem, he thought hazily, that he'd had too much to drink. Again.

Apparently, Harvel, another school chum, thought the same. "Look here, Your Highness, you ought to carry on, hadn't you? Are you not required to attend the ball?"

"I am indeed," Leo said, and put his tankard of ale down with a thud. "As brother of the new duke, as son of the king, as..." He tried to think.

"As squiffed as a bloody prince!" shouted Voltan.

"As squiffed as a bloody prince!" Leo heartily echoed, and lifted his tankard, sloshing a good deal of ale onto the table. He was *indeed* inebriated. So much so that it took him two attempts to push the girl from his lap and find his feet. He stood up, patting down his coat and trousers in search of coins, and finding none. Ah, of course. In Alucia, he had no need of money.

He was feeling a little dizzy and regretting that he'd drunk so much, but his friends were quite amused by his attempts to find a purse and waved him off. "Think nothing of it, Chartier," Francois said. "We'll pay for your ale. Consider it our last gift to a free man."

"What's that you say?" Leo asked, and surged forward, planting his hands on the table. "Do you know something I ought to know?"

"Only what all of Helenamar knows, lad," Francois said. He winked, and all of them laughed. "Go on, then, enjoy an evening of royal repast as is your due, and your loyal subjects will pay for your ale."

"I am in your debt," he said, and with a flourish of his

hand, he bowed grandly. "Where are my guards? I am all but certain I came with guards."

"Here, Your Highness," said Kadro, and put his hand to Leo's arm to turn him about. His other guard, Artur, stood stoically by.

Leo smiled. No, he laughed. "There you are!" he said gaily. *Jmil*, he was drunk. If he didn't dry out quickly, he'd have hell to pay tonight. His father's displeasure was something that could be felt to the depth of one's marrow.

Leo blathered his farewells to his old friends, and God help him if he didn't get a wee bit teary. He invited them all to call on him in England, and they all very earnestly agreed to come.

Leo emerged onto the quiet street between Kadro and Artur, blinking back the late afternoon sun, but managing to walk a fairly straight line to the curb. "Look at me, lads," he said, laughing. "The king will have my bloody head, will he not?" He wasn't so drunk that he didn't notice neither guard disagreed with him.

He looked up and down the street. He'd expected the coach to be waiting—in Helenamar, Leo was accustomed to walking out a door and straight into a waiting conveyance. With all the unrest on the border with Wesloria, maximum caution was taken every time one of the royal family stepped beyond the palace walls. "The coach," he said, as if his guards hadn't noticed it missing. "Where is it?"

There was a discussion between the two guards—something about the driver being instructed to wait at a distance so as not to alert anyone to the presence of the prince in the pub—and then Kadro said, "I'll have a look around the corner, Your Highness, if I have your leave?"

"Have a look wherever you like," Leo said, and watched

rather stupidly as Kadro disappeared around the corner. Behind him, something made a strange noise, like the staccato of gunfire. Artur jerked in that direction. "If you please, Your Highness, wait here," he said, and went striding in the direction of the sound.

Even in his state of inebriation, Leo thought this was all highly unusual, to be left standing on the street without anyone about. He slumped against the side of the building, smiling to himself. He'd had a good day, all in all. Well, save the wretched headache he'd begun the day with. And his father's pronouncement to him. Leo had managed to forget that unpleasantry over the space of a few hours, but now it came tripping back to him, disturbing the buzzy tranquility he'd developed in the company of his friends.

He was thinking of all he wished he'd said to his father instead of bumbling through it and didn't notice the two men darting across the street in his direction until they were upon him. When he realized they were not passing by, it was woefully too late, as they were pulling him into an alley next to the public house. When he understood what was happening, he tried to shout for his guard, but his voice was garbled with his confusion and his inability to make his feet work properly beneath him.

The next thing he knew, he was caught in an alley with two men he'd never seen before. A sick punch of dread hit his belly, threatening to purge all the ale he'd so recklessly drunk.

"What is the meaning of this?" he demanded in Alucian.

"Please be calm, Your Highness," one of them said as they dragged him toward the dead end of the alley, then attempted to prop him up against the wall.

"Calm?" He flailed, waving them away. "Who are you? I have a right to know who or what is about to befall

me." A flurry of watery thoughts and emotions suddenly swirled in him—fear, regret, impatience—and all led to the same conclusion rather quickly: the inevitability of this very thing.

"I'll keep watch," one of the men said to the other in Alucian. He turned and took a few steps toward the alley entrance.

The other man took a tentative step toward Leo.

"See here now, I know death is inevitable," Leo said.

"We do not—"

"And if this is the way I am to die, I will meet it with courage and grace," Leo continued, spreading his arms wide. For a moment—he couldn't hold his balance. "But make no mistake, sir. I will meet my end with a fight. Although I seem to be outnumbered, and I see nothing in this alley that will do for a weapon." He squinted at what appeared to be a cat atop some stacked crates, entirely unperturbed by his imminent demise. "Is that a cat?"

The man turned to look.

"I would kick my own arse for being so blasted drunk if I could," Leo said, remembering his predicament and glancing around for something to swing at the man's head. "And if I survive this hijacking, I shall never taste a spirit again." He paused. "Well. After tonight, I won't. I will be required to drink a toast to my brother, of course."

"Your Highness," the man said in Alucian, and stepped closer to Leo, his arm outstretched, his palm facing Leo. That's when Leo noticed the green armband. It was a Weslorian custom—a band or patch of dark green fitted around the sleeve or pinned to a breast, a lapel, a cuff, to indicate the person was Weslorian.

"You're Weslorian," he said. "I should have known. You mean to murder me, just as you murdered poor Matous.

You ought to be ashamed, choosing the occasion of my brother's wedding to murder me. You might have at least waited until the happy occasion had come to a close. Although, I grant you, it seems as if the happy occasion will never end—"

"Your Highness, please! We mean no harm," the man said, lifting his hands in a placating manner.

"Ho," Leo blustered incredulously. "I may be pissed, but I'm no fool!"

"I beg of you, Your Highness, we haven't much time," the man said, and stepped even closer. He really was quite small, Leo realized. If he hadn't looked him in the face, he would have thought him a lad. His diminutive size merely added insult to this egregious injury—he would be killed or kidnapped by a man half his size.

"We've a message from Lysander."

It was one long ale-soaked moment before Leo was able to grasp what the man had said. *Lysander.* Leo blinked. He rummaged around his thoughts trying to piece things together. Lysander was a man who spent his life righting terrible wrongs. He was a Samaritan, a man who had dedicated his existence to the helping of others. Leo knew a little about him after he famously rallied the people of Helenamar to close the workhouses. Leo had been abroad at the time, but apparently Lysander had caused quite a stir.

"What message?" Leo asked blearily.

"He asks for your help," the elfin man said.

"What? Mine?" Leo asked, pointing to himself. "Why me? For what?"

"He would explain that himself in person. He asks, respectfully, if you would be so kind as to meet him tomorrow afternoon." He smiled.

Why was he *smiling*? It was annoying, given the circumstances. Leo couldn't think properly, but there was no reason the famed Lysander would want anything to do with him. "If he wants my help, why does he not come to me? Why not join us and the cat here in the alley?"

"It was impossible, Your Highness. You and your family have been surrounded by an army during the wedding celebrations. And he is a wanted man."

"Wanted! For what?" Leo asked dumbly. He tried to recall as much as he could about the workhouse riots. Had they not resolved it? Had Lysander not been hailed a hero for bringing the plight to the awareness of the king and Parliament?

"He asks, respectfully, if you might meet him in the palace gardens tomorrow afternoon at three."

Leo snorted. "He won't come here but will meet me in the palace gardens?"

"The walls of public houses have too many ears."

"And the palace gardens don't? If he can't enter a public street, how will he enter the palace grounds? How am I to know that this is not some sort of trap?"

"I beg your pardon, Your Highness, but I can't answer your questions. Lysander has his ways, and I will not pretend to understand how he does what he does. He has determined the palace grounds might be the safest place for him. No one would think to look there for him, would they? He asks that you receive him there, free of advisers and observers."

Leo's suspicions ratcheted. What could the man possibly want with him? "I know nothing of workhouses," he blustered. "I know nothing of anything. I've been in England the last six years. Why did he not send a note? Why have me kidnapped on the occasion of my brother's wedding?"

"It is my deep regret if you believed you were being kidnapped, or—"

"Or murdered," Leo reminded him.

The man winced. "You must know that there are those close to you who would obstruct any effort he made to speak to you."

Leo stared at the man. What was he implying? That there were spies around him? "Who?" he demanded.

The large man behind him whistled. The smaller man started. "Tomorrow, in the palace gardens at three. Please. It is very important," he said, and hurried to the entrance of the alley.

"Wait," Leo commanded. *"Wait."*

But neither of them waited. Leo started after them, but a beat too late. By the time he reached the entry to the alleyway, they had disappeared. He looked around wildly and saw Kadro walking down the street toward him. "Where have you been?" Leo exclaimed.

Kadro looked surprised. "We have the carriage, Your Highness." He nodded to something past Leo. He whirled around—Artur was standing beside a waiting carriage, facing the several people on the street who had gathered to see who the carriage was intended to serve. Leo looked at Kadro again, his confusion mounting. Had his guards known he'd be accosted? Had they been part of it? Were *they* the spies? In London, after Matous's murder, Bas had told him he could trust no one. But Leo had never dreamed that would extend to two men who had been his paid companions for several years now.

He felt uncomfortably confused and said nothing more, but turned and strode toward the carriage, his gait much steadier now that his heart had beat a good portion of the inebriation out of him.

In the privacy of the carriage, Leo leaned back against the squabs and closed his eyes. There was a dull throb at the base of his skull now. This was absurd. He wasn't meeting anyone in the palace gardens on the morrow! He was incensed he'd been cornered like that and incensed with himself for being so careless.

His rage mixed badly with the ale and left him feeling sour.

CHAPTER FOUR

Their Majesties King and Queen of Alucia were pleased to host a royal ball celebrating the nuptials of Crown Prince Sebastian to Lady Eliza Tricklebank at Constantine Palace. The guests included dignitaries and heads of state from European and Asian capitals, and a healthy contingent of English nobility.

The wedding cake was made of five tiers and towering three feet, adorned with marzipan gold doves that appeared to be flying around the cake. Guests feasted on fine Alucian beef and Krantanhange, *a delicacy made of potato, leek and asparagus. The ball was performed by a ten-piece orchestra, and a mix of Alucian dances and the standard English fare of waltz and minuet rounded out the sets.*

A new bachelor has emerged as the most eligible from the fraternity of princes. Judging by the number of Alucian heiresses casting kohl-lined eyes in his direction and flocking to the side of this debonair prince, one might assume with utmost certainty that wedding bells soon will ring again in Helenamar.

It is noted that Alucian women do not shy away from cosmetics to enhance their appearance. Upon observing the beauty of Alucian women, we can highly recommend the application of almond com-

*plexion cream to one's face every night before
sleeping.*

—*Honeycutt's Gazette of Fashion and
Domesticity for Ladies*

CAROLINE'S GOWN FOR the wedding ball was the most gorgeous thing she'd ever seen. The pale blue-and-gold Alucian style was cut so tightly to her figure that she could scarcely breathe. But she didn't care—so many ladies and gentlemen would admire her in it that it would be worth the discomfort.

She'd commissioned the gown for such a dear sum that she'd been compelled to convince the modiste to submit two invoices in two separate months, each for half the amount, so that her brother Beck would not know the true cost. He tended to be very cross when she purchased clothing and sundries. And as the train had not suited her, Caroline had made her own. It was, in her eyes, a work of art.

As she'd readied for the ball, she tried to entice Hollis to admire the gown, too, but as usual, Hollis was bent over paper, writing furiously, capturing every moment for her gazette.

Hollis's periodical had been originally established by her late husband, Sir Percival. His publication had been a once-monthly conservative gazette that highlighted political and financial news in London. After his tragic death in a carriage accident, Hollis refused to let the gazette go. She was determined that the paper survive to honor Percival. However, she didn't know a lot about politics and finances, so she turned the gazette on its head and dedicated it solely to topics that interested women. Now the gazette was bimonthly with more than three times the subscriptions of Percival's and growing.

Caroline took it upon herself to point out how stunning was her gown. "Look at how beautiful I am!" she declared, holding her arms wide. "I think my gown is as beautiful as Eliza's. Don't you?"

Hollis barely looked up. "I can't see the gown, really— I am blinded by your modesty."

Caroline snorted. "Someone must make note of this gown, and if no one will, *I* will."

"The gown is stunning. But Beck is right, Caro—you are terribly vain."

"Well, it's hardly my fault, is it? I've been so long admired that I can't help but believe my appeal."

Hollis looked up, surprised by Caroline's lack of humility.

Caroline laughed. "I was teasing you, Hollis, although you must admit there is some truth to it. *Now* will you look at my gown? Frankly, it's better than even yours, and I thought yours was the most beautiful thing I'd ever seen."

"Your gown is always better than mine," Hollis said, and leaned back, examining Caroline from head to toe. "You're right. It is beautiful. *You* are beautiful."

"*Thank* you," Caroline said, and dipped a small curtsy. She whirled back to the mirror, and in doing so, caused one side of the train to come unbuttoned and fall. "Oh *bother*."

"Come," Hollis said, gesturing her forward like a child. She refastened Caroline's train to one of the buttons meant to keep it from dragging twenty feet behind her. "Remember, no sudden movements. They come undone when you twist and lurch about."

"I do not *lurch*, and *you* remember to put your pencil away tonight," Caroline said. "It's the royal wedding ball, Hollis."

"As my sister is the bride, I am keenly aware of the occasion, darling. And I am dressed for it, as you can see. But I will not risk forgetting a single detail! The only way to ensure that I don't is to write things down as I observe them."

Hollis's dark blue eyes flashed with determination. Caroline knew that she wanted more than anything for her gazette to be taken seriously by everyone in London.

Ah, but Hollis looked so much like Eliza, even though her hair was so darkly brown it looked nearly black, whereas Eliza's hair was the color of spun gold. The sisters were very comely women. If Caroline didn't love them so, she would be envious. "You know, darling," Caroline said slyly, "if you were to look up from your notes, at an event like this it is quite possible that you might meet your one and only."

Hollis gasped as if Caroline had slapped her. "How dare you even suggest it, Caro! Percival was my one and only, and there won't be another! It's not possible there will *ever* be another love like what we shared."

Caroline turned slightly so that Hollis could not see her roll her eyes. The way she went on about her late husband was enough to make womankind across the globe give up any hope of finding perfect love, because Hollis and Percy had taken it and locked it away, never again to be experienced in this world with the same intense passion.

And yet there were some—including Caroline, frankly—who believed that the beautiful Widow Honeycutt had found her next love in her houseman, Donovan. Everyone who had ever called at Hollis's house noted the striking good looks and virile physique of her butler. Or manservant. Or cook—whatever role it was Donovan filled. Hollis was rather vague about it, and Donovan was slavishly devoted to her. Caroline assumed he and Hollis were having a forbidden love affair. *She* certainly would be tempted if she were in Hollis's shoes. A woman of her standing would not publicly consort with a manservant, but behind closed doors, well... Hollis was a widow after all.

"Keep your mind to *your* one and only," Hollis muttered.

Caroline didn't say anything. She supposed it was possible—after all, important gentlemen of all stripes would be in attendance. So would that wretched Prince Leopold, who always looked so detached, as if he thought himself above everyone else in the room. All right, she would concede that by virtue of his very good looks and his princely title he was above most, but he wasn't a king, for heaven's sake. But never mind him. She refused to think about him another moment. She had thought about him entirely too much in the last few weeks when she should have been thinking about much more important things.

She examined her reflection in the mirror. She practiced moving, taking care to dip this way and that, not only because of her elaborate train, but also because her décolletage, dear God, plunged so low that it was entirely possible that everyone at the ball would spot her navel.

Beck would be so displeased with it. She smiled.

She was equally certain that if Prince Leopold saw her, he'd be very pleased with her figure...if he wasn't already swimming in his cups. He seemed to swim in them quite a lot.

It was getting the prince to *see* her that was the bother. Not that she cared if he did, but it was the principle of it. They were practically kin now, and yet she had the distinct impression he didn't care for her. She couldn't imagine why not. She hadn't done anything untoward. She hadn't spread awful rumors about him. She hadn't committed any social faux pas in his presence.

She could never seem to get as much as a moment with him—he was constantly surrounded by footmen, Alucian gentlemen, and women. Scads and scads of women. Why were there so many *women* in the world?

Caroline grew restless, and as Hollis could not be persuaded to stop making her notes, she would not wait politely for Beck to arrive. So she went out of their suite and wandered down the hallway without Hollis even noticing.

Caroline had discovered in the last month that there was a point in the upper floor hallway that curved around an opening beneath a glass cupola in the roof, built to allow light to the floors below. At a particular bend in the hall, one could look over the balustrade and see down two floors below, to the entrance to this part of the palace.

She and Hollis and Beck were housed in a private wing of the palace, where family guests and some members of the extended royal family resided. Caroline liked to watch people come and go without being seen herself, as the shaft of sunlight made it difficult for people below to see up to the top floor. Standing here is where she'd seen Lady Senria Ferrassen arrive one evening in the company of the king's equerry, and the two had parted with a quick and furtive kiss. Another blustery afternoon, she'd seen three chambermaids meet in the foyer and whisper excitedly to one another before all three of them disappeared quickly and in different directions when Lady Senria entered, her hair mussed, her cheeks rosy.

As Caroline was already dressed for the ball, she didn't venture any farther than that point on the balustrade, hiding in plain sight. She wanted her gown to be seen for the first time when she made her entrance to the ballroom, as it ought, for maximum impact. At this hour, however, most were preparing for the evening or had already walked the distance to the main palace ballroom. There was nothing to see below, save the occasional footman or chambermaid hurrying across the black-and-white marble floor.

She grew bored with it and was turning to go when the entrance door swung open and a man walked in. He paused in the middle of the foyer, pushed his fingers through his dark brown hair, then settled his hands on his waist. That man, much to her great surprise, was clearly Prince Leopold. What was he doing at this hour dressed like that? He was wearing plain clothes and his hair was disheveled, and he stood a bit unsteadily, as if he'd just heard some bad news. And then, without warning, he looked up.

He looked up and directly at her with his ocean-blue eyes, and Caroline felt the intensity of his gaze radiating through her. She made a tiny little squeal of surprise and jumped back, clapping a hand to her heart. But she just as quickly surged forward and looked over the railing again. He was still there, and he suddenly smiled so charmingly and with such warmth that she quite lost her breath for a moment. He was actually *smiling* at her. And in response, she felt a very happy smile forming on her own lips. She could feel all sorts of things stirring, really—a laugh of delight. A gasp. A tingle in her groin.

"It would appear you've caught me, then," he called up.

Caroline giggled. She didn't know what to say for once. To agree would be to admit to spying. She would say that she was just passing by, or—

"I've caught you at your pleasure, I should hope," responded a familiar voice.

Caroline gasped and jumped back again. *That* was her brother's voice, and it came from the floor directly below her. He was undoubtedly on his way up to fetch her. She further realized that the prince had smiled so beatifically not at her but at her *brother*. At Beck! Blasted Beck! Always in the way!

"You could say," the prince agreed.

"You're to the ball, are you? I understand there is to be some high-stakes cards in the game room."

Caroline backed away from the railing and began to hurry down the hall as quietly as she could, cursing the rustle of her skirts. She didn't hear what the prince said in response, because her heart was thudding in her ears.

She burst into the suite of rooms she shared with Hollis.

"Lord, Caro, look what you made me do!" Hollis exclaimed crossly, and abruptly stood. Ink had spilled on her paper.

"I'm terribly sorry." Caroline pressed her hands to her abdomen in the vain hope to temper her breathing, trying to catch her breath from the surprise. Where had the prince been, anyway, dressed like that? She'd wondered what had become of him during the reception. She'd been speaking with the Weslorian ambassador to England, telling him the story of the country house party at which a horse had run wild with a man on his back, necessitating rescue by no less than four gentlemen, when she noticed Prince Leopold was no longer visible from the corner of her eye. And when she turned to have a closer look, he was nowhere to be seen. He had slipped out without her noticing! Not that she was watching his every move, because she was *not*. She just had a tendency to notice things.

He'd run off for a tryst. Of course! What else would have taken him from the palace on this day? What else would see him return to the palace looking as if he'd fallen out of bed and right into his clothes? Were men so desperately sexual all the time?

A loud rap on the door was followed by it swinging

open, and Beck strolled in. He paused just inside the doorway and stared at the two of them. "I had hoped that someone might have come and whisked you both down to the ball you're determined to attend and thus spare me the deed. Alas, I see my dreams have been dashed."

"A splendid good evening to you, as well, Beck," Hollis said cheerily.

"*My lord* is customary, Hollis, but I'll allow it in light of your obvious delirium of happiness at your sister's nuptials."

"Where have you been?" Caroline demanded. "I've been waiting and waiting."

"What are you talking about? I was giving you ample time to admire yourself in the mirror," he said. "Are you ready?"

"Is it not obvious? I've *been* ready. We both have. You were expected a half hour ago." She checked her hair in the mirror once more.

"I beg your pardon, but I was out with my Alucian friends. Cheerful lot, I must say. What has happened to the bodice of your gown, Caro? It looks to have gone missing."

"You were with *friends*?" Caroline said, arching one brow, hoping to skim over the fact that her bodice had indeed gone missing, and moreover, she didn't intend to look for it. "What friends? Of which gender?"

"One of two possibilities. Is that another new gown?"

She rolled her eyes at him. "How can you even ask? Of *course* it is—I couldn't wear anything that I've already worn, not to tonight's ball. Even *you* know that."

"Do you think our funds flow from a bottomless well?" he asked crossly as he dropped into a seat. "You buy gowns as if they cost nothing."

"Pardon, but wasn't it you who purchased an Alucian

racehorse just last week, Beck?" Hollis asked as she closed her notebook. "You buy horses as if they cost nothing."

Beck pointed a finger at her. "*You* are not allowed to offer any opinion or observation just now. Did no one ever tell you to mind your own business?"

Hollis laughed. "Many times. But be forewarned—if I'm not allowed to speak my observations, then I shall write them."

To the casual observer, this behavior between Hollis and Beck might have been deemed alarmingly impolite, but Beck had known Hollis and Eliza as long as he'd known Caroline. They were family, really. For years, Eliza and Hollis had summered with them at the Hawke country estate. Caroline was a frequent visitor to the home of Justice Tricklebank, their widowed father, who treated her like one of his own. And when their mothers, the best of friends, had died of cholera—Caroline's mother succumbing after caring for Hollis and Eliza's mother—Beck had treated Eliza and Hollis as if they were his wards, too.

In other words, he paid them no heed most of the time, and they paid him even less.

Beck stacked his feet on an ottoman. "I'm exhausted. All of this wedding business has taken its toll. I could sleep for days—"

"No, no, no," Caroline said quickly. "You mustn't make yourself comfortable, Beck. We're already late! We *must* carry on to the ball—it would be the height of inconsiderate behavior to arrive after the newlyweds. You, too, Hollis. It's time to go."

"Just a moment," Hollis said. "I'm making note about the purchase of a racehorse." She glanced at Beck sidelong.

"Am I never allowed any peace?" Beck groaned. "For God's sake, then, come on, the two of you. What joy I will experience when you're both married and I may be relieved of my never-ending duty to escort you about town."

"What an absurd thing to say," Caroline said as she checked her headdress one last time. "We are the very reason you are able to attend these events without looking as if you haven't a friend in the world. You *need* us, Beck."

"What I need is silence and a bed," he said blithely as he offered one arm to Caroline and the other to Hollis. "Let's get this over and done, shall we, ladies?"

"Oh, Beck, how *charming* you are," Hollis said dreamily. "Just when I think I despise you, I discover I love you all over again."

WHEN LORD HAWKE and his charges had been announced and had entered the crowded ballroom, Caroline looked around for Prince Leopold. Naturally, after his afternoon of debauchery, he was nowhere to be seen.

She was inexplicably exasperated by his absence. Should he not have been here, in the center of attention, doing his duty as brother of the groom? Prince Sebastian and Eliza were due to arrive at any moment, but his brother couldn't be bothered to arrive in time?

And why had he come into the private wing of the palace looking as if he'd been wrestling? The king and queen were here, as were a variety of Alucian nobility Caroline had met in the month she'd been in Helenamar.

Well, no matter—Caroline didn't care a whit. Whenever he did deign to make his appearance, she was quite confident that her stunning dress and her obvious appeal would catch his eye. By then, of course, it would to be too late for him. By then she would be surrounded by admiring gentlemen and have no room for him on her dance card. Being admired was her forte, after all.

She checked her train to make sure it was securely fastened and sallied forth to meet all the gentlemen.

CHAPTER FIVE

With all the excitement of a very grand royal wedding, most would be content to come away with the experience of it. But for the families of several young women, the royal wedding ball was a perfect opportunity to begin talks of a new royal wedding. Alas, while Prince Leopold was seen dancing with no less than a dozen such young women, it is common knowledge that an engagement to a Weslorian songbird has all been arranged, and an announcement will soon be made.

This news did not prevent the only remaining bachelor prince in Alucia from departing the ball before anyone else.

⌒—Honeycutt's Gazette of Fashion and
Domesticity for Ladies

LEO REQUIRED TWO cups of medicinal tea and a cold bath before he began to feel in control of his faculties. He did not feel himself, really—that encounter in the alleyway had left him rattled. From his initial fear of imminent death, to the more insidious fear that someone was plotting against him, to the new fear creeping into his thoughts about what this Lysander fellow needed to say to him, he couldn't seem to find his footing.

Were there truly spies among them? He had hoped that

the cancer had been rooted out after the murder of Matous in London. That the palace had been swept clean of those plotting to overthrow the king. Then again, that sounded awfully naive, to think the palace had been swept clean of plotting and intrigue. Still, plotting and intrigue never had anything to do with him.

What could Lysander possibly want?

As Leo soaked in the bath, he tried to recall the details from the workhouse riots a few years ago. Lysander was a priest from the northern mountains of Alucia that formed the border with Wesloria. He'd come to the capital city, like so many other mountain people, in search of work. According to the reports about him at the time of the riots, he'd found deplorable conditions at the workhouses.

Once, Leo had been riding with friends through the streets of Helenamar. They had happened upon the man standing on an overturned crate, shouting at a crowd of people who gave him their rapt attention. "People are dying!" he'd bellowed. "The people in the workhouses lack clean water and decent food!"

"Did he say workhouse or whorehouse?" Edoard, one of Leo's companions, had quipped. Their friends had laughed. Leo had not laughed. He'd wondered if what the man said was true.

He'd been intrigued by the mountain of a man with the unruly blond hair, and his courage to rebel about those conditions and thereby risk arrest and detention. "Do you suppose it's true?" he'd asked his friends.

"No," Edoard had said immediately. "He wants attention, that's all."

"He's lucky he doesn't have the attention of the metropolitan police," Jacques had said.

"If Helenamar is to be the jewel of Europe, can such

conditions exist for her residents?" the big man had asked the crowd. "If Alucia is to lead the way in economic de velopment, can she treat the most common of her workers like dogs?"

The crowd was riled and began to chant back at him. *Pane er vesi. Pane er vesi.* Food and water.

"Will any of the men at the highest reaches of your government listen to a man like me?" he shouted.

"Noo!" the crowd roared back.

Lysander shook his head. "No. But they will listen to *all* of us."

"Je, je, je, je!" the crowd began to chant.

"Come," Edoard had said. "Before it gets out of hand."

It wasn't until another fortnight had passed that Leo's curiosity peaked, and he found a way to have a look at the workhouses himself—incognito. He was completely unprepared and unaware of the conditions in which common people lived. The workhouses—dank, overcrowded and dirty—certainly had not been part of his education. People *were* suffering without adequate food, clothing or shelter. They were made to work long hours for a meager existence. He'd been incensed on their behalf. He'd been reminded again of how privileged he was. His conscience had been pricked.

He mentioned the conditions to his father one evening during a private meal. "Don't listen to the false prophets, Leopold. The man wants fame. That's all."

Leo had tried to start a conversation with his father about it, but as usual, his father was uninterested in what he had to say. He'd smiled and said, "Worry about your studies, son."

In the end, it was Leo's mother who had turned the tide.

"I don't think you should ignore this man," she said to her husband. "He seems dangerous to me."

Leo never really knew what had happened after that—he returned to England and his very vibrant social life. But the Alucian Parliament took up the cause, and the work-houses were eventually shut down. Now factories provided modest housing for the workers.

By the end of his bath, Leo had determined it didn't mat-ter what Lysander wanted—Leo wouldn't involve himself with it. He wouldn't be in the garden tomorrow, because Leo was setting sail in two nights, no matter what.

There was a soft rap at the door, and then Leo's valet, Freddar, appeared, holding a large towel. "Will you dress now, Your Highness?"

Leo sighed. *"Je."* He couldn't avoid the ball. All eyes would be on Leo tonight, more so than ever before. He was the new prized bull, the one everyone wanted as sire. For years, he'd watched Bas endure these evenings and the endless introductions to all manner of women—short and round, tall and thin. Beautiful and plain. Women with pleasing dispositions and those who were cold as fish. All of them wanting an opportunity to woo a crown prince. Leo was no crown prince, but as of today, he was the next best thing. It hardly mattered that his father had already negotiated a marriage—the wealthy and privileged would present their daughters and sisters to him like gifts from the Magi.

His long black formal frock was embellished with the *dignitatis epaulets* on the shoulders, denoting his rank in the military. A rank that was achieved by virtue of his birth and nothing else. He would also wear a royal blue sash onto which medals of his family's name, military achievements and honors would be affixed. None of them belonged to him personally.

Those medals would complement the larger, ribboned medals that were pinned to his chest, also granted because of his titles and privileges and for nothing that *he'd* done. Such as the large bloom of white ribbon with a gold circle and pearls encrusted in the middle, the Order of the King's Garter. There were more medals that signified his rank in the navy and the army—bestowed on him because he was a prince—as well as the Order of Merit and the Order of the Reeve, given to him by his father. And of course, his father's coronation medal, another large gold piece with dark blue and gold ribbons, that celebrated Leo's royal birth.

He was doused in the symbols and trappings of his family's wealth and privilege, and he'd done absolutely nothing to deserve any of it. How was it fair that by virtue of his birth alone he should have such fortune? How was it fair that another child, born into lesser circumstances, would struggle through his or her life and accomplish far more than Leo ever would, yet not have a single medal worth so much? Any one of these medals on his chest would bring prosperity to a family for several years.

Why me?

That question had plagued him at various times in his life. He was eight years old the first time he'd asked it. He'd befriended a boy in the stables. His name was Tadd or something close to it. Leo couldn't rightly recall his name, but he could still see his face, as if he'd spoken to him only yesterday. He and Tadd had formed a friendship over a horse. Tadd had taught him quite a lot about horses—how to brush their coats and manes, how to clean their hooves.

It had been Leo's idea to sneak the horse from the stables and ride him. The freckle-faced lad was reluctant, but at Leo's insistence, he went along with it.

When they were discovered, Tadd was dragged off the horse and roundly beaten in front of Leo, even as Leo cried for the stable master to stop. And then Tadd simply disappeared. Leo had been left with a searing sense of responsibility and unfairness about the whole thing.

That was the first time he'd been aware of the enormous privilege he enjoyed and how little he'd done to deserve it.

He had learned in the years that followed to turn a blind eye to those feelings and accept his life as it was and be grateful for it. That was easy to do when surrounded by the children of aristocrats who similarly had their lives handed to them. It was easy when he had the luxury to spend his days with his friends, or abroad. He'd grown lazy in that way wealth had of making a man disinclined to lift many fingers. Nothing was expected of him other than to finish his studies and not impregnate a chamber girl. *That* he could do.

He had learned to dull the tedium and the unfairness of it all with alcohol. What he wanted was to go back to England and the dissolute but happy manner in which he lived.

LEO WAS ANNOUNCED with enough fanfare to make his head throb, then escorted by two footmen on either flank to the dais where his parents sat on their thrones. As he walked, people on either side of his path bowed and curtsied. Such ritual, such unnecessary pomp.

Two chairs had been added to the dais beside the king for Bas and Eliza.

Leo greeted his father stiffly. "You look well enough," his father said, his gaze apprizing.

"Where have you been, darling?" his mother asked. "You're late."

"Out," he said, and bent to press his lips to her cheek. Queen Daria looked regal in her diamond-and-sapphire crown. On her gold gown, she wore nearly as many medals as he did. She was a beautiful woman, and when Leo was a boy, he'd worshipped her, held in thrall by her beauty. He'd longed for her attention and her smile, but both had been sparingly applied to him.

She smiled at him now and cupped his face when he leaned over her to kiss her cheek. "It has been the happiest of days to have my children here with me. I can't wait for the day that you will make me as happy as Sebastian has today."

Leo suppressed his groan.

"You'll not wait long, my love," his father assured her.

His mother leaned forward and whispered, "Have you met Lady Eulalie? She's quite attractive."

Leo shook his head. If he spoke, he wouldn't be able to hide his anger.

"She is *illunis*," his mother said, using the Alucian word for beautiful. "I think you will find her appealing."

"Hopefully," he said with a shrug.

"You will! We took into account your likes and dislikes, my darling."

That was absurd. He'd never told his mother or father what he found attractive, and if they had truly taken into account his dislikes, they would know he disliked this exceedingly.

"Ah, here is Sir Ravaneaux," his mother said. He turned to see her private secretary approaching the dais. "Sir Ravaneaux will see to it that the introduction to Lady Eulalie is made."

Would he not be allowed as much as a glass of wine before the task of strengthening the ties between Alucia and Wesloria began? "Should I not congratulate the happy couple first?"

His mother's eyes narrowed slightly. "But you've congratulated them, darling! We all have. Sir Ravaneaux, if you would," she said, and waved Leo away like she did when he was a boy and he'd become bothersome. A flick of her wrist and a firm *Off with you now, Leo.*

Ravaneaux led Leo across the crowded ballroom with the two footmen trailing behind. It was a spectacle, people stepping out of the way to allow him to pass. Leo was keenly aware of the number of eyes on him, the low hum of whispers around him. As they neared the opposite side of the ballroom, an attractive woman came forward in the company of a man who looked to be about his father's age. He was fit, with strong features, his clothing that of an aristocrat. The woman was as small as he was large. She was dressed in silk and jewels, and when she curtsied, she sank low in the way young ladies were taught at finishing schools. She wore the Weslorian dark green pinned to her breast. The gentleman likewise wore the band of green around his arm.

Ravaneaux said to him, "Your Royal Highness, may I introduce Lady Eulalie Gaspar of Wesloria," he said. "And her father, the Duke of Brondeny."

Leo bowed. "Your Grace," he said to the duke. "My lady."

They exchanged a few pleasantries, and the duke offered felicitations on the occasion of Sebastian's marriage, then deftly stepped away under the pretense of speaking to Sir Ravaneaux, leaving Leo and Lady Eulalie alone…except for the attendance of dozens upon dozens of onlookers.

Lady Eulalie had small brown eyes and full lips, and her hair was the color of English tea. She arched a brow as she gave him a very thorough once-over, as if he were the milk cow she was considering purchasing. "I understand we are to befriend each other, Your Highness, and do it rather quickly."

He appreciated her forthright manner and that she'd dispensed with the tedium of asking how he found the weather this time of year or mentioning how grand the ball. "I understand the same."

"I've only recently been made aware of this friendship, so if I may make one small request?"

He nodded.

"I should like it to be quick." She glanced away from him and across the ballroom.

Leo followed her gaze and noticed a stately Weslorian captain staring back at her. Well. At least she was open about her true intentions. He didn't know how he felt about such openness, but he couldn't help but admire it. "I will make this initial meeting as quick as the horse your ambassador boasts about."

She laughed with surprise. "He *does* boast. I'll go first, if I may?"

"Of course."

"May I compliment you on how well your brother looked today? His bride is lovely."

"Thank you. Very kind of you to say."

"She is an English commoner, is she not?"

It was not a question, but a comment that Leo supposed he was to confirm or deny. He didn't suspect Lady Eulalie was doing anything more than attempting to make small talk as the situation required, but the question rankled him nonetheless. He hated that sort of question—it was not meant to inform, but to get at the heart of the matter: who outranked whom. He wished he was at the Foxhound with a tankard of ale instead of playing this game. Mercy, how soon he'd forgotten his vow not to drink. "She is not," he said politely. "At least not anymore."

Lady Eulalie laughed with delight. "Quite true," she cheerfully agreed.

The trumpets suddenly blared from an alcove above their heads, announcing the arrival of the happy couple.

"Ah, here they are now, the handsome prince and his very fortunate bride," Lady Eulalie said, and craned her neck forward to see. A line of English soldiers marched into the room beside a line of Alucian soldiers, and in a choreographed move, they turned to face one another, unsheathed their swords and held them aloft, crossing the tips. The effect was to form an aisle. A moment later, Bas and Eliza entered. Bas was dressed in his full military regalia, and Eliza in a frothy peach gown. She had donned a crown that Leo recognized as belonging to the royal collection. Her hand was on Bas's arm, and from where Leo stood, he could see the slight tremor in her. He hoped one day soon she would become accustomed to all the attention—she would have it all her life.

He, along with everyone else in the ballroom, respectfully bowed to the future king and queen as they passed, and when he straightened up, he looked to his left to follow their progress to the dais. But when he did, instead of seeing the dais, he saw the glittering green eyes of Lord Hawke's sister, the one who was clearly convinced of her own appeal. What was her name, for God's sake? Why could he not recall it?

Leo liked Hawke quite a lot. He'd met him at a gentlemen's club in London one evening some months ago, when they'd ended up at a gaming table together. They'd had a good laugh. They'd seen each other at various occasions since. But it was Hawke's arrival in Alucia that had sparked their friendship. Leo had spent quite a lot of time in the gentleman's company and now considered him a friend.

His sister, however, was a nuisance. Even now, when the entire ballroom seemed to understand that he and Lady Eulalie were to be allowed this moment, she was smiling at him with the eagerness of someone who meant to hop over to his side for a chat.

He averted his gaze. He was quite good at ignoring pointed looks. And women who smiled too eagerly. And women who thought they could merely bat their eyes and he would demand an introduction and offer her a kingdom. He was good at ignoring men, too, particularly those who wanted to know him with a hope for gain. And practiced politicians who wanted to whisper in his ear.

A pretty, green-eyed English miss was no challenge for him.

Bas and Eliza had walked the length of the ballroom to the throne dais and Eliza curtsied. The king stepped down from his throne and took Eliza's hand, then escorted her up to the dais to sit in the chair beside him. Bas took his seat beside her. His father gestured to the couple and began to applaud. Everyone in the ballroom joined in, their applause hearty, shouting, *"Vivat regiis reginae!"*

Long live the royal princess.

The orchestra began to play in earnest, and it was official—against all possible odds in the known universe, Eliza Tricklebank was a Chartier, a member of the Alucian royal family.

"People are staring at us," Lady Eulalie murmured.

"They will always stare," Leo said, trying not to sound bitter about it.

"Yes, I suppose. The two of us have been tossed into a tiny boat on this sea of hopeful diplomacy, and we must make do with each other."

At least she understood the rules of the game. "It would seem so." He glanced at her, but Lady Eulalie's attention was directed across the room, to her lover. Leo supposed he ought to be bothered by her brazen regard for the captain while standing next to him, and maybe he was, but at the moment, he couldn't summon enough heart to care. Maybe they could enter this devil's bargain with no expectations whatsoever. Perhaps he ought to keep more of an open mind about...

Leo was startled by what felt like an elbow or a shoulder to his back. He jerked around and looked right into the eyes of Hawke's sister.

"Oh dear, I do beg your pardon!" She laughed and smiled so sunnily that, for a moment, Leo forgot she'd bumped into him. "How clumsy of me! I stumbled over my train. Oh!" She jerked the train around and, with one hand, reached behind her, he presumed, to fasten it. "I really do so admire the Alucian gowns, but the trains are *beastly* to wear."

Once again, she had approached him without the slightest hesitation given that she was interrupting his conversation with Lady Eulalie. Once again, she was smiling and speaking to him as if they were fast friends. It was beyond his comprehension how the sister of a revered English baron could have so little care for proper etiquette. Not that he was devoted to proper etiquette and the rules that governed courtiers in this palace, but on this occasion, to bump into him and interrupt a conversation with another woman was too much. "Lady…" He paused, struggling to recall her name. His memory, he'd noted, was not helped when he overimbibed every night.

"Caroline," she happily finished for him. "*Caroline*. Caroline Hawke? I am Lord Hawke's sister."

Ah, yes, Lady *Caroline*. "Yes, of course. Lady Caroline." He inclined his head. Where was her brother? Better yet, where was the footman with champagne? Really, Hawke ought to keep a closer eye on his sister. Leo intended to ask her to fetch her brother, but she was leaning a bit to her right to see around him, her smile pointed at someone or something else. He realized then that she and Lady Eulalie had made eye contact. Lady Caroline was like a bird hovering, her head darting back and forth trying to get a good look at Lady Eulalie behind him. This was not how this meeting of his future wife was supposed to go, but Leo had neither the energy nor the desire to stop it. He sighed and said, quite reluctantly, "May I introduce you to Lady Eulalie of Wesloria."

"A Weslorian!" Lady Caroline said with great enthusiasm. "How do you *do*? I've hardly met a single Weslorian. Yes, of course, there's your bit of green. I'm surprised I didn't spot it straightaway. I'm very observant, generally speaking. What an interesting habit it is for all Weslorians to wear a patch of green, isn't it? I suppose it's a bit like the Scottish and their tartan. I wish England were so inclined. We should wear ribbons to signify we are English, preferably yellow, as that is the color of happiness, and frankly, it goes well with my skin coloring. But I suppose the color of the ribbon would be left to the queen, wouldn't it?"

Leo didn't know what to say to the steady flow of words that came from the lady's mouth. Neither did Lady Eulalie, as she was staring dumbfoundedly at Lady Caroline. No doubt she'd been raised, like all ladies, to believe that a woman should be demure in the presence of gentlemen and a prince.

"Lady Caroline Hawke of England," Leo added unnecessarily. "As no doubt you just heard."

Lady Caroline curtsied. When she did, Leo saw that everyone's attention had turned to the dais because Bas and Eliza were coming down. The orchestra began to play an Alucian native dance.

"*Very* pleased to meet you," Lady Caroline continued, rising from her curtsy. "Your gown, if I may say, is *remarkable*. I should ask for the name of your modiste, but I will be leaving for England soon, and quite honestly, I think my brother would have my head if I spent as much as a single farthing on another gown." She laughed gaily, as if her brother's displeasure at her spending habits was a lark. "Isn't the ball lovely? The whole day has been such a delight and I'm very much looking forward to dancing. It is my absolute favorite thing. I *adore* it. Do you, Lady Eulalie? Do you, Your Highness?"

Lady Eulalie blinked. "Ah…" Her gaze flicked between Lady Caroline and Leo, as she obviously tried to assess the acquaintance between them.

Leo needed to dispatch this beautiful bother before she set all tongues wagging. But before he could consider how to do that, Lady Caroline said, "I recall you dancing at Kensington, Your Highness. Quite an admirably high kick you've got."

Had he danced with her there? He'd had too much whisky that night, too, as was his unfortunate habit, and he didn't recall it clearly. Perhaps that explained why she thought they were so familiar. Well. For the second time today, he desired very much to kick his own arse.

"The duke and duchess are starting their dance," Lady Eulalie said.

Bas and Eliza had taken their places beneath one of the dozen enormous crystal chandeliers in the space the crowd had formed around them. Lady Caroline smiled with delight—and then gasped. "Oh dear, her *train*," she moaned, and actually *leaned* against Leo as if to share a secret. "Do you see? It's undone on one side. I'm sure she doesn't know—oh! There is Hollis. Hollis will set it to rights. Hollis takes such good care of her, really. So do I, for that matter. I can't imagine what she'll do once we leave her, can you? She said she will have a lady's maid, but it's not the same, is it? Alas, we must return to London. I have my many friends, as you know, and Hollis, well…" She looked at Lady Eulalie. "Her father needs her desperately. He's blind."

Lady Caroline was astonishing. He hardly knew men as free of spirit and tongue as she was. He had never met a woman who wore her eccentricities with such confidence.

She wasn't paying any attention to him now, as all eyes had turned to the royal couple. The music began, and Bas smiled encouragingly at Eliza as he led her into the first steps of the dance. Poor Eliza's fair face turned as red as the cardinal's robes, and she kept her gaze on Bas's feet as she tried to match his movements.

"Lord, she's as awful as I feared," Lady Caroline said without the slightest compunction. "It's really not her fault. Either one is born a dancer, or one is not, wouldn't you agree?" She looked at him for an answer.

Leo said nothing. He would not dare criticize Eliza so openly.

"I've known more than one lady who has been given any number of dance lessons and can't retain the steps," she continued, and winced apologetically. "Eliza tries very hard, but it's almost as if she can't hear the music."

"Oh dear," Lady Eulalie said with a smile she could not contain.

Lady Caroline blinked as if she'd just realized what she was saying. "Oh! You mustn't mind anything I say. If Eliza were standing here, she'd be the first to admit her poor dancing. She finds it rather amusing."

She should certainly not remark so openly about a royal duchess, and by her given name at that. Even *he* wasn't so irreverent. He felt a strange responsibility to defend his new sister-in-law. "If you would allow, Lady Caroline, I think you meant to say *Her Royal Highness*."

Instead of demurring as he expected, perhaps even apologizing, Lady Caroline's lovely green eyes rounded impossibly larger. And then she laughed. Chortled, really. "I meant *Eliza*, of course!"

Apparently Leo still had a bit of stodgy princely blood running through his veins, because he was appalled. Eliza was the future queen of Alucia, and Lady Caroline obviously didn't fully understand that meant that even she was to afford her friend the respect she was due. If she wanted to call the duchess by her given name behind closed doors, that was one thing. But in a public setting? It could not be tolerated, and he believed he was doing Lady Caroline a kindness by intervening. He turned more fully toward her, so that his back was to Lady Eulalie. "I have no wish to embarrass you, Lady Caroline," he said softly, "but I would have hoped that someone might have explained things to you before now."

The light of the dozens of candles in the chandeliers above them sparkled in her eyes. "What things?" she asked as her gaze wandered his face and settled, somewhat disconcertingly for Leo, on his mouth.

"Your friend is the future queen of Alucia. As such, you must show her the respect that *all* her subjects must show her." He arched a brow to emphasize that point. Part of him couldn't believe he was having to say these things. Certainly he had never been one to defend or promote royal decorum. But he'd never been confronted with such an obvious breach of decorum, either. "That would include how you address her...*particularly* in public."

Lady Caroline's mouth dropped open for a sliver of a moment. And then her eyes narrowed into brilliant slits of ire. "I do beg your pardon, *Highness*. I understand perfectly that Eliza will be the future queen, but I am her dearest friend and I don't think it is for you to say what I call her." One of her feathery brows arched high above the other, daring him to disagree.

Her redress absolutely stunned him. And, on some level, bloody well impressed him. *That* was some cheek for you. But it could not be tolerated, not in this palace, so he glared down at her so that she would not mistake his displeasure. "You should not address the duchess as anything other than *Your Grace*, and you most certainly should not address *me* in this manner."

Amazingly, she gasped as if *she* were the one who had suffered an insult. She squared off against him and lifted her chin. "Do you call your brother *Your Grace* and scrape and bow before him?"

"Of course not. He's my *brother*, and I myself am a royal prince, lest you've forgotten."

"Forgotten!" A burst of laughter escaped her. "I don't know how I could—you wear it like a shield."

His astonishment kept ratcheting. And he might faint

dead away if it continued. "Have you considered that is perhaps because I am, indeed, a *prince*?"

"Oh, I am well aware!" she said grandly. "You told me. In Chichester. Although it was hardly necessary there, either. But in the course of our conversation, you were very sure to mention it."

Chichester again! "For the love of..." Leo glanced back at Lady Eulalie, who was craning her neck to hear every word. He abruptly took Lady Caroline by the elbow and moved her away a few steps so that he could speak privately. With a quick look around them, he said quietly, "Frankly, I wouldn't be surprised if I did mention it, for there are times it seems necessary, and I've no doubt that was one of those times. But please understand me, Lady Caroline—I do not recall *any* conversation with you, and I certainly do not recall meeting you in Chichester, or any conversation there. Frankly, I was far too in my cups to remember anything about that particular weekend at all. You must consider how many soirees and fetes and weekend house parties I attend. You must consider that I frequently meet women and often in groups, and I can't be expected to remember them *all*."

She gasped softly, her plush lips forming a near perfect O. Her eyes filled with shock or fury—he wasn't entirely sure which. "I'm terribly sorry if the truth offends you."

"The truth of what? That you were as tight as a boiled owl?"

He had heard that rather English expression for being pissed. "I wouldn't put it precisely that way, but yes."

"*That* doesn't offend me," she said. "I know a drunk gentleman when I see one. What offends me is that you would lump me in with the all the women you meet *fre-*

quently and *in groups*, like a flock of chickens! I'm *not* a chicken, Your Highness. I am unique."

"Chickens! You miss my point entirely," he said, exasperated.

Her eyes widened to such a degree he thought she might keel over with some sort of apoplexy. But she didn't keel—she rebounded and looked as if she might launch herself at his throat at any moment. He prepared himself for the possibility.

"*You* have missed the point. You may have noticed that I tend to stand out in a crowd."

Leo didn't know what to say. She certainly did stand out in a crowd. She was standing out in all her blazing glory at this very moment. "Are you praising your virtues?" he asked with disbelief.

"I didn't praise them! I merely pointed out what is obvious to everyone but you, apparently."

"What the devil is happening here?"

At last, thank the saints, Lord Hawke had arrived to take her away.

"I believe His Royal Highness and the lady are having a row," Lady Eulalie said excitedly.

Lady Caroline whipped around, nearly colliding with her brother. Hawke bowed his head to Leo. "Your Highness, my sister and I offer our deepest felicitations on the marriage of your brother and our most sincere apologies for anything that might have been said to displease you." He put his hand on his sister's elbow, his fingers curling into her flesh as he drew her back with determination.

Leo inclined his head to acknowledge the apology. His heart was still beating rapidly with his indignation, and that little devil's eyes were shining with her vexation.

Hawke smiled thinly at Leo. "If you will excuse us?"

He pulled his sister into his side and forced her to walk away with him.

Leo silently but smugly cheered his friend on as he watched Hawke march away with his sister. But stubborn Lady Caroline tossed Leo a dark look over her shoulder before disappearing into the crowd.

Leo stared after her a long moment, still trying to understand what had just happened, then remembered Lady Eulalie. He turned to her.

She looked delighted. "Who, pray tell, was *that*?"

"Just an Englishwoman," Leo muttered. The most exasperating, infuriating, ridiculous and *attractive* Englishwoman he'd ever met. Oh, but she was right about that—she did stand out in a crowd, and in more ways than one.

"Ah, the English. They are too isolated on that little island of theirs, I think. They don't know how the world moves around them," Lady Eulalie said.

Leo said nothing. All he could think was what a burden Lady Caroline was to her brother, whom he considered to be a fine man and good friend. She might be beautiful, but unfortunately, that beauty was accompanied by outrageous behavior.

Lady Eulalie was smiling, clearly having enjoyed the show. Many people around them were watching as well, and Leo realized it was time to start the charade of a courtship. "Now that we've dispatched with that, may I have the pleasure of this dance?"

"I'd be honored, Your Highness," Lady Eulalie said gracefully and in a manner that a woman *ought* to address a prince.

Bloody Englishwoman.

As it happened, that was not the last Leo saw of Lady Caroline that evening. He spotted her dancing with Lord

Sonderstein. The old man was practically drooling into her very enticing bodice. She was looking off to the side and appeared almost bored, as if she'd danced with a leering gentleman a thousand times before.

He saw her twice more after that, once laughing with a captain of the Alucian navy as they moved through an Alucian dance, and then with an Englishman Leo recognized from a hunting party he'd joined last autumn.

Later still, Leo thankfully left his supposed fiancée and escaped to the gaming room. He happened upon Lord Hawke and took a seat at his table. As another gentleman dealt him in, Leo said, "I hope your sister's feathers are not too terribly ruffled."

Hawke rolled his eyes. "She's fine. She's prone to dudgeon, that's all."

"Aren't they all," Leo said, and he and his friend and the other gentlemen at the table laughed roundly and loudly.

CHAPTER SIX

The much beloved Duchess of Tannymeade, England's own Lady Eliza Tricklebank, has generously graced her British wedding guests with fine porcelain teapots commemorating the occasion of her marriage to Prince Sebastian of Alucia. Several of the British contingent have found the Alucian silks to their liking, and many trunks were purchased to carry the goods home. Expect to see these stunning fabrics at social events in autumn.

So festive were the wedding celebrations that many wedding guests were reluctant to return home. One English guest in particular found it difficult to leave her new friend, a gentleman very much in his prime. But home she did go, to another gentleman who is rumored to be approaching his prime.

ᔐ—Honeycutt's Gazette of Fashion and Domesticity for Ladies

WELL.

As it turned out, her stunning dress and her obvious appeal were *not* enough to entice Prince Leopold. Not that she'd *wanted* to entice that boor of a man, but that did not crase the fact that he ought to have been. Oh no—she'd had to go to *him*, engage *him*, and how *dare* he say he didn't recall her at all and liken her to the squads of debutantes who swirled around him at every public event?

"Why wouldn't he remember me?" Caroline demanded of Eliza and Hollis the next afternoon as they strolled the palace gardens. "Everyone remembers me. It's so boorish, isn't it? He's a haughty prince, and I, for one, have had enough of his prideful ways."

"Ha," Hollis snorted. "You don't mean that at all."

"I do! Does he truly expect me to call Eliza *Your Highness* after all these years of knowing her? I called her Eliza Picklecake until I was twenty years old."

"Oh!" Eliza said with a fond grin. "I had completely forgotten that nickname."

Caroline ignored her. "What a pompous, superior arse that man was! It was fortunate for him Beck intervened when he did, or I might have…well, I don't know, but I would have liked to—"

"Ask him to dance," Hollis cheerfully interjected. "You were *dying* to dance with him."

"All right, yes, I wanted to dance with him if for no other reason than my gown would be seen. I'm just saying that I don't give a fig who he is—he is rude."

"Caro! Keep your voice down," Eliza whispered, and glanced over her shoulder at the two palace guards who followed several feet behind them.

Caroline made a harrumphing sound at being told what to do. "Really, you know, I don't care if he remembers me or not."

Hollis giggled with disbelief.

"It's a matter of pride, Hollis. Certainly *I* don't recall every acquaintance I've ever made, but I like to think I remember most. And there happen to be two I remember with crystal clarity."

"I wait with bated breath to hear who they are," Eliza said.

"Well, one is His Royal Arse, Prince Leopold, which I should think is rather obvious."

"Caro!" Eliza hissed, looking over her shoulder once more at the two guards who followed them. "You are *in* Alucia! On the palace grounds! You can't go round calling Leo names."

"And the second is the Alucian gentleman with the hook nose," Caroline continued, as if Eliza hadn't spoken. "You remember, don't you, Hollis? I pointed him out to you at the ball."

"Did you?" Hollis asked, her brows knit as she tried to remember. "Oh! Yes, I remember—the gentleman who never *once* looked at you. Is that the one you mean?"

"The very one!"

"It was his loss, darling," Eliza said soothingly.

"It was, wasn't it?" Caroline asked weakly. "Thank you for saying so, *Princess* Eliza."

"Princess? Or is it duchess?" Hollis asked curiously.

"I don't really know," Eliza said with a flick of her wrist. "They've told me, but I can't remember. What does it matter? One is as good as the other to me."

"Well, that's just the thing, Eliza—one is *better* than the other," Caroline said. "How can you not remember if you are to be addressed as princess or duchess?"

"I think if we just address her as *Your Highness*, it covers all of them," Hollis suggested.

Caroline rolled her eyes. "Very well, Your Highness, but you've been Eliza to me since I was three and you six."

"For heaven's sake, Caro, I don't care what you call me," Eliza said. "My only request is that you not speak of Leo with such disdain. It's impolite and badly done when you've been a guest of his family for a full month."

Caroline couldn't argue with her logic. All the other thousands or millions of Alucians had been quite welcoming, and she was being rude. "You're right, as is usually the case," she said with a sigh. "All right, then, consider him utterly forgotten."

That wasn't true, and knowing herself as well as she did, Caroline supposed she would probably continue to be rude as far as he was concerned. But she'd keep it to her private thoughts. *Arse of Alucia. The pouty prince. Leopold the Rude.*

"It's just as well, darling, as the king means to formally announce his engagement soon."

"His engagement!" Caroline said, perhaps a bit too loud. "But Beck said he's returning to England."

"Yes, he's returning to England to pack up his things and whatnot. He's due to return by the end of summer when it will be formally announced. But all the arrangements have been made from what I understand."

Caroline was stunned into silence. For a moment. "Well, good luck to the lady. She will desperately need it. She'll be a royal princess or duchess or what have you, but she'll be married to him. They may call her *Your Highness*, but she'll have him to look at across her breakfast table."

Two women approaching them on the walk stepped out of the path and curtsied as the three of them passed. Caroline looked back at them, still amazed that Eliza Tricklebank could elicit that sort of response from anyone.

"Truthfully? I'd be very happy to be known simply as Mrs. Chartier," Eliza said.

Caroline couldn't help but laugh. That was Eliza—never one to pay much mind to social conventions. "You're impossible, darling! Why should you not embrace your new title and wear it proudly? How will we ever leave you to your own devices?"

"Well, I have Bas now," Eliza said, and her eyes shone in that magical way they had since her prince had come to fetch her from her father's house in London.

"It's not the same," Caroline insisted. "He will flatter you and never find any fault with you."

Eliza looped her arm through Caroline's "I will miss you both terribly, but I will manage. There will be someone at every turn to tell me what to do."

"Then what am I to do without *you*?" Caroline asked, and felt herself turn a bit misty. "Who will find fault with *me*? God knows I need it from time to time. Who will compliment the dresses I make, whether or not they're the least bit good? I need that even more."

"Beck," Eliza said.

Caroline gave her a look of incredulity, and Eliza and Hollis burst into laughter. "Of course not *Beck*," Eliza said gaily. "Hollis will, of course!"

"Hollis! She has her nose in that blasted gazette."

"If you help me, Caro, I vow to compliment you all you like," Hollis said. "But never mind that—I'm desperate to tell you both that I have the most amazing on-dit. This morning, I had my tea on the terrace outside our room. And who do you think I saw flirting shamelessly with the Alucian prime minister?"

"Oh dear," Eliza said. "What is his name? Lord Cebutari?"

"Yes," Hollis confirmed. "They were here, in this very garden, having a walkabout." She stole a look at the guards over her shoulder. "They were so close she was very nearly in his pocket. I can't swear for certain that her hand was not *in* his pocket."

"Who?" Caroline demanded.

Hollis quickly glanced around, then whispered, *"Lady Russell."*

Eliza and Caroline gasped at the same time. *"No,"* Eliza whispered hotly. "He's fifty if he's a day, and she's so young."

"They disappeared behind the hedges," Hollis whispered. "And when they emerged, her hair was mussed. She is *smitten*, I tell you. Isn't it ironic that her husband is rumored to be the next prime minister of England? I hear Peel will be gone soon."

"If she is smitten with the Alucian prime minister, what will she do when we return to England?" Caroline whispered.

"What does any married lady do when she finds true love? Tell her friends, naturally," Hollis said. "And then try like the devil to keep her husband from finding out."

They walked along for a few feet, each of them lost in their thoughts about this new development. "My feet are *killing* me," Eliza complained. "I've been on them far too much this week. I should like a bench to appear just now."

"Your Grace." One of the guards came forward. "If I may, there are benches just there, beyond the bend," he said, pointing to the path ahead. "There is a small clearing in the hedgerow with a fountain for sitting."

All three women stopped and stared at the guard as he moved back to stand with his companion, the both of them at attention.

"Ah…thank you," Eliza said. She turned back to the walk and linked her arms through Hollis's and Caroline's and yanked them close. "Have they heard *everything*?" she whispered.

"I don't know!" Caroline whispered back. "*Lord*, how long is this business with the guards to go on?"

"Forever?" Eliza answered uncertainly.

"There you are, Eliza!"

The familiar voice of Prince Sebastian startled them, and they drew to a halt and looked down a path that intersected the one they were walking on. Prince Sebastian was striding forward, ahead of Prince Leopold, Lady Eulalie and the queen. Behind them, more guards.

"Be kind," Hollis muttered. "That's her. She'll be his fiancée."

"What?" Caroline muttered back as they sank into curtsies before the queen.

"I've been looking for you, darling," Prince Sebastian said. He took Eliza into his arms and kissed her. Caroline's heart fluttered madly, and she inadvertently glanced at Prince Leopold. He was looking at the ground, his hands clasped at his back. He looked a little green around the gills, she thought. So green that if she poked him, she'd wager he'd fall over. It took Caroline a moment to realize that Lady Eulalie was looking directly at her with a funny little smile on her face.

"How are you, dearest?" the queen said to Eliza. As Eliza began to speak of her good health and whatnot, Caroline shifted her gaze to Lady Eulalie again. "Good afternoon," she said with a polite nod.

Lady Eulalie serenely nodded her acknowledgment of the greeting but then stepped forward and said to Eliza, "Your Grace." She curtsied deeply and perfectly, and Caroline didn't know if she should admire her or hate her for it.

"Oh," Eliza said, clearly not expecting a curtsy still. "Thank you."

Not thank you, *Eliza*. Caroline bit her bottom lip and looked at her feet.

"Have you met our Lady Eulalie?" the queen asked. "She comes from a very good Weslorian family. The sort of Weslorians who consider the Alucians friends and not foe." She tittered. Everyone tittered with her.

Caroline tittered the loudest—she was no fool. And when she did, she looked again at Prince Leopold. This time, she caught him looking past her, as if he was bored by this meeting. He slowly turned his gaze to her. Caroline arched a brow, flicked her gaze over him, then lifted her hand, palm up, silently questioning why he looked at her.

His brows knit in a disapproving frown, and then, damn him, he gave her a slight roll of his eyes and looked away.

He rolled his eyes.

That was it. Caroline had given that man all the chances she would give him. It was, as Eliza said, his loss. His very *great* loss.

"Lady Caroline, Hollis…will you allow us to steal my wife away?" Prince Sebastian asked. "We've a little surprise for her."

"A surprise!" Eliza said. "I don't think I can bear any more surprises."

"Oh, I think you'll like this," the queen said.

"I'll see her returned to you for tea, on my word," Prince Sebastian said eagerly, and leaned forward and kissed Hollis's cheek.

"Your Majesty, here is where I shall take my leave," Prince Leopold said, and stooped to kiss his mother's cheek.

"What? Where are you going? Will you not join us?"

"I've a prior engagement," he said, and with a curt nod to everyone, he strode off before anyone else could speak.

The queen watched him go, then sighed and smiled sympathetically at Lady Eulalie. But Lady Eulalie gave the queen a slight shrug as if she didn't mind at all.

Sebastian offered his hand to his wife. Eliza took it with a smile of pure adoration. The affection between these two was beginning to nauseate Caroline. Could two people *really* be so in love? She couldn't imagine it—she'd never once felt the flutterings Eliza had described when she realized she'd fallen in love with Prince Sebastian. She had never felt anything more than a passing fancy, one that generally flamed brightly and died quickly as soon as the next, more attentive gentleman appeared. There had been times Caroline had wondered if there was something a little bit wrong with her in that regard. A heart too small or something like it.

"Come for tea!" Eliza called over her shoulder as her prince led her away in the company of Queen Daria and Lady Eulalie, and all the guards bringing up the rear. Hollis and Caroline realized at the same moment they were suddenly very much alone in the huge garden. It struck Caroline that she and Hollis would be very much alone in a matter of two days when they left Eliza's fairy tale and returned to England without her. "Oh dear," she said, and grasped Hollis's hand. "I'm going to miss her terribly."

"Me too," Hollis said weakly. "Oh my, me too." She sighed and looped her arm through Caroline's. "Shall we return to our suite, then? There are a few notes I should like to make before we begin to pack."

The day was lovely, and really, it was the first bit of air they'd had since festivities leading up to the wedding had begun. "I think I'd like to walk a little longer," Caroline said.

"All right." Hollis let her go. "Is it me, or does it feel strange to walk without a guard trailing behind?"

"It's you," Caroline said, and laughed. "I hope to never see a guard again."

She watched Hollis stride off in the direction of the palace. Caroline went in the opposite direction, pleased to be free and alone, enjoying the sun and the air. After one full circuit of a considerable expanse of garden, she recalled the palace guard informing Eliza of benches at the center. The walking paths had been cut through hedgerows trimmed into various shapes and sizes, and every so often one would pass a seating area cut out of the shrubbery. She began to weave her way through the gardens toward the center. It would be nice to sit and think a bit in peace and quiet. She was in no hurry, pausing to look at various plants, or—blast it—to affix a train that had come loose. But as she neared the point where Eliza had left them, she heard low male voices.

Caroline slowed her step and moved quietly, pausing just outside the seating area. She leaned forward, trying to see through the thick bushes who was speaking.

She couldn't see much of anything and leaned forward a little more. Suddenly, a man moved into her line of sight, his back to her. She surged backward, startled. She looked around, noticed a thinner part of the shrubbery where she might be able to see and crept toward it.

The men were speaking in Alucian. And then one abruptly said in English, "You can't come here with this news."

She froze. *That* was Prince Leopold. She dipped down to see through the shrubbery and saw the back of the man again. Oh, that was Prince Leopold, all right. She'd know that strong, square back anywhere. Or the collar-length dark brown hair brushed back behind his ears. But who was he speaking to?

Prince Leopold spoke again, but in Alucian. His voice was low, the cadence swift, the tone sharp.

Another man responded in Alucian. Caroline craned her neck to see, and when she caught a glimpse of the other man, she was all the more curious. He looked decidedly less privileged than the prince. He was broad, and his clothes very plain. His yellow-blond hair was unkempt and stuck out in a number of directions.

Prince Leopold spoke again, and he sounded slightly frantic. The other man smiled sadly at whatever the prince had said, nodded solemnly and said, *"Je."*

She knew that meant *yes*.

Prince Leopold scraped his fingers over the crown of his head, looked once more at the mountain of a man and then, quite abruptly—or so it seemed to Caroline—walked out of the clearing.

She moved deeper behind the hedgerow. She waited for the man to go, but he dipped down beside a fountain and cupped his hands, bringing water to his face. He scrubbed his skin, then smoothed his scraggly beard. He seemed content to sit and think. Caroline meant to creep away, but when she tried, she found that blasted train snagged on the shrubbery. If she freed herself now, he would hear the rustle of her skirts.

After a few moments, he stood and began to amble toward the entrance of the clearing. By then, however, another sound had caught her attention, and Caroline glanced back to the path. Palace guards were quietly advancing toward the seating area the big man was about to leave. Her breath caught in her throat. She desperately wondered if she ought to warn the man, but before she could speak, it was too late.

The larger man tried to run, but he was no match for the younger, fitter guards, and they tackled him to the ground. Caroline may have cried out with alarm as they wrestled him, but it didn't matter—no one heard her over the tussle. It took three guards to drag the man to his feet while one bound his hands. Two more guards appeared to help drag him away.

After they'd gone, Caroline stood rooted to her spot, still shaking a little. Who *was* that man? Had they arrested him? Had Prince Leopold set the guards on him?

What on earth had she just witnessed?

CHAPTER SEVEN

A supper was held to conclude the royal wedding festivities, attended by the few remaining foreign dignitaries who had traveled from afar to attend the wedding. The Duchess of Tannymeade hosted the supper as one of her first official acts. For the occasion, Queen Daria lent her a tiara boasting sixteen emeralds and matching the emerald earrings the queen had earlier presented her as a gift.

There were many notable figures assembled for the last celebratory meal, and perhaps none so intriguing as the Wren of Wesloria, whose song is believed to have captured the heart of a royal prince. It is said the marriage agreement has already been negotiated. Expect a formal announcement by the end of summer.

Ladies, when traveling by sea, it is best to leave your finer fabrics in your trunk, as salt spray will ruin a good garment and keep your clothing damp.

⌒—Honeycutt's Gazette of Fashion and
Domesticity for Ladies

KADRO, LEO'S GUARD, casually reported that Lysander had been detained. The news sliced through Leo. "When?"

"This afternoon," Kadro said. "In the palace gardens."

After he'd left him? After Leo had strode from the garden with that terrible, heart-pounding feeling of unease?

Leo still didn't know why he'd gone to meet Lysander at all. Maybe because he didn't want to hear Eulalie sing again. He'd sat through two songs and it felt like ants were crawling up and down his legs, so anxious was he to be at anything else.

But his mother had been enthralled. "The duchess must hear," she'd insisted, and away they'd all trooped, in search of Eliza.

Or perhaps he'd gone because he was afraid he would be saddled with Lady Caroline if he lingered. He didn't know if he could engage in conversation with her without wanting to tie his neckcloth around her mouth. He imagined it for one gloriously silly and strangely arousing moment—Lady Caroline's mouth bound while her eyes flashed hotly at him.

Whatever his reasons, Leo had gone.

Lysander was much larger than what he recalled, both physically and in bearing. Leo had immediately told Lysander he had no interest in anything he had to say, and to tell him so for his own good was the only reason he'd come round at all.

"Ah. Then you don't care to know what your future father-in-law might be about?" Lysander had asked slyly. "The Duke of Brondeny?"

Well, that had certainly rattled Leo. He'd only just met the man himself. How could Lysander possibly know anything about the duke? "What of him?"

Lysander then told Leo something so outrageous and unthinkable that he was stunned. He warned Lysander that saying such things was dangerously slanderous. He said he didn't believe it. "Lies. Whoever has told you this is lying."

"When you return to England, there is a young woman who can prove to you what I say is true. She is in the employ of Lord Hill. Her name is Ann—"

"I don't care," Leo had said before he could fill him with any more scandalous news.

But Lysander patiently continued. "Her name is Ann Marble, and she is a maid in an important man's house. She has assisted one of our—"

"You can't come *here* with this news," Leo hissed in English. Then in Alucian he said, "Not *here*, man! Do you think these walls don't have ears?" He'd been so certain of it that he glanced over his shoulder. It felt to him as if the trees were listening.

"*Mans princis*, will you turn your back?" Lysander had asked quietly. *My prince.*

That had rattled Leo even more. Was he anyone's prince? He might have been born into it, but in reality, he was a drunkard with a talent for avoiding conflict, duties and responsibilities. He'd very much wanted to turn his back the moment Lysander called him his prince. He'd wanted to walk away and hear no more of it. But something had kept him standing there. If there was even a scintilla of truth to what Lysander had told him, he couldn't walk away.

But neither could he stand there and hear it. "Meet me tomorrow at the home of Jean Franck, the financier. He is a friend of mine. Do you know of him? His home?" he'd asked as his feeling of unease grew.

Lysander hesitated, but he nodded. *"Je."*

"Two o'clock." Leopold then left, striding away from the anxiety Lysander had produced, his thoughts on what he'd learned. As he neared the palace entrance, four palace guards stepped outside. They bowed to him in deference as he passed. One of them even uttered a greeting.

Leopold looked back at them as they carried on, uncertain what they were about. Were they on patrol? Looking for someone? But they appeared to be strolling along in no particular hurry, as if they were out for patrol. Had they detained Lysander?

Leopold could not shake the uneasy feeling that had come over him yesterday. Since Matous's death, everything out of the ordinary left him feeling uneasy.

He left Kadro to dress for the last dinner with his brother and the few remaining guests. The king and queen would not be joining them this evening, and he was glad for it—that meant the evening would be far less formal and start sooner and end quickly. He wanted time to prepare to sail the next day.

But duty called, so he entered the salon that evening to join the guests.

He was immediately cornered by a Moroccan gentleman, Mr. Harrak. Harrak wanted to discuss the opium trade that shipped through the Mediterranean and how he believed his proposal to intervene in that trade could make them all quite rich in Morocco and in Alucia. "Why should Britain enjoy all the spoils?" he asked.

Leo listened with only half an ear—he had no interest in opium whatsoever. He'd known more than one man brought low by its "medicinal" qualities, and besides, he was no expert on trade—Bas was.

As Harrak ranted against the imperialism of England, Leo looked across the room and spotted Eliza standing with Lady Caroline. His sister-in-law looked radiant in a pale yellow gown. She had a sash of dark green across her breast, onto which two things had been pinned—the sapphire brooch Bas had presented her at their wedding, and a new medal that marked her entry into the royal family. The royal brand, so to speak. She was always charmingly a bit off-kilter, and tonight, the tiara his mother had lent her kept tilting to one side. Every time she righted it, Lady Caroline said something to make her laugh, and it slid a bit again. He considered, as Harrak continued to drone on, that Lady Caroline was the true beauty of the two, at least to his thinking. She had wide-set eyes and that bright smile that curved into two pert dimples.

It was a pity she was part loon.

"Contrary to what the British might think, they don't rule the world, much less the seas," Harrak opined.

"Mmm." Leo watched as Lady Eulalie approached Eliza now with another Weslorian in tow. Eulalie Gaspar was an interesting woman, too, wasn't she? She seemed pleasant, and sensible enough about the reality of the situation they'd been thrust into. And yet he felt a current of something underneath her smile that made him uncomfortable. The odd sensation one gets when someone is laughing behind one's back. But it was unreasonable to think she had any impression of him at all, really—he'd only met her last night, had one dance with her.

Did she know what was said of her father? Surely not. *Hopefully* not. But what if she did?

All right, he was allowing his anxiety pull him into delusional thinking. There was nothing there, behind his back or otherwise. Eulalie was as rattled as he was about this proposed match between them, that was all.

"Will you speak to the king, then?" Harrak asked.

Leo hadn't heard a word the man had said. "*Je*, of course." Another white lie to add to the stacks of them he'd told through the years. *Yes, of course I can help you.*

Yes, whatever you need. Yes, I will bring it to the king's attention straight away.

Harrak smiled. "*Thank* you, Your Highness. Thank you."

Leo smiled thinly and excused himself. People always assumed he had influence in this kingdom, when in fact he had none. If he were to mention to his father that British imperialism was not appreciated the world over, his father would think he'd lost his mind.

"Leo?"

Leo stopped midstride and turned around to the sound of his brother's voice. Bas was grinning. "Bloody hell, Bas," Leo said with a chuckle. "Have you stopped smiling since your wedding?"

"I have not," he said jovially. "I was just off to fetch my lovely bride and have this evening over and done. I won't lie, Leo—I'm impatient for Tannymeade."

"God help you, you're randy."

"Impressively so," Bas said with a wink.

"I envy you," Leo said. "Have you seen the woman who will be my wife?"

"Eulalie?" Bas shrugged. "She's handsome enough."

She was handsome, but she lacked the charm that came to Eliza quite naturally.

"Why the long face, brother? Did you expect your future bride to be suitable in mien and compatible in all ways?" Bas teased him. "Do you recall what you used to say to me?"

Leo shook his head.

"Get her, bed her, put a child in her and be on your way."

Leo winced. He had indeed said that, and more than once. It was easy advice to give, but it was not easy advice to follow.

Bas clapped him on the shoulder. "Come, lad," he said. "Let's have this supper done so I can take my wife to bed."

"My God," Leo complained. Bas laughed.

They joined the ladies across the room. Eliza saw them first, and her smile flashed brilliantly warm. "My darling! Oh my, I still can't believe I can say that before everyone," Eliza said brightly. "Have you met the Duke of Sonderstein? He was just telling us that in Wesloria there is an ancient dial of stones that aligns with the stars and the moon."

"Your Highness," the duke said politely as Lady Eulalie curtsied. Lady Caroline curtsied, too, but Leo noticed she was smiling. Always that incandescent smile of hers, cast at him as if they shared a secret.

"May I offer my personal felicitations on the occasion of your marriage?" Sonderstein asked. "You are a fortunate man indeed to be surrounded by such beauty."

"I am indeed," Bas agreed.

"My good fortune came in the pleasure of the Alucian country dance with Lady Caroline," the old man continued, then did a little swinging of the elbows in a manner that Leo guessed was to mimic dancing.

Lady Caroline smiled pertly at Sonderstein, and said, with a sidelong look to Leo, "His Grace very kindly said my steps were excellent."

"Oh, indeed, they *were*," the duke avowed. "I have rarely danced with such graceful a dancer."

"Were it not for Caroline's instruction, I wouldn't have danced at all," Eliza said.

"Oh dear, I can't claim credit for *your* dancing," Lady Caroline said, and she and Eliza laughed roundly.

"Lady Caroline, you're bound for England soon, are you not?" Lady Eulalie asked abruptly.

"Pardon? Oh, yes! We set sail on the morrow. And you?"

"I'm not due to leave for several days yet. My father has some rather important business to finish with the king." She smiled slyly at Leo.

Fingers of ice raced down his spine. He didn't care for her insinuation. If there was an announcement to be made about him, he'd damn well make it himself. He kept his expression neutral and looked away from the group.

"Should be fine sailing weather," the old duke opined.

"Aren't you returning to England as well, Leopold?" Eliza asked.

"As it happens. I sail tomorrow evening."

Lady Caroline gasped loudly. "So do *I*! What a coincidence! What a delight to share a ship with you, Highness. I am very good at whist, sir, I'll warn you now."

"Oh, Caro… I think His Highness will be on a different ship," Eliza said with a slight wince.

"Really? Are there so many ships sailing to England from Helenamar on the same day?" Lady Caroline asked jovially. "An entire fleet, is it?"

"Well, no," Eliza said. "But I think there is a special ship for, ah…for the royal family?"

Lady Eulalie coughed. She looked as if she was choking on a laugh.

"Oh." Lady Caroline seemed to take that in, then suddenly smiled again so brightly that Leo was a little amazed by it—she was bold as brass and hard to ruffle. "Of *course* you'll need a special ship, Your Highness!" she said. "However could I think differently? I'm such a cake about these things."

"You're not a cake, Caro," Bas said. "It's a mistake anyone might make."

"Perhaps not everyone," Lady Eulalie murmured, and smiled as she toyed with the earring dangling from her lobe. But Leo could see her smile was not one of shared amusement. It was the sort of smile people used on witless children.

"Why should you know how ships come and go?" Eliza added charitably. "It's not the sort of education that is required of proper ladies." She and Lady Caroline laughed again. They seemed to have their own unique sense of humor.

"Your brother will miss you terribly," Eliza said to Leopold. "And so will I, quite honestly. You've been so very helpful to me."

"It's been my pleasure," he said sincerely. He truly had come to adore Eliza.

He noticed that Lady Caroline was smiling at him as if he'd directed his comment to her. Her smile was so dazzling that he realized he might have noticed it a moment too long. He quickly shifted his gaze to Eliza. "I'll return to Alucia soon enough, once I've wrapped up my affairs in England," he assured her. He had no idea what that meant, but it seemed to appease everyone when he said it. "I hope to return to the joyous news of a future arrival of a niece or nephew."

"Ha! Ha ha!" Eliza laughed hysterically.

"By God's grace," Lady Eulalie agreed.

"When the time is right," Bas said.

"Ah, there he is," the duke said, looking over Lady Eulalie's shoulder. "The Weslorian prime minister has arrived. If we may have your leave, Your Highness?" he asked, turning to Bas. At Bas's nod, the old duke offered his arm to Lady Eulalie, and the two of them departed. Bas sighed with relief. "Now that the prime minister has deigned to join us, we might dine. I'm famished."

"Should we assemble the promenade?" Eliza asked. "Lord help me, I've already forgotten the order—"

"Don't trouble yourself, darling," Bas said. "We'll go in informally and ask everyone to find places. Leo, you'll escort Caro, will you?" He turned around and called for the butler. "Jando? Jando!" He waved the butler to him.

Leo glanced at Lady Caroline. She frowned.

"Jando, let them all proceed and find their places. Dinner is served." He presented his arm to Eliza. "The duchess first, of course."

With another glorious smile, Eliza put her hand on Bas's arm and they walked away, completely lost in each other.

Leo must have sighed when he offered his arm to Lady Caroline, because her frown deepened.

"What?" she demanded crossly. "It wasn't *my* suggestion. I don't like it any more than you do."

"I didn't say a word."

"You needn't say a word, as your displeasure is plainly written on your face. Really, why *do* you hate me?" she demanded as she put her hand on his arm.

He arched a brow with surprise. "There is nothing plainly written on my face but the tedium of another wedding celebration. And I don't *hate* you—how could I? I don't *know* you. Well," he said after a slight hesitation. "I suppose I do know you now, don't I? You've made certain of it."

"I understand that the concept of cordiality doesn't come easy to you, Highness, but many of us who don't reside in palaces practice it frequently."

"Cordiality? Is that what you call it?"

"I call it any number of things. Civility. Manners. Conduct becoming a polite society. *Friends*, even, as we are practically related by marriage now. You should look them all up in your palace manual of etiquette. I think you will find some illuminating entries under 'enviable traits of the common folk.'"

He snorted his opinion. "And you may find some entries worth your perusal under 'questionable traits of the common folk,' madam, and particularly, the rules of engagement with royalty."

She gaped at him. "Are you accusing me of lacking *decorum*?"

"I am indeed. Will you walk?"

Caroline moved her feet. "Once again, your grasp of social conduct confounds me! You confuse effortless congeniality with some broken rule of etiquette that has been quite forgotten by the world at large. I do not lack decorum, sir, but I swear on Beck's life you could very well push me to it."

"*Ack*, but you are a bloody obstinate woman, Lady Caroline. On my life, I can think of no other who could react so vainly to a proper chastisement. It's a wonder your brother hasn't told you."

"Ha! What makes you think he hasn't told me so? He is as insufferably superior as you, which I would think you might have noticed, given that your feathers have flocked together with his. I'd rather be vain than ill-mannered like you."

He nearly choked on that. "*Ill-mannered?* Your pride astonishes me at every turn! I am unaccustomed to being so completely contradicted every time I speak. Do you treat every gentleman of your acquaintance in this manner, or do you reserve this behavior solely for princes?"

Lady Caroline's eyes turned a shade of green that he would have described as blistering, had it been possible for lovely green eyes to be blistering. "Well, I would ask the same of you, *Your Highness*—do you treat every lady in your acquaintance with such disdain? I *am* proud! Why should I not be proud? I'm a good friend, a caring person and I happen to be exceedingly personable. *And* I'm an excellent dressmaker, too! So yes, I am proud. Aren't you proud of *you*?"

They had reached the dining room, and he turned to face her. They were standing only inches apart, and her eyes continued to blaze just as hotly as the fire in his chest. She was defiant and beautiful and, bloody hell, he felt a twinge in his groin that was almost as strong as the thud at his temple.

"Am I not demure enough for your liking? Do you find it difficult to establish friendships? Do you think women should be seen and not heard?"

Inexplicably, his gaze dipped to her mouth and her full, succulent lips. And there his gaze lingered a fraction of a moment too long, much like it had lingered on her smile in the salon. He made himself lift his eyes. "Perhaps I have gone about this all wrong. If I may, Lady Caroline, allow me to ask you, as a gentleman and a prince, to stop perpetuating the fantasy of some sort of friendship between us. If it pleases you, you may consider us acquainted."

Those lush lips parted slightly with the sharp draw of her breath. Her eyes narrowed. "Why, *thank* you for clarifying that we are not quite *friends*, as that assumption, apparently, is a stunning lack of decorum. You are so *generous* to allow me to consider us acquainted. I cannot begin to describe the leaps of joy my heart is taking just now. What I *can* say is that I have never in my life been treated so abominably. You may be a prince, sir, but you are no gentleman." And with that, she took a long look at *his* mouth with such intensity that he thought for a split second she might throw all caution to the wind and kiss him.

And for a split second, he eagerly prepared himself for the possibility.

Lady Caroline didn't kiss him. She turned on her heel and flounced away.

He watched her march across the room, find her seat and grip the back of her chair with both hands. When she realized that guests weren't to be seated just yet, she glanced up and caught his gaze. She gave a shake of her head and turned away from him.

Leo didn't know if he should be royally offended.

Or inspired.

CHAPTER EIGHT

London, England

> *Absence does not always make the heart grow fonder.*
> *A particular lady who notoriously enjoys the com-*
> *pany of older gentlemen has just returned from a*
> *wedding in Alucia. It is whispered that her delight*
> *in having the attention of an Alucian gentleman in*
> *his prime has found her husband's heart turned cold*
> *against her, and she's been sent to their home in Kent*
> *so that she may contemplate her bad behavior.*
>
> *At a recent supper party of four and twenty souls,*
> *Lady Elizabeth Constantinople wore a gown of green*
> *silk in two tiers, each tier ending with a wide curve*
> *of Belgian lace that complemented the thinner bands*
> *of lace on the bodice and sleeves. The effect was se-*
> *rene, and we predict the style will be often replicated*
> *by ladies in the autumn.*
>
> *ᢙ—Honeycutt's Gazette of Fashion and*
> *Domesticity for Ladies*

A WEEK HAD passed since Caroline had arrived home from
Alucia. The voyage had been brutal, as the seas were unusually rough and Caroline sick for days. Had it not been
for Hollis's attention, she was convinced she might now
be dead. Even Beck had seemed concerned she might de-

part this life prematurely—she had a hazy memory of her brother entering the cabin and bending over her, his hand tenderly on her forehead, urging her to rally. "I would be terribly displeased if you were to die like this."

"Would you like a more dramatic demise?" Hollis had asked as she'd pushed him out of the cabin.

Caroline thought she was fully recovered from her seasickness by the time they reached London. The weakness that lingered was simply fatigue. After all, she'd hardly eaten a thing in the last week, and her skirts hung loosely on her. And how glad she was to be free of the Alucian train! She had many ideas how to reinvent that train into something a bit more practical to wear.

She'd spent the week unpacking and sleeping longer than normal. In the last day or two, she'd felt as if she'd taken cold. Last night at supper, when Beck asked her why she didn't eat, she said she wasn't hungry, and that he should keep an eye on his own plate. She didn't know why she was so cross with him. With everything, really. Even her longtime lady's maid, Martha, annoyed her, bustling about her room, preparing her toilette before bed. "Leave me, Martha!" she'd cried dramatically as she climbed onto her bed, still fully dressed. "I need quiet."

The next day, she felt even worse. She sent word to Beck through Martha that she'd had a late tea—true—and that she wasn't hungry for supper. Also true. But she hadn't eaten at tea, either. Her head was pounding and her stomach churning. After a few miserable hours of that, she decided she ought to pour something scalding down her burning throat. She could have quite easily used the bell-pull, but she'd now developed the strange fear that after her intense bout of seasickness, and now this cold, her legs might atrophy altogether and she'd be bedridden all her life and would never again dance a waltz. So she'd gamely forced herself out of bed and pulled a dressing gown around her. She used a handkerchief to dab at her runny nose and slowly made her way downstairs. She was alarmed by how dizzy she felt and how useless her legs were already beginning to feel, thus confirming her fears of utter demise.

Just at the top of the grand staircase to the lower floors, she heard voices coming from the salon. Not just voices, but raucous laughter. How many were in that salon? It sounded like dozens. While she'd been wasting away upstairs, Beck had brought his friends to enjoy an evening of debauchery. She ought to die, just to spite him.

Caroline backtracked to the servants' stairs and slowly made her way down with the assistance of the wall. On the main floor, she padded in the opposite direction from the salon, dabbing at her leaky nose. But when she turned into the hall that led to the kitchen, she spotted a man and a woman in the shadows. Her first thought was that she must be hallucinating. It was not Beck's habit to consort with the maids or to bring women into their home. She paused. She squinted. That was indeed a man with his back to her. But that man was not Beck. And there was indeed someone else, too, a woman, one considerably smaller than the man.

The pair was standing with their shoulders to a wall, facing each other. How dare they carry on like this in the halls of this house? They *were* carrying on, weren't they? Or were they? They didn't seem to be kissing, which, frankly, is what she'd be doing if she was so inclined to meet a gentleman in the darkened hallway of someone's house. What other possible explanation could there be? She took another step closer, steadying herself with a hand to the wall. They were *whispering*. Was it whispers of love? She'd like to hear that.

Perhaps it was one of the new maids. Beck had recently hired two from Lord Hill, who had decamped to the country with a vow to never return to London until the air was cleared of smoke and soot. Beck said he'd never return, then.

Caroline crept closer. It wasn't the new groom. The man was too tall. That left only one possibility—one of Beck's wretched friends. But who was he cavorting *with*? Caroline crept closer still, so close that she could almost reach out and touch the tail of the man's coat. But then she was suddenly overcome with a violent sneeze at such velocity that she could not possibly prevent it. That bell-clanging sneeze was followed by two more. By the time she had stopped sneezing, the woman had disappeared, and the man had turned around to face her, his legs braced as if prepared to fight.

Caroline dabbed her handkerchief at her nose and looked at the man in the dimly lit hallway. Her belly dipped—good God, it was *him*. The Arse of Alucia. *"You,"* she said dramatically.

"Also *you*." He relaxed, and leaned against the wall again, his arms folded over his chest. "Well, well, here you are, then, Lady Caroline. I was under the happy impression that you'd gone out for the evening."

"Well, *that* was wishful thinking." She sneezed again. "You're like a very bad dream following me about. Where is your paramour?" she asked, craning her neck to look.

"Not a paramour," he said. "A friend."

"Ha! I may be ill, sir," she said, pointing at him, "but I am no fool."

"I never said you were a fool. I said you were a bother."

Caroline was winding up to admonish him for cavorting with a servant, but his last statement gave her pause. "When did you say that?"

"Oh, I don't know. If I didn't say it aloud, I certainly thought it." He smiled.

It was the first time he'd actually smiled at her—truly smiled *at* her…unless Beck was standing behind her and she didn't know it. But Caroline was fairly confident they were the only two in this hallway, and the effect of that smile made her feel even dizzier. Normally, she would have taken advantage of his smile to charm the wits from him. "In consideration of the source, I will take that as a delightful compliment."

He stepped closer, and Caroline suddenly remembered her state of existence—the dressing gown, the unkempt hair, the puffy eyes and red nose. No doubt her breath smelled atrocious, too. Mortified, she stepped back and away from him, and smacked into the wall. Funny, she had not sensed the wall at her back.

This was *not* how she wanted to look when she put the man in his place. It was always best to dress a man down when one was dressed all the way up. She needed her hair to be curled, to be clothed in one of the beautiful gowns she'd made for the trip to Alucia, embellished within an inch of its life. But the prince leaned forward all the same, squinting at her. "Lady Caroline…you look awful."

"How dare you," she said weakly.

"Have you seen a doctor?"

She gathered her dressing gown around her. "I don't require a doctor."

"You look like you're in desperate need of one to me."

She wouldn't mind discussing her theory of the potential for permanently losing the use of her legs with a qualified medical professional, but she would save that for another time. "Don't try to divert my attention, sir. What are *you* doing in this hall?"

"Hawke!" he suddenly shouted, startling her. He put his hand on her arm as if to steady her.

She looked down at his arm. "What in blazes are you doing?"

"You're wobbling, *Hawke!*" he shouted again, and this time caught her by the elbow.

"I beg your pardon!" She looked up at him and winced at the blinding pain behind her eyes. She was tall, but he was a head taller than her and twice as broad. He dwarfed her. Or was she shrinking? She felt as if she were shrinking. She must be shrinking because he now looked rather concerned. She looked down again and realized he had moved her around so that she was propped fully against the wall. She wasn't actually shrinking, but she was scarcely holding herself up.

"Whoa," he said, and caught her with one arm around her waist.

"What is happening?" She was terribly light-headed. Everything seemed so wavy.

She heard a door open behind her, and then the familiar stride of her brother coming down the hall, the bounce of light from the candelabra he carried. "What is it?" he asked as he reached them, and looked down at Caroline. He recoiled with a gasp. "Good God, you look like death."

"Well, thank you, everyone, but I didn't have time to dress."

"Where is Martha?" he demanded. He put his arm around her and shoved the candelabra at the prince. "Come on, then, back to bed."

"I think she should have a doctor," the prince said, and

held the candelabra aloft so that Beck could lean in and examine her. "She looks a bit green, doesn't she?"

"Disturbingly green. Martha? *Martha!*" Beck bellowed. He pressed a hand to her cheek. "God help me, you're on fire!"

"Beck! You're hurting my ears," Caroline said, wincing. Everything about her hurt.

"Do you need help?" the prince asked, and Caroline wasn't sure who, exactly, he was addressing.

"No," she said at the very moment Beck also said no. But Beck added a gracious, "Thank you, I can manage." He dipped down and picked Caroline up before she knew what was happening and began to march along the hallway.

"I dropped my handkerchief," Caroline protested. "And what of my soup?"

"I employ a host of servants so that someone may bring you soup on occasions like this," Beck said as he huffed along. "Why did you not call one? Why did you not call *me*?"

"You wouldn't have come. You've been out with your friends. Why did you bring *dozens* of them?"

"What are you talking about? There are four of us to dine, that's all," Beck said as he started his ascent of the stairs.

"But why *him*, Beck?" she moaned, and pressed her head to his shoulder.

Beck paused on the first landing to catch his breath. "Lord, but you're heavier than you look. Why him who?" he asked through a pant.

"The Arse of Alucia, that's who."

Somewhere, someone coughed lightly.

"For heaven's sake, Caro. Why didn't you tell me you were so ill?"

"I'm not so ill," she said, but could feel the heaviness of her eyelids.

"Shall I take over?"

Caroline's lids flew open. He'd had the audacity to follow them up the stairs? Worse, had he heard her complaining about him to Beck?

"I've got her," Beck said, and continued his march, bouncing Caroline along as he went.

"That's quite a fever," another man said.

Caroline recognized the voice of Robert Ladley, the Earl of Montford. As if this moment could possibly be any worse, now there were three of them gathered. *"Beck,"* she pleaded.

"This way," Beck said.

By the sound of it, they were followed by a small army. Caroline buried her face in Beck's shoulder again so she'd not have to look at the Arse of Alucia. And so he wouldn't smell her breath or see how parched her lips were. This was, without a doubt, the height of humiliation, particularly as she took such great pride in her looks.

Beck opened the door to her room and strode to her bed, depositing her there, then pulling the cover over her. Caroline dared not look around her. But then she did, and no less than four men were staring down at her with various expressions of concern and horror. It was worse than she thought.

"I'll fetch Dr. Callaway, shall I?" Montford asked.

"I think you ought," the prince said, and touched the back of his hand to Caroline's cheek without asking her permission. "She is burning with fever."

"All of you, out," Beck commanded. "I'll not have her infect you."

"I'll go," Montford offered.

"I'll go with you," said Sir Charles Martin.

"Martha! Where have you been?" Beck said gruffly as Martha came into view. "Why wasn't I informed she was so ill?"

"Oh dear God," Caroline said, and rolled onto her side, away from the spectacle.

"I didn't know, my lord," Martha said, and sat on the edge of Caroline's bed, smoothing back her hair. "She was sleeping when last I looked in on her."

Caroline grabbed Martha's hand and held on for dear life. "Make them go," she whispered.

Martha stood up and said, "Allow me to tend her."

"Yes, well, see that you do," Beck said.

Caroline didn't know how Martha managed it, but she felt the room clear of muttering men. A moment later, Martha returned to her side. "I'll get a compress," she said soothingly. She disappeared again. Caroline's eyes closed, but she felt she was not alone and opened her eyes to see the Arse of Alucia looming over her.

He touched a hand to her cheek and winced. "I've never seen you so quiet."

Caroline wanted to roll her eyes, but they hurt. "I've never seen you so sober," she muttered.

He smiled again, his blue eyes shining with delight.

"Please, Your Highness, allow me to tend her," Martha said from somewhere beyond the bed.

The prince disappeared, and Martha sat lightly next to Caroline and pressed a cold cloth to her head. "Am I dying?" Caroline asked weakly. "Did you see them all? Assembled as if they expected me to go at any moment. If I am to die, Martha, please see that I'm buried in the yellow dress with the green sprigs. I worked so hard on those bloody green sprigs and I'll have everyone take one last look at them."

"You've a fever, that's all, milady. Men are generally unduly alarmed when confronted with illness and all matters female. Pay no mind to their histrionics."

"Thank you, Martha," she said with a sigh. "Will you have someone bring me soup?" she mumbled, but could feel herself falling down that hole of dead sleep.

"Yes, miss," Martha said from someplace far above her.

The weight on her bed lifted, and Caroline heard Martha quietly go into her dressing room. She rallied enough to push herself up and looked across the room to the mirror at her vanity. "Oh my *Lord*," she whispered, and fell back against the pillows. Of all the days for that bloody prince to show up.

Caroline tucked a pillow up under her head and was sliding away again when the door swung open violently and Beck appeared at her bedside. He frowned at her. "You have worried me terribly," he said accusingly.

"Are you friends with him now? *Fast* friends?" she asked. "You and Leopold?"

"Are you still nattering on about that? You must be delirious. To begin, he is *His Royal Highness* to you. And what does it matter if he is my friend?"

"It's awful," she whimpered. The worst of it was that her brother would never understand how disloyal he was being to her by befriending that man.

Beck sat on the edge of her bed and roughly caressed her damp head. "Dr. Calloway is being summoned," he said softly. "Now see here, Caro, you mustn't give me a fright like this. You really must mend yourself. We've already been through this, on the ship."

Caroline didn't care about mending herself now since those gentlemen had seen her in such a dilapidated state.

Martha appeared with a basin and a cloth, and Beck stood up so that Martha could take his place.

"You really *must* endeavor to mend yourself, Caro," he added uncertainly.

With her back to Beck, Martha rolled her eyes.

Beck leaned over Martha, put his hand on Caroline's leg and squeezed softly. "The house would be quite empty without you."

"I won't die, Beck. How could I? You'd be utterly lost without me," she said as her eyes slid closed. "Now will you send everyone away? And I do mean *everyone*. I should not like to see *him* again."

"She's delirious," Beck said, his voice fading. "She doesn't know what she is saying."

Oh, Caroline knew very well what she was saying, but she didn't have the strength to explain it.

CHAPTER NINE

A soirée was hosted by the venerable Lord Russell, our new prime minister, to celebrate his party's victory. The gathering included their Lordships Hill, Eversley and Wellington, as well as His Royal Highness Prince Leopold. Noticeably absent from the celebration was Lady Russell, who has not been seen much about since her return from Alucia. Rumor has it that the new prime minister's celebration went on until the bright light of the following day, at which time several of the guests were seen departing the mansion, with perhaps the notable exception of a prince, who was said to have gone missing just after midnight. Speculation is that he was not alone when he went.

Lady Caroline Hawke, a perennial guest at such gatherings as this, was not on hand, as she recovers from an illness brought on by bad seas and poor London air.

Ladies, a concoction of one part arsenic to every two parts honey will soothe the sorest of throats and fevers.

—Honeycutt's Gazette of Fashion and Domesticity for Ladies

LEO TOSSED THE *Honeycutt's Gazette* aside, and a hotel footman deftly stepped in to pick it up from the table. Leo scarcely noticed him, as the servants at the Clarendon Hotel had been trained to be almost invisible.

Leo had taken half a floor at the hotel on Bond Street, noted for its catering to aristocrats and dignitaries. His father preferred his second son to reside in a house, preferably with an Alucian ally, but Leo preferred the hotel. It was in the heart of London, and there was enough room for his staff, which included his palace guards, Kadro and Artur, his valet, Freddar, who doubled as a houseman in Leo's private suite of rooms, and his private secretary, Josef Pistol. It was Josef who kept his ear to the ground around town and who'd brought him *Honeycutt's Gazette* this morning.

Josef was sitting with Leo now in the library, on armchairs covered in rich leather and stuffed within an inch of exploding. They'd been served tea, and Josef was making quick, efficient notes about the week ahead in his leatherbound journal while Leo drummed his fingers against the arm of the chair, mulling over the bit of gossip from the gazette. The news was more than a week old, and yet, it still rankled Leo.

"Will you be calling on Lord Hawke today, Highness?" Josef asked as he jotted a note.

Leo wondered what else Josef wrote in that journal, always dashing off something across the page. "Yes, presently. Who watches me so closely, do you suspect?" he asked, gesturing in the direction he'd tossed the gazette.

"All of London," Josef said blandly, as if he'd had to remind Leo of this several times over.

Obviously, Leo knew that his coming and going was noted and reported in morning papers. He was a prince and therefore a grand prize in the marriage mart. And in more than one country. He wasn't surprised that it was widely known he'd been a guest at Lord Russell's home. But what he did *not* expect was that anyone, besides Russell himself, would know how he'd slipped out that evening. He'd taken such care of it, too, asking the butler if he could use a service door. Evidently, he was not very good at skulking about.

Frankly, Leo was discovering that the only thing he was even passably competent at was enjoying himself. But when it came to serious matters, he was utterly inept. In other words, his worst fear was being confirmed—he was rather useless. This had been proven to him over the last fortnight, when, in an effort to at least educate himself about what Lysander had told him, he'd blundered through every turn.

"The carriage will arrive at half past two, Your Highness," Josef said, and closed his notebook. "Shall I send someone to fetch flowers?"

"Flowers?" Leo asked. He was still thinking of the on-dit, of that night at the Russell house.

"For Lady Caroline."

"Oh. *Je*, of course." Hawke had only rarely left his home during the course of his sister's illness. Leo had gone round every day, not only because he considered Hawke a friend, but because he needed desperately to speak to Hawke's new chambermaid again, and that, he was discovering, was a hell of a lot easier said than done.

It galled him that he was so inept that he couldn't even manage a meeting with a maid. He had made three attempts to find her, and just when he thought he had, Lady Caroline had stumbled upon them, swaying from side to side with a ghostly look about her. Everything about her looked gray…except her remarkable green eyes, which had seemed more incandescent than ever.

Since the night she'd thwarted him by knocking on death's door, Leo had tried in vain to speak to the Hawke maid, but even as Lady Caroline lay bedridden, she was making that impossible. Every time he called at the house on Upper Brook Street, he felt obliged to sit with Hawke, who fretted like an old woman over his sister, even though the doctor had told him she ought to recover completely. And still, Leo could not manage to talk his way out of that study. Every excuse he offered—to fetch water for Hawke, for example—would prompt Hawke to wave his hand and yank on the bellpull. Or when Leo insisted he needed a chamber pot, Hawke pointed to one in the corner.

Leo was continually hampered by his lack of imagination and Hawke's attention to detail.

Really, how did anyone expect he would know what to do? All he knew was that the woman he reluctantly searched for had once been a maid in the home of Lord Hill. That, and her name—Ann Marble—was all he could recall of what Lysander had told him in the palace garden.

Except that she wasn't employed by Hill. By some hook or crook, she'd moved her employment to Lord Hawke's home, of all places.

Naturally, Leo didn't know that when he'd worked so hard to gain an invitation to Lord Hill's home. He was only marginally acquainted with the man, having met him a time or two at the gentlemen's club he frequented and at formal suppers here and there. He'd never had a proper conversation with him that he could recall. It had required a bit of thinking on Leo's part, but he'd finally come up with an idea to connive an invitation to the man's home. He'd thought himself rather clever, too.

"Your Highness?" Josef prodded him.

"Yes, flowers," Leo said, suddenly remembering himself. "Something bright and cheerful." God knew the Hawke household needed it. "And some whisky for Hawke. Although I think perhaps the time has come that he put down the bottle." He'd passed more than a few hours with Hawke while he numbed his fears with whisky.

Josef bowed crisply. "If I may have your leave?"

Leo sighed. "If you're not going to engage in a bit of tittle-tattle with me, then go about your business," he said, waving him away. Josef went out. He never engaged in tittle-tattle, that one.

Leo had an hour before the carriage would fetch him and carry him to Hawke's house, and this time, apparently, he'd be laden with gifts.

More false pretense.

That's the manner in which he'd called on Hill—with much false pretense. Oh, but he'd racked his brain on what to say to Hill to get his invitation. And then, miraculously, he'd recalled taking part in a hunt one rainy autumn in Sussex. Hill had been there, too, hadn't he? Yes, Leo determined, he had, as his family seat was nearby. Leo was certain that Hill had been present when their hunt party had stopped at a Herstmonceux Castle ruin to rest the horses. Hill had been there.

But how to use this memory to approach Hill? Leo had thought back to the many ways people had conspired to make his acquaintance over the years. Who knew there would be a lesson in it? But there was, and he'd put himself at a table with Lord Hill at the gentlemen's club one day and asked if he recalled the abandoned castle they'd rode past during the hunt a few years ago.

"Of course I remember it," Hill had said.

"Is it for sale?" Leo asked.

Hill had stared at him with confusion. "For sale? That pile of rubble?"

"It has walls yet," Leo reminded him. "I have in mind to restore it."

"Restore it!" Hill had laughed. "It would cost a king's ransom to restore it."

Leo had shrugged. "A bit of a hobby. Can you show it to me again?"

Hill had grinned. "Well, Highness, I suppose that you, of all people, would have that king's ransom. Be forewarned—you'll spend every pence. The wood's surely all rotted and the stone crumbling from the damp. Aye, come to call in Sussex. The owners are my neighbors to the east. I'll speak with them and determine their inclination to sell, if you like."

"I would be in your debt," Leo had said.

A day later, the invitation to Sussex had arrived, and Leo had been very pleased with himself. Perhaps he was cleverer than he'd understood. When he entered the home of Lord Hill in Sussex, it was with full confidence, which he carried with him squarely in his puffed-up chest until the moment he'd asked a footman if Miss Ann Marble could be brought round upon his departure.

"Miss Marble is no longer employed here, Your Highness. She's taken a position with Lord Russell."

That knocked the smile from Leo's face. *That* was not supposed to have happened. He'd gained his way into Hill's house, and she was to be *here*, dammit! Leo had not thought once about the possibility she would not be where Lysander had said she would be.

"Ah. Well, then," he said dumbly.

"Shall I send a messen—"

"No. Not necessary, not at all. Thank you." Leo had

forced himself to smile and then strode away from that footman.

To add insult to that injury, Leo discovered he did not have a very good reason to *lose* interest in the castle now that Lord Hill had gone to considerable lengths to research it for him. He'd left that afternoon with the uneasy feeling he'd just bought himself an old ruin.

He should have stopped then, should have plainly recognized that he was no match for this dilemma. It wasn't as if he could move around London unnoticed.

He glanced disparagingly at the offending gazette the footman had laid on the table with the other morning papers.

Unfortunately, he couldn't stop, because his bloody conscience, which had suddenly decided to make an appearance, wouldn't allow it. The five names in his pocket would not allow it. His dirty little list of five names he could not forget: *Nina, Isidora, Eowyn, Jacleen, Rasa.*

They were the names of Weslorian women who'd been sold into slavery. Or worse. Leo tried not to think about the worst of it.

This was what Lysander had wanted so desperately to tell him in the palace gardens. He'd wanted to explain to Leo that powerful, rich men were working together to purchase young women from poor families and sell them to other powerful men with influence in foreign and trade policy. They were bartering living, breathing human beings for political favor.

Leo was so alarmed when Lysander had told him that he'd not wanted to hear it. "Why are you telling *me*?" he'd demanded of Lysander, feeling desperate to unhear it. "I can't help you."

Lysander's steady smile was eerie. "On the contrary,

Highness, you may very well be the only person who can help me."

But Leo was shaking his head before Lysander finished speaking. "I will put you before whomever you must speak to in order to end this practice, sir, but I can't help you. I am to England on the morrow." Leo could recall pacing that garden, wishing desperately he was already on a ship, away from such wretched tales, away from ceremony, away from his place as a prince in his country.

But Lysander would not let him flee so easily. "One of the men involved is an Alucian lord who has made a fortune developing ironworks here, in Alucia. You might have seen the chimneys just outside Helenamar. You may be familiar with the gentleman, Highness, as he accompanied your brother to England to advise him on the trade agreement. Lord Vinters?"

Leo had stopped in his tracks. Marcellus Vinters was a trusted adviser to his father.

"He has strong ties to England and has arranged to bring British advancements to his business. He is the broker, so to speak."

"The broker," Leo had repeated, not understanding.

"The Weslorians want to share in the advancements. This arrangement is a simple commodity exchange—the Weslorian provides the girls. Lord Vinters trades them for the advancements and favorable trade terms for the Weslorians."

That meant, then, that Vinters was working against the interests of Alucia. It had been almost more than Leo could absorb, but then Lysander had said the thing that changed everything. "The Weslorian broker is the Duke of Brondeny."

Leo's stomach had dropped at the mention of Lady Eulalie's father. That was impossible. His dealings would have been thoroughly scrutinized by the Alucians. They would not risk a scandal like this if Leo was to marry his daughter. Which meant his father didn't know about the scheme? "That's impossible. Vinters is a close confidant of my father. He would not negotiate trade for Wesloria. He would not trade in slavery,"

"You know as well as I that industrialization depends on iron," Lysander had said calmly. "To industrialize is to survive, to be strong. Wesloria must industrialize, and they are willing to pay the price."

"And Vinters? What does he gain?"

Lysander shrugged. "Favor, perhaps? There are many who believe that Wesloria will never be as strong as Alucia without an Oberon on the throne, and more still who believe an Oberon on the throne will be the end of Alucia. Perhaps Vinters is gambling." He'd tilted his head to one side and studied Leo a moment. "You know how these things happen."

"No, I don't know," Leo had protested. "I don't know anything. I am not my brother, sir. I am the spare." That, he thought, was glaringly obvious.

But Lysander stared at him with golden eyes, and Leo had felt as if the man could see to the very bottom of his soul.

"You can't bring me this news here," Leo had added quickly. He might not know about these practices, but he knew what sort of uproar it would cause if anyone close to his father was to hear this. Frankly, Leo wasn't certain his father would take his word over Vinters's.

But Lysander had pressed on, mentioning the maid Ann Marble. Leo had stopped him, had asked him to meet later at Jean Franck's house. They were practically in earshot of the king, for God's sake.

That afternoon, Leo had wanted nothing more than to turn a blind eye to the appalling things Lysander had laid at his feet. And yet, at the same time, he was compelled to know more. If this was truly happening, he had an innate desire to crush those men. Even if one of them was to be his future father-in-law. *Especially* if.

But Lysander never appeared at his friend's house, as he'd been apprehended that very afternoon in the palace gardens. Still, Leo thought perhaps his two henchmen might come.

No one came.

Leo heard nothing more until he was preparing to leave the palace to board his ship. As he waited for the footmen to load his trunks into a wagon, he overheard two government men talking. They said Lysander had been sent to Wesloria to answer for alleged crimes there.

"Aye, let the Weslorians have at him," one of the men had said behind him. "They'll make quick work of him."

Leo had swallowed down a lump. That, then, he surmised, was the end of it. What could he possibly do without Lysander to advise him?

But that was *not* the end of it.

When the ship arrived in London in the middle of the day, the docks were teeming. The crew of his ship was eager to discharge their duties and have their time on shore. As Leo watched men move crates and trunks and God knew what all, a sailor inadvertently bumped into him, touching his hand. Startled, Leo turned and realized that the sailor was slipping a paper into his hand.

"What is this?" Leo asked.

"From Lysander," the sailor said. "Find one, find them all. Bring them home, and let the dust settle where it may."

"Pardon?" Leo looked up, confused—but the man had disappeared into the throng of working men.

Leo unfolded the page. Listed were five feminine names. Those names—and the faces he imagined to go with them—were the reason he couldn't stop his attempts, bungled as they may be, to speak to Ann Marble. She had to know something.

His first instinct had been to send the names to Bas with a note explaining what little he knew. But Leo had quickly discarded that idea. Bas was honeymooning. Moreover, Bas had carried the mantle of greater responsibility between the two of them all their lives. He'd worked to make things better in Alucia while Leo had worked to avoid any responsibility. Bas had earned the reputation of being smart and capable, and Leo had earned the reputation of being a rogue, a profligate. And this…this horrible business was happening in England, right under his nose.

Maybe, after living with such grace and privilege, it was time he did something for someone else.

But he wasn't exactly versed in the practical ways of the world. There was, and had always been, someone close by to do everything he needed. How he might even attempt to find these women was a mystery to him. And what if he did find them? Then what? Was he to command them into his carriage and bring them…where? Here? To this hotel?

He was no hero. If he allowed himself to think too much about it, Leo could drown in a sea of self-doubt. And yet, at some point, it had occurred to him that Lysander was right—he *was* uniquely qualified to do something about this, precisely because he was a useless prince. His title alone gave him entry into practically any house in London that he liked. His title alone attracted the attention of women, and his title alone had afforded him many opportunities to practice his charms. If there was a man who could walk into the houses where these women were kept, it was him. If there was a man who could convince these women to leave with him, to come forward, to speak, it wasn't the hulking Lysander. It was him.

All he had to do was find Ann Marble. Isn't that why Lysander had mentioned her? Leo wished he could remember precisely what he'd said, but he had to believe that if he found Ann Marble, he could find these women. *Find one, find them all.*

Unfortunately, after his visit to Lord Hill, he'd discovered that Ann Marble was no longer in Lord Russell's employ, either. No. She was now cleaning rooms in the home of Lord Beckett Hawke.

What a small world it was.

A LIGHT RAIN had begun to fall when Leo reached the Upper Brook Street mansion where Hawke and his sister resided most of the year. Hawke had said once that in the unbearable months of summer they decamped to a family house in the Cotswolds. Leo was flanked by Kadro and Artur as he jogged up to the door. Kadro reached forward and rapped on the door. Several moments passed before the door swung open and Hawke filled the frame. He was still wearing his dressing gown. Dark shadows accentuated his green eyes, and his darkly golden hair appeared to be standing on end. Leo's first instinct was that Lady Caroline had died.

But then Hawke grinned and said jovially, "Highness! You've come just in time. The fever broke last night."

"That is welcome news indeed, friend."

Hawke threw his arm around Leo's shoulders and hauled him inside. "Come in, come in, all of you. No need to guard him here, eh, lads? We'll have ale. No! Better yet, we'll have gin. A toast to my sister's health. Garrett! Where are you, Garrett?" he bellowed, calling his butler.

Kadro and Artur did not move from their post at the door. Hawke didn't seem to notice. He let go Leo and padded into the salon, barefoot, his silk dressing gown billowing out behind him. "Garrett, come here!"

Leo glanced back at his guards and, with a tip of his chin, sent them outside to wait, then followed Hawke into his study. The place was disastrously cluttered. Books had been tossed onto the settee; more of them, once stacked near the hearth, had toppled over. Morning papers were stacked haphazardly on a table. There was a pile of what looked like clothing, but Leo wasn't entirely certain. On the desk, dishes from a previous meal. It appeared as if Beckett Hawke was living in this room.

Garrett entered and bowed, then offered to take the flowers and whisky from Leo.

"What good news it is to hear your sister has recovered," Leo said.

"She still drifts in and out of sleep. It's to be expected. She's hardly eaten a thing," Hawke said. He made his way to the sideboard, waving off Garrett, who juggled the flowers and the whisky in his hands. Hawke uncorked a bottle and poured gin into two glasses.

"Has she spoken yet?" Leo asked.

Hawke looked at Leo and grinned. "Oh, but she has. She accused me of causing her fever by hovering so close to her side and sent me from her room." He laughed. "That is a *very* good sign. If she is cross with me, she is feeling herself again. Is that not so, Garrett?"

"Yes, milord."

"And the doctor? What has he said of her health?"

"The doctor, the doctor," Hawke said with a shake of his head. "He says the same thing he's said all along. He presses his horn to her chest and says she has a heartbeat as dependable as a drummer boy, that there is nothing to fear." He signaled his opinion of that by flicking his wrist dismissively. "She nearly died, I tell you. Had we not opened the windows to clear her room of bad air, and Mrs. Green had not made a poultice for her feet to draw the fever out, she would have certainly died."

"Then God's grace smiles on you today, my friend, for she did not," Leo reminded him.

"No, she didn't," Hawke agreed, and paused to ponder that. He nodded and looked at Leo. "You've convinced me."

"I've what?"

"Convinced me that her health has returned to her."

"I have?" Leo asked, confused.

"I am to the club! You'll wait, won't you, while I tidy up a bit? I insist you accompany me and tell me what you've been about." He picked up his glass and downed the gin. "I suspect you've been a naughty boy, Your Highness."

Leo smiled thinly. "I would be honored if you would call me Leo when you mean to chastise me."

Hawke laughed. "Then you must call me Beck. Not Beckett—sounds too much like *bucket*, doesn't it? Garrett, have hot water brought to my rooms. And do something with those," he said, gesturing to the most excellent whisky and the flowers. "Caro will like the flowers to brighten her room. Oh, yes, and see to it that His Royal Highness is kept comfortable until I return."

"Aye, milord."

"Do make yourself comfortable, Highness," Hawke—
or Beck—said as he swept out of the room behind Garrett.

Leo didn't know how he'd make himself comfortable
in a room as chaotic as this one. And really, what Leo
wanted to do was sneak out of here and find Miss Marble.
He had a feeling that once Lady Caroline was fully recovered, his access to this house and the servants would be
abruptly curtailed.

He moved closer to the door, so that he could see into
the hallway. He was standing in front of a painting of a
fox hunt. The rider on a black steed, bent over the horse's
neck, was Beckett Hawke. In the distance was a stately
home that Leo supposed was their country seat. He was
studying the dogs racing alongside the idealized version
of Beck when he heard the butler in the hallway just outside the door.

"Susan? Susan!"

Leo leaned forward slightly, listening.

"What have you got there?"

"Linens, Mr. Garrett. We've changed her bed linens."

"Fetch Ann. Have her take these flowers to Lady Caroline, compliments of His Royal Highness Prince Leopold."

Leo winced. Lady Caroline would read far too much
into that, he was certain.

"I beg your pardon, Mr. Garrett, but Ann has gone to
fetch her soup."

Leo's ears pricked up.

"Then you take them," Garrett said. "I must attend his
lordship."

There was a lot of movement, a rustling of fabric, a
small sound of exasperation. But then Leo heard Garrett's
sure footfall move away. An idea suddenly came to him,
and he half leaped to the door before Susan could get away.

He poked his head around the corner of the frame to see the maid standing where Garrett had left her, a pile of bed linens in one arm and his flowers in the other hand. When she saw him, her eyes widened, and she glanced nervously down the corridor. She looked as if she wanted to flee.

"May I be of service?" He smiled his most charming smile.

The maid blinked. "I, ah… I can…this is not…" she stammered.

Leo stepped out of the salon. "Susan…allow me to be of service," he said smoothly.

CHAPTER TEN

A stalwart patron of the opera has recently taken to riding on Rotten Row in the evenings. It is said she will not miss the appointment, for her husband's gift of proper riding lessons has come with the services of an instructor who is not only a competent rider, he has eyes the color of a summer sky. Our lady does prefer summer to other seasons.

The new trend in home ownership, begun by a royal visitor to our shores, is to find abandoned ruins to renovate for purposes that defy this writer's imagination.

Ladies, it is never too soon to introduce obedience into the lives of your children. Experts advise that when they begin to express what they want, either with words or gestures, obedience should be the first lesson taught.

—Honeycutt's Gazette of Fashion and Domesticity for Ladies

CAROLINE FELT AS if she'd been living in a cave somewhere far away from the world and from London, and it left her feeling very tired and cross. "Am I to live, Martha?" she asked. "Please answer truly. I want no false hope."

"You are to live a long and happy life, Lady Caroline," Martha said reassuringly, and rolled her onto her side.

Martha and another maid were putting fresh linens on her bed, which necessitated a lot of rolling her back and forth. "Can this not wait?" Caroline complained.

"No, milady, it cannot," Martha said firmly, and used another cold compress to wipe her face.

Caroline pushed her hand away. She felt grimy and sticky, and when she put her hand to her hair, she felt on the verge of tears. It was a terrible tangle. She imagined it would take weeks to return to her former glorious self.

The commotion around her eventually settled, and Caroline closed her eyes once more, ignoring the whispering as the maids scurried around her. She heard someone mention soup and said, "Yes, soup, *please*."

There was the sound of a door opening and closing, and then, blessedly, nothing. But as she lay there, she became aware of a smell so sweet that she had to open her eyes and see what it was. Well, she opened *one* eye, as her face was mashed against the pillow. She thought she saw the figure of a man standing beside her bed. It had to be a dreamy hallucination. Or the wire dress form, shaped to her figure, which she kept in her room. She'd been working on her latest sartorial creation when she'd taken ill.

She lifted her head so she'd have the benefit of both eyes. That was not a wire dress form, nor was it a hallucination or apparition. No, that was very clearly the Arse of Alucia, smiling down at her and holding her grandmother's vase full of fragrant yellow flowers.

"Am I disturbing you?" he asked pleasantly, as if they were at an afternoon social function, or as if they were just leaving church services and strolling along a path. What the devil was he doing in her room? And why was he holding those flowers? She managed to get herself up on an elbow to look him over. "Do you...do you *live* here now?" she asked uncertainly. She wouldn't put anything past Beck.

He laughed. "No, but I'm very close by. I've taken rooms at the Clarendon."

Caroline let herself drop, and rolled, facedown, onto her pillow. "This is unbelievable," she said into the soft cover, then rolled onto her back. "Have you been here all along?"

"All along?"

"For the two days I've been sick."

"No. But I've come periodically to see after your brother. He's been consumed with worry for you. It's not been two days, however—I believe we've entered the fourth day of the death watch. But you keep defying the odds."

Something about that didn't make sense. "Day *four*?" she repeated. "That's not possible." She turned her head to look at the window. Gray light filtered in through the gap in the drapes. *Was* it possible? Had she really been ill for so long? Good Lord, her legs were probably entirely useless now. She pictured herself in a wheeled chair, being pushed about by Hollis.

"It is entirely possible, Lady Caroline. And once again, you've created quite a stir."

"What do you mean?" She turned her head to look at him.

"Have you forgotten the many stirs you created in Helenamar?"

She thought about that a moment. "I did wear some stunning gowns," she conceded.

"I wasn't…that was not…" He shook his head.

"What are those?"

He glanced at the bouquet he held. "Flowers."

"Yes, but…did you bring them for me?"

He stared at the bouquet as if he wasn't certain why

he'd brought them "They were... Yes." He met her gaze. "I did."

"Oh dear. You really *must* have feared I would die. No doubt you will demand an apology from me for not going through with it, but I won't give it to you."

A wry smile tipped up one corner of his mouth. "I would most certainly think you on the verge of death if you apologized for anything. Can you sit up?"

"Of course I can sit up," she said irritably, and gamely tried to push herself up. But the exertion was overwhelming.

The prince put the flowers on her bedside table and leaned over and slipped his hands beneath her arms and lifted her up. "Stop that!" Caroline cried out with alarm. "I'm perfectly capable."

"No, you're not," he said as he held her up, then shoved some pillows behind her. "All right, then?"

"All right," she grudgingly admitted. She felt entirely conspicuous with him hovering over her like he was. "Must you stand just *there*?"

"Your brother was right. You *are* cross. I'll report to him that you cannot possibly be in any danger of departing this earth. I understand that people on their deathbed are more repentant."

"Whatever would I have to repent?" she asked him, quite seriously. She thought herself rather good, all in all. She wasn't perfect by any means, but she did love her brother, and she loved her friends, and she was generally kind to everyone she met. Even this arse. Well, she'd been kind to him before he'd been rude to her, at least. "Why are you here?" she asked. "I should think you would be on your jolly way after your attempt to defile our servant was thwarted. Who was she?"

"What on earth are you talking about?" he asked with a smile of bemusement.

He stood there looking impossibly handsome and innocent. Oh, but he thought she'd forgotten. Well, she hadn't forgotten a blessed thing. She looked at the flowers he'd brought and pondered his entirely suspect motives. "What a curious place a dark hallway is to meet a proper acquaintance," she said.

The prince leaned casually against a poster at the foot of her bed. "You must have been entirely delirious. You've created a fantasy."

"It was no fantasy, Your Highness. You were in the hallway with a woman, and now you are in my room. But how? Garrett would never allow it."

"He doesn't know I'm here."

She blinked. "What? Where is Beck?"

"Preparing to go out for the evening. Which is why Garrett was not available to bring these flowers. I thought to do it for him."

She flicked her gaze over his magnificently masculine figure. His perfect appearance reminded her of how she must look. She wanted to sink under the covers and hide. "I'm not ready for callers," she said. "I am not at my best. I'm feeling rather weak, so perhaps you'd like to return to the study to wait for Beck."

"I think you will be feeling better very soon. I understand soup is being prepared for you." He smiled slowly, and it was warm and sympathetic, and it made her feel a little tingly in her head.

"I should think the Alucian government would want you as far away from illness as possible."

"I suspect if the government were to get a good look at you, you'd be right."

Caroline tried to snort, but it was impossible due to her stuffy head.

"Your brother has been terribly worried."

Caroline had snatches of memory of Beck leaning over her, his hair dangling across his forehead.

"I lost a sister to fever, you know," he said.

"Pardon?"

"She was quite young, only three years when a fever took her."

Caroline pushed up a little higher in her mountain of pillows. "I never knew you had a sister."

"It was a very long time ago. I was awfully young, too, but I remember it very well. Hawke certainly feared losing you, notwithstanding the fortune he claims you have spent on dressmakers and modistes and cloth merchants."

"Has he complained of it again?" Caroline asked with a weary sigh. "I try to intercept the invoices before he sees them." She actually hadn't meant to say that last part out loud.

The prince chuckled and eased himself onto the foot of her bed. "He takes very good care of you."

That was true. Beck could have made her life miserable if he'd wanted to after their parents were gone. But he'd always been very protective of her. "I take care of him, too. It's been only the two of us for so long now," she said wistfully. For some reason, tears welled in her eyes. *Lord.* "He's been like a father to me. I scarcely remember my real father. You're fortunate, to have your father still with you." She swiped at one tear that had leaked. Is this what illness had done to her? Made her wretchedly sentimental?

"My father was not much of a father, really," he offered matter-of-factly. Caroline waited for him to clarify, assuming he said it in jest. But the prince didn't smile. He merely shrugged again. "Old complaints die hard, I suppose, but my brother had my father's attention. He spent our youth preparing Sebastian for the throne. I was... I was merely there. He scarcely noticed me at all."

Surely that wasn't true. Caroline couldn't imagine having a father who didn't notice her. What little she remembered of her father came with warm, loving feelings.

"Ah, but such are the hazards of being born the second son in a royal family," he added with a wistful smile.

Someone knocked softly on the door. The prince stood as it swung open, and the new maid came in, carrying a tray with a bowl of soup. The scent was so savory that Caroline's stomach growled.

But the maid stopped walking halfway across the room. She was obviously flustered by the prince's presence, as well she should have been, and dipped an imperfect curtsy and almost spilled the soup. "Don't mind him, Ann. He shouldn't be here."

But Ann did mind him. Her face turned red and she so ardently avoided making eye contact that Caroline couldn't help but notice. She couldn't imagine how shy one would have to be not to at least steal a *glimpse* of the man—he was a handsome prince! But Ann Marble was working very hard to keep her gaze averted from him as she carried the tray across the room.

She put the tray on Caroline's lap and almost spilled it again when Beck burst through the door, his hair dripping from being combed wet.

"Caro! You've come to! What a relief it is to see you sitting up. Martha says we ought to apply one more poultice," he said, striding across the room. "The fever has broken, but we must be cautious and draw the last of the illness out of you. So if you have the slightest inclination to help the poultice along, I suggest that you do so."

Caroline picked up her spoon. "How on earth does one help a poultice along?"

"What? I'm not a doctor, darling, so I can hardly be expected to know. But do heed what I say. I hope you are never so ill again. We were desperately close to having you leeched."

"Leeched!" she exclaimed as Beck straightened the tray on her lap.

"You see? That's why I need you to help the poultice along." He gestured for her to sit up and removed some of the pillows from behind her. "Oh dear, your hair," he said with a wince. "Well, Martha will repair it. If she can, that is. It looks as if some of it might need to be cut out—"

"Beck!"

"Ah, here is Martha with the poultice," he said as her lady's maid appeared at her bedside.

Whatever she was carrying smelled bloody awful. "Might I have the soup first?" Caroline begged. "I'm famished."

"Yes, of course!" Martha chirped. "And then we'll put this on your chest." She pushed Caroline gently forward and put the same pillow behind her that Beck had just removed. She smoothed Caroline's hair. "Dear me," she said, wincing. "That will take some work."

This was exhausting. Caroline wanted only to eat her soup and sleep again. She looked around her brother to see if the prince was still standing insouciantly at the foot of the bed. But he'd disappeared.

And so had Ann.

The only way Caroline could be certain the prince had been here at all was by the presence of the very cheerful flowers on her bed stand. She frowned down at her soup as Beck nattered on, proclaiming himself so relieved she would recover in time for the Montgomery ball. "I know how you love a ball," he said, pleased with himself for remembering.

Caroline might have been desperately ill, but she was still whip smart when it came to men, and she still knew when they were catting about.

And that rake of a prince was catting about with one of their chambermaids.

CHAPTER ELEVEN

Invitations have been delivered for the Montgomery
ball, an annual event that marks the beginning of the
summer social calendar. All persons of import will
be in attendance, including the new prime minister.
His wife will not be in attendance, however, as she
is said to be enjoying her cabbage garden in Kent.
Other guests will include a recently widowed earl
who is in much demand and, naturally, a visiting
prince to round out the list.

Ladies, a hint of rouge on your cheeks at dusk will
give you a healthy, youthful glow, which will delight
your husband and keep him at home.

⌒—Honeycutt's Gazette of Fashion and
Domesticity for Ladies

ANN MARBLE WAS a mousy thing, and Leo was mystified
how she came to be involved in this indelicate matter.

He caught her in the hall when Beck had come into
Lady Caroline's room. Cornered her, really, in a manner
he was not proud of, particularly given how frightened she
had seemed of him. "You've nothing to fear," he assured
her. "I need your help."

She looked frantically about, her eyes growing wider. "I
told you, I could lose my position!" she whispered harshly.

Leo was not used to anyone saying no to him and wasn't

quite certain how to convince her she must do as he said without causing a scene. "It is imperative that I speak with you—"

"Not here," she said quickly, and craned her neck to see past him. "In the market on Wednesday." She glanced up at him warily.

Leo stared at her. "The market? What market?"

She whispered something.

"Pardon? I didn't catch that. I am not... I don't know the markets," he admitted. How could he possibly know? Everything he needed was purchased for him.

"Half past two. I'm to buy poultry. The good chickens come on Wednesdays." And then she whirled and dipped to one side, as if she thought he would try to stop her, and fled down the hallway.

Leo stood there like a dunce, confused. What had she said? All he'd heard was half past two on Wednesday and good chickens. But which market? How did he go about finding a poultry market without drawing attention to himself? And bloody hell, as if he didn't have any number of things he must do on Wednesday, the lass had summoned him like a suitor...

All right, he didn't have *so* many things to do on Wednesday. Tea with the Alucian ambassador, that was all. He never had anything of importance to occupy him—he generally filled his days with social calls and gentlemen's clubs. In light of what he was endeavoring to do now, that all seemed rather...indolent. Yes. In light of what he was trying to do now—very much on his own, thank you—it was embarrassingly indolent.

Beck finally emerged from his sister's room, his vivacity and naturally jovial spirit having returned to him, babbling about her renewed health and the fact that she'd lapped up that bowl of soup with the eagerness of a dog. Off they went to the club, where Beck passed around the room, reporting to anyone and everyone that his sister was "much recovered"—although she hadn't looked so recovered to Leo—and "fit as a fiddle."

Then Beck sat and complained that Leo had hardly touched the gin and wondered aloud why that was. "You don't think you've come down with an ague, do you?" he asked. "Caro might have been very contagious."

"I'm perfectly fine," Leo said. He'd lost his appetite for drink, that was all. His thoughts were on the need to discover where one purchased chickens in London, and what one had to do to gain entrance to the market. He was too bothered by this business with these poor Weslorian women and the men who would treat them so ill, and how ill prepared he was to do anything about it. Last night, he'd lain awake, tossing and turning, trying to make sense of his life. It was as if his twenty-ninth year had crept up on him like death and had found his life lacking in so many ways. He'd done nothing worthwhile.

Leo was ashamed of himself. But on the other hand, he wished he had tackled something a little less complicated than freeing women sold into slavery.

He and Beck were soon joined by two other men, Mr. Humble and Sir Granbury, both of whom were eager to celebrate Lady Caroline's return to health, although neither seemed to know her. When the talk turned loud and boisterous and Beck complained of hunger, he insisted they carry on to a restaurant nearby that he claimed prepared a very good beefsteak.

Leo saw his opportunity and blurted awkwardly, "I've had a hangering for good poultry."

The three men looked at him.

Leo looked back.

"I believe you meant to say *hankering*, Your Highness," said Sir Granbury.

"Pardon?"

"The word you are seeking is *hankering*, not *hangering*," Beck supplied, grinning.

"Ah. Thank you." Leo could feel a warmth in the back of his neck. He'd picked up some words in the last few years that he had not learned from his childhood English tutor.

"If it's poultry you want, I've the best in Lancashire," said Mr. Humble. "You'll not see better meat than what is produced on my land. Plump birds." He used his hands to demonstrate just how plump.

"It is good poultry, Davis, I will grant you that," Beck agreed.

"Perhaps something a bit closer than Lancashire," Leo suggested. "Surely there is a market…"

"What have you got all those servants for?" Beck scoffed. "Send them out to fetch good poultry and don't concern yourself."

The three men nodded in agreement. Leo would have, too, because naturally, if he wanted poultry, he would tell someone, and it would magically appear on his plate. "Truth be told, sirs…my man does not have an eye for the fattest hen."

"Neither do I," said Sir Granbury, and the three men burst into laughter. Various jests about the gentlemen's appendages and how they'd like to fit said appendages into fat hens went round the table while Leo tried to think of another way to ask about the market.

When the laughter died, he said, "But is there a market for poultry? Someplace I might send him?"

Mr. Humble shrugged. "There is Leadenhall. Or Newgate."

Leadenhall! That's what Ann Marble had whispered.

"Not Newgate," Beck argued. "Leadenhall for poultry, Newgate for beef. Everyone knows it." He looked at Leo. "Tell your man to go to Leadenhall."

"Yes, thank you—I will." That answered the question of where. But as the four of them prepared to leave the gentlemen's club and seek supper, he moved on to fretting about how he'd convince Miss Marble to tell him what he needed.

ON WEDNESDAY, Leo had to convince his valet, Freddar, that he did indeed want to dress like an unassuming gentleman of English descent. "But the cut of the English suit does not serve your physique, Highness," Freddar had sniffed.

"It serves me well enough. And a hat, Freddar. Not a beaver hat. Something less conspicuous than beaver."

"Less *conspicuous*," Freddar repeated, as if he didn't understand the word.

"I'd like a plain hat," Leo clarified.

Freddar frowned. "As you wish, Highness," he said primly, his curtness signaling that he was being made to do this under duress.

Kadro and Artur, too, seemed to participate in Leo's excursion under duress. He overheard Kadro complain to Artur that the English coats were restrictive.

But Leo rather liked it. And he liked the plain hat with the wide brim. He was able to wander the wide lanes of the Leadenhall market with scarcely a notice.

The market was *fascinating.* So many people, so many animal carcasses! It wasn't that Leo had never been to markets—he'd visited them on occasion in Helenamar. But those ventures were always done with a coterie of royal observers, and the visit arranged so he'd see only what the hosts wanted him to see. In England, he'd had opportunity to enter markets, of course, but there had never been any need to actually do so. The idea of wandering through stalls of meats and leathers and various goods he did not want had never crossed his mind.

Well, he had no idea what he'd been missing! He'd commanded Kadro and Artur to wait at a public house near the entrance of the market, so that he might stroll at his leisure. Just the number of beef carcasses alone hanging from the tops of the stall fronts were a sight to behold.

He was so entranced with the number of people and the sale of the meat that he very nearly collided with an old woman who was carrying the carcass of a sheep wrapped around her shoulders. She looked through him and carried on to her stall, one foot before the other, trudging along as if no one else was in the market.

Costermongers moved in between the shoppers, barking out their wares, singing about their fruits and vegetables, their herbs and flowers. People crowded the stalls, bartering for their cuts of meat. Ale was sold out of carts, and gentlemen strolled through the lanes with tin tankards. An enterprising young man had roasted legs of mutton to sell, too, and the smell made Leo's mouth water.

On another aisle were leather goods. Belts and knife sheaths, saddles and shoes. Leo walked past a heated argument that had broken out at one tanner's post. The gentleman apparently thought the tanner's price for leather to make boots was exorbitant. The tanner accused the gentleman of sullying his reputation and took a swing.

Leo moved on to the poultry stalls, where live chickens and skinned chickens existed side by side, the latter

hanging in rows above the stall. He lingered in this lane,
pretending to look over all the birds, then walked back
and looked again, waiting for a glimpse of Miss Marble.
He was beginning to think that she had avoided him once
again, but then he spotted her. She was walking with another woman, engrossed in conversation.

He had not counted on there being anyone with her.
That was alarming all on its own, but then Leo happened
to notice something else that caused his heart to skip a few
worried beats. Just behind Miss Marble, a very ornate hat
and a tumble of blond curls beneath its brim was moving
steadily toward him, like the prow of a ship making its way
to the quay. Good God, that was Lady Caroline strolling
the market aisle on the arm of a gentleman.

What in blazes was she doing here, at this market? It
had been only three days ago he'd seen her in bed looking
as if she'd just crawled back from the jaws of death. How
in heaven had she untangled the mess of hair he'd seen on
her head, much less coiffed it into curls? And how could
she look so pretty after appearing so emaciated?

Miss Marble and her companion stopped at one chicken
stall and studied the birds. Leo ducked behind a stack of
crates stuffed with live birds and held his breath against
the stench, impatiently waiting for Lady Caroline and her
escort to stroll past. They were not alone, he realized—two
ladies dressed similarly to Lady Caroline strolled behind
them, looking terribly ill at ease.

When he saw the group of them go round the corner
into the lane of beef, he darted out from behind the crates,
very nearly knocking them over, and drawing the immediate ire of the proprietor.

Miss Marble didn't see him at first. She was laughing with the other woman, who, Leo realized as he drew

closer, was also from the Hawke home. Bloody hell, who was next? The butler? Beck himself? He stepped out of their line of sight and bumped into a lad carrying a basket of cakes. He held one up. Leo dug in his pocket for a coin and handed it to him in exchange for a cake.

"A *crown*?"

Leo momentarily turned his attention from Miss Marble and looked at the coin in the lad's hand. "Looks like it is," he agreed.

"The cake, it's a half penny, milord," the lad said.

"Is it?" That seemed awfully inexpensive. "Buy yourself a treat, then," Leo said, and with a friendly pat to the lad's shoulder, he moved past him, following Miss Marble and the other maid as they moved down the aisle while munching on the cake.

He feared he was going to have to resort to extreme measures to separate Miss Marble from her friend, but suddenly, Miss Marble's friend turned down another aisle, and Miss Marble walked up to a poultry seller. Leo quickly hopped forward and sidled up to her. "Miss Marble."

She gasped. Her hand went to her throat. The man behind the stall looked at him curiously, then at Miss Marble.

"Please don't draw attention," Leo muttered.

Unfortunately, Miss Marble could not appear to be anything but alarmed. She seemed frozen with shock. He did not understand her shock. She'd *told* him to meet her here—did she think he would not?

"Say something," he urged her, and forced a smile for the poultry man.

"Something amiss here?" the man rumbled.

Miss Marble managed to gather herself. She said to the man, "Two of your best chickens, if you please. Make certain they're your best—they're for Lord Hawke."

The man nodded, took butcher paper and turned around for his stick to reach the carcasses hanging above him.

"Wrap them well," she said, then gestured for Leo to step into a tight passage between two stalls. She stepped in behind him, glanced over her shoulder, then dipped into a curtsy.

"Oh no, no," Leo said, reaching to lift her up, but drawing back his hand before he touched her, uncertain if he ought to, given the circumstances. "That's...that's *hardly* necessary, given this...ah, arrangement," he stammered, seeking the right word.

"Please, Highness, what do you want of me?" she begged him. "I've done all I can do. I told the gent that I couldn't help more."

"The gent? What gent? Do you mean Lysander? But he gave me your—"

"Who?"

Leo paused. "Lysander, the Alucian."

She shook her head.

Leo frowned with confusion. "But he gave me your name. What gentleman are you referring to?"

"Don't know. I only know the Weslorian girl."

"Who?"

"Isidora Avalie," she said.

Leo's heart lurched. That was one of the names.

"She's the one you want, isn't she? I told you, I can't help you. I told the other gent that, too, when he came looking for her. Lord Hill, he turned us both out, and without any pay. Lord Russell, he didn't like the way Lord Hill had done it, but he was kind enough to take me in until I could find another position. But Isidora, he wouldn't take her, not her, because she was Weslorian, and he said he'd not involve himself in that. There, I've told you all I know, and now I really must go, Highness! If I lose my post, I've nowhere to go!"

"Hawke won't turn you out—"

"He will, Highness, he *will*! Please, let me go."

"Take a breath," he said, realizing it was his own chest that felt tight. He was far out of his depth.

"I tried to help Isidora, on my word, I did, but she... she..." Miss Marble suddenly burst into tears.

"Oh no. Goodness, no," Leo said, putting both hands up. "No, Miss Marble, you mustn't weep. Why are you weeping?"

"She had no place to go, either, and now she…oh, she's *lost*, the poor soul. *Lost!*"

Leo's breath caught. "Do you mean she's gone missing? Or…" He winced. *"Dead?"* he whispered.

Miss Marble looked up from blubbering into her hands and pinned him with a ferocious look. "She ain't *missing* or *dead*. She's working in a house of ill repute, that's what. Right at Charing Cross. What was she to do? I begged Mrs. Mansfield to find something else for her—"

"Who is Mrs. Mansfield?" Leo asked, his head spinning.

Miss Marble's eyes narrowed. "She owns the house where Issy stays now," she said stiffly. "She said Issy was as safe with her as she was in some grand house, and if I didn't leave her be, she'd take me in, too." She glanced over her shoulder and gasped. "Molly's looking for me! Please, Highness, don't ask me again, I *beg* you."

"Just one last question—who is the other gentleman who asked you about your friend?"

"I don't know." She turned to go.

"Wait! Where is Mrs. Mansfield? Where might I find her?"

"Charing Cross," she repeated irritably.

"But Charing Cross is…"

It was too late—Miss Marble had fled, returning to the poultry man to collect her bundle, then rejoining her friend without once looking back.

Leo stepped out of the space between the stalls and looked around him. How the devil was he supposed to find a brothel with nothing more to go on than it was at or near Charing Cross? That wasn't a street—it was a juncture of many streets.

He began to walk, his head down, thinking. He had no idea what he was doing, much less what he meant to do if he found any of these women. He was chasing rainbows and wandering around meat markets.

"Dear God, it's *you*."

Leo instantly stopped walking. He turned slightly and looked directly into the lovely green eyes of Lady Caroline. "I beg your pardon. It's *you*."

She suddenly beamed at him, clearly delighted with her find. She took in his plain hat, his unassuming coat, and her smile turned impossibly brighter. "Well, well, what have we here? What are you about today, Your Highness? Hungry for a leg of mutton, are you?"

It was impossible to imagine that this woman, who had been in bed just a few days ago, could look so beautiful. She was a tad too thin, but the glow of health had returned to her cheeks, and her eyes were glittering with wicked delight. "It may surprise you, Lady Caroline, but I like mutton as well as the next man."

"Do you know what I find interesting?"

"No, but I've no doubt you will tell me."

"That the last Alucian gentleman who dressed like this

was your brother. He was sneaking about, as you may recall. Are *you* sneaking about?"

"I see that your impertinence has returned in full. It's rather astonishing that I must say this aloud, but what I do is no concern of yours. I think the better question is why are *you* here at all? Were you not deathly ill only two days ago?"

"Three," she said. "But I am blessed with a hearty constitution, and I bounce back like a rubber ball." She moved closer. "Why are you prancing about Leadenhall market dressed as a regular Englishman?"

"I am not prancing—I am walking. You can't possibly understand, given that you are not a prince, nor inclined to listen, but sometimes it is easier to go round dressed like a regular Englishman."

"*Is* it," she said skeptically.

"It is," he assured her. "Shall I call someone to help you to your carriage? You oughtn't to be about."

Her brows dipped into a decided V over her smile. She stepped closer. "Will you not humor me and tell me why you are here, Highness?"

He shifted closer to her, too. He could see the deep green specks in the irises of her eyes, dancing little eddies, drawing him in. "Will you not humor me and tell me why it is you think you have license to interrogate me? Why does anyone enter a meat market? I want a chicken."

Her brows rose with surprise and she smiled with delight. She leaned forward. "A *chicken*?" she asked, her gaze on his mouth.

"That's right, a chicken, Lady Caroline," he said to her bodice. "The poultry at the hotel is not to my liking." His gaze moved to the pert tip of her nose. And then to her succulent lips.

"But you have servants."

"You sound like your brother."

"Do I? That is somewhat alarming to hear, but I know that the difference between me and my brother is that Beck would probably accept your explanation without question. I won't." She tilted her head slightly as her gaze moved to his jaw, and up to his ear.

"But that's the rub, madam. I don't need or want your approval." He desperately wanted to take her by the chin and force her to look him in the eye. He leaned so close that she had to look up. "No offense meant," he added impertinently.

She smiled for the long moment it took for her gaze to travel lazily to his lips. "None taken."

"Excellent. Then we may both be about our day." He touched the brim of his hat and stepped around her. But when he did, his hand made contact with hers. It was a very slight tangle of fingers, hardly anything at all, and yet it set off fireworks inside him. "Good day, Lady Caroline. I shall leave you to your bouncing about like a rubber ball."

"You're scurrying away like a rat or a guilty man, Your Highness. What about your chicken?"

"Lady Caroline?"

Leo started almost as badly as Lady Caroline. She abruptly whirled around. "Mr. Morley!" She was breathless, either with surprise or delight, Leo didn't know. "You found me!"

The gentleman was about the same height as Lady Caroline. He'd walked up behind them holding a basket carrying bread and flowers. "I thought I'd lost you," he said with a nervous smile. "It would be quite easy to be lost in here, I think." His gaze shifted to Leo. "I beg your pardon, sir. May I…?"

"Oh, I do beg your pardon, Mr. Morley," Lady Caroline said, and Leo prepared to be introduced as a prince, at which point he'd have to make some elaborate excuse for being here admiring a row of hanging chicken carcasses without a royal guard in sight. "Mr. Chartier, my friend, Mr. Morley."

Leo was surprised and relieved by the tiny bit of charity from her. Why she'd done it, he wasn't certain, and he glanced at her questioningly.

She returned a faint smile.

"I am honored to be called your friend, Lady Caroline," Mr. Morley said, grinning like a lad. "Mr. Chartier, how do you do?"

Leo nodded.

"Are you a Londoner, then?" Mr. Morley asked as the two ladies Leo had seen earlier arrived at his side, each of them carrying a small cake.

"At present," Leo said. "A pleasure to make your acquaintance, but if you will excuse me, I'm in a bit of a rush. Good day to you," he said, and touching the brim of his hat, he turned to leave.

"Good day, Mr. Chartier!" Lady Caroline called in a singsong voice after him.

He could feel Lady Caroline's gaze on his back, and he swore he could hear her laughter. *Impudent woman. Impudent, irreverent, beautiful woman. Impudent, irreverent, beautiful, enticing woman.*

With a mouth he would very much like to kiss into submission.

CHAPTER TWELVE

A crate of squawking chickens delivered to the Clarendon Hotel has upset the genteel patrons to the point of complaint. The chickens were a gift for a prince of a fellow from a Humble admirer in Lancashire. It has been said that the prince is so in search of good poultry that he took it upon himself to visit the Leadenhall market. Perhaps the prince might endeavor to raise his own perfect poultry in the ruins of Herstmonceux Castle.

A recent encounter at Gunter's Tea Shop between a gentleman whose debts have been questioned and the gentleman who questioned them, was devoid of the dictates of polite society and resulted in both gentlemen being ejected from the premises. This serves as a solemn reminder that one must always bow to an acquaintance, even if that acquaintance is one's enemy.

⌒—Honeycutt's Gazette of Fashion and Domesticity for Ladies

CAROLINE WAS FEELING her old self again. The trip to Leadenhall, which Beck was adamant she not attempt, had done her some good after all. She hadn't meant to go along, she hadn't *wanted* to go along—she could think of nothing less attractive than a meat market. But Mr.

Morley and his sisters had called, and Caroline had been desperate to escape them, and had said that she must accompany the new maid to Leadenhall, which she was certain would do the trick. Alas, much to her dismay, Mr. Morley said he would be delighted to accompany her as well, and turning to his sisters, he'd asked if they didn't both need some beef sent home?

The day had been truly exhausting, physically, as she was still recovering, and also emotionally, as she found it taxing to be demure for such long stretches of time. But in the end, Caroline was very pleased that her legs had not lost their usefulness after all. Indications were that she would indeed dance again.

The other happy result of her trip to Leadenhall was the remarkable sight of Prince Leopold prowling around as if he were some inspector of birds. Not the poultry kind, either, as he maddeningly would have her believe.

Caroline had seen him in conversation with Ann Marble. She'd only noticed it because she'd spotted Molly, the kitchen maid, wandering around by herself, and had looked around for Ann. She'd been so intrigued by the intimate little tête-à-tête that she'd stepped away from Mr. Morley and his sisters and slyly moved in the prince's direction.

She knew what those two were about, obviously. She knew the true nature of men, and she particularly knew the true nature of privileged men. He was a rake! The question was, what was she going to do about it?

She wondered what Beck would say if he knew about this despicable affair. Caroline did not intend to tell him…at least not now. She had her reasons. For one, she didn't want to see Ann dismissed. She was good around their house, and besides, from what Caroline had gleaned from Martha, the poor girl was alone in this world. Beck had said as much when he brought her into the house. "Russell didn't want to keep her, and I'd not like to see a young woman put to the street," he'd said with a grimace.

But Caroline couldn't allow this affair to continue. It would be a trifling thing to the prince, but it would ruin poor Ann. That was the thing Caroline had come to understand about men—their desire was so immediate, so intense, that they didn't think of the consequences of what they were demanding. They thought of only the need. They didn't see a person, really, but a feminine shape that appealed to them and their base instincts.

She'd noticed this, *really* noticed this, after her debut. She'd always known she was attractive, but she hadn't realized just how attractive until that night. She had basked in the attention and the compliments, had found it exhilarating. And subsequently, at every party, every soiree after that, she sought the same feeling—of being admired. Of being desired.

But…it wasn't long after that Caroline began to notice that the attention she gained was not particularly fulfilling. She knew what she looked like and how men looked at her. She began to understand that what attracted men to her was her near perfect shape, her face, her mouth, her hair… her exterior, in short. But they were not attracted to *her*.

It was as she told Hollis the afternoon her friend had called to see how Caroline fared after her illness. "No one but you cares how I truly am," she'd complained.

"That is not true!" Hollis said. She was trying on Caroline's latest gown and admiring herself in the mirror.

Caroline was sitting on her chaise, staring listlessly out the window. "But it is. All anyone had to say was how I looked. 'Oh dear, your hair, darling, can it be repaired?'

Or 'your pallor is quite gray.' Or 'your dress is too loose, you must eat something!'"

"All genuine concern, darling," Hollis said. "Surely *this* gown was not loose on you. My God, I can scarcely breathe at all."

"But no one asked about *me*, Hollis. You were the only one to ask if I understood how close to death I'd come and how did it feel to be on the edge of dying."

Hollis paused to wrinkle her nose. "Well, that sounds positively dreadful when you put it like that. But I was curious, and if I can't ask you, who might I ask?"

"That's precisely my point," Caroline said. "You are very curious about *me*, and not the terror of my hair. Of course you can ask me those things, because we are very dear to each other. Do you see?"

Hollis had laughed as she'd pulled her gown over her head. "I think you've a touch of fever yet, Caro."

She did not have a fever. She had an inability to articulate what she meant.

It was her own fault, this feeling of disappointment. She'd made a sort of game with herself—how many gentlemen could she get to flock to her? Which of them would inquire after her interests? Or her thoughts about the trade agreement between Alucia and the United Kingdom? Or even something as illuminating as what age she'd been when her parents had died?

But as the years had ticked by, Caroline realized there was something terribly wrong with her game—she continued to attract gentlemen to her, but the game had taken on a new urgency. She used the game as an excuse, to mask her fear, because Caroline didn't really know what there was to like about her. What if she discovered she wasn't as pretty on the inside as she was on the outside? What if all her ugliness was tucked away, and would spring free if someone got too close? What if she was completely empty on the inside, and all that she had to offer this world was her fine looks?

Fortunately, Caroline had the luxury of wealth and privilege to play her game and she didn't have to delve too deeply into the answers. But Ann had no such privilege, and Caroline meant to protect her.

She needed to think how best to deal with the knowledge of the prince's affair, and until she had determined what to do, she would hold on to this morsel of news and do her level best to keep him from preying on other maids.

He was a rake. A handsome, charming, rake—the most dangerous of them all.

THE WEEK AFTER her visit to Leadenhall, Caroline felt up to accepting an invitation to the home of Lady Priscilla Farrington. Caroline had known Priscilla for an age. She'd married quite young, had three children in quick succession, then watched her husband increase the Farrington holdings with the import of cotton. He'd recently been appointed to the House of Lords.

Caroline had always enjoyed Priscilla's company. She was jovial and quick with a laugh. She had a growing rivalry with Lady Pennybacker, whose husband had likewise received his seat in the Lords.

Priscilla was keen to have Caroline design her a gown, because Lady Pennybacker would not have one. During her convalescence, Caroline had made a pattern for a gown and needed to fit it to Priscilla's robust frame.

When she arrived, she was shown to a salon where she was instantly greeted by four small dogs, all of them eager for a pat on the head. Priscilla was lounging on a chaise with yet another dog. The ornate room looked and smelled a bit like a kennel.

"Darling!" Priscilla trilled, waving Caroline over as the footman followed her, carrying the box with the muslin pattern of the gown. "How well you look! You're recovered from the seasickness, are you? Oh, but you're terribly thin."

"A temporary condition," Caroline assured her. "But I am fully recovered." She made her way through the small beasts and leaned over to kiss Priscilla's cheek. She took a seat on a settee across from Priscilla. One of the dogs hopped up, its paws on Caroline's lap. She carefully pushed it away. It hopped up again.

"You must tell me *everything*!" Priscilla said. "But not yet! Felicity Hancock and Katherine Maugham are coming to tea."

Priscilla had not mentioned this fact in the delivered invitation. Katherine Maugham had been very keen to secure an offer of marriage from Prince Sebastian and had not yet forgiven Eliza for getting the offer she'd coveted. Caroline, Eliza and Hollis called her the Peacock behind her back.

"How delightful," Caroline said, and pushed the dog away once more. But the dog was not to be bested in this, and hopped up and climbed onto Caroline's lap, circled around, and settled in for tea.

"Is this new?" Caroline asked, looking down at the carpet.

"It is! It was made specially in Belgium and delivered to us just last week. Tom has in mind to hire more servants, too, did I tell you? But only foreign ones. Foreign girls are far better than our domestics, don't you think?"

Caroline was not pressed to answer that ridiculous question, because a footman walked in at that moment and announced the arrival of the two ladies. Lady Katherine swept in like a stage actress, determined to be noticed first…until she saw Caroline. She slowed her step, blinking in Caroline's direction. Felicity Hancock stumbled in behind the Peacock, tripping over the edge of the new Belgian carpet.

Caroline pushed the dog from her lap and stood to greet the ladies. "What a pleasure!" she trilled, holding out her arms to both women.

"Lady Caroline, you have returned to us," the Peacock said. "I thought *surely* you'd remain attached to the side of your very dear friend. I feared we'd not see you again. Didn't I say so, Felicity?"

"Who do you mean?" Caroline asked sweetly. "The duchess and future queen of Alucia? Oh, I'll see her soon enough. I intend to return in the spring. I can call on her anytime I like, you know."

"Another voyage, really?" Priscilla asked. "But Tom said it made you so dreadfully ill. Very near death, he said."

"It wasn't quite as bad as that, but even so."

"I want to hear every *word*," Felicity said eagerly, and settled in a cloud of blue on the settee beside Caroline. "Was it as wonderful as *Honeycutt's Gazette* made it seem?"

"Every bit and even more," Caroline said sincerely. It was hard to relate just how beautiful and amazing the wedding had been in words or song or painting or gossip gazettes.

"Tell us, tell us!" Priscilla insisted as she waved at the footman to begin the tea service.

Caroline was careful not to leave out a single detail. She told them how vast the palace, and how Eliza now had two ladies in waiting to tend to her. How the king and queen had bestowed jewels on her as they'd welcomed her into their royal family. How desperately in love Prince Sebastian was with her. Caroline made sure that every conceivable reason to envy Eliza was laid before the ladies and was rather pleased with her effort in the end.

"I still can't believe Eliza Tricklebank should find herself married to a *prince*," Priscilla said, her voice full of wonder. "Eliza *Tricklebank* of all people."

"Why not Eliza Tricklebank?" Caroline protested. "She is the best person I know."

"Because it wasn't *you*, Caroline. If you ask me, you are far more suited to such a match than she."

Well, that was obviously true. But Eliza deserved it far more than Caroline ever would. She smiled and shrugged lightly. "Fate has a way of putting us in the right place."

"Doesn't it," Katherine said slyly. "Speaking of the great hands of fate…what of Prince Leopold? Did you catch his eye?"

Priscilla and Felicity tittered.

"Oh, I'm certain I did," Caroline said nonchalantly, feeling a slight flush in her cheeks, remembering how intent his eyes had been on her at Leadenhall. She'd actually felt a spark of excitement standing there in the midst of all that meat. "Frankly, I found him rather tedious."

"Really!" Katherine put down her teacup. "I fully expected you'd come back with tales of his slavish devotion to you."

"Why ever would you think that?"

"Well…because you said so, darling," Priscilla said gently. "Remember? You said he was quite taken with you and you fretted that you'd have to fend him off when there were so many other gentlemen with whom to acquaint yourself while in Helenamar."

The flush in Caroline's cheeks was heating her skin. Sometimes, she was *too* confident. She did indeed recall saying something very much like that one evening after one too many glasses of wine. "I never said I'd have to *fend him off*," she scoffed.

"You did," Felicity said. "You even demonstrated pushing him away," she said, and pretended to push something away at chest height. "You clearly thought he'd be a bother."

Caroline wished for something to fan herself. Perhaps she could claim to have a touch of the fever yet. But it was pointless—she did have a tendency to boast. Beck said she was filled with her own sense of grandeur. And it was true that before she'd sailed to Alucia, she'd been extraordinarily confident that the prince would be attracted to her. But he wasn't the least attracted to her and now she couldn't help but wonder if she was losing her charm. She was six and twenty, creeping toward the age of spinsterhood, and that handsome prince was more attracted to her maid than her.

"What *happened*?" Katherine asked with far too much joy to suit Caroline.

"I thought him tedious, that's all. And besides, his formal engagement to a Weslorian heiress will be announced by the end of summer. It's been arranged."

All three ladies stopped tittering and stared at her. *"Really?"* Felicity asked, incredulous. "Arranged? But… but I've heard he's been in London sowing his oats."

"Of course he is sowing his oats," Priscilla scoffed. "Everyone is working to gain an introduction. And he's far from home—he can do what he likes."

"But…he and Mr. Frame called on a *brothel* just this week!" Felicity whispered loudly. "*I* heard that he took the woman with him."

Caroline jerked her gaze to Felicity. "I beg your pardon, he did what?"

"Took her," Felicity said. "He left the establishment with the…woman."

"Took her *where*?" Katherine asked.

"You know," Felicity said, her face turning red. "To his…castle, or what have you."

Caroline felt a sour twist in her belly. She thought him a rake, but that was despicable. "Are you *certain*, Felicity? You don't suppose you misheard?"

"Yes, I'm certain! Mr. Frame's sister is a dear friend of mine, and she told me. She had quite a row with her brother about it, which threatens to ruin all of Christmas."

"We are months away from Christmas," Katherine pointed out.

"That's how bad their row was."

Katherine looked at Caroline.

Caroline wouldn't give her the least bit of disappointment. "Well, I'm not terribly surprised. He's a prince, and it goes without saying that he'll soon be engaged, no matter his conduct. But if it were me, I'd not want *my* daughter anywhere near him."

"Not your daughter, but perhaps you?" Katherine asked with a devious laugh.

"After the brothels and maids? Certainly not!" Caroline said primly.

"The maids! What maids?" Priscilla exclaimed as she took the lid off the box and pulled out the pattern Caroline had made.

She hadn't meant to say that. She hadn't meant to tell *all* the man's secrets, particularly as it related to her house. She stood up and walked across the room to join Priscilla.

"I've heard rumors that he has, from time to time, taken up with a housemaid here and there, that's all."

"What house?" Priscilla asked, looking properly offended.

"Oh, I don't know, really." Caroline unfurled the muslin pattern. "My point is that he's a prince in name only. He's a rake by any other name."

"But this is so *damning*," Katherine said as she rose from her seat so that she might have a look at the pattern, too.

Caroline did not miss the look that Katherine exchanged with Felicity. She didn't like that look. It was rather judgmental. Of her? Or the prince? It hardly mattered—Prince Leopold was corrupting her maid, and Caroline was both irate and envious, and suddenly very tired, and she wanted nothing to do with him. Not much, anyway.

"I should tell Lady Montgomery about this," Priscilla announced. "She would not like that sort of scandal at her ball. You know how she is."

Caroline had said too much. "I do," she agreed. "Perhaps we ought not to upset her with gossip."

"Caroline! Are you making this gown?" Felicity asked.
"I am."

"Astonishing! Will you make me one?" Felicity asked.

"Oh, darling, you must!" Priscilla agreed, and passed the dog she was holding to Caroline so that she could hold out the sleeves of the muslin.

When Caroline left Priscilla's salon, she had orders for two more gowns. Both for Felicity, however. Katherine Maugham had eyed the gown with envy but could not bring herself to ask Caroline to make her one.

CHAPTER THIRTEEN

The guest list for the highly anticipated Montgomery ball has allegedly been culled by one. This should be a reminder to us all that even a prince of a man may be hiding some sordid secrets that no respectable young lady would want to introduce to her family.

It is said that a well-heeled gentleman, higher in social stature than most, has been spotted in some unsavory locations. It is rumored that this particular gentleman might have removed a skirt quite light in its appearance and placed it in the kitchen of a fine house. Several theories abound as to why, but the most sordid one is certainly the most plausible.

Ladies, it is suggested, if you are inclined toward canine companions, that you endeavor to open your windows and employ a broom so as not to offend your guests with uncomfortable smells and unwanted hair on the hem of skirts.

ᕙ—Honeycutt's Gazette of Fashion and Domesticity for Ladies

IT TOOK A few days before Leo could persuade Mr. Frame to take him to the brothel he'd bragged about. But Mr. Frame, who had heretofore not shown any inclination toward morality, had suddenly developed one when it came to Leo. He thought it unseemly for a prince to make such a call. Leo didn't know if he should be offended or pleased that a man he hardly knew thought to step in as his moral compass.

In the end, however, Mr. Frame was persuaded by a promise of a rare bottle of Alucian wine to be delivered to his home…just as soon as Leo had it delivered to London.

Fortunately, Mrs. Mansfield, the proprietor of this decrepit house, so wretchedly dark and dank within, did not know who Leo was, other than someone she had deemed important and thereby felt entirely comfortable demanding an outrageous amount of coin to meet Isidora Avalie. "Yes, of course! Winsome lass, that one," Mrs. Mansfield had said, as she'd plucked at the loose threads on the arm of her chair. The woman's girth alone was testament to the success of her despicable enterprise. On a table beside her was decanted wine and a plate of meats and cheeses and nuts, as if she planned to snack her way through the evening while women were subjected to God knew what in the rooms one reached through a very dark and narrow flight of stairs.

"It's quite a compliment to ask for her by name," Mrs. Mansfield continued, eyeing his clothing. "You look familiar, my lord. Have you visited us before?"

"How much for the girl?" Leo asked coolly.

"Well, she's one of my best, she is. She's Weslorian, you know, and they are particularly skilled in the art of pleasure. I get the highest coin for her."

Leo never resorted to violence. Even in his youth, he'd avoided tumbles with friends—the thought of striking someone or something nauseated him. But he'd never wanted to punch someone in the mouth quite like he wanted to punch the leering smile off of Mrs. Mansfield.

He negotiated what was an extortionist's rate for the

lass, and when he handed over the money, Mrs. Mansfield hoisted herself from the chair and beckoned him to follow. She showed him to a small shabby room with a worn red velvet settee that looked as if it had been host to any number of gentlemen's asses. There was a narrow gag-inducing bed in the corner, the sheets rumpled from use. Mrs. Mansfield summoned Isidora Avalie from somewhere behind a door in the room. "Hurry along girl, there's a gentleman asking specially for you."

Isidora entered the room timidly. She looked very uncomfortable, clad as she was in scarcely a dressing gown. She had dark hair and dark eyes, but Leo was struck by how vacant her eyes looked. She stared at him blankly for a moment then cast her gaze to the floor.

"What are you doing standing there?" Mrs. Mansfield said irritably to the girl and pushed her into the middle of the room, so that she was standing directly before Leo.

"You have an hour, milord," Mrs. Mansfield said. "I'll knock on the door ten minutes to, and give you time to dress." And with that, she'd gone out.

Isidora did not look up. She was trembling. *"Bon den,"* he said. *Good evening. "Weslorina?"*

He hadn't meant to startle her; he'd meant to assure her by speaking her native language. But the language panicked her. She'd turned and lunged for the door, but Leo was able to leap ahead of her to keep her from leaving before he could speak. She tearfully begged him in Weslorian and English not to hurt her, to let her go.

"For God's sake, I'm not going to hurt you. I want to help you," he'd insisted.

"Why?"

"Because I do, Isidora. You deserve better than this life.

Help me find the others, help me bring the men who did this to you to justice."

"I don't know what you're talking about!"

"You do," he said gently but firmly. "Allow me to help you and the others."

She immediately dissolved into tears. "I can't," she said tearfully. "They will force my father to give back the money. My family won't take me back, not after this. I'll have no place to go but the street—"

"You do have a place," he said, although he had no idea where she might go—he would have to think of it. But he would think of something.

He gestured for her to sit on the foul settee and tell him how she'd gotten here. Her family was from the mountains of Wesloria, on the border with Alucia, she said. He knew the mountains were an impoverished part of both countries. Most of the men there worked in the coal mines. She said a gentleman had come and offered quite a lot of money to her father for her. She said her father took it to save the rest of the family from starvation.

Leo vaguely recalled his brother talking about the lack of economic opportunity, particularly in some parts of the country. Leo had barely registered the conversation, as he did any topic that seemed too weighty, because he had long been a man who didn't want to bother himself with anything of importance. Isidora had been sold so a man could feed the rest of his children. Leo could not imagine what it must be like to live with nothing, or the sort of desperation the man must have felt that would allow him to sell one daughter to save his family.

So Isidora had come to England to work for nothing. That wasn't enough for Lord Hill, she said—he'd wanted more than her services as a chambermaid, and when she'd rebuffed him, he threatened to send her back to the man who'd arranged it. Ann Marble had tried to intercede and he'd fired her, too, then took his family to the country.

Leo withdrew the five names from his pocket and showed her the list. Isidora shook her head and confessed she couldn't read. So Leo read the other names to her. *Nina, Eowyn, Jacleen, Rasa.*

Isidora knew them all, but knew only where Jacleen and Rasa had ended up. Rasa, she said, was a maid in the home of Lord Pennybacker, a name that was mildly familiar to Leo.

Jacleen, however, had been sent to a grand country estate belonging to the Duke of Norfolk. That news caught Leo by surprise—the Duke of Norfolk had attended Cambridge with him. He'd known Henry many years and considered him a friend. For God's sake, he was married to a lovely woman with three children and a fourth on the way. Surely he had no part in this. "In Arundel?" he asked.

"Je," Isidora said weakly.

His head spun. Who were these men that would use women so ill? How could he be nearly thirty years old and not know men like that existed in his sphere? The knowledge soured his stomach and made him more determined than ever to end this abominable practice.

But first, he had to agree to a price for Isidora. Unfortunately, Leo was not adept at the art of negotiation—when he agreed to the outrageous sum of one hundred pounds, Mrs. Mansfield's little eyes had gone wide with surprise, and he knew then that he'd been outdone.

He brought Isidora to the Clarendon Hotel, ignoring the looks directed at him, and paid for a room for her. The desk clerk could hardly contain his disgust at what he perceived was happening, and at first he refused to grant her a room.

But Leo reminded him how much the Kingdom of Alucia was paying for the rooms he let. The clerk reluctantly agreed to allow one night. Only one night. "Won't have her type here, Your Highness," he'd said tightly.

"Her *type*," Leo had said, "is that of a woman who has been treated very ill by your country."

But the Clarendon Hotel was not a solution, and Leo fretted to Josef. "The lass wants to go home to her family," he lied. "I need a place she might stay until I can arrange it."

As Josef had not seen Isidora, he had no reason to suspect what Leo was about. He thought about it a moment and said, "May I suggest Mr. Hubert Cressidian."

Leo knew of the gentleman, an Alucian merchant living in London, who was, by all indications, richer than Croesus. "Do you know him?" Leo asked. "Can I trust him?"

Josef's expression had remained entirely neutral. "It is my experience, Highness, that Mr. Cressidian may be trusted for a price."

It turned out that Josef's instincts were right. Mr. Cressidian was thin and wiry, with black hair and eyes so brown they appeared almost black. Leo told him he needed a place to keep a young woman safe from harm. Mr. Cressidian didn't ask any questions about Isidora. He didn't seem to care. He didn't seem particularly curious about anything, really. He merely stated his terms: a stipend for her keep, and an introduction to a French shipping magnate Leo knew.

Neither did Isidora ask questions—she seemed resigned to whatever fate had in store for her. But when they arrived at the very large house in Mayfair, she looked at Leo. "Who *are* you?"

She truly had no idea who he was. "I'm no one," he said, and he meant it. He smiled and said, "My friends call me Leo."

Three days later, Josef informed Leo that his invitation to the Montgomery ball had been rescinded.

CHAPTER FOURTEEN

A soiree to be held at the London townhome of the Duke of Norfolk was postponed indefinitely. A friend of the duke has said that the reason might have had to do with one of the guests being unsuitable to dine with someone as dignified as the duke and duchess. Could it be the same gentleman who was disinvited from the Montgomery ball?

Ladies, doctors advise a period of nine hours of complete rest with no distractions or diversions after a period of maternal confinement and birth, with no more than five minutes allotted to one's husband to assure him all is well.

༄—Honeycutt's Gazette of Fashion and Domesticity for Ladies

CAROLINE HAD A habit of entering her home through the back door if she'd been shopping, lest Beck see her packages. Generally, he was none the wiser when she used this method of entry, but this afternoon, he was striding through the kitchen when she tumbled in with her wrapped packages of brocades and silk fabrics. He took one look at the bundles in her arms, then at her. "What are those?"

She tried to think of an excuse that would spare her. None came to mind.

He frowned at her silence. "Come with me," he said gruffly.

Things had reverted to normal between them, with Beck complaining about her spending and the fact that she ate his favorite jam—oh, and that she practiced the piano when he was trying to read. And, of course, his favorite complaint—that she did as she pleased.

"Why?" she asked as she hastily shoved her packages beneath a wooden bench in the small entry into the kitchens.

"Why do you think?" He was holding a wooden tray onto which he had himself, apparently, put cheese and bread. "I rang for you two hours ago."

"I was out, Beck," Caroline said as she followed him down the hall. He was striding purposefully, and she was struggling to keep up as she tried to unfasten her cloak.

"Yes, you were out shopping again!" he said crossly over his shoulder before turning into his study.

Caroline managed to get the cloak unfastened and pulled it from her shoulders, dropping it onto a chair in the hall.

"I have my own money, have you forgotten? And besides, Felicity Hancock is desperate for one of my gowns. Ladies are beginning to notice—"

"I don't care," he said, and dropped the tray onto his desk as she struggled to remove her bonnet. "And need I remind you that your inheritance is in a trust. You are spending *our* money."

"Well, whose fault is that?" Caroline demanded.

"It is necessary, Caro, as you have given every indication you would spend *all* of your trust if given the opportunity."

Caroline managed to remove her bonnet, but it caught a pin in her hair, and one thick tress tumbled down over one eye. "Blast it," she complained, and with a sigh of exasperation, she tossed her bonnet onto his desk, too. "I'll just go and repair my hair," she said, but before she could turn to the door, he stopped her.

"No, no, we'll have this said and done now," Beck commanded her. "I mean to go out soon, and I know your tricks, Caro. If you go up to your rooms, I won't see you for hours, and when I do, you'll probably have brought along Mrs. Honeycutt to verbally assault me."

"Hollis does not verbally *assault* you, Beck. She is careful to say only what is true."

"Oh? So is it true that I was born with the head of a monkey and the heart of an ass?"

"Not *that*, obviously, but the other things she says are true."

Beck wasn't listening. He was waving his hand at her. "Enough about Hollis Honeycutt. If Percy were alive today, he'd have her in hand. He shouldn't have died like he did."

Caroline tried to push the tress from her face. But the way her hair was pinned, it kept falling. "You have no regard for my very dear friends who have been my loyal companions all my life." She swiped up a bit of cheese and stuffed it into her mouth and said, dismissively, "Go on then. What is it that is *so important*?"

"You want to know? I'll tell you, Caro. *You* need to marry."

Caroline froze. Then she laughed. "Not this again!"

"What? You're six and twenty or very near, and it's high time you married and it's high time I let someone else worry about your purchases." He picked up a stack of bills and waved them at her. "As it happens, I've taken matters into my own hands."

That got her full attention. Beck often ranted about the need for her to marry, but he'd never said anything like this. "Pardon?"

"Your reluctance to entertain an offer before now has left half the eligible gentlemen skeptical of you. So, I've let it be known—discreetly, of course—the size of your dowry."

"You did *what*?"

"You can't continue on like this, flitting from one soiree to the next dressmaker without any regard for who you are destined to be."

"How do you know who I am destined to be?" she demanded, fighting the lock of hair.

"Are you mad? Must I tell you that you are destined to be a wife and mother?"

"Who decreed that I must be a wife or a mother? This is precisely the reason I do not entertain the idea of marriage, Beck. Men think they know all there is to know. Perhaps I'd like to be an artist instead."

Beck sat down in the chair behind his desk and leaned back, templing his fingers. "That would be well and good, darling, had you ever shown the *slightest* interest in becoming an artist. I hired an art tutor for you when you were seventeen, you may recall, and you deliberately painted as horribly as you could to chase him away. The only interest you've shown is being invited to the next social gathering."

"At which I excel, thank you. And I didn't say I *will* be an artist. I was making a point. I might like to be a dressmaker. I happen to be very good at it."

Beck snorted. "You will not be a dressmaker. I spoke to the prince about it, and he—"

Caroline let out a bark of laughter before her brother could finish. "Your friend *Leo*? Your dear, dear friend who has been uninvited to everything in the last fortnight? He knows nothing." She swiped up another piece of cheese.

She noticed Beck had stilled. When he didn't give her a snippy little retort, Caroline looked at him. "What?"

"I was about to say, *Caroline*, that I spoke to the prince about it, who happens to be standing just there."

An icy scrape went down her spine. The top of her head buzzed. She stared at Beck for a long moment before she pushed her hair from her face and made herself turn around to see. The prince was indeed standing there, his back against the wall, one dark brow arched. He gave her a half-hearted wave. She hadn't seen him because the door was open and impeding her view, and her bloody hair had obscured the rest of her vision. She whipped back around to Beck. "Why didn't you *tell* me he was here?"

"I should think it obvious, seeing as how he is *just there*," he said, gesturing emphatically toward the prince. "And by the bye, what do you know about the invitations being recalled?"

"Nothing!"

Beck narrowed his gaze.

"And what, pray tell, did the illustrious Royal Highness have to say for my deplorable status of being an unmarried woman?" She knew quite a lot about those invitations, as it happened. It was she, after all, who had suggested to Lady Norfolk that she might want to postpone her soiree, given Lady Montgomery's rather visceral reaction to the gossip surrounding the prince. Priscilla had relayed to Caroline that while having tea with Lady Montgomery, she'd mentioned the prince's unsavory habits, and Lady Montgomery had nearly choked on her crumpet, and screeched for her secretary then and there and demanded the invitation be rescinded at once.

Also, Lady Norfolk was terribly pregnant and terribly cross. Caroline had assumed, on her friend's behalf, that the anxiety would be too much.

"Watch your tongue, Caroline," Beck warned her. "Naturally, he said what any man would say—that it's well past time you married."

"Ah—with all due respect, Beck, that is not exactly what I said," the prince politely demurred.

"It was implied," Beck said impatiently.

"What *did* you say?" Caroline asked, turning back to the prince.

"Caro, please! Do not speak to His Royal Highness as if he were some servant to be interrogated for a missing spoon!"

"It's quite all right," the prince said. "I merely said that in Alucia most women are married by the time they are twenty. It was an observation, that's all." And now he was observing her hair with a curious look.

"And you are *well* past twenty, Caro," Beck needlessly pointed out.

Ooh, she would strangle Beck when they were alone. Why was it she could never meet the prince when she looked her best? Why must she always look so bedraggled? He'd been casually looking on all the while she was standing with her hair half down and stuffing cheese into her mouth.

She slowly turned back to her brother. "You're right, Beck. I should marry. Bring on the suitors, then. Bring them now! If the *prince* says it—"

"Again, I did not say it," the prince said quickly. "I simply had a conversation with a friend—I didn't mean to offer advice."

"But you did."

"Caro! For God's sake, he is a prince of Alucia! Show some respect!" Beck bellowed.

"My lord?"

Caroline and Beck turned toward the door at the same moment. Garrett had stepped inside, unnoticed by them, and interrupted what Caroline felt was the prelude to a brawl. "My lord, there is a gentleman at the door about the horse."

"Ah!" Beck grinned and hopped to his feet. "That must be the stable master where I intend to house my horse when she arrives. Fine blocks of stables they are, too— the queen's Horse Guard is stabled there." He started for the door but paused to look at Caroline. "This would be an opportune time to do something with your hair," he added, his fingers fluttering in the direction of the fallen tress that drooped over her shoulder as he hurried out.

Caroline made a face at his back and remained where she was, her arms folded. When she was certain he was gone, she pivoted around and marched to where the prince stood behind the open door.

He seemed alarmed at first and straightened as if he thought he might have to do battle. But then he quickly clasped his hands at his back, his legs braced apart, and seemed to prepare himself for whatever she had to say.

"How dare you," Caroline said.

"How dare I...?"

"Speak to my brother about my marriage prospects!"

"Once again, I did *not* speak to your brother about your marriage prospects. Or even that you were not married. Your brother asked a question and I answered as I would answer any friend."

"I am not his *ward*, for God's sake. I'm a grown woman and I do as I please."

"Evidently true on both counts," he agreed. And then he smiled.

It infuriated her that he should smile in a way that would make her feel so buzzy. With a quick look at the door, she shifted closer. "I don't have to do as he commands, you know."

"I never dreamed that you did. I can't imagine there is any man on this earth that can tell you what to do."

She shifted even closer. She could detect the musky scent of his cologne, could see a bit of lint on his collar. "Why should *any* man tell me what to do? I am as much a person as him or even *you*, Your Highness."

"Obviously." He picked up the tail end of the loose tress of hair and brushed it along her collarbone before dropping it over her shoulder. It instantly slid forward again.

All the nerves in Caroline's body began to sizzle. She despised this man, but she'd never been quite so aroused as she was in this angry moment. She dropped her gaze to his mouth and the shadow of his beard. "Why are you always *here*?" she demanded. "Are you having an affair with our Ann?"

His eyes widened. He barked out a laugh. "Good God, Caroline, do you speak *every* thought that occurs to you?"

She would ignore, for the moment, that he had used her given name, which meant, she supposed, that they were very much acquainted, thank you, just as she'd maintained all along. She would further disregard how pleasant her name sounded in his melodious accent. And she would not use this moment to discuss how many thoughts did *not* pass her lips, for there were quite a lot of them. "Well? Are you?"

His brows dropped into a dark frown, and he leaned forward. "Hear me plainly, woman. *No*. For God's sake, *no*.

If I were to have an affair, it would be with a woman who is lush, and curved in all the right places, and open to my suggestions for how to debauch her. Not a timid maid."

The sizzle was quickly turning to fire. She couldn't help but wonder what his suggestions for debauching a woman might be. Her gaze fell to his mouth again. She was feeling a little heady.

"My turn. Why aren't you married? Surely a beautiful woman like you, with her own inheritance, and an enormous dowry, apparently, who does not have to do what any man says, would attract quite a lot of gentlemen in this town. Particularly the type who enjoy a great challenge. Or are they all bloody fools?"

Aha—again, she would not be put on her heels by a compliment casually tossed to her. "Of course I've attracted them," she scoffed. "I don't care for any of them. Why aren't *you* married? Been waiting for the right Weslorian to come along?"

He chuckled, and his gaze moved to the bit of lace she'd sewn along the edge of her bodice. "The same as you, madam—I don't want anyone to tell me what to do and I don't want responsibilities."

"Aha! So you *do* prefer maids, then."

He slowly lifted his gaze to hers and held it tight, like he had her attention in his fist. "I prefer women, Caroline," he murmured. "I prefer women who are confident of their place in this world…but perhaps those who hold their tongues when they ought."

"Because you don't agree with everything a woman says doesn't make what she says wrong."

He lifted his hand, and with the tip of his finger, he traced a line from the curve of her shoulder up to her chin.

"Tell me, Caroline—what gives you the right to speak to me in this manner?"

She leaned forward, just an inch or so from him. "I was born with the right to speak however I want to whomever I want. You are not the prince of me."

The prince blinked. "Of all the outrageous—"

She didn't let him finish. She pushed at his chest with both hands, forcing him against the wall, and before he could recover, she rose up on her toes to kiss him. She kissed the prince like she'd never kissed another man in her life. Admittedly, there hadn't been very many, and certainly she'd never kissed a gentleman like this. But there was something about this man that begged for it—he was so high and mighty, so sure of himself. She had *never* taken such liberties, and she'd never been so wholly thrilled with an act in her life. This was fire.

But for a high and mighty man, he seemed not to know what to do. He held his arms out wide, as if he were silently announcing he wanted no part of this. Except that his mouth said differently. Oh, but his lips and his tongue said something else entirely. He wouldn't touch her with his hands, but he nipped at her lips, his tongue playing with hers. He pressed against her, his chest against her chest, and kissed her back as passionately as she kissed him. It was intoxicating, and it wasn't until her hair found its way between their lips that she suddenly pushed him away and stepped back.

She was breathing raggedly and so was he. They were both panting like they'd chased each other around this room. They stared hard at each other for one endless moment. An entire book of thoughts and feelings and unspoken words flowing between them was written in that moment. Caroline felt something open in her, warm and wet and accepting.

But then he said, "What the hell is the matter with you?"

She didn't have a good answer for him. A fever? If it was a fever, it was a new sort of fever, one that struck without warning and consumed her quickly.

He held up his hand, his palm facing her, as if he thought she would throw herself at him again. His eyes were dark, his lips slightly parted. He looked shocked. But he also looked dangerously aroused. "*Never* do that again," he said in a low voice.

"Don't tell me what to do," she said, and wheeled about, fleeing for the door. She leaped into the hall and nearly collided with Beck on his way back in.

"Caro?"

She ignored her brother, picked up her skirts and fled to her rooms with that kiss burning on her lips.

CHAPTER FIFTEEN

Invitations to Lord Pennybacker's ball will be deliv-
ered by the end of the month. Alas, there will surely
be those disappointed by the absence of an invita-
tion in their post, as the number of persons desir-
ing to attend has grown steadily through the month.
Lady Pennybacker has said the ball will be limited
to two hundred souls.

The Duke and Duchess of Norfolk have returned
to their family seat as the duchess enters her pe-
riod of confinement. The couple has enjoyed the
calls of many notable personages, including Lord
Hawke and his sister, who is much acclaimed for
her beauty. So acclaimed, it seems, that a gentle-
man who is expected to formally enter an engage-
ment of princely proportions in a matter of weeks
invited himself along.

It is discovered by many that Lady Caroline
Hawke's talents have extended to dressmaking. La-
dies in Mayfair are suddenly clambering to have an
evening dress designed and fashioned by our dear
friend. She has a unique talent for drawing on the
English- and Alucian-style gowns and creating cov-
eted garments. She is taking limited requests for the
winter season.

᎒—Honeycutt's Gazette of Fashion and
Domesticity for Ladies

AFTER A FULL two days of torment, Leo couldn't shake that kiss.

He was strolling alongside Beck as they toured the stable blocks, and while Beck maintained a stream of commentary about the accommodations for his Alucian racehorse, Leo kept thinking about his outrageous, remarkable sister.

That kiss appeared in his thoughts at the oddest times. When he was alone. In the middle of the night. At breakfast, at lunch, at tea with friends.

He was shocked she'd done it, shocked that she'd so brazenly presumed that she could. And then again, he wasn't surprised at all. He was appalled by her insolence but also admired her pluck. He was angry that she'd taken the liberty but also damn well excited by it.

He was beginning to believe that he'd never met a more perplexing, confounding, beautiful woman in his life. He seemed to be feeling every emotion—good, bad or indifferent—that a man could feel about a woman.

He was also feeling a libidinous desire that was not responding to his usual attempts to keep it at bay. He wanted to do that kiss again. Only this time, he'd do the kissing, thank you.

He had to force himself to think of something else. He turned his attention again to the women he was trying to save. He had intended to speak to his old friend Norfolk about Jacleen at the supper party, but then the supper had been indefinitely postponed. If that bloody gazette was to be believed, it was because of him. It must be true, because more than one gentleman had laughingly congratulated him for his indiscreet call to Mrs. Mansfield's "house."

"Never knew a bloke who could draw so much attention to his activities," said a man he knew only as Hornsby with a guffaw.

Mr. Frame, who had vigorously cautioned Leo about the need for discretion and a moral compass before leading him to Mrs. Mansfield's house of ill repute, had a fat mouth.

Now Norfolk and his family were in Arundel, awaiting the birth of their fourth child. That made things more difficult—Leo couldn't simply drop in on the duke in Arundel. One did not "pass by" a grand English estate in the country, particularly if one had no holdings in that direction... Herstmonceux notwithstanding.

But then Beck handed Leo a solution.

A few days after Caroline had kissed him senseless, Leo had joined Beck at their favorite gentlemen's club for a spot of gin. Out of the blue, Beck began complaining about having to make a trip to Arundel. "The rains have been awful and left the roads almost impassable, I've heard. It will take a full day to get there."

Leo looked up. "You're to Arundel?"

Beck sighed. "I promised Caro. Lady Norfolk is her friend, and she's made a dress or dressing gown or a bonnet, I don't know what, for her time in confinement."

"Norfolk is an old acquaintance," Leo said casually. "We were at Cambridge together. I've spent a holiday or two at Arundel."

Beck didn't bite. He nodded pleasantly. "Grand place, isn't it? I've known the old chap quite a long time myself."

Leo sipped his gin. The taste was too bitter. "When will you go?"

"Thursday," Beck said, and glanced at his watch.

Leo drummed his fingers on the table before them, thinking how to proceed. He could not recall another time he'd been in the position of having to ask to be included. It was he who was always fending off people who wanted to join *his* party. *What a strange new world.* He eyed Beck from the corner of his eye and thought what to do. He thought perhaps the best way to approach it was the most direct way. "Beck, my friend, would you mind terribly—"

"Don't ask it of me, Leo," Beck muttered.

"Pardon? But Henry is my old friend."

Beck shifted uncomfortably in his seat. He looked around, as if seeking a footman, even though his glass was full. "Naturally, Highness, at any other time I would be *delighted*—"

"Ah. I'm a Highness again," Leo said with a bit of a sardonic laugh.

Beck groaned. He rubbed his face, then looked Leo in the eye. "It's his wife. Augusta is…reluctant."

"Reluctant," Leo repeated.

Beck leaned forward. "You've gained a bit of a reputation," he said with an apologetic wince.

"No. Listen, Beck," Leo said quickly. "The things that are said about me are not true. Well, not *entirely* true. That is, they are *true*, but not in the way you or Henry might understand. I know the supper party was postponed on my account, and I should like to set the matter to rest, with my old friend, if nothing else but for the sake of our friendship."

Beck winced again. "She's at the end of a pregnancy and, as I understand it, rather uncomfortable. I'd not want to give her any cause for more discomfort."

"I won't see her," Leo promised. "Arundel is as big as a palace—it is entirely possible our paths need not cross at all. I will do my best to stay out of her way."

Beck leaned back, bracing both hands against the table. He filled his cheeks with air, then slowly released it. "Yes, all right," he said after a moment. "*I* don't believe what is said of you. God knows worse has been said of me."

He paused. "Well. Not *worse*, for what is said of you is wretched. Pardon, but you understand. Yes, of course you must come, Leo. We men must stick together." He smiled.

Leo didn't think men needed to stick together. It seemed to him they had the upper hand in almost everything as it was.

"I ought to send a messenger," Beck said "I should let him know you're coming."

"No, no," Leo said hastily. "He would tell his wife, and the anticipation might cause her undue anxiety. When I call, people tend to be concerned with propriety and having everything just so, as it were."

"Ah," Beck said, nodding sagely. "Of course." He laughed. "I've quite forgotten you are a prince."

Leo laughed, too. "I think so have I."

CAROLINE COULDN'T KEEP the secret of that kiss another moment. She lasted an entire four days before she went to see Hollis and thought her restraint was rather remarkable given the extraordinary situation.

She wanted to kiss him again, but perhaps this time with his arms around her. She was confused by this desire—how could she feel such strong feelings for the worst sort of scoundrel? He was blithely seducing maids and walking out with women of the night! And then charming women like herself into bad behavior.

She arrived at Hollis's house after a brisk walk, feeling as strong as she ever had and rather invigorated by the vexation with herself and that wayward prince. Hollis's home was close by—her late husband, Sir Percival, felled by a muddy road and a carriage accident, had left his widow in very good circumstances. She lived quite comfortably near Hyde Park, in a very large house with minimal staff.

It was true that a rich, attractive young widow was quite a lure, and gentlemen of all stripes had sniffed around Hollis in the almost three years she'd been widowed. But Hollis was never interested.

She knocked on Hollis's door with her usual flair, a series of rapid-fire knocks. A few moments later Donovan opened the door. He stood casually in the doorway, his legs braced apart, his shirtsleeves rolled up to reveal thick forearms. He was holding a silver teapot and worked to polish it as he looked Caroline up and down. "Good afternoon, Lady Caroline," he said. "What a pleasure to see you in good health. I had heard you were all but dead."

"Ha. It will take more than an ague to kill *me*, sir."

He smiled. The man was simply stunning in his masculinity and good looks. "That's the very reason I didn't believe it. Do come in." He stepped aside so that she could enter the foyer.

Caroline removed her bonnet and dangled it from one finger in his direction. "Donovan, on my word, you are an Adonis in the flesh."

"Pardon?" He took her bonnet and tossed it onto a console.

"A Greek god."

One of his dark brows arched. "You are mistaken, milady—I'm but a regular Englishman."

She laughed. "You can't be a regular Englishman, because you are impervious to flattery."

"Not entirely." He smiled again.

Something delightful fluttered in her veins. "Where is your mistress?" she asked with a coy smile.

"In her study, naturally, where she spends most of her day." He gestured for her to follow and led her to Hollis while whistling a cheery tune. He stepped into the room and said, "Lady Caroline is calling."

"Caro!" Hollis called happily from somewhere inside.

Caroline slid past Donovan with a wanton smile. He returned that smile with a smile of amusement, then closed the door behind her as she entered Hollis's cluttered study.

Hollis was bent over the layout of her gazette. She'd turned what had once been a very lovely room into an office, where she pieced together her gazette before sending off a template twice monthly to Gilbert and Rivington for printing.

A repurposed dining table dominated the center of the clutter, upon which Hollis had spread out the pages of the current edition of her gazette. Past issues were stacked around the floor and on shelves that Donovan had constructed. A tabby cat was stretched across the stacks on the floor, and another sat like an ornament on one of the shelves. There were books and strings and scissors and visors that Hollis wore when she worked late in the night.

Hollis had also taken to using a monocle to examine the print layout of her gazette, and at present, she held it up to one eye.

"This looks more and more like a government office," Caroline complained, glancing around her. She took some broadsheets from the seat of the only armchair in the room and shoved them onto a shelf and sat.

Hollis put down her monocle. "What brings you round on this fine day, other than to seduce my household help?"

"I can't help myself, Hollis. Donovan is a beautiful man and he deserves to be admired, and *you* won't do it."

"He is admired, you may depend. Last week, he accompanied me to the market, and there we met a lass who put herself in our path at every turn. She reminded me of you. Very tenacious, that one."

Caroline laughed and stacked her feet on top of a pile of gazettes on an ottoman. "I have news."

"Splendid!" Hollis said. "I've just enough space for a bit of gossip in the next issue. Tell me."

"You know about Prince Leopold and the brothel."

"I do indeed! You came here with the news yourself, remember?"

Caroline remembered. She'd made a mad dash, as she recalled it now. "Which happened only a week after I spotted the prince chasing our maid Ann around Leadenhall market."

"I still can't believe you went there!" Hollis said with delight. "I wrote Eliza straightaway and told her you went to Leadenhall in the company of Mr. Morley and his sisters." She laughed.

"Never mind that," Caroline said. "I suspected the prince was a rake, but the visit to the brothel was the truth. But then Priscilla told Lady Montgomery—"

"Oh! I heard about *that*," Hollis said. "She was incensed he would do something so terrible before her ball."

"And naturally, I told Lady Norfolk, because she would never forgive me if Lady Montgomery banished the prince and she didn't have the opportunity to do the same."

"You did?" Hollis asked.

"I did! It's wretched behavior for a man of his stature." She folded her arms and stared off into space for a moment.

She realized Hollis hadn't said anything and glanced in her direction. "What? Why do you look at me like that?"

"Like what? Like I'm terribly curious about what goes on in your head? I thought you had clearly resolved to be less infatuated with him, darling."

"I'm not *infatuated* with him," Caroline scoffed.

"Really? Because this is the second call you've made to my house since crawling off your deathbed, and both times have been to complain about *him*."

Caroline huffed. "He just confounds me, that's all. That's why I think that ladies of good reputation should steer very clear of him. He can be quite charming, but beneath the surface, this despicable behavior lurks. But the die has been cast, hasn't it? Priscilla said Lady Pennybacker means to reduce her guest list, as well."

"Caro! What are you doing?"

She hadn't really meant to set all these wheels in motion, but Priscilla couldn't stop telling everyone she knew, and Augusta, well… Caroline had been in a bit of a mood during that call. "My friends would not want someone of questionable morals in their homes. I have no choice in the matter, as Beck thinks he and the prince are the best of friends."

"Well. I suppose you know best," Hollis said with a hint of sarcasm.

"I don't know if I do or not, but I'm ashamed that I ever kissed him."

Hollis gasped.

Caroline waved her hand at Hollis as if it were a trifling matter. But it was no trifling matter. Her heart was permanently singed from that kiss. "It was nothing! I was angry, that's all."

"Angry! Why would you kiss someone if you were angry?" Hollis scoffed. "Don't you dare sit there looking so coy, Caroline Hawke. Tell me what happened."

Naturally, Caroline told her everything. That's why she'd come, after all—to unburden herself. She told Hollis about Beck's new determination to see her married, and how he'd been lecturing her in his study, and how she hadn't seen the prince in the room until it was too late. How she accused the prince of meddling and how he'd called her Caroline. She didn't tell Hollis that when he said her name in that low, silky voice of his, it had curled around her like a warm silk wrap and held her there. She explained to Hollis that the act had been so impetuous, that it was almost as if someone else entirely had taken over her body, and she hardly realized what she was doing until she did it.

Hollis sat back, grinning with wonder at Caroline.

"Stop *grinning* at me," Caroline groaned.

"That was bold, even for *you*, Caro. Do you think you're in love with him?"

The question jolted Caroline. "For God's sake, Hollis! Of *course* not."

"Smitten, then. You must admit it, it was very kind of him to bring you flowers while you lay ill."

"He didn't bring flowers for *me*, he brought them for Ann. Honestly, I can't abide him. He deserves Lady Eulalie, if you ask me. I can't imagine why she'd want to bind herself to him."

Hollis laughed. "Can't you? She is binding herself to him for wealth and privilege, and he to her for political alliance."

"But that's not what marriage is for," Caroline complained. "One should marry for felicity and companionship, not to keep from being murdered." She plucked irritably at her sleeve. "I would avoid that sort of arrangement with all that I had."

"You're not a prince and you don't believe in marriage in the best of circumstances," Hollis said.

"That is not true," Caroline insisted.

Hollis shrugged. "All right. You fear marriage."

"I don't *fear* it. Contrary to what you think, I should very much like to be married. But…" She winced. "I want to be wanted for me. Not for my looks. Or the size of my dowry. Those things can't sustain a marriage."

"You bring to mind Mary Pressley," Hollis said thoughtfully. "She fell very much in love with Malcolm Byrd, and he supposedly with her, and she's been terribly unhappy ever since."

"He treats her like a dog," Caroline said flatly. Mary was a childhood friend of Caroline's. A sweet girl, who'd never wanted anything more than to be married and be a mother. She was courted by Mr. Byrd, who had charmed her down to her toes. She fell very much in love with him. She and Caroline would lie on Caroline's bed and spend hours talking about Mr. Byrd, and what her wedding dress would look like and how many children she might have.

But the reality turned out to be quite different from the daydream. Malcolm Byrd was nothing like what he'd presented to Mary while courting her. He was a beast, he was cruel and he didn't hesitate to strike Mary if she failed to please him.

Once, after Mary had given birth to her first child, Caroline had begged her to run from him, but Mary had laughed sourly. "And go where, Caroline? My elderly parents? I have no money, nothing to my name. He would never allow me to take our son. This is my cross to bear." And then she had taken Caroline's hand and squeezed it tightly. "You never know a person until you've shared a bed and a house. It's impossible to know their true nature. Mind you, have a care."

That stark warning had stayed with Caroline. Gentlemen would come to call, perfectly pleasant and polite gentlemen. But invariably, she would wonder about their true nature, and they certainly never inquired after hers. For every marriage like Hollis and Percival's, or Eliza and Sebastian's, she knew a story of another, darker marriage.

But she would concede that she did very much want to be loved.

"I think you should tell the prince how you feel," Hollis said.

"How I feel about what? You're mad, Hollis," she said, and Hollis giggled. "I didn't come here for that sort of advice."

"You came because I am your confessor and your conscience. Want to go round and see Papa with me?"

"I'd love nothing better," Caroline said, and sighed. "But I can't today. Beck and I are to Arundel on the morrow. I promised Augusta I'd call. She's terribly worried about being lonely. She has no one but her children to entertain her, you know."

"Ooh," Hollis said, her eyes rounding. "They may be the least entertaining children I know. Wild little beasts. Always carrying on about a pony."

Caroline stood. She walked around the table to bend over Hollis and give her a hug.

"Farewell, darling! My love to Beck. See you next week, then?" Hollis asked as Caroline started out of the room.

"If not before!" Caroline called over her shoulder.

She grabbed her bonnet from the console where Donovan had placed it and walked out into bright sunlight. She looked up, blinking at blue sky. She didn't *love* Prince Leopold. Just because he was the *only* man in a very long time to have filled her imagination, or to have failed to notice her facade, or had seen past it, didn't mean she loved him or held him in any sort of particular esteem. So why did the thought of him leaving England unsettle her so? Why should she feel a little bit bereft, a little bit remorseful and a little bit heartsick?

Because she was a fool, that was why, with a terrible habit of being attracted to rakes. She would think of the kiss often, but she would not miss him a moment after he'd gone.

She convinced herself that was true and even believed it...up until the moment he climbed into the coach that would ferry them to Arundel.

CHAPTER SIXTEEN

A lady generous in spirit and in person is adding to her household, and happily, it is not another dog. In this circumstance it is the addition of two new chambermaids. It is expected the lady and her lord will entertain many over the coming weeks of summer, beginning with the first garden party of the season.

Ladies, apply a toilet mask to your face each night liberally coated in sheep fat. After two weeks of night use, skin will revive its youthful vigor.

⌒—Honeycutt's Gazette of Fashion and Domesticity for Ladies

LEO COULD COUNT on one hand the number of times he'd actually felt a woman's disdain for him. Actually, he didn't even need his hand, for he counted exactly zero times. Until today.

Today, when he'd stepped into the coach in front of Clarendon Hotel, Lady Caroline's gaze had turned to ice. Leo had expected their first meeting after that kiss to be interesting, but he hadn't expected *that*. It was almost as if she had determined she was the injured party, when in fact it was she who had taken liberties with him.

She folded her arms and glared at her brother. "What is the meaning of this?"

Beck blinked with surprise. "The meaning of...?"

She slid her gaze to Leo.

"Prince Leopold? Well, His Highness is to Arundel, like us, and I offered him to ride along."

"What? He has his guards. Shouldn't they be the ones to escort him?"

"They are escorting us, Caro. They are riding behind, but the coach is obviously more comfortable for the prince."

"For heaven's sake, Beck," she said irritably, and began to fluff the many, *many* flounces on her skirt.

"God as my witness, I never understand you. What is the matter? Has he offended you?"

Lady Caroline's face turned pink.

"*Je*, please tell me if I have offended you, Lady Caroline, and I will do my utmost to atone for it. When last we spoke, I had the impression you esteemed me quite a lot." Leo smiled.

Caroline's color deepened. "I do beg your pardon, Your Highness, if that was the impression I gave you. I was being polite."

"Ah," he said, his smile deepening. "Then I must commend you—you were zealously polite."

"It's called civility, sir."

"Is *that* what it's called." He gave a shake of his head. "I am forever learning proper English."

"What have I missed?" Beck demanded of the two of them.

"Nothing!" Caroline said, and looked away from Leo.

But Leo did not look away from her. He rather enjoyed her discomfit. He was the one who was always back on his heels when they met, and he didn't mind that, for once, she was the unsteady one. He liked how it turned her cheeks an appealing shade of pink, and how it made her green eyes sparkle so brilliantly with vexation.

"It is clearly something," Beck said, sounding confused.

"Really, Beck? Have you forgotten that you started it by seeking the advice of His Royal Highness about what to do with your poor, burdensome, unmarried sister?"

"I didn't ask for his advice," Beck corrected her. "I know precisely what needs to be done. You'll see."

Lady Caroline rolled her eyes. But Leo was interested in what Beck thought needed to be done.

"I've some prospects for you," Beck said.

That caught Caroline's attention. She looked at her brother curiously. "Who?"

"Ladley, for one."

She laughed. "Your old school chum? Robert Ladley has never passed a whisky or an ale he didn't drink."

Beck's brows dipped as this was news to him. "I beg your pardon. Ladley was sober enough to go with all due haste to fetch a doctor the night you almost died."

"I didn't almost die, and is it not true that very recently you had to have the help of two footmen to haul him out to a hackney?"

Beck's brows sank deeper. "*One* time."

"Who else?" Lady Caroline chirped, having dismissed the Earl of Montford as a prospect.

Beck sniffed. "Lord March."

Leo didn't know Lord March, but Lady Caroline clearly did. She slowly turned her head and pinned her brother with a look that made even Leo cringe.

"He's not as bad as you think," Beck said quickly. "I know what is said of him, but just because Hollis prints it doesn't make it true."

"She happens to be exceedingly accurate in most things. Keep thinking, Beck. And really, this seems neither the time nor place to discuss my dismal marriage prospects.

We'd not want to make the drive tedious for His Royal Highness."

"He doesn't mind," Beck said confidently, when, in fact, Leo did indeed mind. "You mustn't think of him as a prince, really, Caro. He's more like…like an uncle."

"An *uncle*?" Leo said, incredulous.

"My point is, you're like family now," Beck said. "You are the brother of Prince Sebastian, married to Eliza, and Caro, you have always said you and Eliza are more sisters than friends. God knows she and Hollis treat me like an outnumbered brother."

Caroline stared at Leo. Leo stared back. He could feel the tension between them, could feel it fill the carriage and press against the walls, could detect the scent of desire mixed pleasingly with her perfume. "Fine," she said. "He's my uncle."

"I am not your uncle," Leo said. "I am no one's uncle," he added for Beck's benefit, but neither of them appeared to be listening to him. Lady Caroline had positioned herself so that her gaze was on the window and the passing scenery of trees and rolling hills dotted with sheep. And Beck, upon seeing the same rolling hills, launched into a tale about a hunt he and Norfolk had participated in several years ago where the dogs had been thrown off the trail of a fox by a dead deer.

It was enough to put a grown man to sleep.

After what seemed an hour of mindless chatter, Leo felt himself sliding off into dreamland when he was suddenly jolted by a strange bounce in the carriage. He sat up. Beck was leaning forward, straining to see out the window as the coach rolled to a halt.

"What the devil? Stay here, the both of you," Beck said sternly. He flung open the door and hopped out, then slammed the door shut behind him. Leo could hear him calling up to the driver, asking if it was a wheel.

Caroline slowly pushed herself upright, her gaze locked on Leo.

Leo leaned back against the squabs. The sound of men talking, or perhaps even arguing, faded into the distance.

"Shouldn't you step out and see what has happened?" she asked. "Perhaps lend a hand?"

"Thank you for the suggestion of how I ought to behave, but I believe I'll remain here and discover why you are treating me like a leper."

"I'm not treating you like a leper."

"No? Feels a bit like it. Whatever you may call it, you are treating me quite differently than you did the last time we met. You do remember the last time we met, do you not?"

The color in her cheeks returned. "Yes, all right, I was ill behaved when last we met, but I was terribly cross. I beg your forgiveness."

"Interesting." He sat up and braced his arms against his knees, leaning toward her. "What a strange thing you do when you are cross. Is it always so?"

"Obviously not. It depends on the person and the injury."

He nodded, amused. "I don't know if you are complimenting me or not."

She frowned. "It won't happen again. I lost my head, that's all. My actions were in no way an indication of any... regard for you."

"Ah. But the color in your cheeks just now and the enthusiasm in your kiss would suggest otherwise. Are you certain you don't have a bit of regard for me?"

She clucked her tongue. "*Completely* certain."

Leo leaned forward in the small space between them.

Lady Caroline pressed back. He placed his hands against the bench where she was sitting, on either side of her knees. "May I offer a bit of advice, Caroline?"

Her lips parted and she drew a slight intake of breath. "I'd really rather you not."

He lifted one hand and touched his fingers to her jaw. "My advice—"

"Which I just said I'd rather not have—"

"Is that you not kiss a man in anger. An angry kiss can be an enjoyable kiss, and certainly yours was, I won't deny it. But it's not as enjoyable as a happy kiss."

She blinked. Her eyes had landed on his lips, and he could feel desire stirring in him. "I suppose I'll have to take your word for it. I understand you're an expert."

"I do know a little about it," he agreed. He couldn't help himself—he touched a dimple in her cheek with the tips of his fingers.

"And I know a little about rakes," she said as he tilted her chin up just slightly. "I know one instantly."

Leo smiled. He leaned closer. "Are you cross, again, Caroline?"

"Yes, *Leopold*, a little."

"Would you like me to move away?"

She hesitated. She pushed his hand from her face, and he thought that was the end of it. He was just about to slide back into his place when she cupped his face with her hand. "Just be warned that if you kiss me, it will mean something. I would advise you think long and hard about that."

"I am thinking long and hard," he said, and shifted closer.

She put her hand on his chest and sighed. "You are the

worst sort of rake, Leopold Chartier. But if you mean to do it, then do it. We haven't much time."

He bit back a laugh of surprise. "Has anyone ever told you how contradictory you are?"

She traced her thumb across his bottom lip. "What the devil are you waiting for?"

Leo moved then, touching his mouth to hers. He kissed her quite differently than she kissed him. She'd pressed her mouth hard against his, her tongue probing. He kissed her softly and carefully, lingering against pillowy lips while the faint scent of florals teased his nose. The kiss was so exquisite that he had to claw his fingers into the squabs to keep from falling into her and nibbling her up like a delicious delicacy. He teased her lips apart with his tongue. She tipped her chin up and opened her mouth to him. The kiss was tender and slow, but the flames in him were not. This was the tiny gasp of air in a hearth before a fire raged.

Caroline lifted her hand and cupped his jaw. The gentle touch of her fingers caused him to shiver—he felt as if he could explode with his desire at any moment. He had meant to tantalize her, but she was luring him in, enticing him to a mystic mountain of pleasure, and he very much wanted to go with this brash woman.

Don't tell me what to do. Her words popped into his head. He wouldn't tell her what to do; he'd let her lead him to what she wanted. He leaned in, pressing her against the squabs at her back. The kiss was quickly sending him off to oblivion—he wanted to touch her flesh, to feel her skin against his. He wanted to put his hand between her legs and feel the damp of her desire.

It was Caroline who reminded him of where he was. She cupped his face with both hands and pushed his head back. Her lips were wet with his kiss. "My brother is just outside."

Beck. His only friend if his life continued to progress as it had the last few weeks. Leo gathered himself. He nodded, pressed his eyes shut for a moment, then fell back across the carriage, adjusting his Alucian coat to hide his enormous erection. He pushed his hand through his hair and smiled at her. "How did you find that kiss, madam?"

A ringlet of her hair had tumbled out of place, and she very carefully tucked it back in. "I found it serviceable." She smiled impertinently.

"I don't believe you," he said playfully. "I think you felt that kiss in a way you've never felt one before." He arched a brow, daring her to disagree and knowing full well that she would.

But she laughed and said, "Now who is proud? Very well. It was very nice, Highness. *Thank* you." Her smile broadened.

She enjoyed the game she was playing. So did Leo. "You little—"

The door suddenly swung open and Beck's head popped into the interior of the carriage. He looked at his sister, who was smiling like a fat little feline. "Bit of a mechanical problem," he said, hoisting himself back inside. "One of the harnesses, as it happens. It's always something with the harness, isn't it?" he asked, and began to talk about the number of times he'd been involved with harness issues.

Leo didn't hear much of what he said. All he could think of was how hard he was for the woman sitting across from him with the most annoyingly enticing and cheeky little smile he'd ever seen.

CHAPTER SEVENTEEN

All of London rejoices with the return of the sun to our skies, but many have already departed for the country. In Sussex, it is anticipated that Lord Hawke will debut his Alucian racehorse at the Four Corners event. He is rumored to have brought the steed to Arundel to be housed there until the racing season is complete.

An afternoon tea at the home of Mrs. Moriarity was remarked because of one particular guest who arrived clad in a morning gown. Ladies, it is important to know how to dress for the occasion, lest you be the one everyone remembers and not for the reasons to which you aspire.

—*Honeycutt's Gazette of Fashion and Domesticity for Ladies*

AUGUSTA, LADY NORFOLK, was in a very foul mood, for which she could be forgiven. She was in the last month of her pregnancy and complained that nothing fit her, her back hurt, and that she hated her husband.

"Augusta," Caroline said with a sympathetic smile. "You don't *hate* Henry." She had fit the dressing gown she'd made for Augusta around her but realized she'd hardly made it large enough. That was her own fault—she'd never been so close as this to a pregnant belly, and it was…quite large. Privately, Caroline worried that Augusta was carrying more than one child in there. It looked like an entire village.

Augusta had collapsed onto a chair with her legs sprawled in front of her. Caroline wandered over to the towering window to gaze out at the vast lawn below. It was a gloriously sunlit day, and she longed to be outside with everyone. Beck and Norfolk reclined in chairs like a pair of country gentlemen. A nursemaid rocked Augusta's baby, scarcely a year old, under the boughs of a tree. And in the clearing, the prince...*Leopold*...was romping with Augusta's two young daughters along with a frisky black-and-white dog.

He appeared to enjoy it. He was laughing with the girls, encouraging them to chase him. Caroline tried to picture him with the children Lady Eulalie would bear him. Little princesses and princes that looked like him.

It made her feel a little achy.

She absently touched her fingers to her lips and remembered again that staggering kiss in the coach. It had been so tender and considerate—not the same desperate passion she'd shown him. And yet her body had bloomed with it. She could feel herself opening up like a flower, wanting more. Wanting all of him.

Good God. Maybe Beck was right and it was time for her to marry. She was as randy as she'd ever been, wanting things she would not take. Caroline was no saint—she'd been kissed and petted and more. But she'd always been conscious of her virtue and the need to protect it. Great families, her mother had said, maintained their stature through their heirs, their morals and their generosity. She warned Caroline about doing anything that could bring shame to the Hawke name. "A man can recover from his mistakes," she'd said. "But a woman will carry her shame to her grave."

For some reason, that warning, said by a mother she'd lost many years ago, had stuck with her all this time. She'd certainly had many opportunities to bring shame to the family name. But yesterday, in the coach, she had seriously considered it.

"What are you looking at?" Augusta asked.

"Oh, just your daughters and your husband in the green below."

Augusta emitted a sigh that sounded a bit like despair. Caroline turned from the window. "Are you all right?"

"I'm fine," Augusta said. Then she shook her head. "I'm not. Henry disappears from me when I am in confinement."

Caroline laughed, gesturing to the window. "But he is here, darling. He's not gone anywhere at all."

"He disappeared from me in the last four months before Mary was born. The moment he discovered I was with child again, he began to disappear again. He is here in body," Augusta said morosely. "But not in spirit. He despises my body in this state." A tear slipped from her eye. "He's entered some sort of arrangement for exports, and as part of it, he brought home a kitchen girl. Can you imagine? She was part of that arrangement. It's not the first time it's happened, either, for him to have a girl tucked away in the servant's quarters. I got rid of the last one."

Caroline was stunned. "What are you implying?"

"What do you think?" Augusta asked tearfully.

"No, Augusta," Caroline said, coming to her side. "That's not true! He is besotted with you."

"Don't try to tell me what he is, Caroline! I *know* what he is and what he does."

Caroline suspected she might, too. Last night when

they'd arrived, Henry had whisked Beck and the prince away, as if Caroline and Augusta didn't exist. When she'd mentioned it to Beck, he'd said it was because Augusta wanted nothing to do with Leopold, and really, did Caroline want to sit with the gentlemen while they smoked cigars and talked about masculine things?

"What are masculine things?" she'd asked.

Beck had frowned. "Masculine things. Use your imagination, Caro." He'd tapped her head with two fingers and had left her to spend the day with a miserable Augusta.

"The dressing gown is beautiful," Augusta said, stroking the embroidered placket.

"The embroidery is Martha's work. She's taught me quite a lot," Caroline said. "She worked on it while I sewed the hem."

"I never knew you had any talent," Augusta murmured.

Caroline laughed. "Neither did I. But last summer, I couldn't find a modiste who was willing to make a train like the Alucians wear. I've always been fairly good with a needle and thought I'd try. It wasn't as difficult as I thought it would be," she said with a shrug.

The door to the salon opened, and a young maid entered, carrying a tray with tea service. She misstepped; the pot clattered against one of the cups.

Augusta took one look at her, and her expression turned dark. "For God's sake, don't be stupid."

The way she snapped at the maid surprised Caroline. She'd never heard her speak so ill to a servant.

"I beg your pardon, milady." The young woman spoke with a slight accent and seemed terrified of Augusta. She put the tea service on a table, then passed close to Caroline to collect a used glass. That's when Caroline noticed something else about her—a tiny patch of green on her collar. Was that bit of color a coincidence, or was she Weslorian?

"Will you need anything else, milady?"

"No. Leave us," Augusta said coldly.

The maid practically fled the room, and when Caroline turned back to Augusta, wondering what she ought to say, Augusta surprised her again by bursting into tears. "Augusta!" Caroline cried, and went at once to her side, dropping to her knees beside her. She took Augusta's hand between both of hers. "What on earth troubles you?"

"That's her," Augusta said tearfully. "That's the girl, the *maid* Henry is sleeping with."

"You must be wrong, Augusta. I'm sure it's all a misunderstanding. Henry would *never.*"

"He would! He thinks I don't know, but they all talk, the servants whisper, and I hear them. She sleeps in a room off the kitchen, and twice now, I've caught him coming up the kitchen stairs wearing nothing but his nightclothes. He doesn't come to me—he goes to *her.*"

"Augusta," Caroline said softly. But she couldn't find words that meant anything. What Augusta described was the worst thing she could possibly imagine and perhaps the very thing she expected. "I don't…men are…well, they're beasts," she said, unable to find the appropriate word for the Duke of Norfolk.

"That's why I don't want him here," Augusta said as tears slid down her cheeks.

"Henry?"

"No, the *prince*! You were right about him, Caroline. He's a rake, and I think he has influenced Henry. They were mates in school, you know. They have a long history. And from what you said, I began to think on it. They've been hunting, and they go round to the gentlemen's clubs.

I heard the prince went to a *brothel*, and took a girl away from it," she said, whispering the word. "He probably dragged Henry along."

Caroline stared at Augusta. She had not a single word to offer in the prince's defense. She'd heard all the same, but he didn't strike her as the type to drag others into his corruption. "I'm so sorry, Augusta."

Augusta turned in her chair and gathered a pillow to her chest and bent over it as best she could and sobbed.

Caroline slowly stood and went to the window. She looked down at the bucolic scene again. Henry was sleeping with that very young maid? Leopold was dragging his friends to brothels? She looked at him, so at ease. He was sitting on the grass now, his legs stretched before him, and the girls were climbing on him. It was hard to look at him now and picture that side of him. It was harder to understand what would drive a man to that sort of behavior. It made her stomach turn a little. Did he kiss those young women like he'd kissed her? Did he smile at them as he smiled at her?

THE LONG DAY with Augusta ended when she claimed a blinding headache and sent word to her husband she would not attend supper. That left Caroline alone to dine with the three men. This was a situation she generally relished. She'd even brought a spectacular green gown, one that had been rather plain three months ago but now boasted a modified train—really, the Alucians wore them too long— and a revised neckline that was more daring than what she typically wore. She had planned to be admired as she always did, but this evening she was feeling out of sorts. She didn't want their attention or admiration. What she wanted was to be home with her cloth and her needle and thread and her imagination. Lord, she was turning into a spinster with every tick of the clock.

The maid who was sent to attend her as she prepared for the evening was a bubbly lass. Janey, she said her name was. She couldn't have been more than sixteen, if that. About the same age as the other girl had appeared to be.

Janey was not shy about admiring Caroline's gown or her looks. She was chatty. Caroline took advantage of that, and as she did a final check in the mirror, she said, "There is another maid here, a young woman with dark hair."

"Oh, there are so many maids, madam! Arundel is the biggest thing I've ever seen. Maybe bigger than Windsor. That's what Adam said. He's in the stables, and he rides with the duke and duchess to London to care for the horses."

"It is indeed a very big estate," Caroline agreed. "But this girl... I think she is Weslorian?"

"Ah, Jacleen! Aye, she's come all the way from Wesloria. Hadn't been in London two weeks before the duke brung her here. It's all so new to her."

"I can imagine it must be *very* new to her," Caroline said darkly. She didn't know if she could look at the duke tonight, knowing what he did, knowing that he'd brought that poor young immigrant here to service him while his wife carried his fourth child.

When she finally went down to supper, Caroline was feeling unusually subdued and unlike herself. Beck frowned darkly when he saw her enter the salon, most likely a result of his displeasure with her décolletage. Caroline ignored him. He ought to be thankful that she wasn't sleeping with a footman like his friend the duke or rounding up her friends to go traipsing off to brothels like his friend the prince.

"Wine, madam?" a footman asked, holding a tray out to her as Beck turned his attention to the duke. Far across the cavernous room, Leopold was sitting in a chair, an open book in his lap.

"Thank you." She took the glass from his tray, then walked to the window and watched the sinking sun wash the countryside in soft gold light. She hadn't stood there long when she slowly became aware of a presence. She glanced over her shoulder and smiled thinly at the prince. She couldn't help herself—the look in his eyes stirred blood, fever and heat. What was wrong with her that she could be so physically attracted to such a rake?

"Good evening, Lady Caroline."

"Good evening, Highness."

"You look…" His gaze traveled down the length of her. "Very well, indeed," he said at last. But his eyes said something more. Or maybe she imagined it, wanting him to mean more. Blast it, she didn't know what she wanted from this man! To leave her be or take her into his arms?

"Will Lady Norfolk be joining us?" he asked.

"I don't think so," Caroline said, turning her attention to the window.

He moved to stand beside her and look out, too. They stood that way for several long and silent moments. Or maybe only a single moment. Caroline was losing track of time—all her senses were trained on his presence beside her. "You like children," she said.

"Pardon?"

"I saw you playing with the girls earlier."

"Ah." He turned around, putting his back to the window so that he could face her. "I do like children, very much. Do you?"

"Yes." She tapped a finger against her wine glass. "Do

you ever think of having your own? What they will look like?"

He gave her a curious smile. "I suppose I have. Doesn't everyone, at some point?"

She didn't, really. She assumed she would have them, but with no real prospect of it, she didn't think much about what her future children might look like, who they might be. "Well... I wish you and Lady Eulalie many happy, healthy children."

Leopold's countenance sobered instantly. "Yes." He glanced away.

Caroline instantly felt contrite. She hadn't meant to be rude; she'd meant to be polite. But given the turn their acquaintance had taken, it sounded a bit...petulant. She'd only said what was in her thoughts. What was so *much* in her thoughts suddenly. "I'm sorry—"

"No, don't be," he said quickly. "It's a fair point." He turned his gaze to her again and smiled sadly. "I find no joy in the inevitability of a match I did not seek."

It surprised her that he would confess something like that to her. Of course it wasn't a match he would seek— princes weren't allowed to marry whomever they pleased. It hadn't been that long ago that the Royal Marriages Act had been passed to keep royals from marrying people deemed unsuitable for the royal family. Leopold's own brother had taken a great risk when he'd chosen Eliza— he could have been stripped of his investiture if his father had demanded it.

She suddenly felt a strange sort of sympathy for Leopold. How awful it must be to know all his life that the most important relationship he might have likely would not be of his own choosing. "Matches rarely are what we seek, I suppose."

He gave her a distant smile. He glanced down at his glass and asked, "What about you, Lady Caroline? Is there a match you seek? Children you want?"

She shook her head. "I should like children one day, of course. But if I am honest, I don't see it happening."

He chuckled, as if she were being precocious. "Why not?"

"I don't know, really, but when I picture my life, I see only me and Beck." She smiled, ashamed to admit that was true. "We're an odd little pair, my brother and I."

"Circumstances have a way of bonding siblings to each other. For me and Bas, it was the box we were forced into as royal sons. For you and Beck, I would think it the tragic loss of parents at such a young age."

That was true and perceptive of the prince—she and Beck had been inseparable all their lives, really. Beck had only been fourteen when their mother had died, their father gone long before that.

"How is Lady Norfolk?" he asked.

"She is…" *Distraught. Devastated.* Caroline shook her head. She was feeling so many confusing things just now. "She is very pregnant."

"Ah. Perhaps she will feel at ease on the morrow when I take my leave." He glanced around them, then said softly, "I heard them arguing last night, so I'm rather clear on her thoughts about me."

"Oh dear." If Augusta had been as plain with her husband as she had been with her, then Leopold knew everything. "I think only the birth of this child will put her at ease, really. She's not herself."

He lifted his glass of wine. "To Lady Norfolk's health."

"To her health." She touched her glass to his and their gazes met—and held. It felt almost as if they were suspended in a space where only they existed. She could feel the same energy thrumming between them as she'd felt when he kissed her in the coach. A flush that betrayed her was creeping into her cheeks.

The spell was broken by the butler, who entered and announced rather grandly to His Grace the Duke that supper was served.

"Ah, splendid," Norfolk said, and strode across the room to offer Caroline his arm. "Shall we?"

In the dining room, Caroline was seated directly across from Leopold. She lost track of the conversation—something to do with horse racing, of course. She kept looking up and catching Leo's gaze on her. She watched how he laughed and teased his friends, how he respectfully offered his thoughts and advice when asked. Who was this man? Was he the same man who took a woman from a brothel for his pleasure? The more she was near him, the more she felt as if she didn't know him at all.

She couldn't stop stealing looks at him. In the glow of the candlelight, she couldn't stop wondering what if.

What if, what if, what if.

CHAPTER EIGHTEEN

The impending birth of a child can be the most anx-
ious of times for the entire household, including
any servants, as they often bear the brunt of famil-
ial discomfort and uncertainty. Word reaches us that
a young chambermaid disappeared from her post
after suffering harsh treatment from her mistress in
Arundel. How curious that the lass would disappear
at the same moment an illustrious and princely guest
took his leave of Arundel.

Ladies, two eggs, whipped to a cream, should be
applied vigorously and directly to the scalp for two
minutes, rinsed with lukewarm water, and followed
by Kaylor's head cream. The result will be hair that
feels like silk and curls much easier.

⌀—Honeycutt's Gazette of Fashion and
Domesticity for Ladies

LEO HAD SPENT a good portion of the afternoon sniffing out
where Jacleen might be, but in this monstrous castle, it was
not unlike looking for the proverbial needle in a haystack.
But Leo had a stroke of good luck when a maid carried in
platters of food and tea for the duke and some of the local
gentry who had come to call. She had a patch of green on
her collar. She was slight and pale, with shadows under
her eyes. She looked rather wan.

He watched her place the platter on a long table as instructed by the butler, and as she turned to go, Leo blurted, "Miss!"

The maid and the butler both turned to him, surprised.

"I've a shirt to be ironed," he said quickly. It was the sort of order he had probably barked any number of times at Constantine Palace. A servant was a servant, there to do what was needed, and he rarely gave it any thought.

"Not her," Henry said, appearing on his right and placing his hand on his shoulder. "She's a kitchen maid. Janey will iron your shirt. Peterson," he said, directing his attention to the butler, "send Janey to the prince's suite." Peterson nodded and gestured for the kitchen maid to go.

Henry laughed at Leo. "Traveling without a valet, Your Highness?"

"It is often more expeditious to leave him in London," Leo said. "But he did warn me this might happen."

Henry chuckled and wandered off to speak to some of his other guests.

Leo was certain that was Jacleen. So she was a kitchen maid. Now what? He couldn't very well appear at the kitchen door and ask for her, could he? Perhaps he could pretend to be in need of something. No, that wouldn't do. Henry had assigned a young footman to tend to Leo, and the lad watched him like a dog, trying to anticipate his every need.

And frankly, Leo was having a devil of a time escaping his host. After Leo had offered his apology for having offended his wife, Henry laughed. "She's easily offended. You mustn't pay the ladies any heed, Leo." He certainly didn't and proceeded to parade his friend the prince before his neighbors.

Perhaps later tonight, he thought. In Constantine Palace, kitchen workers slept near the kitchen. Work began at four o'clock in the morning in a large palace, and it kept them from padding around and disturbing those who were sleeping. He suspected the same was true of Arundel, give or take a half hour.

He settled on that, then. He would say he'd gotten hungry in the night and make his way to the kitchen, if he could find it. He'd already instructed Kadro and Artur to be ready at first light to escort him to London. Which meant he only had twelve hours left to find Jacleen.

Leo was so worried about his plan that he forgot about the shirt. When the maid Janey came to collect it, he was wearing it. Another blunder.

"I'm to iron a shirt, Your Highness," she said cheerily, dipping a curtsy.

"Oh. Ah..." He looked around, seeking something she might iron, and finding none, glanced back at her and smiled sheepishly. "As it happens, it didn't require ironing."

"No?"

"The valet must have done it before I left. Or...or perhaps a footman here saw to it. I do beg your pardon."

"Aye, Your Highness," she said, undoubtedly relieved that she didn't have to add the task to her list of chores. She curtsied again and turned to go.

"Girl," Leo said abruptly. She turned back. "Janey, isn't it?"

"Aye, Your Highness." She smiled faintly.

Leo frantically tried to think of how to ask her where Jacleen might be. But the girl was staring at him, and he couldn't think of a way to ask that didn't seem entirely suspicious. He could imagine her hurrying back to the butler. *Mr. Peterson, I think you should know that the foreign prince was asking how he might find Jacleen's room!* The thought appalled him, and he shook his head and smiled a little. "Nothing. Thank you."

When she'd gone out, he dragged his fingers through his hair. "So, then," he muttered aloud, "you are on your own, sir. For the sake of the kingdom of Alucia, I pray you manage without purchasing a ruin or a crate of live birds, or having to pay another one hundred quid. Or further damage a reputation that was, until recently, at least decorous." He put his hand to his chest and bowed to himself. *"Somewhat,"* he muttered. "Don't compliment yourself too heartily."

He determined there was nothing left to do but wait until after midnight. Leo went down to dinner, joining Beck and Henry in the family's private salon. But he bored of their conversation about racehorses and picked up a book, *La Cousine Bette*. He read until a footman opened the door and Lady Caroline entered the room. She entered like a queen, frankly, in a silk gown that seemed to move like a cloud around her as she walked.

She was lovely, a beauty by any standard. It did seem odd to Leo now that he didn't remember meeting her in Chichester. He was generally very quick to notice beautiful women. So much so that a paramour had once accused him of seeing only the surface of women. Leo had thought about it and had agreed with her, much to that woman's chagrin. But it was a truth—he'd never been in a position to form a meaningful connection with a woman for obvious reasons. He had to marry in Alucia and for Alucia, and any relationship he engaged in, romantic or otherwise, could be exploited. So he'd kept his interests to the physical.

If he was to judge on that criteria alone, Caroline Hawke met all his preferences.

Another reason he might not have noticed Lady Caroline that long ago evening was because of the habit he'd developed over the last few years of drinking far too much. It was a side of him that he did not like to admit to or examine, really, but alas, it was also truth. He drank to fill long, tedious hours of having nothing important to do. He drank to numb his feelings about being the spare prince with no meaningful responsibilities. But since his return from Alucia, he had noticed he didn't have the same desire to fill those hours as he once had. Moreover, this recent change in his long-standing habit had made his mornings brighter and his days more coherent. He rather liked it.

And besides, something else occupied his thoughts now. Something important. He was determined to find these poor young women.

After speaking to Isidora and learning how she'd come to be in a brothel of all places, Leo's mind had been made up. He couldn't fathom men so unfeeling as to participate in such a scheme. And then to learn that one such man had been a friend of his, well…that left him feeling strangely ill. One assumed one knew his friends.

He would find these women and return home with them. He would help them face the men who had done this to them. He didn't know how he'd possibly manage that, either, as he'd never tackled anything of importance in his life, and had deliberately steered clear of responsibility.

There was, as wisdom taught them, a first time for everything.

Which brought him around to thinking about Caroline again, as she, too, was a first of sorts for him. There was much more to her than a beautiful face and flawless figure. She had aroused his curiosity in new ways.

He had begun to realize, as he tried to bumble and maneuver his way through this new life of his, that he'd allowed himself to become intrigued by her. She was brash and impossible. Beautiful and sophisticated. *Interesting*. Furthermore, she'd accomplished something few people, if any, ever accomplished with him, and that was to turn his initial impression of her on its ear.

Since returning to England, he'd actually enjoyed his encounters with her and had found her impertinence strangely tantalizing. Refreshing, even. He had come to adore the spark in her and the way she went about her life in the most outrageous manner she could possibly get away with. And it went without saying that the rather constant thought of kissing her was popping up far too frequently, creeping in beside his more urgent thoughts of how to free the Weslorian women. Those two things made for uncomfortable bedfellows, but he couldn't help it. He couldn't deny his attraction.

Tonight, however, she was not quite as vivacious as he was accustomed to finding her, and that intrigued him. She was somber. Fatigued, perhaps? He noticed that she scarcely said a thing over supper. But then again, neither had he, as Beck and Henry were ridiculously absorbed in all this talk about horses and summer races.

It wasn't until they had decided to have a go at the card game Commerce that Caroline finally perked up. Particularly when she began to win. That was when her eyes began to sparkle again in the low light of the candles. She delighted in winning, and when she delighted in anything, she was especially beautiful. When she laughed, the blond ringlets danced around her face, as if they were delighted, too. And when she crowed with victory and dragged her winnings across the table, she was entirely alluring.

She won three hands in a row and cackled each time. She said they were all "typically male" in being surprised by her win, and that she had "cocked their hats," and had "catawamptiously chewed them up."

"What does that even mean?" Beck had complained. "It's gibberish, Caro."

"It means I beat you, and I beat you soundly," she said gaily.

Beck snorted, "You've been calling on your American friends, again, haven't you?"

"Yes!" Caroline cried triumphantly. "They are *very* interesting women. You should make their acquaintance, Beck." She stood up from the table, sweeping the coins she'd won into her hands. "This ought to purchase a new bonnet. *Thank* you, gentlemen." She curtsied.

"Wait, where are you going?" Beck complained. "That is my winning, too, Caro. I gave you the money to start."

"How right you are. How terribly thoughtless of me." She carefully counted out two pounds and dropped them like pebbles onto the table before Hawke. "There is your investment returned, sir. The rest belongs to me. Good night, gentlemen!"

Leo rose, too. "I think it time I bid you all adieu, as well. I leave at dawn's light and it is well past the time I should be abed."

"What, so soon?" Henry asked. "But you've only just arrived, Highness! I thought we might ride down to the village tomorrow."

His old friend was keen to have him stay, but Leo also suspected Henry would likewise be relieved when he left, given his wife's feelings. "I've some Alucian state business to attend to." Oh, but that wasn't true at all. He had no official business that he knew of, but he had some very pressing unofficial business and he was running out of time.

Beck and Henry said their good-nights, then Henry signaled for a footman to refill their whisky glasses as Leo followed Caroline out of the salon. She paused in the hallway and glanced back at him.

"If you like, I'll carry your coin for you," he offered.

"Do you take me for a fool, sir? A lady learns very early never to hand her winnings to a gentleman. The next thing you know, he'll want to invest it for you."

"Very astute of you."

They began to stroll along as if at their leisure, his hands clasped at his back, her hands cupping her coins. "I didn't take you for a gambler," he remarked.

"Really? I'm very much in favor of it. How boring life would be if one never gambled on anything." She cast a quick smile at him, her eyes shining with amusement. "I sincerely hope, however, that *you* don't sit at the gaming tables often. You played so terribly I shudder to think what the cost is to your royal coffers."

"I beg your pardon, I was dealt very bad hands," he said with a grin.

"Ah, the standard cry of the vanquished." She laughed again and the warm sound of it slid down to his groin.

They started up the grand staircase, moving to one side when a footman went barreling past them in the opposite direction.

"You're leaving on the morrow?" she asked, as she tried to maneuver up the stairs holding her skirt and her coins.

"*Je.* For heaven's sake, Caroline, please allow me to carry your winnings. You may count every coin when we reach the next floor and flog me if any go missing. But you'll never make it up these stairs without the very real danger of falling and cracking your head if you don't have use of your hands."

"You're right." She turned to him, reluctantly pouring her coins into his palm, then carefully closing his fingers around them. Her hand lingered on his. "Don't drop them."

He covered her hand with his free one and squeezed. "I would rather die," he said gravely, and with a soft smile let her hand go.

She gathered her skirts, and they resumed walking up the stairs. "When will you return to Alucia?" she asked as she looked up at a portrait of an ancestor glaring at them from above.

"I can't say for certain, but I'd wager sometime after I've been catatumpously chewed up by England."

"Oh!" she crowed with delight. "*Catawamptiously*, Your Highness."

"Leo."

"Pardon?"

He smiled at her. "I like when you use my given name. My close friends call me Leo."

"Then I shall call you Leopold."

He shook his head. "For the sake of quenching my curiosity...*are* you the most obstinate woman in this land?"

She giggled. "Thank you for your confidence in me, Your Highness, but I think not." She leaned toward him and whispered, "I think Lady Norfolk can be rather obstinate when she's of a mind."

One of his brows rose above the other. "I had that feeling."

She laughed.

"Why do you ask about my return to Alucia? Are you so eager for me to be gone?"

"Oh, in the worst way," she said with a winsome smile. "And I feel it is my duty to warn Eliza when the time comes. I write her every week without fail. I tell her everything."

"I certainly hope not everything." He winked. And then delighted at her blush. "Why bother writing? Her sister can send her gazette, in which, I may vouch, no stone of gossip is left unturned."

"You are wrong about that. There are *always* certain details left out of the gazette," she said as they reached the next floor. "Details the three of us keep to ourselves." She paused. "Would you like to know what they are?"

"I would."

"I thought you might! But I can't tell you." She laughed and turned into a wide corridor.

"Can't you? I might have to employ my technique of teasing information from the most reluctant beings," he warned her.

"It won't work. My lips are sealed." She mimed locking her lips with a key and throwing it away.

A maid hurried by them, also in the opposite direction. They both paused in their walk and watched her practically jog down the hall. They looked at each other; Caroline shrugged.

They carried on.

"What sort of things do you write to Eliza?"

"Everything! I wrote her about my illness and how my funeral had all but been arranged, and that no one had thought to ask me what I should like to wear to my own burial."

Leo laughed.

"I write her about you," Caroline said with a saucy little glance at him.

"About what? Are you spying on me?"

She clucked her tongue at him. "Spying is hardly necessary. *Everyone* knows your news."

"This may come as a shock, madam, but much of what you think you know of me is not true. Most of it, I'd wager."

"Ha," she said with a roll of her eyes.

"For example," he said as they turned another corner into the wing where the guest rooms were situated. "I am not having an affair with your chambermaid, as you so ardently believed."

"You brought her flowers," Caroline pointed out.

"I brought those for *you*, Caroline. I thought you might like something to brighten your room."

Her gaze narrowed skeptically.

"All right, I brought them to Beck to give to you, and he suggested that they would brighten your room. But as they were all occupied in the making of your soup, I took them up myself, because I wanted to look in on you and assure myself that my worthy opponent was not going to desert me."

Caroline paused in front of a door to one of the guest suites. She turned her back to it and faced him. "What a lovely thing to say. I like the idea of being a worthy opponent. And I would almost believe your concern, but then you disappeared with Ann."

She hadn't missed a thing, even as ill as she was. "*Je*, I did. Only because Ann was acquainted with a Weslorian woman for whom I had a message. I needed to know where to find her. That's all I ever asked of her."

"And is that all you asked of her at Leadenhall?"

"That's all, on my word. It required more than one meeting as she was disconcertingly reluctant to trust me."

Caroline's lips curved into a smile. She studied him a

moment, then shrugged and tapped his hand. "My winnings." She held up both palms.

Leo poured the coins into her hands. "There is something else you have wrong about me, if you'd like to know."

"Oh, I highly doubt that, but please do try to convince me."

He waited until she looked up from her hands and into his eyes. "I am intrigued by you, Caroline."

She laughed. "Yes, I am well aware I have that effect on gentlemen."

"I'm not talking about your looks, as fine as they are. I'm talking about you. There is something about you that…" He tried to think of the right English word to describe his esteem for her.

"That what?" she asked, frowning slightly.

"My English fails me. There is something about you that holds my attention in the most urgent manner."

She blinked. A slow, uncertain smile appeared on her lips. Her gaze moved from his eyes to his mouth. To his neckcloth and chest. "Your English doesn't fail you," she said softly. "But I don't believe you."

He dipped down, so that his eyes were level with hers. "Why not?"

"I think I… I think that…" She looked down at the coins she held in her hands, frowning thoughtfully. "What I *think* is…that you…"

She was babbling. He'd surprised her, which, frankly, he would have not thought possible, but she was clearly unable to find words for the first time in their acquaintance that he could recall. Leo couldn't help but smile. "Holy mother, you're speechless." He reached around her and turned the knob on her door and pushed it open.

"I'm not." She stepped backward, into her room. He

stepped forward. "I'm wary," she clarified. "I think there is something you don't know about me, too," she said as she took another step backward, deeper into the room. "And you ought to know it."

Leo moved across the threshold. "I am desperate to know what."

"I will not part with my virtue, not entirely, no matter how you might tempt me. I will not part with it until I'm in love. So don't think you can take it because you're a prince and you've flattered me so expertly." She took another step backward.

"You presume too much, madam. I would not dream of it." Oh, but he would dream of it. He would probably dream of it tonight. He quietly shut the door at his back.

Caroline stepped to a table and kept her gaze locked on his as she deposited her coins. "If you would not *dream* of it, then why are you stealing into my room?"

"Stealing?" He glanced around him. "I walked in as you stood there. But if you like, I will go." He prepared himself to be shown the door before he could touch her.

He desperately wanted to touch her.

He would start with the soft hollow of her throat. Then her shoulders. Her chest. "Say the word, and I'll go."

Caroline folded her arms. "I *do* want you to go."

His entire body stifled his groan of disappointment. He mustered some sort of face-saving smile and bowed his head. "Very well." He turned toward the door. "As you—"

"But I *don't* want you to go, Leopold. I want to despise you, and I can't seem to do it."

His heart filled with hope. He slowly turned back. "Then don't, Caroline."

She bit her lower lip, as if biting back words. And then she sighed heavenward. "There is no point to this," she said gesturing between them. "None at all! It only causes me to desire things that I can't possibly have and shouldn't want."

"Why shouldn't you want it? What is the harm in wanting?"

"Are you mad?" she asked with disbelief. "Yearning is nothing but agony."

"That's not true," he said, stepping closer. "Yearning can result in extraordinary pleasure. But you don't have to yearn or want, Caroline. We can be friends. I am a very good friend to those I care for."

She clucked her tongue. "Robert Ladley is a friend. Even Mr. Morley is a friend. *You* are not a friend. You are a rake, and you've always been a rake. You are something else entirely than a friend." Her gaze slowly slid down the length of him. "I don't know what you are."

In that particular moment, he was indeed a rake, because he was raging with desire. "Would you like to know what I think?"

"No," she said, but then impatiently gestured for him to speak.

"I think an undeniable physical attraction between us has presented itself and has begun to flame. Personally, I find it increasingly difficult to ignore. But I've no desire to ruin you, Caroline. I've no desire to go against your wishes in this. I think too well of you to attempt anything crass. What I want, more than I want to kiss you or…" His gaze drifted down her body. He swallowed. "Or to touch you, is to spend time in your company. I want to discover what makes you so confoundingly original."

One of her brows rose skeptically. "You do?"

"I do."

She smiled dubiously. "I don't trust you, Leopold Chartier."

"So you've implied. You're very cynical," he said with a lopsided grin.

"You would be, too, if you were me. I've been lied to and flattered by more than one gentleman."

"Ah, well, I can't defend my sex. Men are such singular creatures when it comes to women. We are ruled by lust. But Caroline, if I wanted to lure you into my web, I would do it. I would entice you with riches and promises that I didn't intend to keep. I would drape you in flattery. I would gift you with baubles. I've done none of those things, you may have noted. I've not promised you a thing, have I?"

She seemed to consider this a moment. "True…you've not gifted me any baubles and you certainly haven't flattered me."

He laughed. "You don't need to be flattered. You need to be loved."

Her lips parted and she stared at him, as if she hadn't heard him properly. And then she looked at the door and rubbed her nape, as if rubbing off a chill. "Friend or foe, Leopold, it's dangerous for you to be here in this room. My brother is downstairs with the duke."

"Your brother is always close by." He took another step closer to her. "This is a bit like gambling, isn't it? How boring life would be if there was no danger to it?"

Her green eyes sparked with delight. "You *do* listen to me," she said. This time, she was the one to move closer to him. "It would be impossibly boring, I should think. If one doesn't gamble, one must be content with imagining what might have happened."

"What do you imagine might happen?"

"This," she said, and reached for him.

"I knew it," Leo said as she drew him to her. "You like the danger."

"Don't talk—we haven't much time."

This was the second time she'd urged him to get on with it. Lord, but the woman was intimidating without even trying. A lesser man might have been cowed by that command, but Leo was not a lesser man—he was eager and captivated. He put his arm around her waist and pushed her onto an armchair. Caroline landed with an *oof* and a giggle. He landed awkwardly on top of her, facing her, his knee braced against the floor and somewhere between her legs, he thought, although the volume of her gown made it hard to judge.

"How aggressive of you."

"You are the sort of woman a man must aggress."

Her smile deepened into two dimples. "That's not a word." She shoved her fingers into his hair.

"You should be my tutor," he muttered, and kissed her. The dam burst inside him, desire flooding through him, hardening his cock. There was desire, and there was desire that raged, and his was a raging river in his veins.

He moved to her neck and kissed a path from her neck to her décolletage, kissing the swell of her breasts, sliding his fingers under the fabric to touch them.

She giggled as if it tickled her, but Leo didn't care. He kissed her again, demandingly, his tongue dancing with hers, his body pulsing with hers. He felt feverish in his skin, too hot. He was piteously aroused and exceptionally ravenous. He maneuvered a perfect breast from the bodice of her gown and drew the nipple into his mouth and felt himself lose a bit of control when Caroline moaned with pleasure. She dragged her fingers through his hair again, traced a soft line around his ears. "Tell me something, Leopold," she asked breathlessly.

"Anything."

"What would you do to me if I allowed it?"

Oh, madam. He glanced up from his attention to her breast. Her eyes had taken on a sheen that he hadn't seen before, but he knew instinctively this was the deep light of desire. She may hold her virtue in high regard, but she lusted, just like him. Something primal and deep kicked hard at Leo. He braced his elbow against the armrest and brushed a curl from her temple, tucking it behind her ear. "If you allowed me, I would fill you up completely. I would carry you with me on an expedition the likes you've never experienced." He kissed her cheek and whispered, "I would make you sob with pleasure."

Her lips parted with the draw of her breath. Her fingers curled around his arm. "And then, perhaps, I would do the same to you?"

He was mesmerized. Provoked. Her smile was dangerous, and he could imagine how easily he could fall under her spell if he desired it.

She twisted a curl of her hair around her finger. "What's wrong?"

"You," he said. "Everything about you is wrong, and yet there is not enough of you."

She sighed. "How odd that I would feel the same way about you."

He ran his hand along her shoulder, over her collarbone and breast, down her side, and down one leg, to her ankle. He dug his way under her skirts until he touched the smooth silk of her stocking. She made a sound in her throat and wrapped her arm around his neck, rising up to him. Leo sank into her and shifted slightly so that he could follow a path up her leg beneath her dress, skimming over the silk, then sliding onto the bare skin of her inner thigh as he kissed her.

Caroline shifted lower in the chair, her legs a little farther apart, and Leo slipped a finger through the slit of her drawers and into the damp folds of her sex.

"Oh," she said, as if she'd just heard something quite interesting. She closed her eyes as he moved his fingers on her. He could have pleasured her there, but it wasn't enough. He kissed a path down her dress as he slid the hem of her dress up and over her knees. Caroline didn't stop him. She grabbed at the fabric and petticoats, holding them there. She was as eager as he was, and knowing that aroused him even more. He took her by the waist, pulling her forward in the chair, then dipped his head beneath her skirt and brushed his mouth against the spring of honey curls.

Caroline was panting now. Leo nudged her legs farther apart and slipped his tongue between the lips of her sex. Caroline gasped with surprise, her fingers groping for his shoulders, gathering her skirt higher and higher. As he began to lave her, she groaned with the pleasure he was giving her, causing his blood to pound hotly.

He explored her thoroughly. She moved against him, panting for breath, the little cries of pleasure coming quicker and quicker as she neared her release. He stroked her, sucked her, nibbled as if she were a delicacy until she found it, crying out without regard for their privacy, her hands clutching at him, exalting in the throes of release.

And when it was over, she said, quite breathlessly, *"Extraordinary."*

Extraordinary.

Leo sat up and delicately dragged a finger across his lips. He adjusted his clothing and watched with not a small amount of pleasure as her eyes skimmed over his erection.

He carefully pulled her skirts down over her legs. There were desires and feelings he wanted to convey, emotions he wasn't entirely sure he understood himself. The words that came to him were Alucian, and he couldn't think how to say those feelings in English. So he said, "You are remarkable, Caroline Hawke."

She laughed softly and sat up. "I know. But I didn't know that so are you."

Leo grinned broadly. He reached for her hand and pulled her to her feet, kissed the back of her hand as if they'd just finished a dance, then her mouth, lingering there. "I should go."

"You should." She brushed something from his cheek, his hair from his forehead. She didn't ask him any questions. She didn't ask when she would see him again. She said nothing and smiled that catlike smile, looking sated and happy and in need of a nap. "Good night, Leopold."

"Good night, Caroline." He bowed. She curtsied as she bit back a laugh. With one last tug of his clothing, he carefully opened the door and looked out, then stepped into the hall.

He strolled quickly away from her door, but when he turned a corner, he encountered another maid hurrying toward him, this one carrying linens. It seemed an odd time of night for linens, but Leo had no notion of how these things were done. "Pardon, miss."

The maid stopped and awkwardly curtsied. "Yes, milord?"

"I should like some bread—"

"I'll fetch—"

"No, no, you are clearly occupied," he said, gesturing at her linens. "Just point me to the kitchen, will you?"

"It's directly below us, milord. Two floors down."

"Very good," he said with a nod, and continued walking.

He had not forgotten what he had to do, the stirring interlude with Caroline notwithstanding.

CHAPTER NINETEEN

The Duke and Duchess of Norfolk are pleased to an-
nounce the duchess has been delivered of a healthy
baby boy. The news was met with joy across Sussex
and London, as it represents a new beginning. Per-
haps the duke and duchess can put behind them the
terrible row the night of the birth, the likes of which
sent pets and servants scurrying for cover. Gentle-
men would be well reminded that a lady's nerves are
at their most frayed the hours before a birth.

Ladies, it is not practical to invest in belt buck-
les of various shades and colors. Silver and pearl
complement all styles of dress. The investment of a
buckle with a sturdy clasp is well worth the cost if
it keeps one's belt tightly fastened when a husband
has fallen into his cups.

〜—Honeycutt's Gazette of Fashion and
Domesticity for Ladies

CAROLINE WAS STARTLED out of a very restful sleep when
Beck suddenly burst into her room. He strode in and
stopped with his legs braced apart and very nearly shouted,
"Why are you still abed?"

"Why? What time is it?" Caroline asked groggily.

"Time for you to be awake, madam." He strode for the

window, throwing the drapes open. "Lady Norfolk is giving birth."

She abruptly sat up and looked around her. *"Now?"*

"Yes, now. All night, as it happens. Haven't you heard them running back and forth? More towels, more water!" he said, gesturing for her to get up. "The midwife says anytime now. Get dressed, get dressed, Caro! You should be helping!" He moved determinedly out of her room.

"I should be helping what?" she mumbled as the door closed behind him.

Nevertheless, she threw off the covers. She was awake now, attuned to the day, even as the memory of last night flooded her thoughts. She shivered when she recalled the way his hand had felt against her skin, the way his mouth worked on her body. She shivered again when she recalled how dark his blue eyes had turned when she found her release, and time and thought and even air had been suspended.

She smiled as she padded across to the bellpull. She'd never experienced anything like what Leopold had shown her last night. She'd heard of it—Priscilla's older sister once told them that her husband put his mouth "down there." Priscilla and Caroline, who were much younger at the time, hadn't believed it. But then Eliza had confirmed that the sort of thing was true between man and woman and really quite enjoyable. Now Caroline could report—

Wait. She couldn't report any such thing. What was the matter with her? It would not do to talk about it. No, this was a delicious secret she would need to keep to herself. Lord, how would she look at Leopold again, now that this had transpired between them? She'd blush wildly, and everyone around her would suspect the truth, she was certain.

She was still smiling when Janey entered her room to help her dress.

"Good morning, milady!" she said brightly. "What a glorious day it is, isn't it, with another child to be born? They've sent for the duke, so it must be nigh."

"When did the birthing start?"

"Oh, just before midnight," Janey said. She held up a dress from the trunk Caroline had brought. "If you ask me, it started in earnest this morning, just before the kitchen fires were started."

Caroline laughed. "What were you doing about at the hour?"

"Didn't you hear? It's a wonder anyone slept a wink, what with all the shouting."

"What shouting?" Caroline asked as she stepped into her crinoline, and Janey tied it at her waist. She'd slept like a baby—a deep slumber, a contented slumber, she mused, as Janey prattled on. Caroline was slipping back into the memory when something Janey said caught her attention. "Pardon?"

"The midwife," Janey repeated.

"No, before that."

"Oh, aye. My poor mistress, she saw the duke come up the stairs from the kitchen, and I suppose she thought he ought to have been close by, I don't know, but she picked up a vase and threw it at him. The midwife, she said it didn't go far, as it was heavy, and the duchess had very little strength."

"From the kitchen?" Caroline repeated. Her buoyant feeling began to dissipate. She looked at Janey's reflection in the mirror. "Why would he go to the kitchen in the middle of the night?"

Janey pursed her lips and pretended to be fussing with Caroline's dress.

Caroline glanced over her shoulder at her. "There must have been a reason, Janey."

Janey paused in the smoothing of the skirt of Caroline's gown. "I don't rightly know, milady. All I know is that this morning Cook said there was an awful row between the prince and the duke, and…" She quickly looked over her shoulder, as if she thought someone else was in the room. And then whispered, *"The girl Jacleen has gone missing."*

And just like that, Caroline's heart dropped to the floor. She froze, staring at the wall before her, unable to move. Or breathe.

"Milady?"

"What do you mean, she's gone missing?" Caroline asked.

"Took her things and disappeared," Janey said.

"Did the duke send someone to find her?"

"No, milady. He's been pacing the floor outside his wife's chamber. She won't let him in. My mother was that way, too. Didn't want anyone around when she was giving birth. She had fourteen children, can you imagine?"

"No," Caroline said weakly. Her mind was racing. She felt flush. She felt as if she might faint and put her hand down on the vanity to steady herself. Leopold had left this morning. The maid was Weslorian. Leopold had taken that girl and fled. But *why*? "What was the row about?" she asked. "Between the prince and the duke?"

"I don't know, exactly, but the duke, he *struck* the prince."

Caroline gasped.

A loud and sudden knock on the door caused Janey and Caroline both to jump. "One minute!" Caroline called as

Janey lifted the skirt over Caroline's head and let it settle around her waist.

"No minutes!" Beck shouted back. "The baby has come! It's a *boy*!"

Janey gasped with delight. "A boy! An heir to the duke!"

"Go," Caroline urged her. "I can finish dressing myself."

"I shouldn't—"

"Of course you should," Caroline said. "It's the heir," she reminded Janey, knowing full well that in this world of dukes and duchesses, an heir took precedence over everything else.

"Thank you, milady." Janey dipped a quick curtsy and went out. When the door closed behind her, Caroline sank down onto a chair, staring at the floor. Why had he done it? Did he want that girl for the same reason as the duke? But…but it made no sense. If he wanted a paramour, he could bloody well have one. Why did he take up with maids?

And if she doubted it for a moment, Beck confirmed her worst fear when they departed Arundel that afternoon. He fell back against the squabs with a very loud yawn. "A lot of bloody wailing when a child is born."

"Beck! It's very painful to give birth."

"I don't mean the effort Lady Norfolk has put to bringing the boy into the world. The rest of it."

"What rest of it?" Caroline asked.

"For someone who hears every little thing that is said about every person, I'm surprised this has escaped you, Caro. I'm talking about the squabble before the birth, while you were slumbering away like a princess."

"I was sleeping as people normally sleep, Beck. What squabble?"

He snorted. "The maids aren't whispering in your ear?"

"Yes, Beck, that's what the maids of grand houses do in the morning. They gossip with the duchess's guests—"

"Then apparently you don't know your heart's desire has left with a kitchen maid. Henry tried to stop him, but he wasn't successful."

Caroline gaped at her brother. It was one thing to think it. It was quite another to actually hear it said out loud. "Why? How?" she stammered.

"That rogue attempted to steal away with the maid in the early morning hours as Augusta was in the throes of childbirth." Beck shook his head. "Leo is a friend of mine. But I don't care for this side of him." He glanced at her, looking at her appraisingly. "Keep your distance, Caro. He's charming, but it's entirely possible he is rotten at the core. You'll have suitors enough to think about as it is."

Caroline felt sick. She couldn't reconcile what had happened between them last night and Leopold taking a maid with him this morning. What had he said last night? What words had he spoken that she could cling to right now?

"Have you nothing to say?" Beck asked curiously.

Caroline swallowed. "It is…it is appalling," she said. "On the day of their son's birth."

"Yes," Beck said, and shifted his gaze to the window. "Henry was distraught."

"Poor Henry," she muttered. She turned her head to the window, too, and stared blindly at the passing countryside.

It was impossible to fathom why he'd done it. It was impossible to accept that the man who had shown her such pleasure could, just hours later, escape with a maid. How could he do what he did to her, then turn around and take a maid for what she could only assume was his pleasure?

She closed her eyes, thinking of the things she'd told him. That she yearned for him. He had flattered her and she had lifted her skirts, and she'd said things she would not say to another gentleman, and oh, she was such a damn *fool*.

CHAPTER TWENTY

Residents of Mayfair are hosting a flurry of summer gatherings before they depart for the cooler climes of the country.

Warm days lead to long walks in the park and proper courting. We have on good authority that the daughter of an earl who many considered to be too plain to receive an offer has won the esteem of the very gentleman she has most admired.

The sister of a popular baron is thought to be the Favorite of this summer season, as gentlemen are vying for her generous dowry. Bets placed at gentlemen's clubs are running in favor of a young viscount from Leeds.

Ladies, experts advise that the secret to a clear and smooth complexion, be you fair or brown, is to limit excess in all things, including food and drink, exercise and pleasure.

ᔕ—Honeycutt's Gazette of Fashion and Domesticity for Ladies

WHAT A SPECTACULAR week it had been. And not in a good way. The good news was that Jacleen was safely tucked away with Isidora in Mr. Cressidian's large house, but in the course of it all, Leo's reputation had taken a sound beating.

He'd bungled the rescue of Jacleen in Arundel, which didn't surprise him in the least. How was he to have known the duchess was in labor? How was he to have known that Henry would pick that night, of *all* nights, to visit the poor Weslorian girl at four o'clock in the morning? Really, he would think that given the arguing he'd heard between the duke and duchess on the night of their arrival, and given the duchess's precarious state, Henry might have managed to keep his cock in his pants. He'd sorely misjudged his former friend.

Leo had made his way to the kitchen in what he thought would be the dead of night, a quarter to four in the morning. But as he'd neared the kitchen in the dark, he heard the banging of pots and pans. He was surprised to find the cook building a fire under a large hanging pot. She didn't notice him at first, not until she stood and turned. And when she did, she cried out with alarm.

Leo wasn't certain what to say for himself, so the two of them engaged in something of a silent standoff until a footman came in the back door with two buckets. He looked at the cook, then at Leo, then at the cook again. And then the three of them stared at one another until Leo realized he was the only one who could end the stalemate. "Pardon me," he said, and cleared his throat. "I think I'm a bit lost. I'll just show myself—"

Before he could finish his sentence, however, Jacleen appeared. She was tying an apron around her waist as she walked into the kitchen from the same hallway the footman had used. Her dark hair was piled carelessly on top of her head, as if she'd done it in a rush. She paused to take in the scene, and even in the dim light of the kitchen, Leo could see the dark circles under her eyes.

He did the only thing he knew to do and seized the opportunity. "Jacleen," he said, and continued in Weslorian, "I am here to help you."

She looked confused, uncertain. She looked to the cook as if she thought the older woman would explain it all to her.

Leo repeated himself. She still said nothing. He wondered if he might have said something wrong. Alucian and Weslorian were closely related but not identical, and his Weslorian had never been very good. He'd stood there with the servants looking on, feeling alarmed that he'd botch things so utterly in their presence. He spoke again in Weslorian. "Gather your things and come with me. At once."

"Jacleen?"

The sound of Henry's voice was like a punch to Leo's belly. He'd jerked around to see his old school friend standing there in shirtsleeves and trousers. Henry should have been upstairs waiting on the birth of his child, so Leo had needed a moment to understand what he was doing in the kitchen. A very short moment, however, because the blood drained from Jacleen's face.

"Is it time, Your Grace?" the cook asked eagerly.

"What? No, not yet," Henry had said dismissively. His gaze was locked on Jacleen, and Leo couldn't help but notice how the cook and the footman averted their gazes. They had seen this play before, had learned to avert their eyes when the duke came downstairs. And that made Leo irrationally angry—Henry was using this girl like a piece of meat.

So when Henry shifted his gaze to Leo and demanded to know what he was doing in the kitchen at that hour, Leo discarded all the excuses his brain instantly produced and opted for honesty. "I'm taking her, Henry."

Henry blinked. And then he laughed. The sort of laugh

one makes when one finds something very incredible. And when he did, the cook and the footman turned into dervishes of efficiency in filling buckets with hot water, presumably for the birth of Henry's child. "Are you mad? You can't take her."

Leo remembered thinking in that moment that he sincerely hoped he'd not have to fight Henry, because he was certain Henry would thrash him but good if it came to that. He'd give it his best, of course—his father had insisted Leo and Bas learn to box at an early age—but he didn't have the heart for fighting. So he'd braced himself for it, then said in English to Jacleen, "Get your things, lass."

She hesitated. She looked at the cook. The cook was making a tremendous effort not to look back.

"Go," Leo said, and then in Weslorian, "if you want to be free of him, you'll do as I say. I give you my word you'll be safe with me. I won't touch you, Jacleen, but we obviously can't dawdle here, given the situation."

She looked panicked and turned to the cook, her expression pleading. In a bid to buy her a bit of time, Leo said to Henry, "I must admit, I'm rather surprised. I should think a man of your stature need not lower himself to this."

Henry's chest puffed and he glared at Leo. "Oh, *I* see," he sneered. "You've never diddled a servant, then, Your Highness."

Leo was momentarily silenced because while he'd never forced himself on a woman—the regard had been entirely mutual…or at least that's what he told himself—he had indeed diddled a servant. He would examine his bad behavior another time. "At least I didn't buy a servant girl to have at my leisure."

Behind him, the cook dropped something.

"You shouldn't be so judgmental," Henry said. "If you

were married to a woman who is either pregnant or tired at every moment of every day, you might sing a different tune."

"I rather suspect Jacleen is tired, too." Leo turned his head toward their audience, but this time, he made eye contact with the cook in a desperate bid for her help. But when he turned back to his old friend, Henry had advanced on him, and Leo could see the rage in his eyes. He mentally prepared as best he could to take a hit.

"You're high and mighty, Leo. Have you forgotten that I saw you with a serving wench in Cambridge? You held her up against the exterior wall of the public house, you may recall."

"That," Leo said, holding up a finger, "was different." And then he'd tried to think how, exactly, it was different.

"At least Jacleen has a roof over her head and food in her belly."

"How magnanimous of you. What a veritable saint you are, Norfolk."

Henry's eyes darkened. He clenched his jaw and said, "You'll pay the price for this. Your father wants good relations with England, but I can see to it that never happens."

"I am prepared to pay the price," Leo said. He glanced quickly over his shoulder, and to his relief, Jacleen had disappeared. Maybe she wasn't coming back. But then she suddenly reappeared on the periphery of his sight, clutching a small black bag and shaking as if she had the palsy.

"Palda Deo," he muttered. *Thank God.* He stepped away from Henry. "Thank you for your kind hospitality, Norfolk. I will see myself out." And with that, he reached his hand for Jacleen. She was reluctant to take it, so he gestured with his fingers that was what she was to do, then gripped her small hand in his.

Henry made another sound of disbelief, then bellowed, "You can't just walk out of here with one of my servants!"

"She's not a servant—she's a slave," Leo said.

Henry stepped into Leo's path.

Leo groaned. "I really rather hoped we might avoid this," he said, but he knew that he would not avoid what was coming. Henry took a swing and landed it squarely on Leo's jaw. An explosion of pain blinded him for a moment, but by some miracle, he didn't topple over.

He let go Jacleen's hand and swung back, connecting with Henry's chest, and followed that with a slap upside his head. Henry came at him with both hands, but before he could put them around Leo's neck, one of the maids raced into the kitchen.

"Your Grace!" she cried, arms flailing. "It's time!"

Henry did not go to his wife at once but bellowed more things after Leo and Jacleen, mainly about how Leo would never be welcome in Britain again. The poor Weslorian girl was trembling so hard that he worried she'd collapse. But then Henry had seemed to decide he best go meet his child, and the bellowing ceased.

Leo hurried down a very long hall until Jacleen asked in a voice scarcely above a whisper if he meant to go out, for he was going deeper into the castle. "Then if you would be so kind as to direct me to the service entrance," he said. Jacleen pointed in the direction they'd come. Which meant they needed to retrace their steps through the kitchen. With a groan, Leo pulled her along behind him. He avoided eye contact with the cook, who was, oddly enough, still standing in the very spot they'd left her.

At last they emerged from the castle into a service courtyard, and there, just as he knew they would be, were

Kadro and Artur. They were on horseback, and in between them was a saddled horse without a rider.

And quite unexpectedly, there was also a young lad. He spoke to Jacleen in Weslorian, and she turned a panicked look to Leo. "My brother."

"Your *brother*?"

Before he could think what to do, a sudden burst from the kitchen door startled them all. It was the footman who had witnessed the altercation in the kitchen. He had a cloth bundle of some sort, which he tossed to the boy. To Jacleen, he said, "Godspeed," and disappeared back inside.

None of this was in Leo's plans. He didn't really *have* plans, but this was not what he'd anticipated, and it produced such anxiety in him that he thought his heart might give out. But there was no time to wait for that. They had to move. Kadro and Artur had not expected Jacleen or the boy, but when Leo told Kadro to put her before him in the saddle, he did as he was commanded without question. Artur lifted the lad up behind him, and Leo took the third horse.

Leo did not miss the look shared between his two loyal guards. They thought the worst of him, he supposed. He could hardly blame them. Through the years, they'd had to peel him up off floors and drag him out of beds. They knew what sort of sot he was on a normal day and no doubt they thought this was a drunken shenanigan.

But today was not a normal day. On the one end of it, he'd had those few stolen moments with Caroline that still lingered in his blood. On the other end of it, he had a frightened Weslorian girl *and her brother*, who surely thought they were being dragged off to an even worse situation. And in between those ends, he'd hardly had a drop.

He took Jacleen and her brother to Cressidian.

Cressidian met him at the door of his house in a dressing gown. He took one look at Jacleen, and then the lad, and said to Leo, "That's three now, Highness."

"I realize this is an imposition, sir, but I—"

Cressidian interrupted him by throwing his hand up and pointing down the hall. *"Go,"* he said to Jacleen and her brother.

Jacleen looked with alarm at Leo, then took her brother's hand and walked uncertainly in the direction he pointed.

Cressidian glared at Leo. "I need money for their keep."

"More money?" Leo asked, surprised. "I should think what I've given you thus far should suffice."

"You think wrong, Highness. And if you don't want to pay me fairly for their keep, I think the Weslorian ambassador would be interested in what you are doing."

Leo arched a brow. "Beg your pardon, but are you extorting me?"

"Call it what you like. I'm just asking for their keep."

Leo sighed. He looked at the grand house, at the marble floors and gold-plated fixtures, the crystal chandeliers. Mr. Cressidian was a very wealthy man. "I'll have my secretary arrange a stipend."

"A hundred pounds per head," Mr. Cressidian said.

Leo bristled. "They are not cattle, they are human beings."

Mr. Cressidian shrugged. "All the same to me."

So now Leo had a castle, could hear his chickens behind the hotel, had added a young boy he'd not expected to his improbable rescue mission, was paying a very wealthy man one hundred pounds for each of them, and half the town was avoiding him altogether. He would have quite a lot of explaining to do when he returned to Helenamar.

But he still had three more women to rescue. That was

going to prove to be difficult because all of Leo's invitations had dried up. Even the gentlemen who had greeted him each day in the lobby of the Clarendon Hotel avoided him now.

He read about the parties happening around him in *Honeycutt's Gazette*, parties he could no longer attend.

He was reading about one now, as it happened, and he lowered his paper to look at Josef over the top of it. "Not a single invitation?" he asked again.

"None, Your Highness."

Leo shifted uncomfortably. There had been a time in his life here that a party wasn't anything at all to write about in the papers if he didn't attend it. "What of Hawke?" Leo asked glumly. "Has he responded to my invitation to dine?"

Josef was pointedly silent.

Leo had guessed Beck would be unhappy with what had happened at Arundel, but this was more than he'd anticipated. His friend had disappeared from the earth. But Caroline was still flitting from salon to salon, apparently. According to the gazette, some lady was wearing a dress she'd made, and the sleeves were unique and all the rage now.

Leo was completely obsessed with any mention of Caroline in that gazette. When he wasn't thinking what to do with his three wards, and how to reach Rasa, he was thinking about her. He even felt unusual pangs of jealousy at the mention of suitors. *Bloody hell.* What a mess he'd made for himself. He couldn't even get her brother to respond to his invitation.

He sighed and glanced at his secretary. "Well, Josef, I suppose you might inquire of the hotel if one of my chickens might be made ready for us this evening, as I've no place to dine."

"Ambassador Redbane has asked for a moment, Your Highness. He has some dispatches from Alucia."

"Oh," Leo said, perking up a bit. "Is he here?"

"Je."

"Bring him," he said, eager to have some company.

Ambassador Redbane, a jovial gentleman, hailed from the southern border of Alucia—the wine region, where people were known for their hospitality.

Redbane greeted Leo enthusiastically, which gave Leo a glimmer of hope that news of him hadn't reached into *every* corner. The ambassador had very little for him, mainly a letter from his mother the queen, which said very little. "Not a word from Bas or Eliza?"

Redbane shook his head.

Leo studied him. "Do you know what I think, Redbane? I think we ought to have a party and celebrate my time here in England before it draws to a close."

For the first time since he'd arrived, Redbane's smile dimmed. He looked down at his leather pouch in which he carried the official correspondence and winced.

"Oh dear," Leo said. "What's that look?"

Redbane sighed. "I would be remiss," he said carefully, "if I were to allow you to believe that such a gathering would be...well attended."

"Is that so," Leo said. He sniffed back a wave of offense. He was still a bloody prince, wasn't he?

"I mean no offense, Highness," Redbane hastened to assure him.

"Offense taken," Leo muttered.

Redbane's face began to pinken. "It, ah...it has to do with what some perceive as your proclivities."

"My proclivities? I have no proclivities, Redbane. I am proclivitless."

"With housemaids and...*women of the night*." Redbane whispered the last part. "And...and it has been suggested that perhaps you should return to Alucia."

Leo stiffened. "Women of the night, Redbane? You mean prostitutes, for heaven's sake. We are grown men here."

Redbane turned redder. He cleared his throat. But it wasn't this poor man's fault. It was solely on Leo's shoulders, and he couldn't let the ambassador suffer any longer. He waved a hand at him. "Pay me no heed, sir. I've heard the same. Has the king heard the rumors, as well?"

"I can't say for certain," Redbane said carefully. "But I would suspect that he has. I have received word from the foreign secretary that you are to depart for Alucia as soon as is reasonably possible." He handed him a folded vellum, sealed in wax and stamped with the official signet of the king of Alucia.

Leo took the vellum from him. "You've been holding out on me," he said with a wry smile. He didn't break the seal right away. "Fine. But there is something I must do before I leave England." Leo abruptly stood up. "Will you send Josef to me?"

The ambassador came to his feet. He bowed and went out. When Josef appeared, Leo said, "I mean to go round to Lord Hawke's house this afternoon."

"*Je*, as you wish, Your Highness."

What he wished was beyond Josef's capacity to provide. He wanted to find all five women and see Caroline again. Beyond that, he didn't know any more. He couldn't imagine it. He couldn't imagine being married to Lady Eulalie and thinking of a beautiful blonde woman in England every day for the rest of his life, but he feared that was his fate.

CHAPTER TWENTY-ONE

A gentleman who inherited a fortune invested it all so heavily in a defunct railway that now he is left penniless. Reports are that there is keen interest in his Mayfair abode, which now stands empty.

An unfortunate encounter with a candle nearly set Lady Hogarth aflame. It is highly recommended that one not stand so close to the dinner buffet when dressed in formal wear.

The number of potential suitors for the sister of a baron has grown, as word of a sizable dowry has spread like the Great Fire of London.

◦—Honeycutt's Gazette of Fashion and Domesticity for Ladies

FOR ONCE, BECK had proven himself to be dreadfully serious in his quest to see Caroline married, particularly after they returned from Sussex.

Two days ago, he'd wandered into her room and had surveyed the bolts of cloth and dress forms before leveling a gaze on Caroline. She was seated on the floor with her legs crossed, still in her dressing gown, poring over fashion plates.

"What has happened?" he asked, casting one arm out. "Has a cyclone struck? An earthquake? Has a gang ransacked our home?"

"You're so amusing, Beck! As you can see, I am mak ing dresses."

"When did this become your leisurely pursuit? I've never known you to give your attention to anything other than the post and the invitations that might be there."

"That is not true. I've been interested in very many things, but you're so busy with your carousing you haven't noticed. If you are *truly* interested, I've always been fascinated with the latest styles, but my desire to make my own began when the Alucians arrived in town."

"Alucians have been in London since the dawn of time," Beck pointed out.

"You're right—my interest peaked when the *royal* Alucians came to London. Why do you care?"

"Because I'd rather not scare off any potential suitors with bolts of cloth and dress forms and any other indication of your wretched spending habits," he said, fluttering his fingers at the piles of cloth. "Lord March was quite plainly frightened."

She shrugged.

"Robert Ladley and his cousin Betina will come to dine this evening, and next week, we will join the Pennybackers and meet Mr. Trent."

"Mr. Trent?" She looked up at him. "Who is Mr. Trent?"

"He is a gentleman of good looks and moral character, but more important, he's made a bloody fortune in the manufacture of steam-powered agricultural implements."

"Pardon?"

"Thrashers and whatnot," Beck said with a flick of his wrist.

Caroline could not see herself married to a man who made thrashers and whatnot. She wasn't entirely sure what that was, but it didn't sound very glamorous.

Beck sighed impatiently. "He is a wealthy man, Caro. He is young and fit, and he is in need of a wife. *You* are a pretty woman with a generous dowry and in need of a husband. You might as well set your mind to it. I'm determined to do what our parents would have wanted and marry you well. Now, as you know, I am leaving this afternoon for Sussex and the Four Corners race. While I'm away, Uncle Hogarth and his wife will arrive in London with their cousin, Viscount Ainsley. Surely *one* of these gentlemen will be to your liking."

"How can you even suggest it? Do you *know* Mr. Trent or Viscount Hainey?"

"Ainsley," Beck said. He stepped over a bolt of cloth on his way to the door. "I don't need to know them. I need only ensure that they have the means to provide for you and care for you. I'm to Sussex."

"Is that all you need to know? What if you make your grand arrangement and attach the almighty pound to it, and we find we are hopelessly incompatible?"

"Unlikely," he said flippantly.

"Why do you not attend to your own marriage, and leave me be? I am perfectly content the way things are."

"It's not natural. And when you are gone from my care, perhaps I will indeed invite a wife into this," he said, gesturing at her room. "There's no point in arguing, darling! You will be engaged by the year's end." He walked out.

"That's what you think," Caroline muttered darkly, and turned back to her fashion plates. She was not interested in the gentlemen Beck had rustled up for her. Even the two she'd never met, which, admittedly, would normally thrill her. She loved meeting new gentlemen and flirting with them and playing her little game. How long before they were smitten? How quickly could she turn their head? Hollis said she was vain, and Caroline had readily agreed that was true. But that wasn't it, that wasn't it at all. Until recently, she hadn't met a man yet who truly deserved her, whose curiosity had emboldened her to show a different side of herself, to take that chance that perhaps she was not as awful as she feared…and when she did meet that man, he was the worst man on earth.

It vexed her no end that she could scarcely think of anyone else but Leopold. She would be glad when he was gone from their shores, because as long as he was here, she was consumed with thoughts of him. He was a sickness, a fever she couldn't shake. It was maddening to think of him so often and to constantly recall that night and the way his mouth felt on her. It was absurd to pine for a man who would rather dip his wick into the poor maids across Mayfair. It was infuriating to still want to be near him after what had happened in Arundel.

Caroline didn't make sense to herself anymore. She'd never been like this—she'd always known exactly what she wanted and was quick to withdraw her affections or attention the moment a gentleman became bothersome. But not this one—this one, this prince, made her feel ravenous, as if she couldn't get enough of him. As if she'd eaten an entire raspberry cake and still wanted her supper.

Oh, but he'd done it, that scoundrel. He was persona non grata in any respectable house after what had happened in Arundel. Word had spread quickly…perhaps because she'd come back and gone directly to Hollis.

She'd not heard a word from him since their return, either. Every time someone came to the door, she would rush to the railing above the entry and remain just out of sight to see who had come, in the same manner she used to do when she was a girl. In the same manner she'd done

in Constantine Palace. It was never anyone but Beck and
his friends. Why didn't he call? Why didn't he at least call
on Beck? She was desperate to ask her brother if he had
ended his friendship with the prince on principle. That
didn't sound like Beck, but then again, there were occasions when he would step out on principle.

On the other hand, she didn't dare ask Beck a thing
lest she risk him knowing all the confusing thoughts rat-
tling around her.

Whatever had transpired between Beck and Leopold,
it seemed apparent by week's end that they'd gone their
separate ways. Beck hadn't mentioned him at all, and now
he'd departed to Sussex. She was left with nothing. No explanation, nothing but the burning hole in her heart.

WHEN PRINCE LEOPOLD DID, at last, call on the Hawke household, he did so at the most inopportune time. Uncle Hogarth and Aunt Clarissa were in her salon, flanking their
young friend, the perfectly polite and handsome Viscount
Ainsley. Lord Ladley had arrived, too, clearly having heard
of the Hogarth visit from Beck, and clearly not wanting
to lose ground to an interloper who'd only just returned
from America.

Generally, Caroline would be beside herself with glee
to have so many gentlemen assembled in her salon. There
was nothing more pleasing than when a *prince* came calling while others were around to witness. But not this prince
and not this time. The moment Garrett said his name, she'd
wished the floor would open up and swallow her guests
whole.

The five of them were to dine at the Debridges' house
that evening, along with ten other souls. Someone had
brought up the prospect of dancing, and Aunt Clarissa

had lamented the fact that she had not learned the latest Alucian dance making its rounds of London salons. Uncle Hogarth had boasted that Caroline was a fine dancer, and to the merriment of all, Caroline was attempting to show her aunt the dance steps as the gentlemen had a port. They were all laughing when Garrett interrupted to announce a caller.

"Oh?" Caroline said, surprised. "Who is it?"

"His Royal Highness Prince Leopold."

Her heart fluttered instantly, and she was thankful she was standing behind her aunt, because she could feel the heat creeping into her face. "Oh." She wanted to sound light and carefree, but was certain her voice sounded pinched. Her throat felt strained, actually, much like her chest. "Have you informed him Beck has gone to Sussex?"

"Yes, madam. He wishes to give you his regards."

Caroline peeked around her aunt. "Then…"

"Then you must show him in," her aunt said.

Garrett looked at Caroline.

"Yes. That's what you should do," Caroline agreed, and forced a smile. As Garrett went to fetch him, she said, "Do please forgive the intrusion."

"Think nothing of it, Lady Caroline," Ladley said at once. Lord Ainsley looked as if he thought something of it.

But her uncle said jovially, "It will be my pleasure to make his acquaintance. In spite of all I've heard." He chortled.

When Leopold entered, he seemed surprised at the number of people assembled but was clearly practiced in collecting himself. He bowed. "I beg your pardon for the interruption."

"Your Highness, how *good* of you to call after all this time," Caroline said, and sank into a curtsy.

"Thank you. I, ah—"

"You know Lord Ladley," she said, twirling away from him. She introduced her aunt and uncle, and Lord Ainsley, as well. When she'd finished the introductions, she turned back to him. "I regret that we were on our way out," she said.

"Yes, perhaps we ought to be on our way," Ladley said, offering his arm. "Supper is at nine."

"I wish we'd known to expect you," she said. "I could have spared you the trip here."

"Hmm," he said, his gaze steady on hers.

"Shall I give Beck a message when he returns?"

He smiled slowly. Her heart felt as if it was beating out of her chest.

"That won't be necessary, thank you. But if I may intrude for one more minute before you go…might I have a word, Lady Caroline?"

"Well…" She glanced at her guests.

"I won't take but a moment."

"Yes, of course," she said, and gestured for him to speak. His brows dipped. "I had hoped for a word in private."

"Ah. Well, as you can see…"

"Caro, darling, you should hear him," her aunt suggested.

"Of course you must, Caro," her uncle added. "We'll be here when you're done. Take all the time you need."

Caroline shot Leopold a look. "Very well. But I won't need long at all."

The prince stepped to one side to allow her access to the door. She walked out of the room. She supposed Leopold followed. She was so angry and confused and annoyed that she marched down the hall to the small receiving salon near the front of the house. She walked into the room, whirled about and folded her arms.

Leopold entered behind her, quietly closed the door, and smiled. "Well. From the reception I've received from you and your guests, it would appear my reputation is even worse than I feared."

"Oh, it's quite awful," she agreed.

"You're cross with me about Jacleen," he said, pushing away from the door.

Caroline gaped at him. Then she laughed. "How astute of you! I can't believe you would utter her name out loud."

"Why wouldn't I?" he asked as he slowly advanced on her, his gaze moving over her. "Her name is Jacleen Bouvan. She is a Weslorian from the mountains that border Alucia."

Caroline frowned with confusion. Why was he telling her this? What possible reason? Had she been his lover before? Or... Why was he *smiling* at her? "Did you think I would find it amusing that you took a maid from her gainful employment and..." She stopped talking before she said aloud what she feared he'd done.

"No. Did you think so ill of me that you'd believe I'd find such pleasure with you, then only hours later take advantage of that poor woman?"

Did she think so poorly of him? At the moment, she didn't want to think of him at all. But if she *did* think of him, she desperately wanted to think poorly of him. It helped her prepare for his inevitable departure. For his perfidy. "I don't know, Leopold—are you really so different from any other man?"

He blinked. "I left with Miss Bouvan because she was being used by the duke for a purpose that offended me. I wanted to help her."

Caroline was prepared to be indignant and make him understand that she knew the nature of men. But she hadn't expected for him to say what she knew was true—Jacleen *was* being used. She rubbed her nape. "And, what, then the prince swooped in and saved her?"

He looked surprised by that and glanced away a moment, as if pondering it. "Je, I suppose I did. Caroline, you must believe me—I enjoyed your company far too much to ever sully it with a meaningless tryst."

Her cheeks began to bloom. She released a breath she hadn't realized she was holding.

"Did *you* enjoy it?"

Her blush deepened. Surely it was impolite to ask her. But then he lifted his hand and lay his palm against her neck. "What a question," she said softly. "You know I did. Very much."

Leopold's smile was slow. "And yet, it's nice to hear you admit it."

Caroline's blood was heating with his casual caress, but she was determined to give him no sign of it. "But why? Why you? Why must *you* be the one to take her from Arundel?"

He shifted closer, his gaze dipping to her lips. "Why not me?"

He bent his head as if to kiss her, but Caroline put her hand on his mouth. "I have two callers waiting in the salon."

"I won't linger," he murmured, and touched his lips to hers.

Caroline's eyes fluttered shut. His confession wasn't fitting with the story she'd created for herself, the one where she never forgave him and promptly forgot him. And yet here was her hand sliding up his chest, her head angling to better kiss him. Here she pressed her body against his, her hand snaking up his arm, to his shoulder. She wanted him to seduce her, wanted to feel his hands and his mouth on her skin again.

Unfortunately, somewhere in her heart a bell was clanging, warning her. She had proudly protected her virtue for six and twenty years. She was not going to be swayed by how handsome he was, or that his lips felt like butter against hers. Or that he smelled like cinnamon and clove.

She put her hands on his chest and pushed back. "This isn't…there is something not…"

"Something not right, I agree," he finished for her. "About the way you are feeling about me. About the way I am feeling about you. But devil take all if I know what to do about it."

Caroline's breath caught. Had he really just said those words to her? Was he really feeling something for her? Did he feel the same light and fluttery feeling that made her want to sit down and snatch her breath back? "When you determine what to do about it, I'll be delighted to hear it. In the meantime, I should return to my guests. My aunt will come looking for me if I don't. We are to dine at Sir Walter Debridge's tonight."

She moved to pass Leopold, but he caught her hand before she reached the door and twirled her around. He put his arm around her waist and pulled her into him, then cupped her face with his hand. "Caroline." His eyes darted around her face, and he looked as if he wanted to say more. But he didn't speak—he kissed her so hard that everything in her began to tingle and all thought flew out of her head other than how much she wanted this man. And then just as abruptly he let her go, leaving her a little dazed by that kiss. "Best wishes for a lovely evening."

Her skin was sizzling. She forced herself to look down and smooth the lap of her skirt until she could find her breath or a thought that wasn't lustful. She touched her curls to make sure they were in place and no one would detect what she'd been doing, then finally looked at Leopold. "What are you doing to me?" she whispered.

"I honestly don't know."

She sighed. She went out of the salon, but her step was much lighter than it had been going in.

She swept into the salon, beaming at her guests. "There we are—thank you for waiting! Oh dear, look at the time. I'm afraid I've made us late. Shall we?"

Ladley looked past her, to Leopold.

Caroline glanced at him. "Oh! I quite forgot," she blurted. "I invited His Highness to join us this evening. Sir Walter won't mind, will he?" she asked cheerfully, and very carefully avoided the looks of the others in the room. Including Leopold's.

Caroline had no idea what she was doing, either. She'd need a hot bath and a glass of wine and perhaps even Hollis nearby to figure it out. She'd gone from despising him, to despair, to suddenly feeling better than she had in days.

CHAPTER TWENTY-TWO

It is a conundrum of the first order when an uninvited guest arrives at the supper hour, as was witnessed recently at the home of a knight of the realm. Some would advise to refuse the uninvited entry with the claim of not having prepared enough food. But sometimes the uninvited is of such superior social standing that it would cause undue talk. In this situation, one is advised to open the doors of hospitality and endure it.

Might we soon hear the wails of a newborn? It has been observed that a woman of High Moral Character married to a Man of the Cloth has had some skirts altered recently in anticipation of that happy event.

Ladies, science suggests that if you do not satisfy your cravings for unusual foods and in great quantities during pregnancy, the deprivation may appear as a birthmark on your child. When with child, eat well and a variety of foods, and don't give in to those who claim you'll never regain your figure after birth.

*⌒—Honeycutt's Gazette of Fashion and
Domesticity for Ladies*

ONE-HALF OF the Debridges minded very much when Leo appeared quite unexpectedly with Caroline's party. Not surprisingly, given his reputation of late, it was the female half. In fact, Lady Debridge looked positively stricken when he sheepishly entered the foyer, as if he were an ogre come to eat her children.

On the other hand, Sir Walter was quite happy to have an Alucian prince to dine in his home and crowed to the other guests that he'd also had the German cousin of Prince Albert to dine once, and now could add an Alucian prince to that very short but illustrious list of guests. The man seemed oblivious to the looks many of his guests gave him and neither did he seem to notice his wife's anger, nor how many people moved to the far end of the drawing room when Leo entered. Instead, Sir Walter very happily and loudly commanded his butler to add another place setting for their unexpected, but certainly very welcome, guest.

Power was everything, Leo knew, and connections were the lifeblood of power.

Lady Debridge retreated straightaway with Lady Hogarth and Caroline. Leo looked around for a friendly face but found none. Even Robert Ladley, whom he'd known for quite a few years now, seemed annoyed by his presence. When Leo attempted to speak to him, Ladley smiled thinly and excused himself.

So in a strange twist of fate, Leo found himself standing apart from everyone else, nursing a glass of port. He pondered how odd it was that his life had taken this turn. Up until the last few weeks, he'd been the one to avoid the attentions of others. Men wanted to befriend him, ladies wanted to sleep with him, others just wanted him to acknowledge them. When he was a child, he could recall standing on the balcony at Constantine Palace, frightened of the massive crowds below. His father would put a hand on his back and push him forward. "Give them what they want," he would say. Leo had been giving them what they wanted all his life and hiding in the bottom of a bottle to find a quiet place only he could enter.

Vir ingenuus juniperum cadit. The gentleman falls.

He sipped the port and tried not to wrinkle his nose. Port didn't taste as good as it once had. It no longer held any promise of dulling the tedium and emptiness he often felt. He pretended to sip it and surreptitiously watched Caroline move around the room, entertaining whomever she spoke to.

He could be such an idiot. How could he not have thought her charming from the beginning? How could he not recognize at once how unique she was?

Well, well, Prince Leopold. How remarkable that a few words and a few kisses can alter your judgment so.

He noticed that Caroline made a point to speak to each suitor—or at least those he assumed were her suitors. The viscount was in the company of another attractive young woman, but nevertheless, Caroline spoke to him at length. With so much feminine attention, the viscount, predictably, couldn't seem to keep the smile from his face.

Caroline conversed with Ladley, too, whose eyes followed her every move like a puppy. And another gentleman, who laughed too loud and too long when she spoke to him.

But eventually, having made the circuit of the room, Caroline ventured back to him, her smile blazingly brilliant. She looked him up and down, then glanced back at the others. "Why do you stand in the corner all alone, Your Highness?"

"I feel a bit out of place. Or rather, I feel this is my place." He sipped the port. "Dare I ask if you've settled on the lucky gentleman you will allow to offer for your hand?"

She turned around and stood beside him and surveyed the room. "No. I think not."

"No? From my vantage point they seem like good men. And they seem terribly admiring of you."

"Please," she drawled with a roll of her eyes. "Do you really believe so? Lord Ladley has known me for ages and never expressed the least bit of interest until recently."

"Perhaps that's because he's come to see you as a grown woman and not Beck's younger sister," Leo suggested. He could imagine that every man in attendance tonight would see the woman.

Caroline laughed. "Perhaps." She turned her glittering gaze to him. "But might it also be that his father has amassed a large debt the family cannot pay, and he would benefit from a large dowry?"

Leo lifted his glass in a mock toast. "Entirely plausible, madam. What of the viscount? Your uncle seems to think his having been to America recommends him well enough."

She giggled. "Uncle Hogarth is obsessed with all things American. He was there as a boy and hasn't forgotten a moment of it." She gazed off in the direction of the viscount. "Ainsley *is* rather charming."

"Charming, is he?"

"And handsome, too, wouldn't you agree?"

He didn't want to agree, but even he could see the man's appeal. "Perhaps," he said grudgingly.

She smiled pertly, then bumped her shoulder into his, like they were old chums. *"He put all his money into tobacco,"* she whispered.

"I beg your pardon?"

She nodded, her curls bouncing gaily around her face. "Hollis told me all about him. He went to America to make his fortune, taking all the money from his estate that wasn't otherwise entailed. *All* of it. Can you imagine? Apparently, he meant to make a fortune in trading tobacco. But his first ship ran aground. The crew was rescued, but the ship was scuttled and the cargo lost. All that investment sitting at the bottom of the ocean." She shook her head.

"That's unfortunate," Leo said sincerely.

"A terrible tragedy that my dowry could possibly repair. Unfortunately for him, as he's just come back from America, Lady Katherine Maugham, otherwise known as the Peacock—"

"Pardon?" Leo asked, smiling.

"The Peacock. Do try to keep pace, Leopold. Hollis and Eliza and I gave Lady Katherine that name because she is a peacock, always showing her feathers."

He choked on a laugh. "Isn't that a bit of the pot calling the kettle black?"

"Well, yes, but I'm genial about it," she said, her eyes dancing with merriment. "She's just there, with my aunt, do you see?" she said, nodding to a point across the room.

An attractive woman a head shorter than Caroline was in conversation with her aunt.

"Katherine has set her sights on the viscount, and she will not lose him to me."

"Is she in a position to decide?"

"You may trust me it would be war if he were to seriously pursue me. Oh! There's another potential suitor," she said, leaning slightly forward to look to Leo's right. "Mr. Bishop. Don't look."

Leo turned to look.

"Don't look!" Caroline said, giggling.

"How am I to know who we are speaking about if I don't look?"

Caroline stole another look. "All right. But do it *quickly*. He's tall and thin with fine blond hair that is thinning on the crown."

"That describes half the men in London."

"But only three of the gentlemen here tonight. *Now*."

Leo looked. He spotted the man in question and turned back to Caroline. "I've spotted him, I've seen his thinning hair and his height. What does Mr. Bishop lack as a suitor?"

"Oh, nothing. He's very kind and has no debts to speak of. Unfortunately, he aspires to the clergy."

"Oh dear," Leo said with a smile.

"Exactly," she whispered. "I can think of no one less suited to being the wife of a vicar than me. Can you?"

"Not a single name comes to mind," he agreed.

Caroline laughed. "Prince Leopold, I think you know me better than I allow. Look, here comes Lady Debridge. Supper will be served soon. She will have sat you as far from her as possible and say only a lowly footman may serve you." She winked. "Enjoy your supper, Your Highness," she chirped, and walked away, pausing to speak to a couple who were bent over an open book.

A moment later, Sir Walter announced supper was served.

Caroline was right—Leo found himself seated at the very end of the table next to Sir Walter and across from Mr. Franzen, a German banker. On Leo's right was an elderly woman whose name he never could quite decipher. She curled over her food like a question mark.

Caroline was in the middle of the table, surrounded by all the youth and beauty in the room. Or at least it seemed that way from where Leo was sitting. Ladley was on her right, his attention to her every need. On her left, another gentleman Leo had not met but who also seemed capti-vated by Caroline.

Or maybe it just seemed that way to him because he was captivated by her, too. Perhaps more than all these gentlemen combined. Too captivated. His enchantment had all the signs of potentially getting in the way of his goals and his duties.

He would have been content to sit quietly and contem-plate these thoughts, but Sir Walter was very keen to de-lineate for Leo all the things he'd done in his life, and desiring, apparently, to compare them to experiences Leo might have had. Sir Walter had excelled at archery. Had Leo?

"Ah…well, I was certainly taught the art, but I must admit my brother was better."

"And riding, sir? I'm sure you are an expert rider. I sus-pect princes are trained from an early age to ride."

"I am a passable rider."

"What of your military service? I myself spent four years in Her Majesty's Royal Navy. Best four years of my life."

"Yes," Leo said. He was bored with this game. "I was four years in the navy."

"Four years! Admirable, Your Highness," he said, as if congratulating a boy on the cricket field. "And you've been in England now for…how long, is it?"

Leo sipped his wine. "A very long time, as it happens. So long, in fact, that the time has come for me to return to Alucia."

Mr. Franzen chuckled. "The time does come to put away childish things, does it not?"

Leo didn't know if this was a comment on the life he'd led in England, or merely an observation, but he could feel the heat rising beneath his collar nonetheless. He used to laugh about his dissolute life, but now it seemed sad to him to be a man of nine and twenty years and have nothing to show for it. He thought about the Weslorian women and what they'd had to endure while he'd lived so carelessly.

"But isn't it everyone's duty to marry?" The question, posed by the woman Caroline had dubbed the Peacock, rose above the other conversations, and, curious, Leo looked down the table.

"Why are you asking her?" Lady Debridge asked. "Lady Caroline believes that a lady need not set her sights on marriage until she feels completely at ease with it." She gave a good roll of her eyes to indicate her apparent opinion of that.

"Lady Debridge," Sir Walter said. "If that is Lady Caroline's opinion, she is welcome to it."

"It may be her opinion, but it's wrongheaded," Lady Debridge said. "A woman's good years are limited, and she must marry sooner rather than later if she is to produce an heir."

Caroline laughed. "That's rather my point," she said. "Why should I marry for the sake of producing heirs if I don't wish to produce them?"

"Oh *Lord*," Lady Hogarth muttered. "Caroline, darling—"

"What are you saying, precisely, Caroline?" the Peacock said, sitting a little straighter.

"I think the topic too indelicate for the supper table?" Sir Walter tried.

"Of course it's not, Walter," his wife said. "We're all adults here, are we not? That is the way of the human race. You marry, you produce heirs and life goes on. Why ever would any young woman of good health and moral standing wish otherwise? Lady Caroline, surely you don't mean to imply that you don't want children?"

"Not at all," she assured Lady Debridge. "Of course I do."

But the words didn't match her expression and Leopold rather wondered if she really didn't want children.

"The truth is that I haven't given it much thought, as I have not yet found the gentleman with whom I should like to share that blessed event."

"Darling, look around you," Lady Debridge said. "There are gentlemen here tonight that would delight in sharing that blessed event with you, I've no doubt."

Several of the guests laughed. Caroline smiled as she looked around. "Such admirable gentlemen, too. But I should hope that a gentleman's interest in me would extend beyond the size of my fortune."

There were audible gasps around the table. Leo almost laughed. Once upon a time, he would have led the way in the gasping and gnashing of teeth and the outward display of indignation at her cheek, but this evening, he sat back to enjoy it. The woman refused to guard a single word. He admired her for always being willing to speak the truth.

Even now, she looked around at their shocked faces. "I beg your pardon, have I spoken too bluntly? I probably should not have said what we all know to be true." She laughed softly.

"Caroline," her uncle said sternly. "Have a care."

"I will, Uncle." She smiled and leaned forward. "But whose feelings am I sparing? If anyone should be offended, it should be me, shouldn't it?"

"Oh my *Lord*!" Lady Hogarth said heavenward.

"What you say may be true, Lady Caroline," the Peacock said. "After all, the only reason anyone in London knows the size of your dowry is that you've made certain of it."

"Not me. But I can't say the same for my brother."

Someone at the table chuckled.

"Well, I, for one, have no regard for your dowry, Lady Caroline," Lord Ladley avowed.

"I should think Prince Leopold has no regard for it, either?" the Peacock said, and cast a smile at Leo. "It must be rather small compared to what he might command."

Lady Debridge snorted a laugh. "The prince is not a suitor, Katherine."

"As I said," Ladley interjected. "I don't care about the size of your dowry."

"Thank you, my lord," Caroline responded.

"For what it's worth, I agree with Lady Caroline," the viscount said quietly. "A dowry is an important part of a marriage bargain, and the amount must be taken into consideration. Any gentleman who claims otherwise is fooling himself," he said, and looked pointedly at Ladley.

"But a dowry is not a substitute for love," Lady Hogarth pointed out.

"Perhaps not always," Lord Ainsley said.

Leo could see the amusement in Caroline's eyes. She enjoyed starting this little fire.

When the meal was concluded and the guests invited to repair to the drawing room, Leo took his leave. He said a quiet good-night and thank you to Sir Walter. He stepped out of the drawing room door and almost collided with Caroline and another woman he'd already forgotten.

"Oh!" Caroline said, smiling up at him. "Are you leaving, then?"

"Je."

"Excuse me," the other woman said, and darted into the drawing room.

Caroline watched her flee with a laugh of surprise. "What do you suppose was the meaning of that?" She turned her smile to him again. "I hope you enjoyed yourself this evening, Your Highness."

He wanted to kiss her. "Immensely." He wanted to take her by the hand and lead her out of this place. He wanted to take her to his bed and remove her clothing one piece at a time.

"Shall I tell Beck you'll come around?"

He didn't answer. He had a sudden burn in his chest. He knew what she did not—that he would leave very soon, and with five women if he could manage it. And when he left, he likely would never return to England. At least not for a very long time. There didn't seem much point going round to 22 Upper Brook Street again, except to kiss her. He wanted to kiss her so much that his heart was beating like a drum in his chest.

Her smile turned brighter, almost as if she sensed the burning in him.

"I'll come around. I must if I am going to enlist your help in gaining an invitation to the Pennybackers' ball."

"Oh dear. Has your invitation gone missing?" She leaned closer. "Are you a rake?"

"Guilty as charged."

She laughed. She leaned forward, lifted her chin and murmured, "Find your own way to the Pennybacker ball." With that, she moved away from him and in the direction of the drawing room. She brushed her fingers against his as she passed, and cast a smile at him over her shoulder before disappearing into the room.

He waited until he couldn't see her anymore, then made

his way to the door and received his hat and cloak from a footman.

Leo felt odd. Like his body didn't fit his skin. He felt like something was blossoming in him.

He felt like he was falling in love.

CHAPTER TWENTY-THREE

One never knows what the sea wind may carry into London with it, but for a peacock with an eager wish to land a match, it has brought a gentleman who has been away from England's shores for some time. Whether or not the gentleman desires a match remains to be seen.

Savile Row, a street for the most fashionable of addresses, has added a new clothier for fine gentlemen's tailoring. Should one's husband require formal evening wear, one simply must call on Mr. Henry Poole.

Ladies, perfume liberally scented with ambergris will mask the body's unpleasant odors when the heat begins to rise.

⌒—Honeycutt's Gazette of Fashion and Domesticity for Ladies

IN THE WEEKS that followed the bad sea voyage and her terrible illness, Caroline had made some lovely dresses that were so well received that she'd gained a list of names wanting her creations. Dress forms and bolts of cloth and spools of thread filled her sitting room. Beck complained about it, but he stubbornly refused to hear any mention of her opening her own dress shop.

She was actively considering how she might maneuver around him.

"Fine ladies do not engage in trade, Caro," Beck had huffed. "Leave that sort of thing to Mrs. Honeycutt."

Caroline hadn't argued with her brother—she'd learned that sometimes it was better to do and then seek his approval.

Today, on her way to pay her weekly call to Justice Tricklebank, she'd gone down Savile Row to have a look. Why should it be the street of bespoke tailoring only for men? She should very much like to have a dress shop with a lovely window on this street.

The other thing that had happened in those weeks after Eliza's wedding was Leopold. Oh, but she was a blessed fool for involving herself with him. Had it been Hollis or Eliza in her shoes, she would have strongly cautioned them against getting caught up with someone like him. Well, she *had* cautioned Eliza, but Eliza had stubbornly followed her heart, and look where that had gotten her.

But Caroline was not Eliza, and Leopold was not his brother, and Caroline knew she was walking on the very edge of a cliff. But she'd meant what she'd said—life was so boring if one didn't gamble a bit.

On this bright, sun-filled day, she had to swallow down a giggle every time she thought of him. She couldn't help herself. She couldn't help anything where he was concerned.

When she reached the judge's modest home, she fairly leaped from the carriage and jogged up the steps to the door, rapping a staccato burst of eagerness that sent Jack and John, the two terrible terriers, into paroxysms of alert. Their barking sounded like an entire kennel on the other side of the door.

Poppy opened the door. Poppy had been a housemaid since Caroline was a girl and was really more sister than servant. Her face lit with delight, and she threw her arms around Caroline, smashing Jack and John between them as she hugged her tightly. "I thought you'd all but forgotten us! Oh, but we've missed you, Lady Caroline. The judge asked about you just yesterday. 'Has Caro forgotten us,' he said."

"How could I ever forget any of you?" Caroline exclaimed as she squatted down to greet the dogs properly with a good scratch behind the ears. "I've been terribly busy. So *many* engagements." She sighed loudly, as the work of attending soirees and supper parties was as taxing as pulling a plow. "I'll confess, Poppy," she said as she gained her feet, "I seem to be in vogue this summer. It's not unlike my debut. You remember that, don't you? It seemed as if suitors and callers were falling out of the ceiling rafters."

"I don't remember that exactly, no," Poppy said thoughtfully. "But of course you're in vogue. Look at you!" She held Caroline's arms wide to see her gown. "Did you make this dress? It's stunning."

"I did indeed. I mean to make you one, too, Poppy. I think a dark red would suit you. But you'll have to wait until the end of the summer season—the invitations come one after the other," she said breathlessly as she followed Poppy down the hall.

"It must be so difficult to juggle so many invitations," Poppy said with genuine sympathy. She'd always been an ardent supporter.

"Thank you, Poppy. No one but you really cares how taxing it all is for me."

She walked into the drawing room and paused to look

around. The room, as familiar to her as her own home, was just as Eliza had left it. There were two well-worn armchairs in the window, with stacks of books and gazettes on a table between them. A settee with lumpy seating from years of use was in the middle of the room. Clocks in various stages of repair sat on the mantel—Eliza had a peculiar hobby of repairing them. Near the door was a small desk stacked with papers and ledgers. The judge's chair was before the hearth, and next to it, a large basket of yarn on the floor, into which the black cat, Pris, had wedged himself today. The judge liked to knit. It was the thing he could do by feel.

Hollis was here, standing on a footstool at the bookshelves that lined one wall, and appeared to be attempting to tidy them up. Caroline didn't think it was possible to tidy a room as cluttered as this, but she respected Hollis's willingness to try.

"Is that Caroline?" the judge asked, putting down his knitting, training his sightless eyes to the middle of the room.

"Yes, Your Honor! It is me, in all my glory, which, today, I don't mind saying, is quite incomparable," Caroline said as she sailed across the room and bent to kiss his cheek. "Have you missed me?"

"Almost as much as I miss dear Eliza," he said, and smiled as he patted her cheek with his hand. "Hollis tells me you have been entertaining a prince of your own."

"Entertaining him! Certainly not. *Avoiding* him." Caroline laughed as she reached for Hollis's hand to squeeze it.

"Ha!" Hollis said. "Every time I see you you've had some encounter with him that you can hardly keep to yourself."

"I can't deny it," Caroline admitted, and ungracefully

fell onto her back on the settee, nestling her head against a faded pillow on one end, and stacking her feet on the arm of the settee at the opposite end, letting them fall naturally to the side. "This summer has been a *storm* of activity, I tell you. I'm exhausted from it all."

Hollis hopped down from the stool and settled on the floor beside Caroline. "So? What news have you brought us today?"

"Well, I've gone and made a terrible mess of things for Beck."

Hollis laughed with delight. "How grand! I am forever amused when things have been made a terrible mess for Beck."

"Hollis, don't be unkind," the judge said. He'd resumed his knitting, and the cat was trying to catch the line of yarn that went up to his needles. "Beckett Hawke has been very good to you."

Hollis glanced heavenward. "Yes, of course he has, but that does not change the fundamental fact that he is Beck."

"Beck wasn't even there when I made the mess. He's gone to Four Corners to race the horse he brought from Alucia. Did I tell you? I heard him say he'd wagered one hundred pounds. Can you imagine?"

"I cannot," the judge said.

"Poppy!" Hollis called out. "Will you bring us some tea, darling?"

They all heard Poppy's indiscernible reply from some other part of the house.

"All right, tell us," Hollis urged her.

Caroline turned onto her side and propped her head onto her palm. "Since we returned from Alucia, Beck is determined to see me married. I told him that no one would court me, not really, as I've turned down every eligible gentleman in London. Haven't I, Hollis?"

"I wouldn't say *all* of them."

"Do you know what my brother did? He whispered the size of my dowry to his friends, and suddenly every gentleman with a debt has come to call."

The judge laughed. "That's one way to accomplish it."

Poppy banged into the room with a caddy which carried a tarnished tea service. "All at the ready," she announced. "Cook has made a new batch of gooseberry jam."

"Oh, I'll have some," the judge said.

"Serve the tea, darling, then take your own and sit," Hollis said. "Caro is about to tell us all how she's fended off an unprecedented number of suitors."

"Do tell!" Poppy said eagerly.

Caroline sat up while Poppy served tea, stroking Pris, the cat, who had made his way onto her lap. And then she proceeded to regale the Tricklebanks about the night she had two gentlemen callers and a third unexpected one, and how they'd all trooped off to the Debridge supper, where she had announced she wanted a suitor to find his interest in her, and not the size of her dowry.

"My God, you *didn't*," Hollis said with an expression that could be construed as either horrified or admiring.

"I *did*. Why not? It was true and everyone knew it, including the peacock Katherine Maugham. And do you know the only person who was *not* shocked by what I said?"

"Who?" Hollis asked.

"Prince Leopold, that's who. He laughed."

Hollis giggled. "Papa, I wish you could see how *sparkly* Caro is just now. At every mention of the prince, another spark shoots right off of her," she said, squeezing Caroline's knee. "She's in love with him."

Poppy gasped. "Another royal wedding!"

"Good Lord, not another one," the judge moaned.

"Rest assured there won't be another one," Caroline said confidently, even if the mention of it sent a wave of shivers down her spine, just like those she'd felt at Eliza's wedding.

"Why not?" Hollis asked. "It's a lovely fairy tale dream to be an ordinary person and be swept off your feet by a true prince."

"It is indeed a fairy tale, which is precisely why nothing will ever come of it. But I don't mind, really. It's been quite a lot of fun, and honestly, the reality hasn't kept me from kissing him."

Poppy and Hollis squealed at the same time.

"Heaven help you, Caroline Hawke!" the judge said disapprovingly over their shrieks of delight. "That sort of talk will see you ostracized from the very society you love to rule!"

Caroline laughed. "I haven't yet gone out into the square and announced it, Your Honor. And really, is it so terrible? Men and women do share kisses. I've seen it happen time and again. I saw Lady Munro kiss Mr. Richard Williams at Kew Gardens just before we departed for Helenamar."

"What? And you're only telling me this now?" Hollis exclaimed.

"My point, if you will hear it, is that sort of affection should be reserved for husband and wife," the judge said sternly. "Or at the very least, if you cannot contain your lust until you are married, for the gentleman who is to *be* your husband. What would Lord Hawke say to this?"

"He'd lock me away. For God's sake, we must all swear to never tell him!" Caroline said, laughing.

"But…but aren't you concerned about the maids, Caro?" Hollis asked.

"What maids?" the judge asked.

"Prince Leopold is notorious for a rather untoward preference for housemaids."

"What?" Poppy exclaimed.

Hollis sighed. "Does no one in this house read my gazette? Did you not hear what happened in Arundel with the Norfolk maid?"

"No! Tell us!" Poppy said, inching forward on her seat.

"Hollis! You make it sound dreadful," Caroline said. "The prince explained it to me. Norfolk was the one who was behaving badly. He was visiting the poor thing at night, if you take my meaning, and showering her with the sort of affections she did not want. And the prince, well…he helped her to escape. She was a Weslorian and I think he felt obliged."

"Why would he feel obliged to help a Weslorian?" the judge asked.

"Well…" Caroline started, but paused. She didn't quite know why.

"What did he do with her?" Hollis asked.

"What do you mean?"

"If he helped her to escape, what did he do with her? Where is she now?"

Caroline didn't know the answer to this, either. She'd been so ready to accept his explanation so she'd not have to think poorly of him. "I…I really don't know." Her sparkle was rapidly dimming. What *had* he done with her? And the other one?

"Caro, you'd do well to keep your distance. Who knows what the man is about, really," the judge cautioned her.

"Don't look so distressed, darling. I didn't mean to intrude on your joy in being the one and only Caroline Hawke," Hollis said cheerfully. "Tell us, what's next on your social calendar?"

"Oh, the, ah…the Pennybacker ball next week." At the mention of the ball, she rallied out of her disappointment. "I have a new dress. The blue one, Hollis, remember?"

"It's beautiful. I intend to wear the same dress I wore to Eliza's ball— Oh! I nearly forgot. We've a letter from Eliza." She went to the desk to fetch it and handed it to Caroline to read.

My dearest beloveds, I hope this letter finds you well and in good health. Papa, have you taken the willow-bark tea, and did it help the pain in your fingers? The queen swears it has reversed her own pain and sends her best wishes for you.

My husband and I have been at Tannymeade long enough that it is beginning to feel a bit like home. I have a dog now, a very big one. His head comes just under my hand, and there he keeps it most of the day. I've named him Bru, which in Alucian means loyal. It is quite beautiful here, but I will confess the ocean smells terribly briny in the afternoons and I have asked for the windows to be shut against the stench. It leaves us feeling too warm, but my prince has assured me that when the season turns to autumn, the smell will dissipate. Speaking of my husband, we've been trying diligently for an heir, and with God's blessing, we might report happy news very soon.

News has reached us of Prince Leopold's bad be-

havior, and the duke frets over him most days. He
shall see his brother soon enough, I expect, as he
said the king has sent word he is to return to Alu-
cia at once.

The Alucians are very fond of their eel and dine
on it at least twice a week. I can scarcely tolerate it,
and one night, I grew so green when I saw it that my
husband demanded they bring onion soup straight-
away. The master of the kitchens has been terribly
apologetic, and has attempted to serve that foul beast
in different dishes, but alas, it does no good. I can't
tolerate it. I assured the poor man that I will delight
in anything he prepares, save that wretched eel.

Eliza continued on about Tannymeade, and a clock she'd
found in one of the staterooms that was not working properly, and how everyone around her had twittered with unease when she insisted she would like to fix it. She reported
that the clock now resided in her dressing room, and she
was spending her spare time in the repair of it. There was
more, but for once Caroline did not hang on Eliza's every
word. The words relaying the message that they knew of
Leopold's "bad behavior" and the king had sent for him
danced before her eyes.

When Caroline finally took her leave, she grew steadily
despondent in the carriage ride home. She wasn't ready for
him to leave, in spite of all the questions about him. What a
strange, perplexing feeling it was to have doubts and questions about a person and still desire them. But when she
thought of his leaving, the doubts gave way to complete
despair. How would her life be then? What would amuse
her? And how could she ever hope to look at another gen-

tleman and feel the same sort of excitement and anticipation she did when he was near?

Caroline was such a fool. She'd known since Eliza's wedding that it would lead nowhere, and after his treatment of her in Helenamar, she hadn't even liked him very much. But oh, how she'd kept at it until she *did* like him. Until she *loved* him. And she did love him, she could feel it deep in her bones.

The truth was that she'd be desperately wounded when he left and she'd be forced to marry a stranger and pretend to esteem him and wish every waking day that that stranger was Leopold.

It was the most dreadful fate she could imagine.

Caroline was so lost in thought that she didn't really notice the two gentlemen standing outside her home when she disembarked from the carriage. She smiled and nodded and moved to pass them on her way to the gate of her house. But then one of them said, "Lady Caroline?"

She paused and glanced back at them. "Yes?"

"Mr. Drummond, at your service," said one. He looked like someone's kindly grandfather, tall and stately. He touched the brim of his hat as he handed her a calling card. She looked at the inscription. The gentleman was from the foreign secretary's office. She frowned with confusion and glanced up.

Mr. Drummond's smile turned kinder. "Oh—this is Mr. Pritchard," he said, nodding to the silent man behind him. "Same office."

She stared at them, trying to understand this intrusion.

Mr. Drummond stepped forward. "If you would be so kind as to indulge us, Lady Caroline?"

"Shouldn't you speak with my brother?"

"Oh, undoubtedly. But we would like a word with you, as well."

Caroline's pulse began to race. She glanced uneasily toward the gate.

"We could speak here, if you like. It won't take a moment. We should like to ask a few questions about an acquaintance of yours."

"Who?"

"His Royal Highness Prince Leopold of Alucia."

Caroline was stunned that she gave no reaction to his name at all, because in her mind, she shrieked and fell back against the gate. She didn't know what this was about, but she was certain she didn't want to have this conversation. "What of him?"

"An…accusation has been made against him."

Good God, what had he done now?

"It's a bit complicated, but to put it succinctly, there is some suspicion that the prince might be plotting with the Weslorians. With his uncle Felix, specifically."

She had no idea who they were talking about. Who was his uncle Felix? Plotting what? Oh, how she'd wished she'd listened more carefully to Hollis on the voyage to Helenamar, when she'd tried in vain to educate Caroline about the history of Alucia.

"His uncle is the half brother of his father the king. I am sure you are aware of the rift between the brothers?"

She did know something about that, but at the moment, she could hardly say what.

"Recently, here in England, we've uncovered a plot by the prince's uncle in Wesloria to dethrone the prince's father. You may recall the unfortunate murder of an Alucian gentleman last year?"

Caroline stared at this man in disbelief. Of course she remembered it. "Yes."

"There is some...speculation that Prince Leopold has aligned with his uncle."

"Impossible," Caroline said immediately.

"Oh, I should think so," Mr. Drummond agreed, all too readily. "But so that we may end any speculation, might we ask you a question or two?"

Caroline's head was spinning wildly. The maid in Arundel was Weslorian. But what could a Weslorian maid possibly have to do with this?

"Lady Caroline?"

She started.

"Have you known the prince to have met with or mentioned any Weslorian nationals?"

Caroline slowly shook her head.

"No one? A woman, perhaps?"

Her pulse was racing so quickly now that she couldn't seem to breathe. She shook her head again.

Mr. Drummond was still smiling his grandfatherly smile and stepped closer. "If I may, Lady Caroline...this plot, if it exists, could have far-reaching implications for England, and especially for the Duchess of Tannymeade."

Caroline's breath caught. "What? How?"

"Imagine if there were to be a coup in that country. How do you think the rebels would treat the duchess?"

Caroline gasped softly. She slowly lifted her hand and gripped the gate handle to steady herself.

"Do you think you might keep an open ear to his conversations? We've noted that he calls here more than any other house."

A cold shiver radiated through Caroline. What else had they noted? Were they looking in windows?

"If you could see what you might learn for us?" he asked, smiling in that strange, grandfatherly way, while his eyes remained as hard as flint. "Think of it as helping the duchess."

Caroline could hardly get a breath. This was all so confusing and alarming…but she knew when she was being manipulated and whirled about to the gate. She fumbled with it, fearing they would try to stop her, perhaps even attempt to take her with them. She managed to get through the gate and closed it resoundingly shut behind her.

The two men hadn't moved from their spot on the sidewalk. Mr. Drummond tipped his hat again.

Caroline ran up the steps and into the house. She closed the door and pressed her back to it, breathing deeply, her hand to her chest, then two hands to her face as she tried to make sense of what had just happened.

What they said wasn't possible. She could believe many things about Leopold Chartier, but she would not believe for a moment this was true. He was a lothario, but he was not a traitor.

But what of the maid? Was it really mere coincidence she was Weslorian?

What if it wasn't coincidence at all?

CHAPTER TWENTY-FOUR

Sources report that a summons from King Karl of Alucia for his son to return home has been delivered to the prince. Those with knowledge of the situation expect the prince will depart London in less than a fortnight.

The repercussions from the ventures of a rail enthusiast continue to be felt across London. Some of the gentleman's investors have lost as much as two hundred pounds in the scheme.

Married ladies with fragile constitutions who wish to prevent a rapid increase in the growth of her family may consult Madam Bessor of Greenwich Street, a female physician, for a preventive powder.

ᗡ—Honeycutt's Gazette of Fashion and Domesticity for Ladies

BECKETT HAWKE HAD apparently determined he wanted to maintain his friendship with Leo, as he sent word to the Clarendon Hotel asking him to come round for tea that afternoon. Leo was relieved. He enjoyed his friendship with Beck and didn't want to lose it over the incident at Arundel. But moreover, he was desperate to have an excuse to see Caroline.

Leo had enough to keep him occupied what with his imminent departure to Alucia. He had noticed in the course of preparations that Josef, Kadro, Artur and Freddar all seemed quite eager to go. Of course they were—these men were not Britons. They were Alucians, and they wanted to go home.

Leo was not eager to go for obvious reasons. Three things kept him up at night: One, that he hadn't found a way into the Pennybacker house to find Rasa. Two, that he still didn't know where Nina or Eowyn were. And three, he could hardly bear the thought of leaving Caroline.

It really had come down to this—of all that he loved about England, she was the thing, the person, the feeling he would miss the most. He desperately needed to steal a few moments with her. He desperately needed to kiss her again.

But first, he had decided to pay a visit to the ladies he had tucked away at Cressidian's and probe their memories. Hopefully, one of them might remember something that would help him find Eowyn or Nina.

He sent word to Cressidian in advance of his departure that he intended to call.

But when he arrived at the Mayfair mansion, the butler coolly informed him in Alucian that his master had gone out for the day. Leo was taken aback by that news. He would think that the gentleman would accommodate his prince. Would accommodate the man who had *paid* him to see after the ladies. "I should like to see the maids, then," he said flatly.

The butler's eyes widened slightly. "I beg your pardon, Highness, but—"

"But," Leo quickly interjected and stepped into the doorway, crowding the smaller man, "I am your prince, sir, and you will allow me to see the Weslorian women who are housed here. Assemble them at once." And then he pushed past the man and strode into Cressidian's house. Like a bloody prince, thank you.

The women and one lad assembled in a small room near the back of the house that looked to be used by servants, judging by the mean furnishings. None of the rich upholsteries or fine rugs or marble or gold seen in the public parts of the house were evident here. They had a plain wood floor, a long table with six wooden chairs and two more before the hearth. The women entered in service clothes, which Leo didn't like. He'd paid for their keep. They didn't need to work for it.

With his hands on his hips, he surveyed the three of them. Isidora and Jacleen stood side by side, and the boy before Jacleen, her arms securely around him. The three of them viewed him warily, which Leo found disconcerting—he had rescued them, after all. Did they think he was like the men who had bartered and sold them?

He sighed. He pushed his fingers through his hair. "There is no need to look at me like that," he said, gesturing at them. "What are you afraid of?"

Isidora and Jacleen exchanged a glance. Isidora stepped forward. She cleared her throat and ran her hands down the sides of her skirt. "Your Highness," she said in Weslorian, "may we inquire…what you mean to do with us? Mr. Cressidian doesn't want us here, and he said…" She paused and glanced at Jacleen and her brother. Jacleen nodded, encouraging her. "He said you mean to take us to Alucia."

She did not seem to be pleased with the prospect, but seemed rather alarmed. "Don't you want to go home, then?" he asked.

She bit her lip. "There's no work in Wesloria, Your

Highness. Our families…they won't have the money to return."

"Your families will not need to return the money. After you speak against the men that did this, you—"

Jacleen gasped so loudly that she startled Leo. She and the lad and Isidora were suddenly talking at once—to each other, to him—in Weslorian and broken Alucian and English. The cacophony of voices was reaching a fevered pitch, and he threw up his hands and demanded they stop. "All right, then," he said when he lowered his hands. "One at a time, if you please. What is it that causes you distress?" He pointed at Jacleen.

She gripped her brother's shoulders before her. "We don't want to speak out."

"Why not?"

"They will kill us."

He recoiled at that. "*Who* will kill you?"

"The men who done this," Isidora said.

"They said they'd kill us if we told the truth," the boy said.

"What? What is your name there, lad?" Leo asked.

"Bobbin," he said softly.

"Bobbin, they will *not* kill you," Leo said. But the two women started talking to him at once. "Ladies!" he said loudly. "Have you no faith in me? In my word?"

Isidora steadily held his gaze, but Jacleen looked to the floor. And Bobbin looked frantically at his sister. How old was he? Seven? Eight?

"So that's the way of it," Leo said flatly, inexplicably annoyed with them. "I am a prince of Alucia. Has that escaped your attention? I have a certain amount of power and integrity."

"But…but what can you do, milord?" asked Isidora. "If

we speak, they'll send us home and they'll find us there. They'll find our families—"

"No," Leo said firmly, holding up a hand. "They will not." God, he hoped he was right about this. "Is this the life you want?" he asked Jacleen. "Is this what you want for your Bobbin? I thought you were relieved to flee Arundel."

She flushed. "Aye," she whispered, and wrapped a protective arm around the boy.

"And you, Isidora? Were you not relieved to leave Mrs. Mansfield's den?"

She quickly nodded her head and took a small step backward.

"More important, ladies, do you want other young women—or children," he added, gesturing to Bobbin, "to discover what awaits them in England?"

"No," Isidora muttered.

Leo rubbed his nape. He looked at them again and said solemnly, "I understand. I know I'm not the prince you want to come to your rescue. I am not a hero. And I have a certain reputation that should not recommend me to any part of society."

Jacleen nodded along as if that was fact.

"But you have my word that you and your families will be protected. If you don't believe me, then believe my brother."

Isidora perked up. "Prince Sebastian?"

"*Je*, Prince Sebastian," Leo said. "He will assure you are all protected. But you must help me. What has happened to you is an abomination, and those responsible must be held accountable. Such a despicable practice can't be allowed to continue, and the only way to end it is to bring down the men who have arranged it. We, my brother and I, will need your cooperation."

The women looked at each other.

"Do we have it?" Leo asked.

"Aye, Your Highness," Isidora said, and looked starkly at the other two, as if daring one of them to argue.

After a suitable amount of silence, Leo nodded. "But I must find a way to free Rasa, and even then, we won't leave without Eowyn and Nina. How do I find them?"

"Mrs. Brown," Jacleen said.

"Who is Mrs. Brown?"

"The cook, Your Highness."

"Whose cook?" Leo asked, confused.

"She's the cook here, Highness. She's the one who readies them to send."

A wave of nausea went through Leo before he even understood. Something in the back of his mind told him he was the biggest fool to have ever lived. "What, *here*? Mrs. Brown readies women from Wesloria—"

"And Alucia," Isidora interjected.

"And *Alucia*?" he asked, in spite of the answer already forming in his head. "When you say she readies them…"

"To be sold," Jacleen said flatly.

Leo felt himself sinking down onto a chair at the table. He stared at them in disbelief. "Are you telling me, then, that women who have been sold to English gentlemen come through *this* house?"

The women stared at him. Isidora said, "We thought you knew. You brought us back here. We thought…" She looked at Jacleen. "We thought we were to be sold again."

Cressidian, that bloody bastard. No wonder he was as rich as he was—he was a double-dealing scoundrel. Leo suddenly saw it all very clearly—the women, sold by their parents, were brought here, where Cressidian sent them out to the homes of influential gentlemen in exchange for a friendly vote or what have you. And Leo, the hero in this tale, had brought them right back into the place that had sold them to begin with.

He wasn't a knight in shining armor to them—he was just another man who would use them.

"Well then," he said. "We need to get you out of here, don't we? Ladies, Bobbin, gather what things you have. We're leaving."

"Where are we going?" Jacleen asked.

Leo laughed wryly to the ceiling. "An excellent question. I haven't quite worked it out yet, but you'll not stay another moment in this house."

IT WAS SURPRISINGLY easy to leave with the women. The butler seemed unfazed when Artur and Kadro entered the house and escorted the two women and the boy out to the waiting coach. Leo joined them in the coach and sat on the bench opposite the two women and the boy squeezed onto one bench. He thought about pointing out they'd be more comfortable if one of them sat next to him, but he had a feeling that none of them wanted to be very close to him.

He didn't blame them. Men like him must haunt their dreams now.

"Where to, Highness?" Artur asked through the open door.

Leo needed time to think. He looked at Bobbin. "Have you seen the park? No? You should." He instructed Artur to drive them around Hyde Park while he frantically thought what to do.

But after two trips around the park, and another half hour where he commanded the carriage be brought to a halt and had all of them step out and take some air, Leo had no better idea what to do with them.

It was likewise clear that Isidora and Jacleen knew he had no idea what to do. They kept exchanging glances, then leaning forward to look out the window, as if trying to find their bearings. They were thinking of escape.

"Don't fret," he said softly. He needed help. He knew only one person whom he might trust to help him. He pulled down the trap door that covered a funnel that went up to the driver's box. "Twenty-two Upper Brook Street," he commanded.

When the coach pulled up in front of the mansion, Leo told the women to wait. "It might a bit of a wait, I'm afraid, but please, do not leave this coach."

Isidora nodded, and he hoped that meant they had agreed to give him a chance.

He asked Kadro to see to it that no one left the coach, before walking up to the front door.

Leo was not himself. It was as if part of his brain was trying to wrangle all the facts and place them into a semblance of order, while another part of his brain attempted to look reasonable and present and, most important, not hapless or frantic. It was the frantic that had him feeling at sixes and sevens.

But when he walked into the salon and saw Caroline sitting on the settee in a cloud of cream and white, another part of his brain pushed the rest of it aside. His heart quickened and he felt relief.

Caroline stood and gave him a tight smile as she curtsied. She seemed guarded. Uncertain.

It was then that he noticed Beck, who stood from behind a desk and came striding forward, his hand extended. "Your Royal Highness Prince Leopold," he said jovially.

"Garrett, we'll have that tea, then. Leo, you are looking well!"

"Thank you—"

"You've come just in time. I've been returned to London only a day, and this one," he said, gesturing at his sister, "has just now graced me with her presence."

Caroline said nothing and resumed her seat.

"She's not speaking because she knows that, for one, I've seen invoices for more bolts of cloth," Beck said. "Why is it that ladies will not be satisfied with a pair of serviceable dresses?" he complained. "And two, that I've heard what occurred at the Debridges' while I was away."

Perhaps that was the reason she appeared so chary.

"Leo, whisky?" Beck asked, and Leo realized that he'd been gazing at Caroline and hadn't noticed that Beck had moved to the sideboard.

"Pardon? No, thank you," Leo said.

"No? What has happened to you, man?" He poured himself a generous whisky, then turned to face the two of them again, Caroline on the settee, Leo still standing just inside the door. Beck pointed his glass at Caroline and said to Leo, "She's spurned my friend Ladley."

Caroline frowned at her brother. "I warned you."

"But I don't see why. He's a good man. You can't keep turning away all the good men, Caro," Beck said impatiently, and to Leo, "Can you imagine, Leo, what our poor parents would say if they knew I'd allowed her to remain unmarried for so long?"

"*Allowed* me?"

Leo didn't have time for the bickering, and apparently neither did Caroline. She suddenly stood and went to the window to peer out. She seemed unusually restless.

Beck looked at her and shrugged, then turned his attention to Leo. "You, my friend, missed a spectacular horse race," he said, and launched eagerly into telling Leo of how his Alucian racehorse had performed at Four Corners. The telling took some time, however, as Hawke was determined not to leave out a single detail. Leo made all the appropriate remarks, but he realized that he wasn't listening at all. The butler wheeled in the tea, and Beck craned his neck to see around him, still talking. Tea was served, and Leo realized he was gripping one hand tighter and tighter until he had a fist worthy of a blow to Beck's mouth if he didn't stop talking.

"Caro, the tea," Beck reminded her, and Caroline came back from the window and accepted a cup from Garrett.

"I've the race results," Hawke said, and patted down his chest, as if he'd pinned them there. "Where are they? They must be in the study. Excuse me," he said, and strode out of the salon.

Leo put down his teacup and looked at Caroline. "What is the matter?"

"Nothing."

"It's not nothing, clearly."

She glanced across the room. Garrett was standing patiently at the door. "I need to talk to you," she said softly.

"And I desperately need to talk to you," he murmured.

"Here they are!" Beck had returned and was waving a piece of paper in his hand. "You'll be as proud when you see how the Alucian horse fared." He sat next to Leo and proceeded to go over the race times of all the horses entered in the race.

Caroline put down her teacup. "Beck, darling, aren't you forgetting? You're to dine with Lord Ainsley this evening and ascertain if he intends to offer for my hand."

Beck started. "Good Lord, I am. Thank you, Caro. Leo,

will you please excuse me?" he said. "The time got away from me. My apologies, Leo. I got a bit carried away. Caro, you'll see the prince out, will you?" Beck asked as he came to his feet.

"Garrett!" Beck called, striding from the room. "Send Jones to me! I don't want to be late!"

When he'd gone, and the butler with him, Caroline said, "Have you ever in your life known someone more obsessed with horses?" She abruptly stood from the settee and went to the window.

Leo did, too. He didn't know how to broach this delicate situation with her. "Looking for someone?" he asked, peering out the window. He could just see the top of his coach.

Caroline turned around and leaned up against the window frame.

"Caroline, I—"

"May I ask you something?" she interrupted.

"*Je*, of course."

"I've heard you're returning to Alucia quite soon. Is that true?"

He'd long since learned not to question how things were known about him. They simply were. "Who told you so?"

"Does it matter?"

"No, but I—"

"Is it true?"

He stared into her shining green eyes and tried to find words. There were so many bloody emotions bubbling in him. Emotions he needed a drink to dull, but alas, had foregone the opportunity. "*Je*. It can't be avoided."

Something flickered in her eyes. It was like the flame of a candle sputtering out.

"You knew I would return eventually."

"Yes. But I thought it would be the end of summer." She bit her lip and looked down at the floor.

Her reaction was disconcerting. There was one thing about Caroline Hawke he could entirely depend upon—she was not afraid to let him know exactly where she stood or what she thought. She never looked sad. Leo dipped his head to see her face. "I will mourn you. Every day."

She glanced up.

"You don't believe me? Oh, but I will mourn you more than you know, Caroline. I've come to depend on your company."

"Really?" Caroline asked softly. There was a different light in her eyes now. They were both dull and shiny. She was looking at him through unshed tears.

"*Very* much," he said earnestly and shifted closer to her. "May I ask you something else?"

Je, I love you, Caroline. I love you. "Ask me anything. What is it you want to know?"

"Don't lie to me, I beg you. Do you plot with the Weslorians to overthrow your father?"

He couldn't have been more stunned than if she'd slapped him. "W-what?"

"Are they spies? Have they come here to plot with you? For the life of me, I don't understand, and I've tried, but nothing makes sense."

"Has *who* come? What spies? What the devil are you talking about?"

"The maids!" she whispered loudly, and looked toward the open door.

He stared at her, trying to make sense of this. "Are you asking me if the maids are *spies*? That is absurd."

"Then *why*, Leopold? What have you done with them?

They're Weslorian, aren't they? And you took them and where are they now?"

He blanched as all plausible explanations went out of his head. Bloody *hell*, he wished for a vat of whisky just now. Something to dull this discomfort. But he was not that man anymore. He hadn't been that man since he met Lysander in the garden. "I will admit to being many things, but I am not a traitor. Christ Almighty, you think I'd plot to overthrow my own *father*?"

"Then please explain it to me," she begged him.

Leo was torn by this request—he did love Caroline, and he wanted to protect her from knowing what evil there was in this world. She was light, she was happiness and he would prefer the ugliness not touch her. But it was more than that. He didn't want her to look at him with pity. To see what he suspected she and everyone else knew—that he was a prince with no true talent other than drinking. That he was on a mission that was impossible for someone like him. That he was so bad at it that he now had to ask for her considerable help.

But his reluctance to speak caused her to jump to conclusions of her own. "Dear God, it's worse than I thought."

"No, Caroline, *no*," he said, lifting his head. "The women—girls, really, these maids—are not spies. They are slaves. And I've been trying—bungling, really—to free them."

She stared at him. "Slaves?"

Leo nodded.

"Where are they?"

"At present, they are just outside, in the coach."

Her mouth parted with her shock. *"Here?"*

He put his hand on her elbow. "Please sit and allow me to explain."

He told her everything. It felt good to say it to someone, to tell another living soul how he'd been waylaid in Helenamar, then given this list of names. To describe how difficult it had been for him to find these women quite on his own. That as a prince, he wasn't inconspicuous. And that as a prince, he'd discovered he was ignorant of the ways of the world. He told her how he'd made such a mess of things that he'd bought a castle, was paying blackmail to an Alucian businessman who had double-crossed him, had exposed an old friend for the scoundrel he was, and had rescued, quite unexpectedly, a young boy along with the women.

And of course, the crowning detail—that the Weslorian gentleman involved in this scheme was his future father-in-law.

Caroline had turned pale by the time he'd finished. "What are you going to do?"

"I plan to take the Weslorian women to Helenamar with me and have them speak out against the men who did this to them."

"But what about your engagement? Won't your father be angry?"

His father would be livid, of that, Leo was certain. "Possibly. Probably. I don't know what all will happen, Caroline. All I know is that I am determined to take these women to Alucia and have them speak against the men who had bought and sold them for political favors. I intend to expose them, the consequences be damned."

She stared at him for a long moment, and then her eyes began to well with tears.

"What's the matter?" he asked, reaching for her hand.

"Those poor women. And *you*, Leopold. What a noble

thing you're doing, and yet everyone thinks...they assume..."

"I know what they assume. I'm not noble, I happen to be in a unique position, that's all. Do you believe me?"

"I do." She sniffed back a tear. "The Duchess of Norfolk told me about her husband. I never dreamed there were more women like that poor girl. But Leopold, what of your reputation? It's all but ruined, and I...oh Lord, how I regret it! I helped it along. I gave Hollis gossip to print—"

He squeezed her hand. "Darling Caroline, think nothing of it. My reputation was not a grand one to begin."

She shook her head and looked away from him for a moment. "You said there are more women?"

He nodded. "I know of one in the Pennybacker house. The other two... I've not yet discovered where they've gone."

Caroline gasped. She squeezed his hand. "You must attend the Pennybacker ball, Leopold. That was all my doing, and I will undo it. Nancy Pennybacker can be persuaded, I am certain. Leave it to me. You will accompany Beck and me. Beck swears he won't attend, that balls are a colossal waste of time, but I know he will if you come."

"Caroline..." Leopold was so moved in that moment, that she would want to help him in this, that he leaned across the space between them, put his hand to her nape and kissed her.

She pushed back. "Garrett—"

"God help me, but I can't help myself. I will mourn you when I go, Caroline. You have...you have enlightened me. Shown me what it is to live freely in one's skin. You have made me feel things I've never felt—"

"Leopold, there's more," she said quickly. "You're being followed."

CHAPTER TWENTY-FIVE

Mayfair is abuzz with anticipation for the Penny-backer ball. No expense has been spared, and curiously, the invitation list has recently been expanded by one noble name. Even more curious is that the expansion occurred the morning after the select list of invitees for a supper at the home of Lord Farrington were delivered. There is no explanation for this change, but we all know that rivalries die hard.
          —Honeycutt's Gazette of Fashion and
                    Domesticity for Ladies

AMAZINGLY, LEO DIDN'T ask who was following him or why right away. He sighed wearily, as if this was not completely unexpected.

Caroline got up and hurried to the door to the drawing room. She looked out into the hall, then quietly shut the door.

"What—"

She put a finger to her lips, listening for footfall in the hallway. When she heard none, she breathed, and went back to the settee and sat next to Leo. "They were gentlemen from the foreign secretary's office. They asked me to…to keep an eye, really, and said there was reason to believe you were plotting with your uncle to overthrow your father."

Leo drew a breath that flared his nostrils. "Bloody *hell*"

"I can fend them off," she said confidently.

He snapped his gaze to hers, alarmed. "These are not parlor games, love. You must tell Beck."

"Are you mad? He'd not let me out of his sight, much less allow me to attend the Pennybacker ball. Listen, we haven't any time to spare. I must call on Nancy Pennybacker and gain you an invitation—"

He suddenly wrapped his arms around her and drew her into his chest, cupping the back of her head and pressing it against his shoulder. "For God's sake, don't do anything. I told you about the girls only because I wanted you to understand—not to *involve* you. I love you, Caroline. I would never put you in harm's way."

Caroline gasped. She pushed out of his embrace, with a strength born from a sudden and wild mix of emotions. Had he *really* just confessed his love for her? And did he *really* think she would be so easily put off? She took his face in her hands and made him look at her. "I am going to help you, Leopold, and you can't command me to do otherwise. I am the only one who *can* help you."

He caressed her earlobe with his thumb. "You're right. I came here because I need your help. In fact you are the only one who can help me, the only one I can trust. I need to hide them."

That was not the sort of help she had in mind. "Where? *Here?*"

"It's better than the Clarendon Hotel. Can you imagine the speculation?"

Oh, but she could. "Not here," she said, her thoughts churning. "Beck—"

"*Je,* of course," Leo sighed and bowed his head. "I knew it was asking too much, but thought it worth the chance."

"Not here. Hollis's house."

Leo's head snapped up. "I won't involve her, either, Caroline."

"You can't take them there, obviously, but perhaps you could send them with one of your guards?"

"Caroline! Hollis Honeycutt knows nothing about this. I won't do it."

"You won't, but I will," Caroline said. "Hollis will help in any way that she can. And she will because I ask her, Leopold. She loves me as I love her."

He looked as if he wanted to argue. But he didn't. He said, "As God as my witness, I have done nothing in my life to deserve you. I do love you."

He couldn't possibly know what those words meant to her—more than life itself in that moment. But they were almost too painful to hear. She couldn't bear to hear him confess his love, then set sail for a marriage in Alucia. "Don't say that," she whispered. "Please don't say that."

He didn't say it again. He pulled her to him and kissed her. It felt to Caroline as if the room closed around them, shielding them from the world. She could feel an eruption at the core of her with all the yearning she'd felt for him since that night in Chichester, a tiny volcano of want and need and hope. That was the first time she'd really noticed how handsome he was, how tall he stood, how finely he dressed, how his smile seemed to radiate from somewhere inside him. And then all the yearning she'd had the day Eliza married, when she'd seen him standing so regally beside his brother.

And in these last few weeks, all the yearning she'd suffered every time he'd touched her or kissed her. His lips were the beacon, his warmth the shelter, his strength the fence around them. Here she was again, aroused by all those feelings for him, his lips banishing any doubt or concern or fear in her. Everything faded away but the two of them, and the only thing that remained was a deep desire to hold him and love him. She desperately wanted to love him.

Her arousal scorched her blood. She pressed against him, into the hard planes and angles of his body. She touched the corner of his mouth with her fingers, angled her head so that she could deepen this kiss between them. She could feel his arousal, could feel the tension of his desire in the taut way he held his body, in the restraint that radiated from him.

He held her tightly to him, and part of her hoped he never let go. She hoped they never left this room, never ended this kiss. But Leo did end it. He nipped at her lips, kissed her cheek, her forehead, then lifted his head. "Caroline, *mang leift*, my love, we can't continue this," he whispered. "I have three poor souls waiting for me."

Everything in her hummed. The caress of his voice, his hand...but she nodded. Her body was pulsing and wet and she felt like she could explode with a single touch, and she couldn't let that happen.

But neither did she want it to end. Because the moment they opened that door, it could very well be the last time he touched her.

Leo stood up and held out his hand to her to help her to her feet. He kissed her once more, this time with particular tenderness. "It would be the end of you and possibly the death of me if anyone of your household was to find us like this," he whispered. He dropped his hands and stepped away and walked to the door. He glanced back at her, his gaze full of longing. "Tonight? Eight o'clock?"

Caroline nodded. And then she pressed her hands against her belly and watched him walk out the door.

When he'd gone, she stared up at the ceiling and the papier-mâché scrolls there, blinking back tears. She didn't hear Garrett come in until he spoke.

"Madam?"

Caroline was a master at recovery, she discovered. "Ah, Garrett, there you are. A cloak please. I'm going round to call on Hollis, and I won't be home for supper."

She knew herself well enough to know that she was in desperate trouble. Her heart was headed for collision with reality, and it was going to shatter into pieces very soon, because Hollis was right—she loved Leopold. And now he was going to ruin everything by being a good man.

Her heart would be irreparably broken, she was certain of it. But until the moment of its death, there was nothing to be done for it—she had to help him.

A DAILY MAID let Caroline into Hollis's home. She found her friend in the drawing room, not in her office. Hollis was perched on a chair before the hearth, reading a broadsheet, a serious look of concentration on her face. Caroline took the chair beside hers and looked around the neat room. It was quite a contrast from the clutter of her office. Even the two cats seemed to be in their places, curled up together on the end of the settee. "Where is Donovan?" Caroline asked.

"I don't know," Hollis muttered.

Caroline bent forward to catch Hollis's eye. "Good evening, Hollis! How are you? What are you doing?"

"Reading the *Daily News*." Hollis sighed and lowered the broadsheet. "It's edited by Charles Dickens. Do you know him?"

"I've not met him."

"He's printing things that are...*worthy*, Caro. Items of

news that ought to be spread around. Not on-dits. Did you know that Parliament means to establish an entire new system of county courts?"

Caroline laughed. "I certainly did not, and I refuse to know it now. Darling, put that away. I need you just now."

Hollis blinked. She put the broadsheet away. "Why? What's happened?"

"I must have Leopold invited to the Pennybacker ball."

Hollis stared at her. And then she laughed. She laughed so hard she fell back against the settee. "Caro, *you* are the one who made certain of it he was *not* invited."

"Yes, I am well aware, thank you, Hollis. But now I realize it was a terrible mistake."

Hollis wasn't through laughing, however. "The seeds you sow, dearest. Shall I venture a guess? You *do* love him."

Caroline didn't have the patience to be coy today. Time was of the essence. "Yes! I am in love with Prince Leopold. There, are you happy now? Will you help me?"

Hollis was still giggling. She reached for Caroline's hand. "I *am* happy now. You're a perfect match. You, too bold by half and terribly impetuous at times, and him, too fond of his ale. All right. But it will require a little cunning." She stood up and began to pace, one hand on her waist, one finger tapping against her lip. "Ah. Here we are, then. Lady Farrington's husband has come into quite a lot of money, as I am sure you know."

Caroline snorted a laugh. "*Everyone* knows. Priscilla makes certain of it."

"Nancy Pennybacker can't abide it when Priscilla has something she doesn't have. If Nancy knows that Priscilla is having the prince to dine—because you tell her—she will have the prince to her ball. No matter what she thinks of Prince Leopold, she will not allow Priscilla to have royalty into her house before she does."

A slow smile spread across Caroline's lips. "That is positively *diabolical*, Hollis."

"I study the on-dits, darling. But you must convince Priscilla she ought to have him."

Caroline stood up, "That's the easiest thing I might do this week. But Hollis, there is more."

"No," Hollis said, and fell very ungracefully into her chair, and propped one foot against the fire screen. "I can't help you with Lady Norfolk."

"No, something else—I need a rather large favor. I need you to take in two young women and a boy. But only temporarily," she hastily added.

Hollis dropped her foot and sat up. "Caroline? What have you done?" she asked gravely.

"Nothing. At least not yet."

Hollis leaned forward. "Tell me."

Caroline told her everything. Hollis said not a word as she talked—she gaped at her, her eyes round with shock. When Caroline finished, Hollis leaned back in her seat and stared at the ceiling for a very long moment, taking it all in. "I wouldn't have thought Prince Leopold of all people would be the one to save them from that."

"No," Caroline said with a sheepish laugh.

Hollis suddenly surged to her feet and began to pace again. "This is precisely what I was talking about, Caroline. This level of corruption among government officials can't be allowed to continue! It should be exposed. I mean to write an article—"

"Hollis? The girls?" Caroline asked.

"What? Yes, yes, Caro, of course," she said with a wave of her hand. "But do you see what I mean? Instead of publishing who has worn what, or the invitation to whose soiree is the most coveted, I ought to publish the *real* scandals— Oh! Donovan, there you are. We're to have guests. Two young women and a lad."

Donovan had come into the salon with wine. He put the bottle and two glasses on a table between the two chairs. "Very well."

"Shall we put them in adjoining rooms? How long will they be here, Caro?"

She squirmed a little. "Until the prince sails?"

"Ah. Yes, adjoining rooms."

"I'll take care of it," Donovan said, and turned about and walked out whistling under his breath.

Hollis continued giving Caroline her very firm opinions about what a gazette ought to be until ten past eight o'clock, when at last, a knock was heard at the front door.

"They're here!" Caroline whispered, and she and Hollis leaped from their seats and smoothed their skirts as if they were meeting royalty.

Moments later, Donovan came into the room with two women and a lad. "Is this who you were expecting, madam?"

"I think they are. Thank you, Donovan."

He said, "I'll just take their things up to their rooms, then."

Thank heaven for Hollis, as Caroline was quite speechless. The two women looked exhausted. They were both terribly thin, but it was the sort of thin that didn't come by choice, judging by the pallor of their skin and the lankness of their hair. And the boy, oh! The poor lad was swallowed in the coat he wore and clung to the hand of the woman— girl, really—Caroline recognized from Arundel.

The three of them looked frightened and wary, and

Caroline's world of experience did not extend to the sort of life they must have led so far. To try and imagine what they'd endured made Caroline feel ill.

Hollis laid her hand on Caroline's arm. "Would you mind terribly, Caro, darling, to run and ask Emily to bring tea and sandwiches? I think our guests are hungry."

"Yes!" Caroline said, grateful for something to do. She hurried out of the room, tears blurring her vision for the second time today. She felt such sorrow and despair for those women. But she also felt a swell of pride. Not for her—for Leopold and all that he'd risked to help them.

CAROLINE HARDLY SLEPT that night, her mind wandering back to Leopold, and the women who were sleeping under Hollis's roof.

The revelation of what was happening in the very houses she visited left her feeling sad and strangely shallow. When she thought of all the hours and days she'd spent worried about nothing more than what to wear to this party or that supper, while women in meaner circumstances worked hard to just be safe, she felt angry. With life, with herself, with her bubble of privilege, with the meanness in the world.

She desperately wanted to help Leo find the other women. To help in *some* way. And she desperately needed to turn her mind to something other than the idea he would be leaving soon.

Caroline called on Priscilla that afternoon to finish the fit of the ball gown she'd made for Priscilla to wear to the Pennybacker ball. It was a yellow gown, which, in hindsight, had the effect of making Priscilla's skin seem sallow. But Priscilla didn't seem to notice and was thrilled with it.

"It's beautiful," she breathed.

"You will be among the most envied, Priscilla."

Priscilla turned her attention to the mirror, admiring herself. "Nancy is wearing lilac. It's not a good color for her. Makes her appear chalky."

Caroline suppressed a roll of her eyes and busied herself with arranging the skirt around Priscilla's ample frame while nudging curious little dogs out of her path.

"She thinks she is better than all of us, you know," Priscilla confided in a whisper. "You should have heard her at Madam Brendan's."

"Madam Brendan? The hatmaker?"

"We ordered gloves from her and had gone in to be measured. And as we waited for the lady before us to finish, Nancy began to talk rather loudly how all of London looks forward to this ball. 'We never meant it to be the most anticipated event of the summer, but here it is,' she said, as if she were the queen herself."

"The hem is too long in the back. I should pin it," Caroline observed. "Have you a box or a stool?"

Priscilla rang a delicate little bell next to her vanity. "She claims not to have a single regret offered. *All* the replies were affirmative."

"Not everyone will be in attendance, will they," Caroline said. "The Alucian prince has not been invited."

Priscilla snorted. "No one cares about him, darling. You yourself told us that."

Yes, she certainly had. There was never a time she wasn't prattling on about something and it occurred to her that she perhaps ought to learn the art of prudence. "Well," she said airily as she shooed another dog away with her hands, "it happens that it wasn't entirely true. The prince dined with the queen's husband just last week." That was an absolute falsehood, and one Caroline instantly hoped was not easily proved as such. She felt awful for lying to her friend…for a full minute. But then, it had the desired effect. One must never underestimate the power of royalty upon those who wish to be included in that vaulted circle.

"Did he? I haven't heard that said. Tom would know if he had, I should think."

Caroline flushed with a bit of panic. "Yes, but…but how could Tom know, really? Prince Leopold is not receiving invitations from anyone but Buckingham, so I think no one really knows what he is about. That is, besides Beck." She pretended to study the hem of Priscilla's gown.

"Really," Priscilla said.

"Mmm. I'd have the prince to dine myself were it not for Beck. He goes back and forth between Sussex with that blessed horse of his. I never know when he will be home to have guests to dine. I think he prefers to dine with horses."

Several moments passed. Caroline feared the subtlety of what she was suggesting was lost on Priscilla. But then Priscilla said, "I could have him to dine."

Caroline almost let out a shout of small triumph. She glanced up, wide-eyed. "What? You could?"

"Yes, why not?" Priscilla asked airily.

"But…his reputation?"

"Darling! If the gentleman is good enough to dine with Prince Albert, he's certainly good enough for *me*."

Caroline crouched down and petted one of the dogs to hide her smile. "But you haven't any suppers planned, have you, darling?"

Priscilla lifted her chin. "Tom's been very keen to have all the right people to dine since he's taken his seat in Parliament. He has very big plans, you know."

Oh, yes, Caroline and everyone else in Mayfair knew. His ambition was well-known. "What a clever man, your husband. The prince is precisely the sort of connection he'll need, isn't he?"

"Yes," Priscilla said, as if she'd thought it all along. "Where is that girl?" She rang the bell again.

A young woman with dark brown hair hurried in. "Beg your pardon, mu'um," she said with a slight accent.

"A stool, girl, and be quick. We haven't all day," Priscilla said.

The girl went out but reappeared a moment later with the stool and two dogs trotting behind her. She set the stool in front of Priscilla. But because of Priscilla's ample figure, and the many dogs milling about, she couldn't quite see the stool, and commanded the girl to give her a hand up. The girl lifted her hand so that Priscilla might take it, and when she did, Caroline's eye was drawn to the linked hands—and a flash of forest green. It was scarcely even a patch of green at all, but there it was, on the cuff of the girl's dark service gown.

Weslorian green.

Caroline stared at the girl who, relieved of her duties, had stepped back, her eyes downcast. What was it Priscilla had said? Something about foreign servants being better than English servants. *Foreign* servants. Weslorian servants. Did that mean... Was Tom... Caroline's breath caught. She could hardly move as the possibilities began to crowd into her head.

"What do you think?" Priscilla asked.

"Pardon? Oh, it's beautiful," Caroline said. "It's perfect for the Pennybacker ball."

"The hem, darling."

"Oh! Right." Caroline sank down on her knees to have a look at the hem. She took a pin from the cushion on her wrist. "For your supper, I think you should wear the blue."

"You think I should?" Priscilla asked.

It all made sense. Tom's dear friend was Henry, the Duke of Norfolk. If Tom was using this girl, Caroline was determined to get her out. And the other one, at the Pennybackers'! Yes, of course! Lord Pennybacker and Tom were friends, too, and if Priscilla had a new foreign servant, Nancy would have insisted.

"No one looks as good as you in blue, Priscilla," Caroline chirped as she put a few pins in the hem to mark where to take it up. "And do you know what else? I think you ought to have your supper after the Pennybacker ball next week, but before everyone begins to leave for the country. It will be a palate cleanser after that dreadful ball, won't it? And you'd not want Nancy to escape to the north for the summer and not know until autumn that you had the prince to dine, would you?"

"Oh, I hardly care what Nancy Pennybacker thinks of anything," Priscilla said, which was laughably untrue. "But if I were to have it next week, who else should I invite?" She began to rattle off names that she ought to invite while Caroline's head spun. Somehow, she managed to chat along, agreeing that this person or that ought to be invited, when all she cared about was how to get news of this to Leopold.

"I'll serve lamb," Priscilla said, waving the girl over when Caroline had finished pinning the hem. "The butcher in Newgate has taken a liking to me." She took the girl's hand again, and Caroline leaned closer. There was no mistaking that Weslorian green.

She watched the girl go out with the stool.

"Caroline! Where are you?"

Caroline started and whirled around. Priscilla had presented her back to be unfastened out of the gown. Caroline was breathless. *She'd found a Weslorian.* "What about marzipan cakes?" she suggested.

How would they rescue this poor girl? *They?* Yes, of course, they! She and Leopold. He'd come to her for help and she was going to help him. She had to do it. For him, and for herself.

But the other thing suddenly beating in her chest was the knowledge that once Leopold had them all, he meant to leave.

He would be leaving very soon. Too soon.

CHAPTER TWENTY-SIX

The Pennybacker ball was held in Mayfair to much fanfare. At midnight, a light supper of ham and potatoes was served, as well as ices to keep the guests from sweltering.

The best of summer evening gowns made their appearance at the ball, the most desirable including the latest in French fashion of having elaborate bows cascading down the front of the dress.

Prince Leopold of Alucia has announced his imminent departure from England. He is expected to set sail in a matter of days and return to Helenamar to formally announce his engagement to a Weslorian heiress. It shall come not a moment too soon, as Lord Pennybacker has accused him of trying to seduce one of his maids during the ball.

ᴖ—Honeycutt's Gazette of Fashion and Domesticity for Ladies

LEO WAS INDEED being followed. The day after Caroline had told him about the two men from the foreign secretary's office, he'd noticed a man walking briskly behind him. Kadro and Artur were strolling behind him, too, but either they hadn't noticed the gentleman, or…or was it possible they were part of the conspiracy against him? Leo wouldn't have believed it, but then again, he wouldn't have believed there was a plot to kidnap his brother last year, either. And yet there was. What possible reason would anyone have to plant such a terrible rumor about *him*? To keep him from discovering the identity of these women?

He didn't know how or what, but he knew instinctively that it had something to do with Cressidian.

He decided he would think about it when it was necessary. For the time being, he had something pressing to think about. Time was running out to find the last two Weslorian women and free Rasa from Lord Pennybacker's shackles. He had to at least find the women he knew about. He couldn't begin to guess how many more there were that he didn't know about. Young women. Poor women. Helpless women.

He hoped to have Rasa in hand very soon. Tonight was the night of the Pennybacker ball, and somehow, Caroline had managed to see him invited to attend.

Last week, a footman from the house on Upper Brook Street had delivered a note. It said simply, *Please do accept any and all invitations you might receive.* He'd thought it odd advice, seeing as how he wasn't receiving *any* invitations, his name having been struck from all the rolls of suitable guests. But then, curiously, an invitation to dine at the Farrington home arrived a day or two later. In spite of Caroline's note, he was rather surprised by it—he scarcely knew Lord Farrington. Nevertheless, Lord Farrington had issued his invitation and seemed eager to make Leo's acquaintance. The date was set for Saturday next.

The invitation to the Pennybacker ball arrived the day after that, along with a personal note from Lady Pennybacker, begging His Royal Highness's forgiveness for not having sent the invitation sooner. The ball was to be held in just four days' time, and three days before the dinner at the Farringtons'.

The note said the invitation had been "inadvertently misplaced."

"Inadvertently misplaced," Leo repeated. How the devil had Caroline managed it?

"Shall we accept?" Josef had asked, his expression inscrutable. "It is Wednesday evening, and your calendar is free."

Leo resisted directing a withering look to Josef. He wanted to say of course they would accept, as he was being followed and suspected of treason against his own father and appearances were desperately important. *"Je,"* he said simply. "I should appreciate the diversion before we depart this land. You should take the night for yourself, Josef. Take in the theater, perhaps."

"Thank you, Your Highness."

It was the sort of vague response Josef always gave him. Neither a yes or no, but a simple thank you. Would he take in the theater? Or would he plot against his employer?

Leo had been looking at Josef a little more closely of late. He suddenly didn't trust him. Josef had always been unreadable, but now that enigmatic posture seemed suspect, especially in light of the fact that Josef had been the one to suggest Cressidian to him.

Leo recalled how Bas had felt in London those days after Matous was murdered—he trusted no one but Leo, and a pretty woman who lived in a modest town house who liked to repair clocks. He was becoming more like his brother every day.

"I shall notify Freddar that you will need formal clothing for that evening," Josef said, making a note in his leather journal.

Leo wondered about that leather journal. What other notes did it contain? "Thank you. You may go."

Josef glanced up. Leo rarely was the one to end their appointments—generally Josef was bustling off to take care of this or that. But he gathered his things and stood, then bowed his head. "Send Kadro to me," Leo added, his gaze once again on the invitation.

"*Je*, Your Highness."

Kadro entered a few minutes later and bowed.

Now Leo studied his guard. Kadro had been with him for six years now—surely he would have noticed something along the way if Kadro was involved in something nefarious? Or had he spent so much time at the bottom of a bottle that he wouldn't have noticed anything at all? Entirely possible. "Have you noticed anyone following me?" he asked.

Kadro looked confused. "No, Your Highness."

"Perhaps on the street as I've trundled about," he said, gesturing lazily with his hand.

Kadro's brows knit into a frown. He shook his head.

Leo slowly stood. "Well, someone has been following me. I've seen him, and I wonder why you haven't. I should like to know who he is."

Kadro's feelings about this flashed across his face in a look of confusion, then alarm and then doubt. But he nodded and said, "*Je*, Your Highness. Artur and I will keep watch."

"And keep an eye on Josef," Leo added.

Kadro blinked. He looked as if he wanted to speak. He clearly wanted to understand what had prompted this warning. But Leo wasn't going to tell him more.

Kadro nodded curtly.

"Thank you. You may go," Leo said, and turned away from his guard.

He felt unlike himself. A wholly different person from the man who had occupied this skin for twenty-nine years. He didn't like living with dull suspicions and the need to look over his shoulder. He didn't like it at all.

Yesterday, a note had come from Hawke:

Your Royal Highness, greetings and salutations. I am writing to invite you to attend the Pennybacker ball with Lady Caroline and myself. She assures me an invitation has been extended to you and feels very much that you should not enter that "den of rumormongers and anxious mothers" all alone. I have suggested that my sister is chief among the rumormongers, and she has said some very unkind things to me in return. But it is her wish, and I extend this invitation because I have proven time and again that I am powerless to deny her. Therefore, it would be our great honor if you were to attend the ball in our company, if for no other reason than to keep brother and sister from maiming each other. We look forward to your favorable reply. B.H.

Leo couldn't help but smile as he imagined the scene between brother and sister. The Hawkes were the only bright spot in this strange new world he'd created for himself.

He'd sent his favorable reply. He was ready to attend and free Rasa.

He was, however, unusually anxious, given that his previous attempts to free the maids had not gone smoothly. Part of him wished that he could enjoy the ball as he might have a year ago—with an abundance of wine, dancing, perhaps a card game or two.

A larger part of him was relieved those days were behind him.

He had one thing to do before he arrived at the Hawke household. Much to Freddar's dismay, he insisted on a large overcoat to cover his formal clothing and a dreadful hat with a brim so wide one would have to dip down to see his face. He needed to make a pair of calls on the way to Upper Brook Street.

The first was to Cressidian's house. It was time to think about that scoundrel.

Mr. Cressidian looked surprised to see him. He looked a little bleary-eyed. Leo knew that look—it was the look of a debauched lifestyle. He guessed Cressidian would rouse himself with some food and drink and have another go this evening.

"Your Highness," the scoundrel said uncertainly when Leo was shown into his study. "I wasn't expecting you."

"I suspect not. I won't keep you. But I'm curious, sir— how much did they pay you to slander me?"

One of Cressidian's brows rose. "I beg your pardon?"

Leo sighed with impatience. "Come now, Mr. Cressidian. You are a master at lining your own pocket. When you told the men who are in the despicable business of selling Weslorian women that I knew about the scheme, how much did they pay you to slander me?"

The blood drained from Cressidian's face. "I don't know what you're talking about," he said coolly.

"Bloody hell, you don't."

"I will thank you to take your leave," he said, and sort of lurched toward the door, throwing it open, then looking into the hallway, where he probably suspected Alucian men were standing, waiting to take him. They would come later for him, Leo would see to that.

Leo slowly walked to the door, but he paused before the man. He could smell the sour stench of fear and drink on him. "One day, Mr. Cressidian, you will be called to account for your crimes. If I were you, I'd get on my knees and beg for mercy."

"Fine advice coming from a royal wastrel. Get on your own knees."

"What makes you think I haven't?" Leo asked with a wry smile. And then, with speed and strength he hadn't known he possessed, he punched Cressidian squarely in the jaw and sent him tumbling backward. He gave a laugh of surprise as he went out—he wouldn't have thought himself capable of such a stunning blow.

The next call he made was to the home of Hollis Honeycutt. He needed to see that his wards were comfortable and prepared to leave at a moment's notice. He arrived at the address where he'd sent the ladies and knocked on the door. The man who opened the door to him in shirtsleeves and an apron was as tall as he was, and a bit broader. He might have been the most handsome man Leo had ever seen.

He must have been staring in confusion, because the man said, "Aye?"

"Pardon. Is Mrs. Honeycutt at home?"

"She is," he said, looking Leo up and down. He didn't move from filling the door.

"Who's there, Donovan?"

Hollis Honeycutt appeared at the door, ducking under the arm the man had propped against the door frame. She was dressed for the ball. "Oh! Your Highness!"

The man arched a brow.

"I beg your pardon, but I had a moment of opportunity and I thought I might see after your guests?"

"Come in," she said, smiling. "They're dining just now.

My cook has gone away for the weekend and Donovan made a lamb shank. He's an excellent cook."

Leo squeezed by the man and into the foyer. He was instantly struck by the smell of something delicious and something even more amazing—the sound of laughter.

An hour later, Leo arrived at Upper Brook Street with Hollis, who would also accompany the Hawkes to the ball. He shed the overcoat and hat and straightened the cuffs of his sleeves. He was wearing his finest formal wear, and for the first time since perhaps his brother's wedding, he had cared what he looked like. He wore a blue silk sash with his royal medals and had Freddar tie an Alucian knot in his neckcloth. He wore the formal Alucian coat and combed his hair neatly behind his ears, also in the Alucian style. If he was going to leave England in disgrace, he would do it with his head held high.

Garrett showed him into the family drawing room. Beck was impatiently pacing the hearth. "I've been waiting for Caro a half hour," he said impatiently. "What is it that women *do* in their boudoir? It seems fairly straightforward, does it not? A petticoat, a few pins in the hair," he said, fluttering his fingers at his head.

"Are you complaining again, Beck?"

"Caro!" Hollis exclaimed as Leo and Beck turned toward the door. "Your gown is gorgeous!"

"Thank you, Hollis! And you are beautiful in blue, darling. You should wear it always."

Leo's breath was snatched from his lungs—Caroline looked beautiful. She *always* looked beautiful—but tonight there was something about her that sparkled. She wore a headdress made of gold and sparkling crystals that looked a bit like a crown, and from which three gold feathers rose up on one side. Her dress was a brilliant shade of gold, so light that it looked a bit like stardust. The skirt, a diaphanous layer of silk over another layer of heavier silk, was embellished with tiny seed pearls. She wore a choker of pearls around her neck, and another, larger pearl brooch pinned to her bodice. A wrap of the same material as her dress was draped loosely around her arms.

She was elegant, resplendent—he felt like a crow, and she the shiniest of objects. He couldn't look away.

"It was well worth the wait, then, darling," Beck said. "You and Hollis will outshine all the other ladies."

"That's an unexpectedly kind thing for you to say, Beck," Caroline said with a curtsy. She turned her smile to Leo and he felt it sink into his bones and lodge there. He hoped he never forgot that smile. "Your Highness! How do you do this glorious evening? The weather is so fine, I think they will have the doors open, won't they?"

"I am…ah." He felt a little tongue-tied. "I'm very well, thank you." He smiled. He was speechless. Utterly bewitched. In love.

Her smile deepened, too, as if she understood what he was thinking.

Beck said, "If the two of you will stop gawking at each other, we might be on our way." Beck and Hollis had already moved to the door and Leo hadn't noticed.

The ride to the Pennybacker mansion was quick, as it was only a few blocks away, but the wait on the street to disembark was interminable. When at last they pulled in front of the house, Beck stepped out first, then helped Hollis and Caroline down. Leo brought up the rear. Hollis took Beck's arm, and Leo escorted Caroline inside. It was the first opportunity he had to speak to her privately. "You are a vision," he murmured. "A lovelier sight I have not seen."

She smiled with delight. "And so are you very dashing, Your Highness. A true prince. I shall be the envy of everyone here on your arm and I don't know how we'll go about the business of finding a maid—I can't imagine anyone will look away from us." She smiled and nodded at a pair of acquaintances, then whispered, "I have an idea of how to find her, the maid."

"I don't want you to involve yourself tonight, Caroline. It's too risky."

"Really?" she said as they climbed the steps. "And how on earth do you think you will manage without me? This place is too large for you to go wandering about. She's probably a retiring room attendant, poor thing."

She had a point. The ball would be so crowded, it would be impossible to ferret out one maid. He hadn't really thought how, but he suddenly had an image of him wandering around in his princely attire, asking after Rasa.

"I've a surprise for you."

He glanced at her. "Well. My curiosity knows no bounds."

She giggled. "I'll tell you all when no one is about. Perhaps when we dance." She glanced up at him with sparkling eyes. "You meant to invite me to stand up with you, didn't you?"

He looked at her, at the shimmering green eyes, the full lips. The smooth, porcelain skin. She was the stuff of men's dreams. "I meant to invite you."

They stepped into a receiving line, and inched along with the throng waiting to greet the earl and his wife. Hollis and Beck were engaged in a lively and somewhat heated discussion, which, curiously, seemed to do with eggs. Caroline spoke to several people as they moved, greeting friends, pausing occasionally to introduce someone to him. But as they neared the earl and his wife, and Caroline had run out of acquaintances to greet, she leaned into him and whispered, "My surprise for you is that I've found another one."

"Another what?" he asked. He glanced around them, expecting another officer of the foreign secretary to step up and accost him.

"Another Weslorian!"

Leo's heart slowed. Then rapidly began to beat. "What? Here? Where?"

"The Farringtons'." She smiled, pleased with herself. "It was quite by accident! I had gone to see my friend Lady Farrington and convince her to invite you to dine, because, of course, if *she* had you to dine, then Lady Pennybacker would have you to the ball. And there she was."

"What?" he asked, confused.

"My lord!" Caroline suddenly slipped into a curtsy. Leo realized only then that they had reached the Pennybackers. This was the second time this evening people and space and time moved around him while he'd stood still, captivated by Caroline.

"Lady Caroline, you grace us with your presence," Pennybacker boomed. "Your Royal Highness, welcome," he said, and clasped Leo's hand in both of his and shook.

"Thank you," Leo said. "I must thank you for the kind invitation. I shall consider it my last opportunity to see friends before I go."

"So the talk is true, is it? You're returning to Alucia?"

"It is true."

"Well. Don't take any of my maids," Pennybacker said, and laughed heartily. Leo forced himself to laugh, too.

After he'd greeted a decidedly standoffish Lady Penny-backer, and they'd been announced into the ballroom, Caroline was pulled away by three ladies, all wanting to admire her gown. Leo stood alone in that crowded room, marveling at how studiously everyone avoided him. Before the royal wedding, he'd been swarmed with people wanting introductions at events like this. Tonight, he received several curious looks, but no one approached him. He was a pariah.

Soon the dancing was in full swing and Leo caught up to Caroline and asked her to dance.

"I should be delighted," she said. "Everyone is looking at us, so don't look around to see if they are."

"I won't," he said with a fond smile for her. He wanted to ask her what she meant about finding another Weslo-rian, but he wanted to dance with her more, to experience the feel of her in his arms with music sweeping them and their mutual esteem along. He bowed to her before taking her hand and stepping into a waltz. As they moved, he looked into her eyes. He didn't care who looked at them.

"You are a fine dancer, Prince Leopold," she said. "I suspected you would be."

"So are you, madam."

"You really shouldn't look at me like that."

"I shouldn't look at you with adoration?"

Her eyes sparkled more. "Is *that* what it is? No, you really mustn't. Tongues will wag and ladies will smolder with resentment. We can't have them smoldering."

"Let them, I don't care."

She laughed. "They will all wonder if you've seduced me. If I have been taken in by your princely charms and spurned all others for you. They will wonder if you are seducing me even now, with your eyes."

"I'm trying," he said. "How do I fare?"

"Very well, indeed." Her smile suddenly dulled. "Oh, Leopold. You may think me mad for saying it, but I will miss you so when you…when it's over."

He twirled her around, pulling her a little closer into his body. "I will miss you, too, Caroline. Words fail me to convey just how much."

"I've never known anyone like you, really. Well, your brother, of course. And Eliza is a bit like you, sort of careless and carefree. But really, no one like you, and I'm certain I never will again. That makes me unpardonably sad."

He sighed and squeezed her hand. "And I have never known anyone like you. You're rather incomparable, madam."

Her smile returned. "That is exactly the sort of flattery I adore."

"That is exactly what I love about you." Her eyes were locked on his, and she tried to keep her smile, but as they twirled around that dance floor, it was as if all the unspoken words and promises between them were swirling, too. It felt like they were on a tiny planet of two, spinning around and around on their own special axis.

But as the dance drew to a close, Caroline's eyes glistened in a darker way. "We're star-crossed, aren't we? Why couldn't it have been us?"

He didn't ask what she meant; he understood. Why could it not have been the two of them to meet and perhaps marry?

"More than anything, I wish it could have been us," he admitted.

The song ended. She stepped back and curtsied, then walked away from him. She hadn't taken more than a few steps when Lord Ainsley intercepted her, and after a brief exchange, she returned to the dance floor and disappeared into the crowd of dancers.

Leo needed air. But as he was walking out of the ball-room, Hollis caught him.

"There you are!" she said brightly. She linked her arm through his, and when he looked down at her hand on his arm, she said, "We are practically brother and sister. I've said so to nearly everyone, so they won't think the least about us strolling along. Now, then, Highness, everyone is watching you and Caroline—she's terribly good at draw-ing attention, isn't she? She's drawing attention right now, as it happens, dancing with Viscount Ainsley, and draw-ing the ire of the Peacock, who thinks his offer for her is imminent. It will keep everyone's attention for a time. In the meantime, I have found your friend."

"My friend?" he asked, momentarily confused, think-ing she meant Beck.

"Your *friend*," she said again, looking up at him. "She's running about with towels for the retiring room and I know precisely where to find her, so if you will come with me?"

"Hollis… I don't want you to get involved," he said as she led him down the hallway before turning into another hallway.

"I *am* involved. Do you think I haven't talked to my guests? Smile, Your Highness! You look far too serious. People will suspect you're up to something or have re-ceived terrible news."

Leo forced a smile for her.

There were servants in the hallway, and a pair of retir-ing rooms for the ladies, judging by how many of them were coming and going from the two rooms. There was also a linen closet. Hollis turned him about so that his back was to the main hall and said, "Pretend we are speaking of our sister and brother as we would, and I'll keep an eye— Oh! Here she is." She suddenly stepped away from him and blocked the path of a maid with red hair and a cap that was slightly askew.

"Pardon," the maid said.

"Excuse me, miss, I should like to introduce you to Prince Leopold of Alucia. He has something he would like to say," Hollis said smoothly.

"Pardon?"

Hollis took the maid by the arm and dragged her to stand in front of Leo. "Hurry," she urged him.

"Good evening, Rasa," he said in Weslorian.

She dropped her towels. Hollis quickly scooped them up and pressed them back into her arms. "Step into the linen closet!" Hollis insisted.

The girl looked frantic. "But I—"

"Step *inside*, darling," Hollis said more firmly.

The girl stepped inside the narrow closet. Leo didn't attempt to crowd in with her, but he blocked the entrance. "Forgive this intrusion, but I've come to collect you," he said in Weslorian.

"Collect me for what?"

"I'm taking you and the other women who came to London with you to Alucia."

Her mouth gaped. She clutched the towels to her. "But why?"

She was not understanding him. "Rasa…you've been poorly treated. You've been sold into slavery and I mean to free you. If you will gather your things and meet—"

"I don't want to go!" she exclaimed. "I like my post here! Lord Pennybacker, he gave me his daughter's clothes she'd outgrown."

Leo was confused. "But doesn't he… I beg your pardon, but I must speak plainly. Doesn't he want something…and by that I mean, *you*…in return?"

She didn't seem to understand at first, but when she did, she gasped. *"No!"*

"Come now, Your Highness," Hollis whispered. "We have company."

Leo stepped closer. "Do you understand, lass? You were bought and sold by powerful men."

"I wasn't! I begged my father to accept the offer, Your Highness. He's ill, and my mother has to feed my brothers and sisters. How are they to survive? I *like* London. I've my own room, my own shoes, my own bed."

Leo stumbled over the idea that she had not had her own shoes.

"Please leave me be," she begged him. "I don't want to go back to Wesloria. I want to stay here."

He hadn't anticipated this and didn't know what to say.

"Ah, Your Highness!" Hollis said suddenly. "Are you lost again? Come, I'll show you the way to the ballroom."

Leo ignored Hollis and leaned forward. "Rasa, please reconsider."

She shook her head and stepped deeper into the closet.

"You must be looking for the gaming room," Hollis said, her voice at a high pitch.

Leo reluctantly stepped back and turned to Hollis. He was surprised and annoyed to see Lady Katherine Maugham in the hall, watching them curiously. He said to Rasa, "Thank you. Mrs. Honeycutt has rescued me and will return me to the ballroom." He smiled at Lady Katherine. "I seem to have lost my way."

Lady Katherine was no fool. She stared at him shrewdly.

Hollis looped her arm through his and said, "You've had a bit too much ale, haven't you, Highness?"

He hadn't had a drop. "*Je*, too much," he said jovially.

Lady Katherine curtsied. "Good evening, Your Highness."

"Mrs. Honeycutt, if you will kindly direct me to the gaming room and the nearest tankard of ale, I should be delighted." He pretended to stumble and Hollis called out a cheery, "Good evening, Katherine." The two of them headed for the main hall.

"Well?" Hollis whispered as they strode down the corridor.

"She refuses to leave. She likes it here. She claims Pennybacker treats her well."

"Oh," Hollis said, surprised. "Well…perhaps if she is happy?"

Leo didn't understand how a woman could be happy under those circumstances. She had no freedom. She was a commodity. Because she was comfortable now didn't mean she always would be. But he didn't want to debate Hollis. She'd done enough for him, and he didn't want to involve her further. When they reached the gaming room, he bowed to her. "Thank you, truly, for your help. If you would be so kind as to pass the news along?"

"Of course." Hollis smiled sympathetically. "You tried, and that's what matters."

Leo wasn't sure of that. Trying didn't seem quite enough to him.

He watched Hollis disappear into the crowd, then walked into the gaming room and found Beck. His friend had had entirely too much to drink and was feeling very verbose.

Leo sat, his head spinning, his thoughts whirling

around, grappling over what he should do next...until Pennybacker came into the gaming room and demanded in a loud whisper what Leo wanted with his Weslorian maid and asked him to take his leave.

CHAPTER TWENTY-SEVEN

A certain peacock, whose feathers are easily ruffled, is nonetheless fanning them fully to attract the attention of a bachelor viscount. We have high hopes that someone will offer for the little bird before she molts.

Two ladies were spotted in gowns designed by Lady Caroline Hawke. There is some talk that Lady Caroline will invest in a shop so that she might share her talents with all the ladies of London.

Ladies, it should not have to be stated that gray is not a suitable color for a summer ball, and perhaps should be reserved only for a period of mourning.

—Honeycutt's Gazette of Fashion and Domesticity for Ladies

IT REQUIRED BOTH Leopold and Garrett to engineer Beck into the house and to his bed, with Caroline hurrying ahead to remove any obstacles to their progress. When he was at last on his bed, one leg sprawled off the side, Beck lamented the amount of money he'd lost at the gaming table.

As Garrett was in his nightshirt, Caroline said, "See to Beck, Garrett. I'll see the prince out."

"Wait, wait, *wait*," Beck said from the bed and struggled up onto an elbow. "Leo…promise me if anything were to happen to me, you'll take care of Caro."

"Beck!" Caroline exclaimed. "Nothing will happen to you. You're drunk and talking nonsense."

"Promise me, man," Beck insisted. "I know you keep an eye on her—don't think I've not noticed," he said, wagging a finger at empty space.

"*Je*, friend, I promise," Leo said with a grin.

"Come and fetch her if you must. She'd be better off in Alucia than she would be with these jackals." His eyes slid closed.

"My goodness," Caroline said. "Your Highness, shall I see you out?"

They walked out as Garrett attempted to remove Beck's shoes.

In the hall, as Caroline closed the door to Beck's room, Leo leaned against the wall, smiling ruefully. He'd undone his neckcloth and looped his sash over one arm. He was so appealing standing there that her heart began to skip. She grabbed his hand and tugged him along, hurrying down the stairs and into the drawing room.

The hearth was cold, the drapes drawn. She groped on a table for a candle and found one, struck a match and provided a small bit of light. She held it up and turned around.

He took the candle from her hand and placed it on the table, then took her into his arms.

She didn't know what she was doing, other than she couldn't bear to lose a moment with him. "Everything has turned on its head, hasn't it? Hollis told me what happened, but not before Katherine Maugham came to tell me that out of concern for my feelings, she thought I ought to know that she saw you trying to seduce a maid, and I should not believe that your attentions to me were anything but for show."

"She said what?" he asked, incredulous.

Caroline waved a hand at him. "She delighted in telling me, you may trust."

"She delighted in telling Lord Pennybacker, as well," he said wryly. "It doesn't matter. Rasa refused to go. She likes her post. I told Pennybacker that the poor lass had rebuffed my advances and fled."

"Leopold!"

"What was I to say? I couldn't risk the blame falling to her." He stroked Caroline's face. "I have tried my best, but I think I must accept that I can't save them all. Rasa has refused me, and the girl at the Farringtons' may, as well. And that leaves one missing yet."

"Maybe the girl at Priscilla's will know where the other one is?" Caroline offered hopefully. "I'll help you in any way that I can."

But Leopold was already shaking his head. "No matter what happens at the Farrington supper, I will depart a day or two later, depending on the tide." He stroked his thumb across her cheek.

That was it, then—the end date. Caroline lifted her hand and wrapped her fingers around his wrist. "Leopold…" She couldn't bring herself to say the words that were in her heart and on her mind. She suddenly threw her arms around his neck to kiss him. He caught her by the waist, making a sound like a laugh into her mouth. But this was no laughing matter to Caroline. She had found the one she wanted. The man who made her want to leave everyone else behind. The man who had made her think beyond herself, who had seen something in her beyond her looks.

The need for him struck her almost violently. The swell of adoration for him was so powerful it left her dizzy, almost like a waking dream.

His arms circled tightly around her, his tongue seeking

hers. Her desire enveloped her like a blanket of torment and pleasure—her heart ached and swelled and pounded against her ribs. She felt as if parts of her were cracking open, and the heat of him was seeping into her marrow. She clung to his body, to his lips, and her thoughts deserted her.

Leo groaned from somewhere deep. He lifted his head, gripped her arms tightly. "Don't, Caroline. I have reached a point where I can't continue like this, not without..."

"I won't stop," she said, and eagerly sought his mouth as her fingers tangled in his hair.

Leo suddenly lifted her off her feet and moved to the settee. He dipped down to the hollow of her throat. "I haven't forgotten what you said. That you will defend your virtue until you marry," he said roughly, and shoved his fingers into her curls, pulling some free.

She pushed against his shoulder and made him look at her. "That's not what I said. I said I wouldn't part with it unless I was in love."

Leo's blue eyes darkened in that low light and he sank back. "Are you in love?"

"Do you really need to ask?" She cupped his face with her hands. "I love you, Leopold. I ardently admire you. I *adore* you. If you were any other man, I would beg you to ask for my hand."

Leopold's expression turned wild. He grabbed her hand and pressed her palm against his chest so that she could feel his wildly beating heart. The force of it surprised her. He looked almost pained as he caressed her face, her shoulder, his fingers trailing over the swell of her breasts. "I love you, Caroline. I don't know how it happened, how you crept under my skin and into my heart. I don't know how you inserted yourself into my every waking thought.

It wasn't supposed to be like this. It was never meant to be like this."

"I know, I know, but I don't care," she said breathlessly. "I know I can't have you, Leopold, but I can't let you leave and not say or experience these raging feelings for you. I'm desperate with want. Aren't you?"

"Desperate," he muttered. He stroked her face, his eyes searching hers. But then his gaze fell to her lips. "Close your eyes."

Caroline closed her eyes and lay back on the settee, giving in to her desire and to him. He moved his mouth over her skin, his touch burning a trail in its wake. She felt white-hot inside, desire thrumming and pulsing in her, anticipation and such incredible longing shimmering out through her toes and fingers.

He slid his hands down to her ankle, then his fingers beneath the hem of her gown and on her calf, and then up, to her thigh, to her sex. She skated her hands over his shoulders and his chest, insistent. She kissed him and pressed her body against him, wanting more, wanting everything about him.

His kisses turned blistering, and his hands were between her legs, stroking her. But it wasn't enough for her this time. Caroline slid her hand down his body and stroked his erection. Leo grunted and pressed against her, so that she could feel how hard he was, how he wanted her.

It was extraordinary that desire could burn so fiercely in her that she could abandon the barriers she'd erected to keep her virtue. He had easily torn down the doors of her defense and made her his. All that Caroline knew was that she'd never felt anything as urgent, as imperative, as the desire to have him.

He filled his hand with her breast, kissed her chin, her

throat and the spill of her flesh above the bodice of her gown. He moved down her body, kissing her stomach through her dress and her corset, then moved up, sank his fingers into her cleavage and released a breast. He suckled it, then rolled the tip between thumb and forefinger. Caroline gasped with pleasure.

"You must be *sure*," he said, pressing his forehead against hers, his breathing as ragged as her own. "You must be certain this is what you want, because God help me, I am not man enough to help you decide. I am but a breath away from ravaging you. Do you understand me, Caroline?"

He was a good man. A decent man. She drew up on an elbow and kissed his mouth. "I'm not asking you to help me decide anything, Leopold. I'm asking you to take me."

The light in his eyes seemed to shimmer in the darkness. He muttered something in Alucian and lowered his head to hers, kissing her tenderly, reverently. But the tenderness quickly gave way to heat, and his hands and his mouth were everywhere. He ripped the coat from his body, grabbed the shirt and pulled it over his head. Her hands touched the flesh of his chest for the first time and Caroline groaned.

He reached his hand between her legs and began to stroke her, moving his fingers inside her, helping her body to open. She was wild and uncertain what to do, or where to put her hands. Her breath was so shallow, as if she'd run for miles to him. She could feel the inevitable release building in her, and she grabbed his nape, pulled his head to hers, kissed his lips and bit the bottom one. "It's time."

"God, woman, you drive me to madness," he said. "Be still now. Be easy," he whispered.

She couldn't be easy. She could be anything but *easy*.

She closed her eyes, dug her fingers into his neck and chest, and allowed herself to sink into the pleasure he was giving her. His fingers slid deep inside her and back again in primal rhythm, as he moved his mouth over her cheek, her lips, her eyes, gliding so lightly that her skin simmered to the point she could scarcely endure even the whisper of his kiss. When he dipped his head to her exposed breast again, she felt herself sliding off a cliff and falling through space.

She knew he fumbled with his clothing. She gasped when he guided her to touch him. But nothing compared to the moment he slid the tip against her dampness. She was lost. It was pain, it was pleasure. It was a sensation beyond anything she'd ever known.

Leo dragged her hand up above her head and held it, then kissed her tenderly as he began to slowly, carefully, push himself inside her.

Desire and love intermingled and began to drum in her. She was inflamed by this intimacy, and despite a bit of discomfort, she would do this again and again with him. But as he moved deeper, pressing up against her maidenhead, she realized how profound this was, this moment in her life, with this man. She would never again feel so deeply for someone. Never in her life would she experience something so remarkable.

"Draw a breath," he whispered, and as Caroline drew it, he pushed past her maidenhead. Her body tensed to absorb the discomfort, but then something remarkable began to happen—she could feel her body adapting to his.

He stroked her face, kissed her lips and began to move in her. He was whispering encouragement to her, but at some point, he stopped speaking. His breath deepened and he moved with more deliberation. Caroline began to move with him. It was as if her body knew what to do, how to reach the end with him, and all she had to do was ride along.

Her body raced toward release, her heart pounding in her chest. And then he put his hand between her legs and began to stroke her in time with the movement of his body. A moment later, her release poured out of her.

His followed—he pulled himself free of her at the last possible moment, then collapsed on top of her.

Caroline softly pressed her lips to his neck, her hand to his chest. She was speechless. She couldn't imagine this with another man. She couldn't imagine this with anyone but Leopold.

Which presented a bit of a problem, but one that Caroline would think about tomorrow. At present, she wanted only to revel in the feel of this man's body with hers.

"I love you," he said against her shoulder. "I need you to know it." He lifted his head. "I love you, Caroline Hawke. And no matter what happens, I always will."

It was too dark for him to see the tears in her eyes. "I love you, Leopold. I do, so desperately."

They held each other for a very long time. But eventually, Leopold stood. He took a handkerchief and cleaned them both, then fastened his clothing. Her hair had come undone, and her beautiful gown was wrinkled and the overskirt torn in one place. She hardly cared.

He helped her up from the settee, then wrapped her in a warm embrace. "Caroline, I…" His voice trailed away, as if words had failed him.

"I know," she whispered. She didn't want to hear him say he had to go. She didn't want to be reminded that they were hurtling toward the time he would leave her forever.

He kissed her cheek. Her mouth. Her hand. He kissed her lips and lingered…and then walked to the door. He looked over his shoulder, his gaze sweeping over her before locking on her eyes. She felt not of this earth. The candle had almost burned out, and he was in the shadows, like a dream. Her summer dream.

Caroline stood in the very spot he'd left her long after he'd gone. She couldn't seem to make her feet move. She couldn't seem to do anything but breathe, and scarcely at that.

Caroline was still abed the next morning when Martha came in and told her she had callers. Caroline groggily sat up. "Who?"

"I don't know, miss. Garrett sent me to fetch you."

Her heart started. Was it Leopold? She grinned and threw off the covers. She dressed in a simple day gown, left her hair hanging down her back in a tail and hurried downstairs, eager to see him. But when she burst into the drawing room, the very room where she'd experienced something so very profound just hours before, she didn't see Leopold at all. It was Mr. Drummond, from the office of the foreign secretary, and a very green Beck.

CHAPTER TWENTY-EIGHT

An intimate supper party at the home of a newly ap-
pointed lord erupted into chaos when a maid new
to the household was discovered to have run away
in the middle of the evening. The party was quickly
disbanded. In the following days our intrepid host-
ess and family departed for the country for the rest
of the summer and has not been heard from since.

Ladies, for the bit of dust in corners that does not
come away with a good feather duster, balling up a
slice of brown bread and dabbing in the corner will
do the trick.

⌒—Honeycutt's Gazette of Fashion and
Domesticity for Ladies

AMBASSADOR REDBANE CALLED on Leo in the common room
of the Clarendon Hotel quite unexpectedly the morning of
the Farrington supper. He seemed agitated, as if he'd been
chased by a pack of wolves.

"Good morning, Redbane," Leo said, looking up at him
from the morning papers. "Is everything all right?"

"Your Highness," Redbane said, clutching his hat. "It
is imperative you leave for Alucia on tomorrow's outgo-
ing tide. The royal ship stands at the ready."

Leo froze for a moment. "Tomorrow? Why?"

Redbane removed a letter from his pocket. "The British

foreign secretary has requested it. They have some outrageous idea that you may be plotting with the Weslorians against the king, or involved in something even more nefarious. They have come to me, asking that the king remove you from England at once."

"I beg your pardon?" Leo tossed the paper aside and stood up. Redbane handed him the letter.

Leo quickly scanned the contents. It was a formal request to be presented to his father that he be removed at once for reasons of "poor conduct."

"Poor conduct?" Leo asked.

"It is a more palatable excuse for their accusations that you are plotting against your father. They want no trouble, Your Highness. They can't have any sort of plot being hatched here."

"I am not plotting against my father," Leo said. "And if anyone suspects that is so, they need only follow me back to Alucia, where I will reveal the truth about my activities here," Leo said curtly. He rubbed his eyes. "Has a dispatch been sent to my father?"

Redbane nodded.

Well, this certainly put a damper on things. Leo suspected his father would give no credence to the talk of treason, but he knew he'd give quite a lot of credence to the charge of poor conduct.

"It is in the best interest of Alucia," Redbane added.

"Fine, I understand I must go. But on Monday."

"But Your Highness—"

"There is nothing that will sway me, Redbane. There is one last thing I must attend to before I go."

Redbane pressed his lips together.

"Is there anything else?" Leo asked.

"No, Your Highness."

"Then you may go," he said irritably, gesturing the ambassador away.

He was made distraught with this news. He still didn't know where one of the women was, and he didn't know what would happen this evening. But it was the thought of losing Caroline that made him feel so ill. He'd known this moment would come, that he'd have to say goodbye, but he'd fought to keep himself from dwelling on it. He had to face it. She'd come to mean so much to him. She'd come to mean *everything* to him. She was the light his soul needed. How could he leave? He didn't know how he could go on, knowing that he wouldn't see her for a very long time, and when he did, it would be in Alucia and he'd likely be married. If not to Eulalie, then to someone else.

His mood soured over the rest of the day as he tried to think his way clear of this dilemma. He dressed for the night, but he had that odd feeling again of not fitting right in his own skin. As if this new person he'd become didn't fit his body. As if loving a woman was something he wasn't built to do. He burned for her. He did. He even lifted his shirt, half expecting to see a mortal wound there.

What had he done? Had he taken the virtue of a woman he truly loved only to leave her? At the time, it had seemed imperative, the only thing that was right between them. Today, with this banishment hanging over his head, it seemed entirely wrong and selfish.

He glanced at Freddar, older than him by twenty years. "What do you say, Freddar, are you ready to return to Alucia?"

"*Je*, Your Highness. I miss my family, I do."

Leo didn't miss his family. He would miss Caroline more. *So much more.*

HE WAS GREETED at the door of the Farrington house by Lord Farrington himself. "Welcome, *welcome*, Your Highness. Thank you for coming," he said as Leo handed his cloak to the waiting footman. "I hope you won't mind that we are a small group tonight. I look forward to speaking with you this evening, as I've been working very closely with Mr. Vintors of Alucia."

Leo paused as he removed his hat. "Have you?" he asked. That was the name Lysander had given him. His father's most trusted adviser and peddler of human flesh.

"He's a clever man, that one. I think we might find numerous avenues of cooperation between our two countries. Trade, naturally. But in the arts, as well. I'm very keen on that idea in particular." He smiled broadly.

"A noble pursuit," Leo muttered.

He followed Farrington into a large drawing room that seemed to have been recently decorated, judging by the smell of plaster and the pristine condition of the rugs and drapes. He was greeted by Lord Ainsley, and Lady Katherine Maugham and her mother, Lady Maugham. Lady Katherine would not meet his eye.

Hollis and her father, Justice Tricklebank, had come, and he was introduced to Mr. Edward Hancock and his wife, Felicity Hancock. And of course, Caroline and Beck. Oh, but he was a poor actor—he couldn't keep the smile from his face when he saw her. She wore yet another beautiful gown of shimmering green. "A lovely dress, Lady Caroline," he said politely as he bent over her hand.

"Do you like it? I made it myself." She smiled coyly. "We've not seen you in two days, Your Highness. Have you grown weary of us?"

"Quite the contrary. Unfortunately, I've been too well occupied."

"All right," Beck said. "If you please, Caro, go and keep the judge company, will you? I should like a word with the prince."

"Really? What word?" she asked.

"Does it not stand to reason that if I wanted you to know, I would invite you to stay? Go," Beck said, fluttering his fingers at her.

She cast a brilliant smile at Leo and walked across the room to join Hollis and her father.

Beck indicated with his chin a corner of the room.

"Is something wrong?" Leo asked when they had separated themselves from the other guests.

"You're being watched," Beck murmured, his eye on the others. "Gentlemen from the foreign secretary have come round. They seem to think Caro might know something about a plot to steal your father's throne." He shifted his gaze to Leo. "They think you may have confided in her. What the devil is going on, Leo? Why do they think my sister might know of your plans? What *are* your plans?"

"Beck," Leo said. "I don't have plans. I'm not plotting against my father, for God's sake. I love him. I don't even know my uncle."

Beck looked dubious.

"It is something else entirely."

"What?"

Leo considered what he ought to say. "It has to do with betrayal in my father's ranks, but I really can't say more. I'm asking you to trust me, Beck."

"And Caroline?"

Leo swallowed. He would not lie to his friend. "She has helped me meet some people who were useful to know." It wasn't a real answer, Leo knew, and judging by Beck's dark frown, he didn't think so, either. But Leo wouldn't say more. He would not risk implicating Caroline to anyone.

Beck pressed his lips together and looked across the room to where Caroline was standing. "Look, I don't know what this is all about, but these men were serious. My advice is to depart Britain as soon as you can."

"I plan to leave this week," Leo said.

Beck put his hand on his arm. "Listen to me, Leo. It doesn't matter what is true—it matters what they perceive. And people perceive you to be rotten at the core."

"I understand." He did. The people behind this would look for any scapegoat to keep their profits. How the devil had he gotten himself in this mess?

"For the sake of my sister, I hope that you do," Beck said. He walked away.

Leo reluctantly turned back to the others. He wanted a word with Caroline, but it seemed as if all eyes were upon her, watching everything she did. And she, of course, was holding court as only she could do.

At supper, he was seated across from Caroline. She laughed and talked as she normally did, almost too beautiful to behold. She looked for all the world like nothing had happened between them. He would have been perfectly content to watch her all night, but Lady Katherine Maugham and her friend, Mrs. Hancock, wanted otherwise. They peppered him with questions he found confusing and silly, and he was certain he appeared as bored as he felt.

The only saving grace was that every so often he would catch Caroline looking at him with a sparkle in her eye. He would carry that delightful sparkle and brilliant smile with him always, imprinted on his heart. He would look back on this night and remember her and imagine what might have been.

She laughingly accused Mr. Hancock of wanting to steal their driver, apparently after a mix-up of carriages on Park Avenue one day. She congratulated Mrs. Hancock on her dress. She regaled the entire table with a tale of three young girls who had gone out when they shouldn't have and gotten lost in a thicket.

"Where did this happen?" Lady Farrington asked.

"Oh, our home in Bibury. We used to summer there, all of us."

"What I remember was taking a switch to the three of you," the judge said.

"You never took a switch to them that I recall," Beck said with a laugh. "Admit it, my lord. You indulged them terribly."

"No worse than you, Hawke," the judge agreed.

Talk turned to the new county courts that were to be established. Justice Tricklebank confessed he'd like to retire to one.

"You can't desert us for the country," Caroline protested. "What of me and Hollis?"

"The two of you will be married by then. That is my fervent prayer," he amended to much laughter.

"Your prayers clearly haven't been fervent enough, Papa," Hollis said with a laugh.

When the plates had been cleared, Caroline asked to be excused. All the gentlemen stood and she left the dining room.

At the door, she glanced back at Leo so briefly that he might have imagined it. And then she was gone. He looked down at his plate. His stomach was roiling with nerves. He didn't want his time here to end this way. And then again, he'd come this far. If he could save one more of them, wasn't it worth the risk?

"Perhaps all the ladies should retire and leave the gentlemen to their cigars?" Lady Farrington suggested when Caroline had gone out. The ladies agreed and made their way from the room.

The smoking portion of the evening stretched interminably. Leo didn't smoke but stood at the window, listening to the gentlemen discuss those things they enjoyed: hunting, racing. Women. His nerves kept ratcheting up. He felt a little ill. He wished for whisky.

He finally turned from the window and excused himself.

"We've got a piss bucket in the corner for you, Highness," Farrington called out. The man had drunk too much, and so had most of his guests—they erupted into laughter.

Leo laughed, too, but carried on, stepping into the hall and pulling the door shut behind him. He glanced around and saw Caroline standing just at the door in the drawing room. She was waiting for him, he realized. She glanced back into the drawing room, then quickly stepped out and hurried over to him. "Last door on the right," she whispered, pointing.

Leo looked in the direction indicated.

"She's waiting for you." Caroline moved as if she meant to return to the drawing room.

But Leo caught her hand. "Caroline, wait—I must speak to you."

"Yes, of course. But you must go speak to her first. She's frightened, but she wants to flee." She disentangled her fingers from his and skipped across the hall and disappeared into the drawing room.

Leo looked down the hall to last door on the right. *One more*. One more to rescue, and he could stop playing the hero.

CAROLINE WAS CERTAIN no one had noticed her step out of the drawing room, and when she returned, no one glanced up—they were all chattering away. She was glad for it—she was at sixes and sevens, her nerves frayed. She went to the window and tried to see out, but it was dark, and all she could see was her shadowy reflection. She couldn't seem to keep a breath in her chest and kept taking little gulps of air.

"There you are, Caroline. Where did you get off to?"

Caroline started. She turned to look at Lady Katherine. "Oh. The retiring room."

"Ah. I should like to avail myself before the gentlemen join us. Is it just down the hall?"

Caroline panicked. There was nothing down the hall but a study, and right now, Leo was there with Eowyn. "Oh, I wouldn't just now. I think they mean to clean it."

"*Clean* it? Now?"

"Well," Caroline winced, then put her hand to her belly, "I'm afraid supper didn't agree with me. I think it was the fish. You never know how long it's been sitting in those market stalls."

Her distasteful little white lie worked like a charm. Katherine looked stricken. "Oh dear." She glanced to the door. "Surely they've had time to clean it."

Lord, this woman! She was a pest, forever watching Caroline. She wanted to put her hand over Katherine's mouth and beg her not to speak. But here was Katherine, sticking her nose in once more. Obviously suspicious. Wanting to catch Caroline at something she could gossip about.

"You may be right. I'll go and check for you, shall I?"

Katherine tilted her head to one side. "That's not necessary."

"I'll be back tout de suite." Caroline smiled. It was a flimsy excuse, but Caroline didn't know what else to do. She moved around Katherine and out the door, hurrying down the hall, glancing back once to make sure Katherine didn't follow her. Just as she reached the study, she heard the gentlemen. They were preparing to rejoin the ladies, and it wouldn't be long before someone noticed she and Leopold were both missing.

In her panic, Caroline dove in through the partially opened door of the study and startled both Leopold and the girl. Eowyn was sobbing. Leopold spoke to her in Alucian, his voice calm and soothing. Then he looked at Caroline.

"They are...you've been missed."

He understood immediately. He turned to the girl, put his hand on her arm and spoke to her in Alucian. But Caroline could hear voices coming down the hall toward the room. She closed the door. "They are coming now!" she warned them.

"Go and get your things. Come round to the side of the house," Leopold instructed Eowyn. "Take only what you can carry and speak to no one."

The voices were drawing nearer. Caroline recognized Tom, Priscilla's husband, and she was all but certain she heard Katherine's voice, as well. "It's too late! Hide, Eowyn!"

"Caroline!" Leopold said as Eowyn dove behind a chair.

There really was no place for the poor girl to hide. They would spot her right away, and they would assume the worst of her and Leopold. Caroline heard Farrington at the door. She knew instinctively the only way to hide that girl was to create a diversion. She ran to the prince. "I'm so very sorry," she said, then threw her arms around Leopold with such force that he stumbled backward and had to catch her. Just as the door opened, Caroline kissed him. She kissed him with all the regret and longing she would carry with her the rest of her days.

Leopold returned her kiss with all his regret and longing. They were locked in a lover's embrace. Their last embrace. Their last kiss.

Caroline heard Katherine's cry of alarm, heard Farrington bellow for them to stop it at once. Caroline shoved away from Leopold and lunged toward the door. "It's not what it seems!" she cried.

"Bloody hell, it's not!" Farrington shouted. "And you, Highness, debauching this young woman!"

More people were coming, and Caroline moved toward Farrington. "I welcomed it!" she cried, and grabbed the man's lapels.

"Caroline!" Leopold thundered and rushed after her. They all spilled into the hall, Caroline sobbing that she'd done nothing wrong, she'd merely followed her heart, and Leopold begging Farrington's forgiveness. Everyone was shouting, Priscilla's dogs were barking and Katherine was crying, which confused Caroline. Somehow, Hollis had reached her, had taken her hand and squeezed it, her face ashen and wide-eyed.

It was Beck who scared her the most. She'd never seen him so angry. He dug his fingers into her elbow and yanked her forward. She didn't know what he said to their hosts—she tried to turn around, to see Leopold, but Farrington was railing at him, threatening him with the demise of good relations with Great Britain as he, too, tried to make his way to the entrance. And Priscilla, her good friend Priscilla, staring at her in horror. "In my house, Caroline? In my *house*?"

Somehow, Beck managed to force Caroline outside and into a waiting coach. She waited, fearing she would be ill, trying to see out the window at what was happening. But it was dark and she couldn't make anything out. Several minutes later, Beck entered the coach, and he pounded the ceiling so hard she thought he'd put a fist through it.

"I can explain," she tried, but Beck threw up a hand.

"Don't," he said, his voice deadly and low. "Not a word, Caroline. Not a damn word from you."

They rode in an uncomfortable silence all the way home, and once there, Beck didn't bother to help her from the coach. He leaped out and strode through the gate and up the stairs to his suite of rooms. The slamming of his door reverberated throughout the house.

Caroline slowly made her way to her room. Her legs felt heavy, and her heart ached. She fell listlessly onto the bed, facedown. She was exhausted, emotionally drained. She had ruined her reputation, she might never see Leopold again and she didn't even know if Eowyn had escaped.

When the tears finally started to fall, they were not for her ruin. They were her grief at losing Leopold.

CHAPTER TWENTY-NINE

Quite a few people have come and gone from a particular house on Upper Brook Street in the last two days. One might assume someone had taken ill. It is entirely possible that is true, given that the events at a friend's house left many hard and confused feelings among close acquaintances.

Ladies, if your husband is experiencing lethargy and an unwillingness to work, a teaspoon of licorice root to one's tea is guaranteed to restore vitality. Carsons' Licorice Root is available in measured doses for the unsuspecting husband.

↣—Honeycutt's Gazette of Fashion and Domesticity for Ladies

CAROLINE CRIED HERSELF to sleep and into the night between tears and sleeping. On the following day, she was dragged awake by the sudden streaming of sun in through her windows. She threw an arm over her eyes and moaned. "What time is it?"

"One o'clock," Martha said from somewhere across the room.

Caroline opened her eyes. They were swollen from sobbing, and her head felt as if it were caught in a vise. She slowly pushed herself up, and a curtain of hair shielded her view of Martha.. "The most terrible thing happened last night, Martha."

Martha didn't speak at first. Caroline squeezed her eyes shut then pushed her hair aside and looked at her lady's maid.

Martha gave her a piteous look "I heard, madam, Another maid has gone missing, and the tale of how she went missing was quick to spread. They say it's a love triangle."

"A love triangle?"

Martha glanced away. "You, the prince, and the maid."

"Oh, good Lord," Caroline whispered. "I'm ruined, aren't I?"

Martha didn't dispute her. She sat next to her on the bed and put her arm around her shoulders as she'd done many times through the years. "Don't fret, milady. His lordship will make it better."

But Beck didn't make it better. He couldn't make it better, no matter how he might have wanted to. If he wanted to. He summoned her to his study later that afternoon. He looked older to her somehow. His eyes were shadowed with exhaustion, and the lines around them were more pronounced than she'd ever noticed before. She stood meekly before him, her arms wrapped around her body, equal parts ashamed and tired and defiant.

Beck sighed. "What am I to do, Caro? *What*, pray tell? Your reputation is in tatters. I went round to the club this morning and everyone had heard what happened at the Farringtons'."

A shaft of light broke through the clouds and landed between brother and sister, like some sort of invisible barrier.

Caroline felt as if she'd climbed mountains. Her legs and arms felt wobbly. She sank onto a settee. "I was trying to help."

"By *seducing* him? That's what they will say, you know. The fault always is assigned to the female in these situations."

"I didn't seduce him. It wasn't like that."

Beck came around from his desk and pulled a chair up to sit before her. "Then what was it like? Tell me, Caro. Help me to understand."

Caroline didn't have the strength to spare Beck any detail. She told him everything—about the Weslorian girls and the terrible thing that had happened to them, and how Leopold was doing his best to save them. She confessed she'd fallen in love with Leopold, and that it wasn't infatuation but true love, and he had come to feel the same for her. She told Beck that last night, when it looked as if Leopold would be caught and the girl sent off to her rooms and to God knew what sort of punishment, she'd done the only thing she could think of in the moment and created another scandal to cover the one blooming in that study.

When she had finished, Beck understood. He had softened considerably. He sighed and leaned back in his chair, rubbing his chin as he looked at the window. "Why didn't you tell this to Mr. Drummond when he called?"

"I didn't know if I could trust him, and I wouldn't do anything to harm Leopold."

Beck spread his fingers wide on his knees. "Well, then. You'll have to go away from London for a time."

"Why? I won't go out, I promise."

"Caro…don't you understand? I won't allow to happen to you what happened to Eliza. This society you love so much is like a rabid dog. They will turn on you and pillory you at the slightest opportunity. You and Martha will go to our country home in Bibury, and hopefully, with the passage of time, the talk will ease."

Her chest constricted painfully. She couldn't imagine living in the country indefinitely. What would she do? How would she survive without friends? What about her dresses and her plans to open a dress shop? What about suppers and balls and gentlemen callers, all threads in the tapestry of her life? Who was she without those things? "But…but what of Leopold?"

"No, Caroline," Beck said sharply. "I am sorry, darling, I know you love him. I've suspected it for some time, really. But you mustn't ask about him, you mustn't think about him. He is sailing tomorrow and he will not be back. His reputation is in worse tatters than yours." He surged forward and grabbed her hand and squeezed it. "I understand, darling. I've known heartbreak. But it will ease with time and a change of place. You will gradually think of other things."

Caroline didn't believe him. She couldn't imagine she would ever think of anything but her prince.

HOLLIS CAME THE following morning. Beck met her in the grand hall and told her that now was not a good time.

"It's never going to be a good time, Beck," Hollis said. "Move aside."

"Do you really think you're in a position to come into my home and order me about, Hollis Honeycutt?"

"I do, Beck! I do! She is a sister to me and I will not allow you to stand in my way."

Beck huffed. "Why is it that you are incapable of listening to me?" he demanded. "Why are you *all* incapable of listening to me?" he called as she marched past him and up the stairs.

Hollis ignored him. Her face was upturned to Caroline, who had watched it all from above. "Darling!" she cried. "Oh, Caro." She reached the first floor and looped her arm through Caroline's, whirling her about and pulling her into Caroline's sitting room, where dresses in various states of construction were lying and hanging about. She pulled Caroline down onto the settee, took both hands in hers and said, "Caro…he's gone. He boarded the royal Alucian ship this morning with three maids and a boy."

She gasped with relief. At least they'd managed to do that. "How do you know?"

"I sent Donovan to help them all. No one else would."

Caroline couldn't breathe.

Hollis squeezed her hands. "He told everyone the truth before he went," she said low. "He called the Alucian ambassador to him as well as the men from the foreign secretary's office. Mrs. Parker was at the Clarendon Hotel with her husband when it happened, and she said that he explained to them that he'd discovered a nefarious plot. She didn't hear all the details, as her husband sent her from the common room, but she heard enough to know it involved young women. She said the government men didn't believe him, and wanted to question him further, but the tide was going out soon and he said if they didn't have cause to detain him, he was leaving, and that he did. He boarded a ship for Alucia with the rest of them. Donovan said he's a hero."

Caroline felt herself choking on her breath. He *was* a hero. He was kind and compassionate and he felt things, and made her feel things, and Caroline couldn't *breathe*. "I'll never see him again, Hollis. And if I do, he'll be a man with a wife and children and I… Oh my God."

"Darling, he tried to see you, but Beck wouldn't allow it. He told him he'd done enough and it wouldn't do."

"He was here?" she cried. While she'd been sobbing herself sick, he'd come.

"But this morning, a man appeared at my door with a letter. One of his guards, I think. Anyway, he said the prince asked me to see it safely delivered to you." She pressed the folded paper into Caroline's hand. Tears began to fill her eyes, and she stood. "I must be gone. I mean to expose this corruption." She leaned down to kiss Caroline's cheek.

Caroline didn't know what she meant by that and lacked the energy to ask. She stood woodenly and followed Hollis out onto the landing, the letter clutched in her hand. She watched her dear friend rush down the curving staircase, watched her speak to Beck, then surprisingly, watched them embrace. It was as if she'd died.

She returned to her sitting room and shut the door, staring at the letter. She drew a breath. Then another. And then she read it.

Darling Caroline, by the time you read this letter I likely will have set sail for Helenamar. Given events, I am obviously no longer welcome in England. I have agonized for you and regret that there wasn't a moment to speak.

There seems quite a lot that should be said, but time restricts me, so I will write this: I never believed love would find me. I never believed that in my position, I would know the luxury of love. My world was a fog of pleasure and privilege, but then you came along and pierced that fog.

I never dreamed I would meet someone like you, much less love someone like you. I fear this love I hold for you will drive me to madness. I think of you every day and I will for the rest of my life. I will hold dear what we have shared.

I will never have the strength to feel this way again, and I want you to know, no matter what else, I loved you beyond compare and will burn for you for the rest of my days.

So did she love him beyond compare. So would she burn for him until she was all burned up.

She didn't care if she was sent to the country. She didn't care about anything anymore.

CHAPTER THIRTY

Bibury, the Cotswolds

Everyone who is able has left the dreaded summer heat of London, but a few souls remain, including a peacock, who lost a few feathers this summer and reportedly hasn't the energy to fly.

Lady Caroline Hawke announces she will not be taking orders for dresses, as she has decided the London air is unkind to her constitution and has determined to take some time to recuperate in the country.

After a scandalous departure of one maid, a certain lady whose husband is a rising star in politics has taken two more new servants into the fold. The lucky young ladies are Londoners.

Disturbing rumors of a slave ring operating at the highest reaches of British government continue to swirl, and we'll be keeping our eyes and ears open to bring you more news of it.

Ladies, new studies in physical health suggest that calisthenics should be incorporated into every woman's daily routine.

~—Honeycutt's Gazette of Fashion and Domesticity for Ladies

THE THREE LADIES gathered in the drawing room at the Hawke country house had come from the parish village.

Two of them were seated politely on the settee. One of them stood on a box, her arms held out as Caroline measured her.

She'd been in the country for four months now. Summer had long since departed and a cool autumn had taken its place. She'd taken to wearing her hair long and in a single tail down her back—it didn't seem worth the effort to coif and curl when she had no society to impress. She likewise wore a plain skirt and one of Beck's old shirts tucked into it, as well as one of his older sweaters that hung to her knees.

Around the drawing room were dresses in various stages of construction. She didn't care to wear them anymore, but making them took her mind off...other things. "You will look lovely in blue, I think, Mrs. Carter. Do you like the blue silk?" she asked.

"Oh, but it's beautiful," the woman said.

"You may lower your arms," Caroline said. She looked at her notes and smiled at the three women. "All right, then, I have three dresses to be made for the Yuletide. One red," she said, pointing at one of the ladies on the couch. "One in the green-and-cream-striped silk, and the blue."

The women all nodded their heads in agreement.

"Wonderful!" Caroline said, and nodded at Martha, who stood from her desk and walked over to the ladies. "Thank you all so very much for coming."

"Thank you, Lady Caroline," Mrs. Carter gushed.

Martha escorted the ladies to the door. She paused to chat with them, something about the new doctor in the village, and then saw them out. Martha liked it here, Caroline could tell. She'd taken to baking, and she and the cook who came from Bibury four days a week had become fast friends.

Caroline liked it here as well as anywhere, she supposed. Perhaps even more. Strangely enough, she didn't miss society. In fact, she often wondered why that elite social circle had been so important to her. It seemed rather vacuous to her now. *She* had seemed vacuous. She'd allowed herself to empty out, to think of only her shell, too fearful to see what ticked inside her. Well, now she know.

A lot had changed for her these last few months. It was as if being away from London and the constant swirl of parties and suppers, she'd finally come to terms with who she was. As if the cocoon of London she'd created had helped her avoid her true feelings about everything.

Since Leopold had left, she'd slowly realized that so much of her life was devoted to superficial things. Now she knew what she wanted. She wanted a love like she'd shared with him. She wanted her life to mean something. She wanted to make Beck proud of her. She wanted to spend her days doing something more important than dressing and being seen and admired. She wanted to help others. She wanted purpose.

She hadn't heard from Leopold, which she'd expected. He was an honorable man and he would not correspond with her as he prepared to marry another woman.

Ah, but she'd heard plenty from Eliza and Hollis.

Eliza wrote that Leopold arrived in Helenamar as rumors swirled about his supposed treachery. But then he'd exposed the plot to sell the poor Weslorian women, and some Alucian women, too, Eliza believed, into slavery. *He is a hero, Caro. Everyone says so. He risked his reputation and his engagement to expose that horrible plot.* Eliza said he was being feted for his noble deeds. She said the entire court was talking about him, as he was not the person anyone expected to care so deeply about anything.

Caroline smiled when she read that part. She wondered what Leopold thought of it all.

Hollis brought her news from town when she came to visit one long weekend. She'd been very kind to Caroline in her gazette, but others had not been kind. All sorts of rumors had surfaced about Caroline and her loose morals. Whispers of the gentlemen she'd entertained, of trysts, of lies she'd purportedly told to hide these things. And the one that stung the most? That she'd *not* made the dresses she had so very graciously handed around to her friends, but had employed the secret services of a trained modiste.

Hollis had more news—Lord Ainsley had offered for a coal heiress, and once again, Katherine Maugham was left in the cold. Caroline felt a little sorry for her, really. Katherine desperately wanted a match and to be married. Hollis also told her that Mr. Cressidian, the Alucian gentleman, would be tried for his crime of slavery. She said that facts came to light indicating that not only had he profited from brokering the sale of women, but he'd also offered to slander the prince for a price. "It's so disturbing," Caroline said.

"It's horrible," Hollis agreed. "Do you know what I think is the most remarkable thing about it?"

Caroline shook her head.

"That Prince Leopold would allow his standing to suffer as he did for the sake of those women. Eliza said he has vowed to find all the young women sold into slavery if it's the last thing he does."

"I always knew he was a good man," Caroline murmured.

Hollis laughed. "No, you didn't, darling. You despised him."

Caroline smiled wanly. "I mean I always knew he was *after* I despised him. Oh God, Hollis, I miss him so."

Hollis had moved to sit beside her and laid her head on Caroline's shoulder. "I know, darling. I still miss Percy."

CAROLINE HAD STARTED gardening in the late autumn, intrigued by the way the roses managed to bloom in spite of the early frosts. Eliza wrote again with news that, at first, surprised and elated Caroline. The engagement with Eulalie Gaspar was ended, as her father was implicated in the slavery scheme. Nothing would happen to the Duke of Brondeny, of course, as the Weslorians accused Leopold of manufacturing such slanderous details about him. Neither would anything happen to Mr. Vinters, as the king relied too heavily on his counsel. *This has displeased the prince greatly, and I think my husband, as well. It's difficult for them to understand how their father would want the counsel of a man engaged in that sort of scheme.*

Caroline understood it. To men like that, the women they'd harmed were just girls. Nothing to get upset about.

But her surprise and elation at the news about Eulalie soon vanished. She realized that Leopold would simply marry someone else. It would never be her. She could take some solace that the smug little face of Lady Eulalie would be smug no more.

But it would never be her.

She continued making dresses into the early winter, more than there could possibly be demand for in a village as small as Bibury. She took long walks in the afternoon to the extent that her boots began to wear at the heel. The weather was colder, so she began to wear Beck's buckskins, belting them at the waist. And she continued gardening, shoving her hands into dirt, turning it over, preparing it for spring.

Beck came to call from time to time. He remarked one evening that she seemed different.

"How so?" she asked him as she stacked her feet into a chair at the dinner table and picked up a cheroot.

"More mature," he said. "You've always been sure of yourself, darling, but now you are…comfortable somehow. I can't rightly put my finger on it. It's as if you don't really care that smoking a cheroot is unacceptable and would ensure you'd not receive another invitation."

She laughed. "I only mean to try it, Beck. Life is so boring without an adventure here or there."

Beck leaned forward. "Are you happy, Caro?"

She shrugged. "I'm not unhappy. I suppose I'm as happy as I can be for the time being." She drew from the cheroot and coughed violently. "You mustn't worry about me, Beck. I always find my way."

"I have no doubt of it, darling."

The days grew short and now there was a bitter nip in the air each day. Caroline wrapped a shawl around her neck and wore Beck's hunting coat when she walked. She had two dogs as companions now, having stumbled on them in a village market. They'd seemed happy to come along on her adventure, trotting along after her as if they belonged to her.

Today, Caroline hadn't walked a mile when she realized that the dampness on her cheek was snow. She and the dogs turned back.

She cut through on a forest path and came down a hill to where the Hawke estate was spread below them. Caroline happened to notice three riders approaching the house. So did the dogs. They raced ahead, barking at the intruders. Lord, she hoped whoever it was would carry on. She did not like the idea of playing hostess to strangers on a snowy evening. She and Martha liked to play gin rummy on nights like this.

But as she walked down that hill, a strange little current slipped down her spine. The first rider suddenly spurred his horse forward, galloping ahead of the other two. Heat began to fill her chest and rise in her cheeks. She stared at the rider, certain it had to be an apparition. She had to be imagining it. Wouldn't someone have told her?

But there was no mistaking the Arse of Alucia, her beloved. She threw off her hat and began to run, slipping and sliding down the hill to the road.

He leaped from his horse and raced toward her, pushing his way through the dogs and up the hill. They met midway, where Caroline vaulted into his arms. He caught her, spread his hand against her face and kissed her. He kissed her so hard that they tumbled to the ground and rolled a bit until he managed to stop them. When at last he lifted his head, he grinned at her.

"How?" she asked.

"Oh, that is a long and boring story, but suffice it to say I have returned against my father's wishes and I'm fairly certain I'm not welcome in Constantine Palace at present. Or in Mayfair."

Caroline sat up. She put her hands on his face, on his chest, feeling him to see if he was real.

"I went to Beck first," he said as she continued to assure herself he was real. "He told me where you were. He warned me that you'd changed, and that you might not want to see me."

"He doesn't want you to see me," she said breathlessly.

"He does," Leopold said, and caught her hands. "Caroline, listen to me. I have spent the last many months wishing for you every day. Every bloody day. I've not been able to get you out of my head. Not for a moment."

She laughed because this was so fantastic, so extraordinary. She had literally *dreamed* of a moment like this.

He cupped her face in his hands. "Do you understand why I'm here?"

"Eliza said you'd vowed to find all the women they abused."

He laughed. He stood up and pulled her to her feet. "I have. I *will*. But I'm here for you, Caroline. Only you. I don't know where we will go, precisely, but I've bought an old castle ruin, and I've a lad, Bobbin, who has come along to serve me—seems he was rather taken with me on the voyage to Alucia—but never mind that. I don't know what else I can offer you but my heart, my love, my undying devotion."

Caroline blinked. "Beck won't—"

"He will. It was the only way he'd let me see you."

Her heart was suddenly hammering in her chest. "This is a dream," she murmured.

"It is no dream, *mang leift*. I am here, before you now."

"But Leopold… I'm not her anymore," she said. "Look at me! I'm not her, I'm someone else now. Everything changed. *I* changed."

He ran his hand over her head. "So have I. I know what I want now. I know what matters."

She was momentarily confused because he'd just voiced thoughts she herself had had. "And you have never looked more beautiful to me than you do now, Caroline. If it weren't for Kadro and Artur just behind us, I'd show you just how much I love you here and now." He abruptly sank down onto one knee.

Caroline gasped.

"Lady Caroline Hawke." He pressed a hand to his chest. "I am a prince without a home. A man without a calling. I can offer you very little but a castle ruin, but I will live my life devoted to you. You are the woman I want to spend the rest of my life with. You are the woman I want to raise my children with. You are the woman who has made me wake up to life and understand it's worth living and is to be cherished. If you will have me, I should very much like to be your husband."

If this was a dream, Caroline never wanted to wake from it. She had a sudden image of the dress she would make for her wedding. She smiled and turned her face to the sky to savor this moment. Snowflakes were falling all around them. The dogs had come back to investigate and were sniffing around her prince. One guard stood on the road with the horses, the other one had lain on his back, pillowing his head.

"This is an agonizingly long wait for an answer," Leopold said.

Caroline looked down at him. She leaned over, wrapping her arms around him. "Yes, Leopold. *Yes*. Forever. In a ruin, in a palace. In a beautiful dress or a feed sack. In this life and the next. All of it. *Yes*." And then she sank to her knees and kissed him.

They fell onto their sides in that kiss and continued on until the dogs began to lick their faces and make them laugh.

EPILOGUE

One month later

The wedding of His Royal Highness Prince Leopold of Alucia and Lady Caroline Hawke of London was conducted in the Church of Saint Mary in the village of Bibury. Given the time of the year and roads made impassable by heavy snows, the guests were limited to immediate family.

The bride wore a gown of her own creation, made from a combination of her late mother's recently discovered wedding gown and a pale cream silk imported from France. The gown was embroidered with tiny rosebuds that cascaded down the bodice and the train.

His Royal Highness wore the Alucian style of formal dress, embellished with the medals and pins of his country. Lord Beckett Hawke served as best man and Mrs. Hollis Honeycutt stood with the bride. The happy couple will make their home at the Hawke house in Bibury until such time Herstmonceux Castle can be renovated for use as a private home. We all join the couple in our fervent wish that the castle can indeed be renovated before Jesus calls them home.

The happy couple have donated their time and funds to a new school to be built adjacent to the church. They have been seen working side by side with villagers to complete the building before the new term.

In other news, the Foreign Office announced this week that Her Royal Majesty the Queen will host a peace summit between the kingdoms of Alucia and Wesloria at the end of this year. The Alucians will be represented by His Royal Highness the Duke of Tannymeade. Accompanying him will be the Duchess of Tannymeade and, with God's blessing, the royal baby, who is due to make his or her appearance in the spring.

The Weslorians have not as yet named their representative.

Thanks to the efforts of this gazette, the Metropolitan Police announced that a Mr. Hemphill of Marylebone has been charged with theft in the case of the missing parish funds, collected by the parishioners of Saint Mark's Church of England in Mayfair, and dedicated to the orphanage. Mr. Hemphill has admitted to wrongdoing.

Ladies, doctors caution that if one indulges in the habit of a heavy evening meal during the winter, one must have care to allow sufficient time to pass before entering the marital bed. The consequence of poor timing could result in a stroke.

> *—Honeycutt's Gazette of Fashion and Domesticity for Ladies*

* * * * *

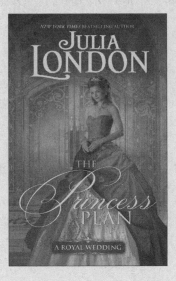